Judgment at Verdant Court

JUDGMENT AT VERDANT COURT

WORLD OF PRIME BOOK THREE

M. C. PLANCK

an imprint of Prometheus Books
Amherst, NY

Published 2016 by Pyr, an imprint of Prometheus Books

Cover illustration © Gene Mollica
Cover design by Liz Mills
Cover design © Prometheus Books

Inquiries should be addressed to
Pyr
59 John Glenn Drive
Amherst, New York 14228
VOICE: 716-691-0133
FAX: 716-691-0137
WWW.PYRSF.COM

20 19 18 17 16   5 4 3 2 1

Library of Congress Cataloging-in-Publication Data

Names: Planck, M. C., author.
Title: Judgment at Verdant Court / M. C. Planck.
Description: Amherst, NY : Pyr, [2016] | Series: World of prime ; book 3
Identifiers: LCCN 2016023992 (print) | LCCN 2016029941 (ebook) |
      ISBN 9781633882294 (softcover) | ISBN 9781633882300 (ebook)
Subjects: | BISAC: FICTION / Fantasy / Epic. | GSAFD: Fantasy fiction.
Classification: LCC PR9616.4.P56 J83 2016 (print) | LCC PR9616.4.P56 (ebook) |
      DDC 823/.92—dc23
LC record available at https://lccn.loc.gov/2016023992

Printed in the United States of America

ALSO BY M. C. PLANCK

Sword of the Bright Lady (World of Prime, Book 1)

Gold Throne in Shadow (World of Prime, Book 2)

CONTENTS

1

REUNITED

"Colonel." Corporal Kennet snapped off a crisp salute while his men stood at attention. In front of the grand ivy-cloaked building under the bright summer sun, they looked exceptionally bedraggled, having endured days of hard riding and worry. All because Christopher had behaved stupidly. Of course, the severe young corporal was too loyal and disciplined to complain.

"You should not have left us behind, sir."

Or not.

"You're right, Corporal. I owe you an apology, but instead I will give you something better: a promise. I will not do it again. You have my word on that." The blonde troubadour Lalania had conned him into letting down his guard, and promptly delivered him into mortal danger. He should thank her. It was the best lesson he could have asked for. "Let's saddle up."

He realized he didn't know where the stables were. Luckily, Kennet was already walking off, so all he had to do was fall in behind him. He didn't get ten steps before another one of those accursed women accosted him, blocking his soldier's advance with a smile. It seemed likely that every one of them had some equally valuable instruction to offer, but after Lalania and the Skald he wasn't sure how much more education he could take right now.

"My Lord Vicar, I thought you wished to visit our library," the curly-haired Loremaster said. She stood in the shade of a tree, looking entirely innocuous now, though the last time he had seen her she had been pointing a steel crossbow at his face.

He'd been trying to escape since the moment he woke up here, and yet he never seemed to make any progress. He looked longingly toward the horizon, where he imagined refuge lay, or at least a temporary respite from the weight of Secrets Man Was Not Meant To Know. The Skald had told him the true history of the Kingdom, and its horrifying and inevitable future. That seemed enough burden for the moment. "I've got a long ride home. I'd like to start while it's still morning."

"All the better reason to visit now, rather than having to return. And your men and horses are exhausted. We are in your debt; allow us to at least offer you hospitality."

He looked over his troop again and had to admit she was right. If the men looked this bad the horses would be utterly spent. They needed a rest, and he would regret having walked away from a library without at least peeking at it. The Cathedral had a library: it had almost sixty books, half of which were useless treatises on archaic laws. Who knew what would be in a troubadour's library?

Although if it was nothing but sex manuals, he was going to crack a few heads.

"Corporal . . . do you feel the situation is safe enough that we can stay here for the night?"

"Only if we can put a guard on your door, Colonel."

Christopher didn't see how that would help, but whatever made the man happy. He owed them that much. "Sure. Let's plan on riding out at dawn tomorrow. Until then, put your men at liberty."

"As you will, sir." Corporal Kennet turned to the Loremaster. "Lady, my men have not eaten this day. Where is your kitchen?"

Gracefully waving her hand, she directed them to a less noble-looking building off to the side. "Simply inform the staff of your needs, and they will meet them as best they can."

Kennet nodded in thanks, and trooped off with most of the men in tow. Two stayed behind, standing at attention.

"Aren't you guys hungry?" Christopher asked them.

"Sir! We're on duty. The corporal will replace us in an hour."

"All right, Lady . . ." Christopher would never get used to the way people didn't use their names here. It was as if their rank was the only thing that mattered.

"Please, my Lord Vicar, call me Bricina."

"Only if you call me Christopher." He regretted it as soon as he said it. He wanted to keep some distance between himself and these all-too-clever women. The aged but razor-sharp head of this den of musically adept prostitute spies, Lady Friea the Skald, had just taught him that in a rather painful conversation, and apparently he had already forgotten.

"This way, if you will, Christopher." She held out her hand, and he had no choice but to offer her his arm. Together they walked down the cobblestone path to another building, one made of stone instead of timber. The door was bound in iron and as heavy as it looked, as Christopher found out when he wrestled it open.

Inside was a treasure-house. A single large, round room, with several small alcoves branching off of it, kept bright and cheery by a dozen light-stones. The main room was filled with shelves, and the shelves were filled with books, scrolls, and loose sheaves of paper.

"I must ask your guards to wait at the foyer. We have many old and delicate manuscripts, and a perpetual fear of fire."

The two young men peered around suspiciously, but from the entranceway they could see everywhere in the room. Christopher would not be out of their sight.

"It'll do," one of them said to Bricina. "Grab us a couple of chairs and we'll be fine."

"I trust you for that much, Ser," she said with a smile. "Help yourself."

"Not Ser," said the other one. "Just Goodman."

"Of course, Goodman."

Christopher opened his mouth to chide their churlishness, but Bricina tugged on his arm and led him into the room.

"You need not fear for my dignity, Christopher. They are not impolite, by our standards. Merely . . . unusual."

"Unusual how?" he asked automatically, but he already knew the answer. Sheer confidence. They swaggered as broadly as a baronet, treating a ranked noblewoman no differently than they would treat a peasant girl.

No wonder the peasant girls went mad for them.

He moved on to a more interesting question. "Do you approve?"

Bricina stopped and glanced up at him. "I don't know. I have not considered the fact long enough to form an opinion."

Great. He'd finally found somebody who thought like a scholar, and she was a professional flirt in a too-tight bodice while wearing delicate green eye shadow. Then he got distracted by the books. One of them had a dragon on the cover.

"You won't like it," she warned. "It's merely fable. We do have some information on dragons, but not enough to fill a book."

"Ah." He saw another book with strange writing on the cover. It was the first foreign language he had encountered, other than the languages people used for casting spells. As he reached for it, she put her hand on his.

"I thought you would want to start with this one." She guided his hand to a book on a lower shelf.

"Why this one?" he said, moving his hand away.

"It deals with an explosive compound."

Damn it, he did want to start with that one. More disconcerting than the flirtation was the fact that she was right.

"But, Christopher, before you begin, I must explain the price to you."

He let the growl in his throat rumble loud enough for her to hear. Maybe a little intimidation was overdue.

She ignored him politely. "We are a cooperative library. To gain access to all of our knowledge, all of the learning you see in this room, we ask only a small price, well within the resources of a man of your wisdom."

"Stop flattering me and get to the point."

She briefly bowed her head. "The price is a contribution. Write us a tome, scroll, or paper containing knowledge we do not possess, and you are welcome to what we do."

"How am I supposed to know what you don't know?"

"Begging your pardon, but I do have a suggestion. Our knowledge of mundane explosives is limited. Thus we are quite interested in your sky-fire."

"What's wrong with this one?" He tapped his hand on the thin, leather-bound volume.

"The substance it yields is absurdly delicate. Merely dropping it on the ground induces it to explode."

"Hmm . . . is it a liquid?" Did they have nitroglycerin?

"No, a crystal. It has another disadvantage: it requires quicksilver to manufacture, where your sky-fire appears to be made from manure. Yes," she said to his frown, "we have a basic idea of your process. But we would prefer that you share your knowledge with us voluntarily. Stolen recipes tend to miss important details."

Fair enough. But of course she knew he would think that.

"Fine. But I can't write out the whole process in an afternoon." He wasn't sure he could write it out at all; Fae, his tamed wizard, was doing the day-to-day work.

"We will take you at your word, Christopher. Agree to provide us with a manuscript within the year, and the library is yours. Should you want a copy of any volume, we will set one of our clerks to the task, and deliver it for only the price of labor and materials."

Materials would mean paper, which around here was worth its weight in gold.

"You know, I make paper. At a tenth of the cost. Maybe we could make a deal?"

Finally he had surprised her. "You would sell us goods at the same rate you sell to your Church?"

"Sure. Why not?" The more he made, the cheaper it was to make, thanks to economies of scale. Another secret for their library.

Maybe later, when he needed another favor. Right now the secret he was giving them wasn't costing him anything. He wanted the art of making gunpowder to be widespread—eventually.

"I will ask the Skald what we can offer you in exchange for the favored price on your paper. In the meantime, please make yourself at home. Should you require anything, send to the main building. We are at your disposal."

All he wanted was a comfortable chair and a chance to dig into something intellectual. The last twenty-four hours had been physically and emotionally draining; reading a boring technical paper sounded downright fun. He flopped into the leather-covered padded armchair and cracked open the book.

Bricina bowed and left, smiling graciously. Christopher, absorbed in his reading, barely noticed.

Three hours later, he put the book down and massaged his temples. It was only forty pages, but it was convoluted, tedious, and written in a cramped, tiny cursive. He had, however, put a name to the compound—mercury fulminate. He wasn't entirely sure why he knew that name, but it had to be for something commonplace. There weren't very many chemical substances he could remember at the best of times, and he'd spent the last year and a half in a world where salt was considered the height of chemistry.

What else could he remember? Sulfuric acid, because, like all boys, he had been fascinated with it. Other than dissolving things, it was used for . . . batteries. Car batteries had acid in them. Then there was Drano, another dissolving compound. Except that was a brand name, not a chemical.

Primers. Now it came back to him: mercury fulminate was used in making bullets. The ignition system he had devised had a miserable failure rate. At least one out of every twenty rounds failed to fire when the hammer fell. Mercury fulminate would be a technological advance. It was difficult to make, but he was certain he could simplify the manufacturing process with a little trial and error. For example, he knew that "three drops of maiden's blood" was a completely unnecessary ingredient. In any case, it would be Fae doing the work.

He was hungry. There hadn't been any time for breakfast, with all the shenanigans going on. Walking to the foyer, he noticed his guards had been replaced.

"So you know where the kitchen is, right?"

"Yes, sir. And a right good kitchen it is."

"Lead on, then."

The dining room was rustic but clean and bright. He was given a plate by a young woman who might really be a shy maiden, or might be the deceptive, seductive, and slightly crazy Loremaster Uma, the Skald's second-in-command, in yet another disguise. At least she was properly clothed, and unlikely to poison him this time.

On the other hand, this would be the perfect opportunity to put certain precautions into practice.

"See that I'm not disturbed," he told his guards. Pulling his legs up into the lotus position, he went into the meditative trance that would renew the spells stored in his head. A strange place for meditation, perhaps, but he needed the practice. He would be on battlefields again, soon enough. If he couldn't ignore his cooling lunch and a few pretty girls, how could he hope to ignore cannon fire and the constant threat of invisible, rabid dog-men?

An hour later, he opened his eyes, strangely refreshed at the abstract experience. Dealing with his god's avatar, a suit of armor ani-

mated by an artificial-intelligence personality, had restored perspective to his emotional state.

Lalania was sitting on the other side of the table. She smiled
weakly at him.

"I'm so sorry, Christopher."

"They tricked you, too, Lala." Or at least, the Skald had said they
did. He decided to believe her. He really didn't want to be angry at the
woman. On the other hand, the Skald was fair game.

"I'm still sorry. But I brought you presents to make up for it." She
put a rolled-up parchment and a small purple stone on the table.

He reached for the stone first.

Lalania explained. "The tael from the Bloody Mummers. The
Skald asserts I am entitled to a share, since I fought at your side, but I
do not ask for it, since I tricked you into being there in the first place."

"I was hoping it was the tael from my assassin."

"No." She did something unusual with her face. It took him a
moment to realize it was shame. "Your assassin eluded us, again. She
locked the inn door with magic and fled out the back, stealing a horse
and your soldier's life. Someone must be supplying her with spells.
You must have a greater enemy than merely her spite."

That wasn't news. He had a lot of enemies.

"What's the scroll?"

She handed it to him, still blushing.

"My penitence, although I cannot complain of it. For the first
time in sixty years, a member of the College will swear service to a
lord. We jealously guarded our independence, perhaps too much so
since we have gradually become irrelevant, but now we sell our ser-
vices for paper. Or, more precisely, merely the right to buy paper at
your ridiculous prices. For that privilege I am at your command, until
you tire of me. And through me, the entire College will serve you in
our common purpose."

Lalania was referring to the coming battle against the hidden monsters known as the *hjerne-spica*. Assuming, of course, that there really were *hjerne-spica*, and that entire story wasn't simply another web of half-truths and suggestions designed to lead him down the garden path. The Skald had admitted that no one else in the Kingdom believed in them. Here, aboveground in the bright sunlight, it all seemed a bit unreal.

"So you're mine, now? Without a salary and without a share of the tael?" Terms she would never have agreed to a day ago. He knew this, because back then he'd been trying to hire her. Now, just when he'd been ready to walk away, she was throwing herself at his feet.

And he would catch her. She knew, obviously had known, long before he did. In retrospect it was obvious. He desperately needed her help and expertise in precisely the areas she had just tripped him up.

On top of all that, despite everything, he still thought of her as a friend. Even now she acted the part, and he believed her.

She was watching his face, waiting for him to work through the logic. "Yes," she said, once his indrawn breath signaled his surrender. She might have gone on to make a salacious comment, to suggest that she was his in any way he wanted her, that her duties did not stop at sundown. But she didn't. She bit her lip, and said nothing. Something else she would not have done a day ago.

He didn't know if it was due to her promise to stop trying to seduce him, or if it wasn't funny anymore now that he had the power to command her. It didn't matter. She would leave his tangled emotions and aching desires alone, and he would breathe easier for it.

So would his soldiers. "You've reassured the men that I was chaste, I assume? You know how much that means to them." It came out bitterer than he had intended.

"That you dare to say it, with your affiliation binding you to honesty, is more compelling than any song I can sing. And more grist for your legend. You walked into a nest of vipers and emerged without a scratch. No merely mortal man could have exercised such self-restraint."

Already she was earning her diplomatic keep. Her language was too carefully chosen. Glancing around, he noticed his guards would not catch his eye.

"For crying out loud . . . already?" It wasn't even noon yet.

"Allow my College a little pride, Christopher. Let us at least hold the interest of ordinary men."

She had revealed the information in a way that would make it easy for him not to punish the men. And he shouldn't. He hadn't explicitly told them to refrain from extracurricular activities—not that he had thought it necessary to specify such an order between the hours of breakfast and lunch—but the fact was he had set them at liberty. On the other hand, if he wanted to instill a little discipline, Lalania would not oppose him.

She had proven her worth, as if it had ever been in doubt. He opened the silver vial he wore around his neck and took out the purple rock inside. The stone she had given him had already merged with it, forming a single large lump, but it was a trivial matter to carve off a specific amount.

"Is that enough?"

Lalania was, for once, quiet. She nodded her agreement, without speaking.

"I assume you'll be even more useful to me as a minstrel? And that promoting you won't invalidate our contract?" He thought of something cruel to say, a way to pay her back for all the times she had tread on his moral uprightness, knowing he wouldn't be able to lie. "As my advisor, do you think this is an effective use of our resources? You'll tell me if it isn't, right?"

She stared at him with agony and, underneath it, a definite streak of respect for the cleverness of his revenge. "Yes, I would tell you. I cannot lie to you for personal gain. And yes, it would make me more effective, granting me a new rank of magic."

"Such as?"

"Such as the power to change my appearance."

There wasn't really any need for that; she was already distressingly attractive.

"Just think of all the money I'll save on hair dye." She was smiling now, making jokes like usual, but he could see the hunger in her eyes. Remembering the first time he had walked on air, he had to sympathize. Magic was fun.

"And what else?"

A wince. "A spell you have reason to despise. But understand, I am not a rapist. Any man I cannot tempt into my bed by ordinary craft I do not deserve. The spell has legitimate uses—talking your way past a suspicious guard, or gaining the trust of a suspected informer."

Both Christopher and his most loyal friend and subaltern Karl had been subject to the charm spell. It was an absolutely painless procedure, but the idea of it left a foul taste that was hard to erase.

"I cannot deny how much I want this, Christopher. There are only half a dozen minstrels in the realm. None won the rank before their thirtieth year."

"And how old are you?" There was a real test of her new oath. No woman liked to reveal her age.

"I don't have to tell you everything, only what you need to know. But I brought up age, so I will tell you this time. I am twenty-three."

The woman was cynical and world-wise enough to be twice that age. It was a sad fact of medieval life that people became adults too young. On this world, with its bloody feast of souls and rigid hierarchies of power, it could only be worse.

He pushed the purple stone across the table, letting it come to rest in front of her.

"I've decided that your new powers are worth the cost."

She lifted the stone gently, like a luscious, delicate fruit. Looking at tael always made his mouth water. Although it had no taste or smell, the idea of eating it was universally appealing. Lalania parted her lips and put the little purple ball on the tip of her tongue. Taking away her hand she let it balance there, before curling her tongue into her mouth and swallowing.

Christopher coughed and looked away. His guards were not so disciplined: they stared at the woman in slack-jawed lust.

"Thank you, my Lord Vicar," she said. "On behalf of my College, I thank you for your investment in us. We will not disappoint you."

He hadn't done it for her College. Nor did he give two beans about her new rank of magic. He had done it for himself. The institution had assigned him her service; he had already won her friendship, but now he owned her gratitude. It was a position of debt she would have never let herself be placed in yesterday. The woman who so freely gave away her body had always understood that accepting a promotion would bind her against her will. He had bought her, but only after she had volunteered the price. He had manipulated her in such a way that she would never blame him for it, but would think it her own choice.

That ancient crone of a skald was not the only one who could play the game.

With a brief word, he said the blessing over his meal that would render it harmless and toxin-free. The meat had long gone cold. He didn't ask to have it warmed. Right now he didn't feel like he deserved it.

He spent the rest of the day in the library, reading books at random, trying to get a feel for the intellectual history of this world. Their obsession with the supernatural was aggravating: far too many books would state some difficult problem, and then appeal to the reader to commune with gods or demons for the answer.

The other notable topic was significant by its absence. The dreaded *hjerne-spica* hardly made an appearance. The Black Harvest was presented as a bogeyman, waiting in the dark to snap up undeserving realms with weak kings and foolish nobles. The Skald had spoken of it as historical fact; the books described it as myth.

As history, it explained a lot of observations Christopher had already made. The level of technology, the lack of ruins, the uncommon fluidity of their feudal society. They simply hadn't had time to build very much, and before they would get the chance, the harvest would reduce them to starting over. It also helped explain the nonexistence of genetic diversity—everybody he had seen looked like they had stepped out of a Norwegian tourist video, which made sense if they were all descendants of a small group. It was the sort of topic he'd really like to discuss with an outside observer—like, for instance, his erstwhile patron Marcius. Why hadn't the god mentioned any of this stuff in the first place?

When he realized he was doing the same thing the books did—turning to the supernatural for explanations—he decided it was time for bed.

When his guard detail opened the door, he was surprised to see it was dark. The Loremasters had let him read through dinner. There was a covered plate of food waiting for him in his room. The College had found the perfect solution to the problem of dragging him out of the library to eat or explaining to his guards why he couldn't take food into that room of irreplaceable paper.

This was exactly the kind of diplomatic skill he needed to wage his covert revolution. Recruiting the College to his side was worth the trip. He'd made the right decision. As he drifted off to sleep in the downy comfort of the feather mattress, with its silk-lined sheets, he wondered whose idea it had really been.

When Christopher stepped out of his chamber in the morning, he was surprised to see two soldiers standing outside the door.

"Were you there all night?"

"Not us, sir, but some of us were. We switched off every two hours."

"That probably wasn't necessary. I'm sure the security of the

College is adequate." No doubt it was better than what two unranked men could provide, despite the firepower of their carbines. There were all sorts of spells that could only be defeated by sheer rank.

"It was them we were protecting you from, sir."

He started to argue with the guard, until he realized they weren't protecting his life.

Karl had warned him. His celibacy was no longer his choice. It had become part of his contract with his men.

Remembering that one of them had recently died in his service, he decided he didn't have any room to complain.

"Thank you, soldier. Let's get some breakfast for the road." The sooner he left this place behind, the easier his life would be.

Lalania was waiting for him in the dining room, accompanied by Uma and an absurdly attractive raven-haired woman with an awe-inspiring bustline who brought a bowl of porridge to his table.

"Remember that you are welcome here at any time, Christopher." The dark-haired woman spoke with the Skald's voice. "We are honored by your presence."

He had last seen her in the presence of a null-stone, where she could not hide her age behind magic—and where Uma could not hide her disfigurement. Here, in the hard light of day, they were both younger and more beautiful than Lalania. His love of honesty warred with pity, until he remembered what they did with their illusions.

"Thank you, Lady Friea. Your hospitality has been . . ." He looked at his men wolfing down bowls of porridge while pretty women brought them milk and honey, giggling and touching them familiarly. ". . . superfluous."

"We try," she said with a wink. "We are sorry that you must rush off. We had to hurry through Lala's graduation ceremony."

Lalania was dressed more modestly than usual. She also had a new instrument in her hands, a gold-painted harp of some kind. She bowed, showing it off.

"I've given my lute to another student, with best wishes and high hopes for her education. The lyre is the instrument of the minstrel. It advertises my status, to your credit. Or it would be, if I wore your colors."

He didn't have any colors. His men dressed in brown, which was a neutral, meaningless shade in this hue-obsessed world, where supernatural affiliation and personal moral development were measured in primary colors. The color he was entitled to was white. He had a suit of armor painted like that, but he couldn't imagine anything made of cloth staying white for more than five minutes in the swamplands his army now occupied.

"We could get you one of our coats, I guess." The huge, floppy leather duster would render Lalania just another shapeless form in his army.

Come to think of it, that was a marvelous idea.

Lalania didn't seem quite so sold on it. "As your advisor, I have to tell you that a man of your rank would normally dress his companions differently. Such as a white fur cloak, trimmed in blue, with fastenings of ivory or pearl."

"Blue?" Uma said. "Wouldn't blood red be more appropriate for a war-priest?" Blue was the color of law; red was violence unchecked. Green and yellow were the more common, muted degrees of good and evil. Christopher understood this well enough now to frown at Uma's jibe.

"Enough, ladies." The Skald smiled indulgently, belying the authority in her tone. "The Vicar is not interested in fashion, only practicality. Brown serves for him, and it will serve for you, Lala."

"Of course," she said. "I will be honored to serve as you see fit. But you might want to invest in a real wardrobe, in case you are ever called before the King."

She really meant, in case *she* was ever called before the King. Christopher already had been, and he'd worn his army uniform.

"I'd rather not." He left it to his audience to determine which, exactly, he'd rather not.

"It may be unavoidable," the Skald warned him. "Your path takes you through Kingsrock."

He and Lalania had ridden off the roads and through Black counties to avoid that place. Except, of course, they had really been riding to the Bloody Mummers.

"So Nordland's not a danger anymore?" He tried not to sound too annoyed at having been misled.

"I would not go so far as that," Lalania said, doing a very good job of not being ashamed. "But you have a dead man to escort to your Cathedral. No one can find provocation in that."

"How long will it take?"

"Two days to Kingsrock, another day and a half to Knockford. Assuming you wish to ride a hard pace, and not a killing pace. Your horses have burnt weeks of fat in the last three days. They need time to recover, as do your men."

The men had the temerity to snicker over that.

"Well, let's get moving." He was starting to worry about his fort, out there in the swamp. It had been many days since he had left. What if the ulvenmen had returned? "I've got an army waiting for me."

"Give us an hour, Christopher, and we can set your mind at rest on that score." The Skald had pitched her voice for his ears alone.

He almost asked how, but of course the answer would be the same as it always was. Magic.

Turning to Kennet, he issued the order he'd been trying to give for the last twenty-four hours. "Corporal, be ready to ride in one hour." He stood up from the table. "Lady Friea, is there anything you need from me?"

"Your presence would indeed be helpful. After you have dined, please join us in the east parlor."

He picked up his bowl, now gone cold. "Lead on. I'll eat on the way."

"Your first lesson in scrying," Lalania whispered to him. "Names have power."

The Skald recited a list of names with the same cadence Christopher would have used on a phone number.

"Karl Treyeingson, son of Aelf, in the reign of Treywan, the Church of Krellyan, the army of Christopher Sinclair."

So this was why nobody used their names. Christopher had been handing out his supernatural address to everybody he met, setting himself up for an unknown amount of unwanted attention.

Murmuring in a strange tongue, both liquid and harsh at the same time, the Skald lit candles of various sizes and set them around her crystal ball in a complex pattern. The flames changed color as they burned; their reflections and refractions in the crystal coalesced and danced until they took shape, forming a suddenly clear image in the center of the ball. Karl, frowning at a group of soldiers.

"You call that clean?" he barked. "Try again. This time you have only thirty seconds."

The men fell about their rifles with ramrods and patches. Christopher nodded approvingly. The swamp was filthy. He hadn't invented bluing yet; mud in the barrels would rust his guns like a plague.

"Are you reassured all is well?" Uma asked him. She was doing the talking now that the Skald was busy maintaining her concentration on the spell.

"Can you scan the surrounding countryside?" Why send scouts into danger when they had this?

"No," Uma replied, dashing his hopes. "We need an individual to target. If you are satisfied, we have a long list of other people we'd like to check up on."

"The ulvenman shaman. You should check on him." Christopher would love to know what that monster was up to.

"Does he have a name?" Uma was being sarcastic; she knew perfectly well the two had never been formally introduced. Christopher could not even be sure it was a he. "Bring us a name, or series of names, that identifies your foe and no other. Until then, you have given us too little to waste our time on. Even if we could create a link to an ulvenman shaman, how would we know it was *your* ulvenman shaman, and not some other creature that threatens some other kingdom in some other corner of the endless expanse of the plane of Prime?"

That was another question he really wanted to ask, but didn't dare. How big was this world? The Skald had apparently reassured herself that Christopher wasn't a magically disguised brain-eating squid, but she still didn't know he was from another planet. If he started asking about cosmology, she might figure it out.

Uma had already dismissed him, turning her attention to the Skald. He let Lalania lead him out of the room, while she finished Uma's list of disclaimers.

"Do not ask us to scry on peers, priests, or wizards. The spell can be detected, so we do not normally look in on those we don't wish to offend. They generally do us the same courtesy in return."

He was beginning to appreciate why she was always so careful with her words. Who knew who was watching? The choice of location for the other night's conversation with the Skald made more sense now. Under the protection of the null-stone, they could speak without fear of being overheard.

The second lesson Lalania was trying to impart to him was more immediate: don't annoy people with high ranks and unknown powers. Climbing into the saddle at the head of his column of men, he hid his rueful grin. Lalania would be no more successful at educating him on that topic than Cardinal Faren had been.

2

HOME TO ROOST

Riding the highways with a dozen armed men presented only one danger, and that was to his purse. Feeding, rooming, and stabling the horde was expensive, and even Lalania couldn't bargain for a better price. He traveled like nobility, so he paid like nobility. His men and horses were locusts, consuming everything in their path and leaving behind nothing but gold. His gold.

As they climbed up the road to Kingsrock, the city sparkled above him in the twilight. If he ignored the smell of horseflesh, and the absence of the sound of traffic, he could pretend he was back home.

The illusion lasted until he reached the gates. Surly men in chain mail, wielding halberds, glowered at him. Nothing modern about that.

"Do you not recognize peerage?" Lalania glowered imperiously back at the men on the ground.

One of them answered her with a jocular leer. "Fancy dress don't make a peer, or we'd all be bowing and scraping to the tailor's dummy."

"Would you like the Vicar to demonstrate his rank?" Lalania asked sweetly. Her horse took two steps forward.

The guard drew back slightly, unconsciously moving his halberd a few inches to the center, as if it were a shield that would protect him.

"Sure, and why not? We could use a show."

Lalania whipped out her thin sword. "Bring your ugly mug over here. After I stab it, the Vicar will heal you, and then you'll know he's really a priest."

"Dark gods, you crazy bitch!" he exclaimed, as his fellows leapt to the ready in a jingle of chain mail and the rustle of wooden shafts in leather-gloved hands. Now the guards stared at the mounted party down the ends of their halberds.

Christopher's men did nothing. As if that weren't insulting enough, one of them chuckled.

"May we pass?" Lalania asked, still saccharine sweet.

The guardsmen fell out to either side of the gate, opening a path. Christopher rode through the forest of polearms and baleful glares. If the guards were planning an ambush, it was a perfect setup. They could fall on the mounted column from both sides, while the horses were in single file.

They knew it, and they knew he knew it. It was another test of courage and trust. On Earth, you shook hands; here, you bared your throat to a naked blade.

It was just a formality, though. Christopher's men outnumbered the guards, and if it really came to a fight, they would be hard-pressed to kill him alone.

"Is it always this difficult?" he asked.

Lalania did that thing with her eyes, the earnest look she always gave him when he was being stupid. "That was a good thing, Christopher. The King's common guardsmen do not bow and scrape to any wandering rank. This shows his strength, and their faith in him. Why, the only greater honor they could do him is to carry themselves like knights."

Christopher glanced back to where his young bravos on fine horses were winking languidly at the girls and grinning insolently at the men on the street.

"Damn," he muttered.

"Damned indeed," she answered. "Luckily, there's only a dozen. Everyone will assume you've knighted them. It would be the normal thing to do with a personal retinue."

They weren't a retinue; they were just an ordinary cavalry troop on guard detail. All of his men would act like this. He had been worried about their attitude last spring, and now, after the ulvenman battle, he was petrified.

"It also explains why you're reviving them." One of the horses in the train carried a body bag instead of a rider. "People will see what they expect to see, as long as you let them. I suggest you let them, as long as possible."

Lalania was the authority here. He sighed, knowing the answer would somehow cost him money.

"What should I do?"

"You are a peer. Act the part enough to not draw attention to yourself. That means"—she grinned at him mischievously—"dressing me in silks and furs. Any lord would want to show off such an appealing addition to his party. Other men like looking at pretty girls in fine clothes, even if you don't."

He glared at her. She did a lousy job of pretending to be chastised.

"The College has chosen not to keep my appointment a secret. Mostly because it will eventually come out anyway, and being clandestine would only draw attention to it. Also because they felt you needed their support. Your Church is your one loyal ally at court, but they are a weak voice, for all their rank."

"The College is a strong voice?"

"No," she admitted. "We are old and established, so we convey gravity. But we have little political clout."

That seemed hard to believe, given that they had such a strong intelligence-gathering ability. Could the Skald have mismanaged their affairs that badly?

"Are you sure I'm the one profiting from this?" Maybe the College needed his prestige. He was the one with the victorious army.

"Yes." She glared back at him. It failed to be intimidating, radiating out from her pretty eyes, which happened to be sky blue today. "We could have allied with any of the Aesir, if we wanted to. Indeed,

Nordland will probably view our choice as yet another insult you have done him."

"So . . . why?"

"You already know. It is a plain fact that our influence has waned over the years. It is, however, a question as to why. Now we have made you an enemy of whatever power works against us. Perhaps in moving against you, it will reveal itself."

"Thanks for nothing," he said. They could have told him this before he accepted the deal.

She lowered her voice. "It was always destined to be your enemy, Christopher."

If there really were octopus-headed monsters grooming the Kingdom for a harvest, Christopher's plans to turn peasants into fire-spitting dragons would not make them happy.

He turned into the stables of the Cathedral with relief. In all the Kingdom, this was the safest place he could be. And the cheapest. His men would not be served by pretty wenches, but they would be fed and stabled for free. The only price would be Guard Captain Steuben's disapproving clucks.

"I see you travel in style now." Steuben already had a cluck ready for him. "A remarkable change from when you rode to our door, begging for money."

"What, this lot? I'd trade them all for another Karl." Karl had opened that door for him. The Saint had trusted Karl's judgment, not Christopher's promises.

"Even her?" Steuben frowned at Lalania. "Why did you bring that strumpet into the grounds of the Cathedral?"

"I honor your Vicar," she answered. "I have been attached to him as minstrel-in-service."

"You honor the wrong god, as far as I am concerned. Go back to your Blue-draped altar and split your legal hairs. We don't need your distractions here."

This was very confusing, since Christopher happened to know that Lalania was actually Green and the Captain himself was Blue. But he understood the Church they chose was more important than their personal level of moral development.

Lalania disagreed with even that much. "We do not serve the Aesir, Ser. We serve the Kingdom."

"Not any bloody better," Steuben growled.

"Ser!" Lalania pretended to be shocked. The words were close enough to treason to trip even Christopher's unsubtle warning alarms.

"What is the realm coming to, when a man can't speak his own mind in his own stable?" Steuben blew out his cheeks and glared.

"Your loyalty to your Saint is commendable, but the Saint is loyal to the King. So you have no need for concern." Lalania smoothed over the conversation. She was always doing that, either covering things up or digging things out. It made Christopher dizzy. He decided to change the topic.

"Can I see the Saint? I have a soldier to revive."

"Gods, man! We've just revived three score for you. Can't you stop killing them long enough for us to catch our breath?"

Steuben was a warrior, not a priest. He hadn't done any of the work. Christopher decided to needle him back a little. "How did it go? Did I lose any?"

The Captain glared at Christopher with real annoyance now. "No, you did not. They all returned, even that prancing pony from the Near Wild. You should have told us there was a Ranger in the lot. They won't be pleased that you've corrupted their lad with your civilized ways."

Christopher wasn't sure if the Captain was angry because of his faux pas or because, once again, the laws of probability had bent on Christopher's behalf. His men were highly motivated to return to the world of the living, and they did so with a frequency that could not help but disturb the Captain's sense of proper order.

"Well, let's go," Christopher said when it became clear the Captain wasn't going anywhere soon.

"Go on in. You're old enough now you don't need a nanny. I'll see to your boys for you, get them some bunks and a proper meal. The harlot can stay here in the stable, I suppose."

Christopher frowned, but Lalania shook her head at him.

"If the Captain wishes to keep me under close surveillance, I can only praise him for his wise precaution. No doubt he desires to keep his capable eyes on me himself. If you could arrange to send me a meal, I'll try to convince the Captain of my good intentions over dinner. Oh, and perhaps you could send out a tub and some hot water? The road clings to me, and I am in need of a bath."

Steuben had brought this on himself. Christopher tossed his reins to a stable-boy, and left the Captain to lose his battle of wits on his own.

After settling his latest account with the Saint, he wanted to spend the rest of the day in the church library, reading, of all things, law books. He couldn't leave until tomorrow anyway, forced as he was to wait for the revived soldier to be well enough to ride. He'd barely figured out the indexing scheme for the legal codices before Lalania interrupted him.

"Did you know one of the best tailors in the realm is just down the street?"

"What are you doing in here?" Hadn't Steuben made a big deal of keeping her out of the Cathedral? Guiltily, Christopher realized he'd been looking forward to the peace and quiet.

"I've taken the measure of the man, and stitched together a solution that pleases us both. By the way, I must warn you, the Captain is not the iron-hard soldier he fancies himself to be. His bed is too soft for that."

"Oh, for crying out loud!"

He did, then, his eyes watering. Lalania had slapped him.

Red-faced and furious, she told him off. "Call me to your bed, and you can tell me who to bed with. Until then, *shut the hell up*."

Would it be cheating to cast a spell and take the sting out of his face? "I'm sorry, Lala. I just . . . Do you think it's wise?"

"I am not you, Christopher. I have needs. I can't sleep with your soldiers anymore. Steuben is a puffed-up fool, for all his steadfast loyalty. If I can put him on my side—our side—while consoling my loneliness, then yes, it is wise. He is handsome enough, strong as a bull, and he has that certain quality I apparently find irresistible. Namely, that he is so full of his own righteousness that he cannot see past the end of his nose."

Had she really said *anymore*?

"Am I so bad?"

"Worse, because most of the time I find your righteousness compelling. You risk blinding me as well."

He sought for a peace offering. Valuing her contribution was the best he could come up with. "Tell me how soft we're talking."

"He has spent too long in comfortable security, without considering danger. You heard him in the stable. We all have our own loyalties, but to openly speak of favoring them over the King is . . . troublesome."

"It wasn't that open." Weren't they talking about it pretty openly right now?

"A stable offers many places for eyes and ears to hide. Scrying is not the only way to spy on people. Now if you are truly contrite, you could take me shopping by way of apology. It is not fit that a minstrel should dress as a troubadour, even if you will not feather me as a songbird."

So now his conversations with Lalania would be both painful *and* expensive. He had to hand over an entire purse of gold to get rid of her.

～〇〇〇～

Riding between Copperton and Fram, he was temporarily gratified to see that at least the road in this part of the Kingdom was professionally built and well maintained. Until he remembered he had paid for it. They spent the night in Fram town, where he spent just as much gold on innkeepers as he had on the way to Kingsrock.

Consequently, he was in a bit of a mood the next day, and so they skipped Knockford, doing no more than waving politely at the gate guards as they rode past. Knockford hadn't had a gate until he'd shown up. The Vicar Rana hadn't been happy about building one, and Christopher would spend just as much feeding his men in her town as he had everywhere else. Best to ride on home to the village of Burseberry and feed the men out of his army kitchen, where food was charged by the ton instead of the plate.

They came up to the village in late afternoon. He could feel the peacefulness settling on him. Old Pater Svengusta would laugh at him, Helga would bake a pie, Big Bob would serve bad ale, and everything would be as it should be. A week of calm, orderly boredom, while he wrote up his treatise for the College and fattened up his horses. Nobody would sneak naked into his bed; the village girls were much too tame for that. His assassin did not dare trouble him here, while he was surrounded by squadrons of soldiers and the unyielding loyalty of the peasantry. No other nobility would deign to make the trip, since Burseberry was utterly lacking in anything remotely interesting to the upper classes.

Except himself. His nameless assassin and the dreadful Baron Black Bart had both come out here just to kill him. So had horrible Ser Hobilar, twice, and the wizard Flayn. The knights Cannan and Gregor had traveled this way, intent on depriving him of his sword. In fact, a barrelful of nobility had rolled into Burseberry with no better reason than to bother him.

So it was with little surprise that he found a woman in green silks sitting on his chapel steps, waiting for him. His troop brought their mounts to a halt at the edge of the village green, the horses pawing at the ground in a display of impatience, the soldiers frowning in suspicion and their hands close to their carbines. It was with equally little grace that he trotted up to the woman on his imposing warhorse, and growled from the saddle, "What do you want?"

"You are the Lord Vicar Christopher, High Priest of the Marshal of Heaven, are you not?" Her voice was melodious, but all he could register was that she had laid on the titles with a liberal hand. That meant she wanted something from him.

He shrugged, his identity unmistakable.

"My son tells me you have pledged vengeance upon the kin-slayer Cannan."

He twitched his warhorse's reins, telling it to stop prancing. He slapped down his own embarrassment at having been so churlish. This woman must be the mother of Ser D'Kan, his young Ranger, who was also brother to the Druid Niona, who had once been married to the knight Cannan, who had saved his life on more than one occasion and who was now accused of his wife's murder.

"I counted your daughter as a true friend, Lady, and I would see justice done."

"Then I bring you glad tidings." The green-clad woman stared up at him with hard eyes. "We have found his trail."

3

A DISH SERVED COLD

It wasn't Christopher's idea of good news. *Hey, we found your friend, now let's go kill him.* He hadn't expected to have to make good on his promise to D'Kan so soon.

To be honest, he hadn't really considered it at all. Finding Cannan had seemed like a remote possibility, safely confined to a distant future. People could disappear into the wilds back on Earth by accident, and that was with helicopters and satellite-photography maps. If Cannan wanted to vanish here, all he had to do was walk a day or two in the wrong direction.

That was before he'd known about scrying. Why hadn't he asked the Skald to look for Cannan? Why hadn't Lalania reminded him to?

So many questions. He settled for one that would be less likely to annoy his audience. "Where?"

"South, and east. Days of hard riding, through untamed wilderness, fraught with peril. Best you should rest, and leave in the morning."

"The Vicar sets his own schedule, Lady." Torme, his knight turned assistant priest, had come out of the chapel doors. Christopher was immensely relieved to see him.

"Torme, invite the Lady inside and offer her some refreshment while I stable my horse." No point in leaving her sitting on his chapel steps.

"I have, my Lord Vicar, these last nine hours. And the day before, to no avail."

Christopher frowned at his attaché, surprised at his failed hospitality.

"Do not blame your servant," the woman answered in his place. "I did not wish to profane your chapel."

Now Christopher was annoyed with her. "Any Bright is welcome in any church of the White. We are all on the same side."

She matched his gaze with her glittering eyes. "As it please you."

"It pleases all of us, Lady Io. We are indeed all on the same side." Lalania's tone was formal without being either stiff or obsequious. "Now we must see to our beasts, who have served us well today. Please excuse us."

"Of course." The lady did not smile, but she turned away graciously enough.

Christopher flicked Royal's reins, and the horse happily trotted toward Fenwick's, where he had once lived in all the luxury of a favored pet. Christopher decided not to argue. Fenwick's boys would take good care of him. Lalania followed him while the rest of his troop went off to the new cavalry stables south of the village.

Inside Fenwick's barn, while he was unsaddling his horse, she told him what he faced.

"Her husband is a Ranger, ranked as a baron, but the druids have no titles. Though she is equivalent to your Curate rank she will answer only to Lady or druid. If you want to seem friendly, call her Lady Io."

Niona had never introduced herself as anything but Niona. She had told Christopher her life story, but somehow had left out the part about being the daughter of a peer.

"Isthalia is one of the smaller counties of the Near Wild. Beric, her husband, failed to achieve the rank of Lord Ranger by a decent age, and no doubt never will. Nor will the Lady Io ever hold the chair of High Druid. All they have in this world are their children, and you have stolen two of them away."

"Two?" By his count, he'd returned one without taking any.

"The Lady last saw her daughter two years ago. You saw her within the year, and held her affection. And yet you let her walk into the Wild with a dangerously unstable man."

That seemed unfair, to both Cannan and himself. He opened his mouth, but Lalania silenced him with a finger.

"I tell you how she will see it, Christopher. Now her son is seduced away from their religion and serves you like any ordinary knight. She will not thank you for reviving him, any more than she will thank you for getting him killed in the first place."

Christopher yanked on the girth, and Royal snorted at him.

"Sorry," he muttered, trying again.

"Indeed," Lalania answered for the horse. "If you're done feeling sorry for yourself, you might ask me what to do next."

"Okay. What do I do next?"

"Be polite, but do not think she is your friend simply because she is Bright. Remember that in her eyes you have wronged her, yet she knows that in the eyes of the world you have not. This means she cannot seek compensation. Which means there is nothing you can do to appease her."

"Except killing Cannan."

"Yes," Lalania said, frowning at him, "which I know you do not intend to do. That might not be wise."

Christopher met her gaze. For all the bard's skill at reading character, she had misjudged him.

"I don't *desire* to kill him. That's not the same thing."

"It may come to it. You will need all your strength to fight the monster he has become. You cannot afford vacillation."

A change of subject would be nice. "Why didn't you ask the Skald to scry on Cannan?"

Lalania vigorously brushed out her horse's mane. "Because I didn't care about Cannan. The High Druid can scry her own problems."

Of course everybody else had their own magical TV set. Christopher wondered how many of them had been spying on him. If the number was high, should he be worried or flattered? "So why did it take them this long to find him?"

She sighed. "I imagine they looked in on him every day. And to what avail? One patch of forest is much like another. How could they tell from his immediate surroundings where in the great Wild he was?"

Christopher waited a moment, until he realized she wasn't asking a rhetorical question. Then they went inside to find out.

Lady Io perched on the edge of a chair in his lecture hall, underneath the wooden gaze of the carved frieze of Marcius, as uncomfortable as a canary in front of a cat. To Lady Io, the god Marcius wasn't a remote employer, a curious alien, or possibly an impressive piece of computer programming. He was a person, a real individual with goals and fears, likes and dislikes. He might be watching her right now, looking for any hint of offense. The distant, impersonal force that passed for modern deities back on Earth was unknown here. This was what it must have been like for the Greeks: gods who lived, loved, and hated, rarely seen but only a mountain away.

A strange set of thoughts, no doubt brought on by his recent discovery that unknown parties could be watching him at any time.

D'Kan stood behind her, looking equally uncomfortable.

"Ser D'Kan!" Christopher reached out to shake the young man's hand, happy to see him alive and well again. D'Kan stared at the outstretched hand in perplexity.

"I, uh . . ." Christopher stalled, trying to think of an intelligible explanation for his odd behavior. Sighing, he gave up, as he usually did, and put his hand in his pocket. "It's good to have you back."

The young Ranger turned another shade of miserable.

"Lady Io," Lalania smoothly interjected, "since time is short, perhaps we should cut to the quick. Where is Cannan?"

"Close at hand, yet where we cannot reach him. He ranged far afield, trying to flee beyond our ken, but he found the world of the living a hostile place to one so foul as he. He has run to ground where only his own dark kind dare tread: the Moaning Lands."

Christopher, still waiting for some kind of definitive answer, looked to Lalania. The bard had an unhappy grimace on her face, as if she'd eaten a bug. "So you've heard of this place?" he asked.

"Legends," Lalania answered. "I'm not sure I credit them."

"You should," Lady Io admonished her. "The truth is worse. The land is haunted by creatures of night and darkness that cannot be touched by iron. Our law forbids us from entering the region, but even if it did not, common sense would stay us. The murderer is protected by his wickedness, but any Bright who trespasses on that cursed land risks awakening horror."

Tapping his finger on the tabletop, Christopher made his own grimace. "Then what do you expect me to do about it?" His guns shot lead. It seemed unlikely that monsters immune to iron would be discomfited by a metal a few steps over on the atomic chart.

"Servants of the Mother are masters of the living. But you are a priest." Lady Io sat back, having served her devastating comeback.

When she finally realized he was still waiting for her to explain herself, he scored his first point. She arched her eyebrows in surprise.

"Go on," he said.

"Surely you jest? Your divinity grants you the power to repulse or even destroy the soul-trapped. As you must know, this is barred to me, being the province solely of the priesthood."

Oh. Now he remembered driving animated skeletons out of his chapel, holding his glowing sword in front of him. He'd followed Pater Svengusta's lead without knowing exactly what he was doing. Later, it hadn't seemed important to follow up on. He didn't encounter skeletons on a regular basis.

Lalania still wasn't happy. "The Vicar is only sixth rank. I'm not sure how much evil he is proof against."

Lady Io didn't care. "More than we."

"Where is this place?" he asked, although he was pretty sure he'd already asked that question once. "Wait, let's get a map, and then you can show me." It would be a lot more helpful than more of her verbiage.

The only maps he had were of the Kingdom. But Lady Io pointed to a spot off the south end, and D'Kan offered a reference point.

"Due east of your fort, my lord. On clean ground, a day's hard ride. In that swamp, four days or more."

He'd figured out how to not get killed by ulvenmen, and now they were trying to get him killed by . . . well, he didn't know what exactly. The skeletons had been creepy, but they were plenty vulnerable to iron. And dynamite.

"What am I looking for?"

"You will know the land by its absence of any warm-blooded creature. Only insects live there. Bring your own provender, for you will find little otherwise. The murderer occasionally strays out in search of meat, but mostly he stays at the center of the taint. Look for a long and narrow path free of scrub-trees: the Avenue of Fear. He will be close at hand."

Christopher wasn't sure he could find a patch of swamp in the middle of a swamp. It was all swamp to him.

"How will I find him, when and if I do find this place?"

"I know his track," D'Kan said. "I will lead you to him."

Lady Io sprung to her feet. "No! You are forbidden by our law. You cannot tread there, not even to hunt the criminal."

"What Cannan did was forbidden by our law, too. Yet he did it all the same." D'Kan was standing up to his mother, although Christopher didn't think comparing himself to a murderer was a particularly judicious tack.

"Lady Io," Christopher said, "D'Kan should be safe with us. I mean, with me."

"It is folly to sunder one law to redeem another. There will be no more talk of it: the boy cannot go into the Moaning Lands." She was harder-edged than the Vicar Rana, and Christopher had thought of that old lady as made of flint.

Lalania stepped in to help. "The Vicar might be able to use his magic to locate Cannan once near, but he will be hard-pressed to find the Moaning Lands at all. Perhaps D'Kan could take us to the edge, but no farther?"

Lady Io glared at her. D'Kan glared as well, though for an opposite reason. Like any good compromise, it left no one happy.

"Ser D'Kan pledged his service to me," Christopher said. "I can't expect him to break your law, but I can ask him to stop just short of it. If he'll take me to the edge, I'll go in and try to drag Cannan out."

"No," said Lady Io, but her boy had become a man.

"I will do this," he told her. His face was on fire, but his voice was steady. "I gave my oath, and I loved my sister. I have already paid too high a price to turn back now."

"Men and their pride—may the Mother weep mercy for them." Lady Io didn't sound merciful. "See that you do not step even a toe into the haunted realm, lest you be dragged under. There is no honor in destroying a mother's love. Swear to me that you will not risk your very soul, or I will take you home against your will."

Christopher looked at the slight, middle-aged woman threatening the lanky young man towering above her, and tried to remember she was fifth rank.

"I swear it," muttered D'Kan, looking as miserable as a middle-school student promising to do his homework.

"I hold you to this oath also, Vicar." Lady Io had plenty of motherly scorn to share. "As his master, your honor is bound up in his."

"Okay," Christopher said. "All right, already. D'Kan won't enter the bad place, we'll take our own food, and I'll scare off the spooks and find Cannan by myself." It seemed like a pretty tall order.

"Then I shall depart. If the murderer flees to other lands, I will contact you. I thank you for your hospitality." She hadn't touched the cup of water Torme had brought. "I thank you in advance for your justice."

That part, at least, she seemed sincere about. After stepping outside, into the fading twilight, she stood on the chapel steps and looked at her son. For a moment Christopher could see the woman under the rank, the mother under the Servant of the Mother.

"We can find you a place in town, if you don't wish to stay in the chapel." Christopher was trying to be helpful, but as he was saying it he realized she'd already been there one night. She must have already made accommodations.

"Thank you," she said, smiling politely, "but I found your woods to be fair haven. Knowing that my daughter once slept there gave me solace."

Then, stepping off the stone steps into empty space, she transformed, her form running like stirred oil, and she was gone. In the place she had occupied, an eagle beat its wings, lifting into the air.

Christopher stared in openmouthed awe as the bird did two turns above them, cawing to D'Kan, and flew out into the darkening sky.

"Wow," he said.

"That is true shape-change," Lalania said wistfully, "not the petty glamour I can do." She had deep black eyes today, with remarkably long and thick lashes.

"How am I supposed to get Cannan, if she can't?" He'd promised to do a lot of tasks that he had no idea how to do, and the polymorphic druid seemed more capable than he had ever imagined.

"You know," Lalania said, "most people who make sixth rank already know how to use their powers. But then, most people get there after years of study, effort, risk, and single-minded devotion. Luckily, I am here to provide the education you skipped."

"Can you teach me to do that?" Didn't hawks fly sixty miles an hour? He could cross the whole Kingdom in an afternoon as a bird.

"No." Lalania laughed at him. "Never. You will have to settle for reviving the dead as your signature power. Try not to be too disappointed."

There were three score young men, a half dozen wagons of supplies, and several teams of replacement horses going south to the fort. Torme had already seen to it all. Christopher's only responsibility was to salute the men as they formed up to march.

Men. They were only a year older than the recruits gawking at them, but the difference was palpable. These young men had already lived a lifetime. They had watched their life's blood run out in the slavering fangs of a howling dog-man, their broken bodies and cries of pain buried under smoke and the din of battle. They had died and come back.

Now they stood silently, in neat rows, waiting for the order to march back into the thresher. Christopher's parting joke died on his lips, and he said something else instead.

"I'll see you down at the fort." Except he probably wouldn't. The wagons would take five long days to reach the new southern extremity of the Kingdom. Christopher and his cavalry escort would do it in three short ones. By the time the revived men got there, he would be off on his idiot hunting adventure.

He turned his horse onto the road and started south. Behind him Lalania, Torme, D'Kan, and the dozen cavalrymen fell into a double line, their horses lightly loaded. They would buy food on the way, sparing the animals that had been working so hard for days.

"You need to tell him," Lalania said, when they were out into the open country.

"Tell me what?" Christopher looked over his shoulder. D'Kan was looking ill again, and Torme was staring intently at his horse's mane.

"The Lady Io is unaware of the favor you have extended to Ser

D'Kan." Whenever Torme was that formal, it meant he was trying not to make Christopher angry. Usually, it worked. Every time he thought about how Torme had lived under Black Bart, where a single slipped phrase could cost a man his tongue or his life, Christopher found himself unable to get angry.

Not this time. "Dark Hells, Torme. How could you not have told her?" Now *he* would have to tell the woman, and she'd scratch his eyes out. Or turn him into a newt. Cripes. She might actually turn him into a newt. He wasn't even sure what a newt was.

"The subject did not come up, my lord. I barely spoke to the Lady, except to tell her three times a day that you had not yet returned."

Christopher swallowed the rest of his curses. "Then why didn't D'Kan tell her?" He swiveled his head around to look over his other shoulder.

"I did not wish to undo your fine work, my lord." D'Kan coolly stared back at him. The boy who had blushed in front of his mother had become the stiff young hero who first waltzed into Christopher's camp. "She might have suggested that I undergo the Mother's judgment, and that would have taken time we do not have to spare."

That was reasonable enough, except for the first part. "What do you mean, undo my work?"

Lalania chimed in. She could always be counted on to deliver the most unpleasant facts. "It means they would have killed him again, and let the Mother judge what form he should return to life as."

"You can't be serious," he said automatically, even though he knew she was.

"I considered it." D'Kan spoke as if he wanted everyone to know how coolly he'd face a second death. "My father's totem is a bear. If I were to return in the body of a great brown bear, I might be able to defeat Cannan by myself."

"Then why didn't you?" It was a stupid question, but Christopher asked a lot of those.

D'Kan shrugged and patted his horse's mane. "Bears cannot ride."

Bears cannot marry and have human children, either. But Christopher wasn't graceless enough to say that out loud. Aside from the misery of spending life in animal form, not being able to produce heirs would certainly remove D'Kan from the line of succession. He would never be Lord Ranger then.

Christopher scratched his head and wondered why he was thinking like Lalania. "What about after we get Cannan?" He still needed the Ranger's skills in his army.

"We may very well all perish in the Moaning Lands. Worrying about the future is premature."

"Hold on, sonny. We are not all going in there." Christopher had enough to apologize to Lady Io for. Breaking his word was not going to be added to the list.

"You will never—" D'Kan tried to argue, but Torme interrupted him.

"The Vicar gave his bound oath. There will be no more discussion on the matter."

D'Kan scowled, but Torme was a man of rank too. Christopher had to step into this dispute.

"Go ahead, D'Kan. Ask us how we're going to find Cannan without your tracking skills. I'd kind of like to know the answer myself."

"As usual," Lalania said, "there is a spell for that."

The men welcomed him back into the swamp without fanfare. Not that they had any fans, or trumpets, or confetti, but they didn't make a big deal out of it. Holding down a fort in the middle of ulvenman territory was just another job they did now. He hoped they weren't getting jaded by danger. There was a fine line between courage and stupidity.

He turned in the saddle to ask Lalania what she thought of his fort, and caught her looking at Ser Gregor and the priestess Disa, standing together near the tents that passed for the officers' quarters. The bard's face did not twitch; her smile was as genuine as any he had ever seen, but he knew her now, and he had far too much first-hand knowledge of loneliness. In the hollowness of her eyes he finally understood what should have been obvious weeks ago.

He had told Gregor to see if there was more to their relationship than sex. And Gregor had discovered the answer was, "No." Now the knight stood too close to a woman who had never, to Christopher's knowledge, done anything but argue with him, shifting uncomfortably under Lalania's welcoming smile.

When Gregor had asked for advice, Christopher had given the best he had, even at the risk of loosening the tie that bound the knight to him. Now it appeared he had simply changed the color of the leash. He did not appreciate the way it made him feel.

"Welcome back, Colonel." Karl saluted him crisply.

"It's good to be back, Major, but we won't be staying long. The druids have found Cannan's trail." He saluted back, and the men standing in orderly rows dispersed, returning to whatever tasks they had been doing beforehand. The sentries on the wall had never stopped their appointed duties. Christopher wanted an army that worked, not one that looked pretty on a parade ground, and Karl had given him what he asked for.

"Any excitement while we were gone?" Christopher was feeling guilty for hoping the answer was "Yes," and thus possibly giving him a reason to put off hunting Cannan, but Gregor ruined it as usual.

"Not a bloody lick. Neither hide nor hair of ulvenman, dinosaur, or anything larger than a blasted mosquito. How about you? Did you go off and have fun without me again?"

"Um . . ." Christopher stalled, unwilling to lie. He knew perfectly well that Gregor would consider the fiery incident at the inn as "fun."

His evasion was wasted. The cavalrymen were grinning from ear to ear. Within hours their sojourn at the College would be all over camp. Gregor probably would have considered that fun, too.

"That's it," Gregor swore, looking at the men's faces. "You are never leaving me behind again."

"Surely you found other ways to entertain yourself?" Lalania asked, her gay and lilting tone wholly at odds with the meaning of the words.

Gregor blushed, but Disa didn't flinch. A slip of a girl she might be, with less combat effectiveness than a teenage boy, but she was made of courage.

"Welcome to our camp, troubadour. We have missed your music."

"It's minstrel now," Lalania said, strumming her lyre. "But let us not stand on ceremony, Patera." Christopher had never actually heard the female version of *pater* before. Everyone in his camp called the woman "lady." When there was only one around, there wasn't any chance of confusion.

"Congratulations." Disa smiled as if she meant it. "By the way, it's prelate now, but as you say, ceremony is unnecessary. We are all friends here. Rank will not change that."

"Prelate?" Lalania turned on Christopher. "You have been generous."

"More than you know," Gregor admitted. "He made me a viscount."

Lalania didn't miss a beat. "Finally, Christopher, you act sensibly. You need a retinue. Your enemies are no longer confined to an over-zealous assassin and Invisible Guild pawns."

"He's not my . . . retinue." Just saying the word made Christopher uncomfortable. "He doesn't owe me anything. We were under siege, and we needed his strength for the next day. That's all it was."

Lalania cocked her blonde head at him. "I don't see it that way, and neither does he. My job is to protect you. I'm going to do it with whatever tools I can. Ser Gregor, your friend rides tomorrow into darkness and danger. Will you honor us with your company?"

"I just *said* he wasn't going to leave me behind again," Gregor grumbled.

"When do we leave?" Disa said.

"You don't," Lalania answered. "You belong to the regiment. Christopher cannot haul you along on his private adventures."

"The Vicar can do whatever he likes with the regiment," Torme said. "Outside the realm, his word is law."

A sticky situation. Christopher didn't want to cut Lalania off at the knees, but he couldn't tolerate this squabbling among his staff.

"Karl will decide who goes and who stays. Now I'm going to get out of this saddle." He directed his mount to the pens, where Gregor's huge warhorse Balance snorted and flattened his ears at their arrival. Royal, in a surprising fit of noble tolerance, only whinnied softly in reply.

"My father was right," D'Kan muttered while he dressed down his own horse in the next stall. "Two women in camp is too many."

It was such an unlikely thing for the young Ranger to say that Christopher burst out laughing.

Dinner was served out of huge kettles by insolent privates, amid the jostling of young toughs who were none too clean, using language that was downright filthy. The contrast to the College was startling for Christopher. He'd almost forgotten what army life was like while floating in that sea of luxury.

Lalania dropped her spoon after the first bite and cursed.

"What?" Christopher said, fearing poison, treachery, or cruel pranks gone wrong.

The bard dipped her spoon into Christopher's plate and stole a bite. Her face stayed sour.

"I'm afraid it's always like that," Disa said, commiserating. Gregor didn't say anything, which was probably wise, but it left Christopher to defend his men alone.

"It's not that bad," he said, and dug in. It required an act of will not to spit it out again. He'd forgotten what army food was like, too.

"They won't let me cook," Disa explained. "And they won't learn anything from me. Karl only assigns cooking duty as punishment, so they refuse to even try."

"No doubt you won't let me set a separate table for you, Christopher." Lalania eyed him hopefully.

"No," Karl said, emptying his bowl with grim efficiency.

"Very well. But can I have permission to at least endeavor to make a skill of it?"

Christopher choked down his second bite. "Yes . . . Karl, see if you can find some other unpopular duty for discipline. Anything at all."

Karl was implacable. "Cooking is women's work. There is nothing lower in the camp to do. Even shoveling manure is a man's job, in peasant eyes."

"Then tell them they can't get *off* kitchen duty until they do a proper job of it," Lalania suggested.

They sat in silence for a moment, watching D'Kan at the end of the table struggling manfully with his bowl.

"Fair enough," Karl agreed.

In that moment they were a family again, all divisions forgotten. They left the mess tent with jokes and laughter.

But when Christopher went for his final walk along the wall, greeting his sentries and looking out over the dark marsh, he found Lalania sitting alone in a crenellation, pretending to tune her lyre.

In turn, he pretended not to notice the streaks that ran down her face, glistening in the flickering illumination of light-stones. There was nothing to say, so he just stood there, sharing the silence with her.

"Good night, Christopher," she said after a while.

"Good night, Lala." He finished his patrol, and went to bed. Alone, as always, while he tried to forget the feeling of her back pressed against his, when they had slept together under the stars.

4

HUNTING BARBS

Lalania got her way. Christopher didn't want to know if it was because she was right, or because she'd bamboozled Karl somehow. It didn't really matter. He wouldn't have allowed Disa to go under any circumstance.

The men that rode out with him were all his, not the draft's, a half dozen of the cavalrymen Karl had recruited from the gutters of Kingsrock. Gregor and Lalania too, just like old times, if you ignored Disa's fervent embrace, and the gentleness with which Gregor peeled her hands away. The knight's relationship with Lalania had been bright and hard, like a shiny coin. With Disa, he was like a man tending a flower garden.

D'Kan rode in front, scouting, as he called it, but Christopher felt he needed the space to hide his face and his feelings. Going to confront the man he once had thought of calling brother-in-law, and now must call kin-slayer, stretched the young Ranger as taut as a funeral drum.

Torme's face was as inscrutable as it always was. Watching him leap expertly into the saddle, Christopher was reminded of how little he knew the man. And yet they were tied together by their service to Marcius, the only priests of the Marshall of Heaven in the entire realm. Torme was no fool. Surely he must guess that Marcius's reemergence was significant. A herald of change, an omen of troubles to come. Torme had heard that trumpet call and responded, while others were still wondering at a faint and distant sound.

Not all others. Karl rode out with him, too, bound as tightly to his cause by his innate character as Torme was by his oath to the god. Christopher was surprised to see him leaving the army behind. He had come to think of Karl as not just part of the regiment, but as the embodiment of it. He had come to think of Karl as his inevitable replacement.

Listening to the young man issue orders to the mercenary cavalry, watching them obey without hesitation, Christopher realized why Karl had to come. This was all too traditional. Christopher had a retinue, whether he wanted to admit it or not. He was surrounded by elites, by people with ranks and powers. All of them had gotten a rank from his hand, and could therefore reasonably expect another.

Karl would not. Karl would ride into this haunted swamp, face terrors that had no name, and come back again, just plain Karl. Goodman Karl, never Ser. The ordinary men who rode with him would know that they were coming back the same. For all the tael Christopher had given out, to everyone from craftsmen to wandering minstrels, he had never made a knight out of a common man. He had essentially promised Karl that he never would.

Christopher didn't know if Karl was there to hold him to his promise, or to make it easier to keep. As long as Karl was not knighted, no one else could expect to be. Karl was going to eliminate the aristocracy through sheer example.

They hugged the marsh for a few miles before it ran out into trackless bush. Then they plunged into the swamp, D'Kan now only a few paces ahead. Christopher struggled to keep Royal from taking the lead. Somehow Gregor had convinced Balance to take the rear of the column, a position soon lost to the close-hanging vines. The scrubby trees looked like they were weeping, bound to the earth in chains of green. Christopher slapped a mosquito and blinked, startled, at the sound of ringing metal. He had forgotten he was wearing his plate mail.

D'Kan glanced over his shoulder, frowning. Christopher frowned back. The sweltering, deadening armor was not his idea. Only when Gregor had donned his own had Christopher given up the argument and accepted his imprisonment. If they were attacked, the armored men would naturally be the first targets. It was simple fairness, since they were the most likely to survive, having several ordinary lives bound into their tael.

The tactical notion of hiding their principles no longer applied. They were revealed as players of significance by their mere presence in this untamed swamp.

They camped on ground that could only be called dry by virtue of not being underwater. D'Kan made them set a watch, two men at a time. Only the soldiers surrendered their sleep for this duty. The ranked were treated like prized boxers, coddled until it was time to step into the ring. Christopher would have found this disturbing, except in this particular case the coddling meant an extra hour lying on soggy, saw-toothed grass that managed to be slimy and sharp at the same time, and using all of his powers of concentration to ignore the insect zoo that crawled, slithered, hopped, and flew around them, seeking an exposed patch of flesh to feed on.

D'Kan steered them expertly. They only had to backtrack around a pool, quicksand, or impassable thorny hedge a dozen times. Once, they came across a float of crocodiles in a shallow pond. One of the beasts began drifting purposefully toward the horses; D'Kan shot it in the nose with a blunted arrow. It thrashed its tail in annoyance, but kept its distance. The men lowered their rifles while D'Kan rolled his eyes. A single gunshot would have revealed their presence for miles.

The days began to blur together, in one hot, miserable streak, but on the fourth day D'Kan came to an abrupt halt, and Christopher automatically drew his sword.

"What is it?" he whispered.

"Nothing," D'Kan answered. "That is the problem."

Christopher was covered in a sheen of sweat and raw skin from wearing the unaccustomed armor. Worse, he couldn't scratch half the places he itched because they were protected by steel plates. He was in no mood for riddles.

"Fine, then. What isn't it?"

"What it is, my lord, is the absence of ordinary fauna. We are in the Moaning Lands."

Instinctively he looked behind to see where the border was, but all he could see was swamp.

"Damn it." Another broken promise he might have to pay for.

Lalania had ridden up to see what the delay was.

"Relax, Christopher, no one is in danger yet. One fact we do know of the Moaning Lands is that it is haunted only by night."

She hadn't known that a week ago. Christopher was guessing the Skald could talk through the scrying ball as well as listen. Lalania's stray bits of useful information seemed a lot less serendipitous now.

D'Kan's horse started to move forward again.

"Whoa," Christopher said. "You're not going any farther. You have to get out of here before nightfall."

"The murderer could be in the next grove." D'Kan stopped to argue. "We might seize him and return before dark."

"Or . . . not." Christopher jerked his thumb over his shoulder. "Head on back. Take some of the riflemen, set up a camp, and wait for us." He put on his best minatory glare. This time, damn it, people were going to do what he told them to.

D'Kan sulked, but only briefly.

"Very well, my lord. But I'll be far safer alone than with your blundering smoke-and-thunder men. I can hide from much more than they could kill."

Christopher eyed him speculatively. Was the Ranger telling the truth, or was he trying to weasel out from under Christopher's watchful eye?

Lalania's latest lesson had application here. Splitting his forces was unwise. If the Ranger was false, assigning common men to guard him would only cost them their lives; if he was true, Christopher would want the men with him to hunt the murderer.

"Can you find us again, when we come out? We'll need you to get us back to the fort." Glancing around at the trackless swamp, it occurred to him they might have trouble even getting back to this place.

"I could find you with a bucket on my head. But if for some reason I fail you, simply head north. Eventually you will bump up against some part of the Kingdom. For now, travel due east until you find the Avenue of Fear. The murderer will be drawn to the center of the taint. So will you, for that matter."

D'Kan pulled his horse aside and watched them pass. Christopher let two cavalrymen take the lead, trying not to wince at hiding behind their mundane flesh. The memory of Lalania's lecture when they had ridden through Dark counties burned his ears. Here he was, clad in plate and tael, hiding behind men who had only one life bound to their bodies. But there was no help for it. If the men stumbled into some horrible trap, they could be revived. Though Christopher could be revived too, death would reduce him by a rank; at his current status, replacing a single rank would cost more than reviving half the regiment. Perversely, he was less prepared to survive death now than he had been when he'd first arrived.

They rode for hours while the sun crawled across the sky. Despite the light the marsh was cloaked in muggy gloom. The insects here seemed even larger and more aggressive. Huge blowflies, black and glittering, assaulted their faces so relentlessly that soon they had their heads wrapped in scarves despite the heat. Clouds of gnats blinded him every dozen steps, and the horseflies were so vicious that Royal began snapping at them when they flew by. It was a futile war. The flies could trade bite for bite for a thousand years and still win.

As twilight crept up on them, the insect swarm began to thin. Christopher breathed a sigh of relief, until Torme spoke up.

"The flies abate. The taint must be stronger here. Perhaps you should try your detection spell."

This was their grand plan. Christopher's latest rank gave him access to a spell that would guide him unerringly to an object, if it were within several hundred yards. He wasn't sure why the ability to find lost car keys was on the same level as curing cancer—but in this particular case he was glad to have it. They knew Cannan still had the magic ring wrested from Black Bart; it was far too valuable to part with, and in any case the druids had apparently observed its effects in action while spying on him. Christopher fixed his mind on an image of the ring, bright gold and black onyx, and said words in Celestial, the language of his god.

Somewhat to his relief, nothing happened. But the respite was only temporary. With a sigh he untangled his feet from the stirrups and his hands from the reins, preparing to launch into flight. He could cover an astonishing amount of ground that way, flying just above the treetops so that Cannan couldn't see him coming while his magic radar swept the ground for the ring.

"Not tonight," Gregor said. "Wait for the light."

"I concur," Karl agreed. "We should look for a place to sleep."

Christopher looked ahead and behind, and made a startling realization. They had been traveling in a straight line for the last several minutes. Around him he could see the others reaching the same conclusion.

"Welcome to the Avenue of Fear," Lalania said, her voice uncharacteristically hushed and heavy.

It was drier and clearer than the rest of the swamp. With a shrug, Karl dismounted and began pitching camp.

Someone shook his shoulder. Gently at first, but when he tried to ignore it, the touch hardened.

"What?" he said, opening his eyes. For a moment he wasn't sure where he was. The sky glittered above him, with its impossible profundity of stars.

"Something comes. Get up." Karl's voice was flatter than usual. Christopher sat upright, and Karl pulled him to his feet.

"What?" he asked, less querulously this time.

Karl shrugged. In the dim light, his rifle barrel was a black void.

"Colonel," said a voice from the edge of their camp. One of the cavalrymen. Christopher had thought they were hard as iron, but this man sounded frightened. He went over to reassure him.

When he got there, he could hear what spooked the soldier. A distant mumbling, low and sad. The horses heard it too, and whinnied in complaint.

"Shh," Christopher tried to tell the horses. They ignored him. The moaning grew louder, and Christopher knew it was coming toward them.

"Stand your ground. If rifles can't kill it, Gregor and Karl can." The two men were bearing magic swords. Lalania had sworn the enchanted blades could slay incorporeal beings, even ghosts. Christopher didn't understand how, but then, he didn't understand how a being could be incorporeal in the first place. Gregor was also in full armor, having volunteered to sit watch for the entire night. Ghosts were not the only thing they feared here.

With a sickening lurch of fear, Christopher realized that the shadow of a scrub bush had moved. Before he could convince himself it was an optical illusion brought on by low-light conditions and nervousness, the shadow rose up to the height of a man, blocking out stars on the horizon.

Several soldiers leveled their guns, and the sound of hammers cocking rang through the camp. The shadow ignored them while it took form, a ghastly, twisted humanoid shape.

"Mmmmmmmmmmmmmmm," it moaned. There were words in there, if only Christopher could tease them out. He put his hand on the cavalryman's shoulder, to delay him from firing for a moment, and listened harder.

"Mmsmlmmsmmlmmlsmmslmslsmlslms." The sound was unnerving, like a sick old man in a hospital ward mumbling to himself. The urgency of the message was unmistakable, though. Christopher cocked his head and tried to separate the endless whispering string into pieces.

The world grew gray and then black, but Christopher, intent on understanding the ghost, barely noticed. Every time he got close to a coherent message, it slipped away from him, and he had to struggle twice as hard to get back again.

Underneath the babbling speech, now so loud it drowned out the calls of night birds and the whining of the shuffling, disturbed horses, there was a different sound. It was annoying, bright, and swirly and marching up steps, only to jump down at the end. It kept getting louder, even though Christopher was trying to ignore it. Then he realized it was a lyre playing.

He pulled his attention away from the moaning and the lyre, trying to make his tongue work again. He wanted to tell Lalania to knock it off. But extracting himself from the ghost-babble was proving very difficult. Panicked, he stepped back, his muscles straining as if he were stuck in molasses.

Consciousness returned. The shadow was directly in front of him, its blobby arms outstretched and grasping his head with an intangible touch that was nonetheless dry and cold.

Staggering away, out of its reach, he tried to think of something more intelligent to do, but his brain was as deadened as his limbs. The ghost followed him, its whine now hideous and terrifying instead of sad and curious. Lalania was pounding on her lyre, singing at the top of her lungs, tears of fear pouring down her face.

All around her, men began to come out of their trance. Torme was quickest; he spoke in Celestial, and his carbine began to give off an unearthly light.

Christopher, trying to run backward, stumbled and fell. As the shadow loomed above him he felt himself giving way to unreasoning panic. Then Torme stepped over him and began firing, streaks of light tracing out the path of the bullets as they flew through the babbling shadow.

The moaning turned to shrieks of grief and loss. Christopher rolled, over and over, until he got control of himself. Climbing to one knee, he saw Torme slowly retreating, emptying the carbine into the wailing, thrashing figure. With his last shot, the ghost began to dissipate, like a column of smoke fading into clean air.

Christopher did not even have time to think a congratulatory thought, let alone say one, before more shadows rushed in and engulfed Torme. They were different, their outlines more distinct and their insides darker. They mobbed Torme while he screamed in pain, blackness flowing between their touch and his body. Christopher was amazed at how much noise one man could make, until he realized other people were screaming too.

The camp was in pandemonium. Men and horses shrieked in unnatural terror. Above it all he could hear the tie-lines snapping as the horses panicked and bolted. In an instant they were swallowed up by night, thundering back up the avenue. Lalania had stopped playing her lyre, and was doing a funny kind of dance. Christopher got his sword all the way out of his scabbard before he understood that she was dodging shadowy lunges.

Torme fell to the ground without twitching, having died on his feet. The shadows abandoned his corpse and welled outward, looking for more victims.

Gregor's sword began flickering blue light as he battered at the insubstantial figures, chasing them off Lalania. Men were firing guns, but without magic, they did nothing. The ghosts ignored them, clustering around Gregor. Karl dashed into the fray, his hands full of his huge black sword, and put his back to Gregor's. Together the two men tried to hold the shadows at bay. They were doing pretty well, until the shadows began coming up through the ground at them.

Christopher was desperately trying to think of a spell to help them, but he couldn't seem to settle on the best one. He fell back to old tricks. Grabbing a cavalryman by the shoulder, he cast the weapon blessing on his carbine. Then he pointed at the unnatural duel.

White-faced, the man swallowed and breathed hard. Christopher wanted to slap him back into rationality, but he didn't have to. The man took three steps forward, and began firing.

Immediately several shadows peeled off and mobbed him, but the guns fired as fast as a man could pull the hammer back and let it fall; the cavalrymen prided themselves on their speed. He emptied the gun before he started screaming, and Christopher was sure another shadow had dissipated, but seconds later the man was crumpled on the ground, unmoving. Instantly the shadows began flowing back to where Gregor and Karl were busy losing.

No wonder the man had been frightened. He knew that Christopher had signed his death warrant. Why hadn't that occurred to Christopher?

He tried to make himself think. Looking around, he saw that the men were on the edge of panic. Their rifles were useless; they were, once again, helpless peasants in the face of unworldly evil. Any second now they would break and run, following the horses out into the night, to die lost and alone in the trackless swampland.

Christopher raised his sword. "To me!" he cried, and then he switched to Celestial. It didn't matter what words he used. It was the intent that counted. These monstrosities were unnatural and absurd, abominations of darkness. The Marshall of Heaven would not abide them. Christopher told them that, with all the conviction of his heart, as he walked purposefully toward them, now cloaked in a shimmering light.

The shadows retreated, leaving the two fighting men gasping in their wake. There were only four or five shadows left, milling about a few yards off the avenue. Christopher stopped advancing only because Gregor leaned on him for support.

"What do I do now?" Christopher was close to panic. The radiance would not last forever. Sooner or later the favor of the god would fail, as it always did. Then the creatures would swoop in to finish their feast.

Christopher remembered he had another weapon blessing he could cast.

"Give me a gun," he stammered.

"No," Karl said. He pulled a round, black object from his belt. "Do this instead."

Christopher obeyed without thinking. He cast his spell on the grenade, and then looked fearfully out at the shadows again. Still clutching his sword, he held it in front of them like a barrier. He was very disheartened to see the blade shaking.

Karl pulled the pin and lobbed the grenade into the midst of the shadows. They casually moved out of the way, somehow managing to exude contempt for the feeble attack despite the lack of any facial features or, indeed, any features at all. Once the grenade hit the ground, they ignored it.

Christopher was thinking how ineffective that was, until he remembered that grenades explode. Then he fell to the ground so fast he almost impaled himself on his sword. Everyone else was already down, with their arms over their heads and their faces in the mud.

The prone humans were shielded from the blast by the thick shrubbery close to the ground. The ghosts, floating a foot above the earth, were ripped to pieces, their insubstantiality mixing with smoke and fading away.

Gregor tried to stand, and failed. "Get this cursed plate off me." He flopped in his heavy armor, too weak to even roll over. Lalania bent over him and began ripping into the laces that held it on.

Christopher felt himself surge from terror to racking jealousy. He turned away and found a place to sit down, fighting to get his trembling, seething emotions under control.

"Casualty report, Colonel." Karl knelt next to him, studying his face carefully. "Three dead. Ser Gregor is crippled by some form of magic: he can barely stand. Several other men are weakened, but to a lesser extent."

"And you?" Christopher thought it wildly unfair that the handsome young man should be unscathed despite his reckless heroics.

"I am one of the weakened." Karl put his hand on Christopher's shoulder. "And you?"

"Yes. There's something wrong with me. I don't know what it is, but there's something wrong." It felt good to confess his confusion and fear. His eyes began to tear up.

"We should move," one of the cavalrymen said. "All of that gunfire. They'll know where we are now."

"We're not moving in this darkness," Lalania snapped at him. "You can barely walk. You'll fall into a pool and drown. And besides, nothing we fear in this tainted land will be woken by noise."

"Then what? What woke them up?" Christopher was astonished to hear how close to whining he sounded.

She softened her voice. "You did, Christopher. You blaze like a beacon of light. You and Gregor. So if we move, we risk waking even more of them. Let us hope this area is now clear, at least for the night."

"And tomorrow?" He couldn't be patient. He had to know right now.

"Tomorrow we flee. There can be no hope of taking Cannan now."

"You underestimate the power of our guns." Karl still wasn't afraid. Christopher found that amazing, and gaped at him in awe.

Lalania didn't. "Karl, we *rode* into this taint. We have to *walk* out, carrying our wounded. We don't have time to fool around with some idiotic vengeance quest."

"What she said," Christopher agreed. "That's right."

Karl stood up and spoke directly to Lalania, over Christopher's head. "His orders can't be trusted anymore."

"I know, Karl. That's why I'm arguing with *you*."

"Hey," Christopher said. "Hey, I'm right here."

Lalania knelt down beside him now, and put her arm comfortingly across his shoulders. This was a lot nicer than when Karl had knelt next to him.

"Christopher, everything is going to be fine. But you have to do what Karl says, all right? Can you do that for me?"

He felt a desire to please her flow through him like a warm fountain. Intellectually he knew she was doing that damned charm spell, but the information was swept away on a tide of puppy love.

"Okay. I can do that. For you."

Karl looked down at him. In the darkness it almost looked like disgust. "Rest," Karl ordered everyone. "We have a long march in the morning."

Gods, but Christopher was tired of long marches. But he could fly now. Snickering, he imagined the outrage on Karl's face tomorrow, when everyone else was trudging through the mud and Christopher was sailing far above, bright and clean where nothing could touch him.

After breakfast Karl and Lalania went through the saddlebags, separating out what they would take and what they would leave behind. Bored with waiting, Christopher cast his flight spell.

Nothing happened. He had cast magic the night before, but only first-rank spells. Apparently anything more advanced than that was now beyond him. This was the second time he had been robbed of his magic, and he found it terrifying.

"Take a day's worth of rations; leave the rest, and all the tack. We will be burdened enough as it is." Lalania was giving orders.

"I can walk," Gregor asserted, leaning on his sword for support.

"Of course you can, my hero," Lalania said. "But someone else will have to carry your sword."

"And my armor?" Gregor looked too stricken by the facts to respond to Lalania's baiting. He turned to Christopher and smiled weakly. "You always did want to get rid of it."

Christopher nodded in satisfaction. Now they'd have to dump his armor, too, and Karl couldn't make him wear it anymore.

Lalania looked around and frowned. "What about the bodies?"

Christopher stared at the corpses. They were wrapped in ropes, as if someone had been afraid they might get up and walk away. Come to think of it, in this horrid place, maybe they would have.

"They are for the fire." Karl hefted a small sack. "Only their fingers will come home with us."

"At least we don't have to haul Cannan out," Christopher said. "Thank the gods for small blessings."

"Why, I do believe I deserve the credit for that particular boon," a different voice answered. Ragged and hollow, it was still instantly recognizable. Christopher looked to the edge of the grassy avenue, to the figure standing there.

His armor was holed and faded, hanging in tatters. His face was gaunt, cheeks sunken in hunger. His huge red sword had turned rust brown. Despite all of that, the man still projected power and raw menace.

Cannan smiled at them, grinning like a fevered skeleton. "Not only did you bring me breakfast, but you brought me a woman. How thoughtful of you."

5

RETURN OF THE BARONET

This wasn't working out quite like Christopher had planned. He had intended to descend upon a frightened and cowering Cannan, with guns, swords, and magic at his back. Instead, it was Christopher who was having trouble stopping his knees from knocking. He hadn't had a chance to refresh his spells. Without the weapon blessing, he couldn't enchant his sword to bypass the power of the ring. Absent magic, Gregor was the only equal to Cannan in their camp, and Gregor was barely equal to the task of standing up.

The blue knight had lifted his sword at Cannan's arrival, but now he had to let the point rest on the ground. Cannan laughed at him.

"Can't keep it up anymore, Ser? Then I'll be doing your woman a favor."

"Shut up," Lalania said. "Put your sword down and surrender, or you'll die."

"To what? A few commoners, an old man, and a cripple? You used your magic in the night. I heard it. You have nothing left."

"We have plenty enough left to kill you," Lalania answered.

"No. There was too much screaming for that to be true." He looked directly at Christopher. "You shouldn't have come, Pater. You should have left me here, with my own kind. With the shadows. But now you're here, and I'm going to eat you. I'm so darking sick of lizard meat."

There was a strange spinning quality to Cannan's voice that was making Christopher dizzy. The man was clearly insane.

The man was also bent on violence. With a death's-head grin,

Cannan advanced on Christopher, clearly relishing the sword fight to come. Christopher was terrified. His mundane sword would be almost useless against the ring. Cannan would cut through his tael in a few brutal strokes of his huge blade. Karl had a magic sword, but he was weakened, and Cannan could kill him in one blow in the best of times. Gregor was as dangerous as a kitten. All Christopher had left to face the monster with were guns.

Now that he thought about it that way, it didn't sound nearly so bad. What the heck was wrong with him? What had the shadow taken instead of strength?

"She's right, Cannan. Don't make me kill you." Christopher's voice sounded courageous enough, at least to him, but he still couldn't stop his katana from quavering. "And I'm not a Pater anymore."

"Pity, you. It only means it will take you longer to die."

The three remaining cavalrymen stepped forward, one wobbling a bit, but the others showing no fear.

"Surrender now, Ser," Karl said, standing beside them.

"To commoners with clubs? Did the ghosts eat all your wits?" Cannan laughed, and Christopher realized the red knight did not know what guns were. He'd left before Christopher had made the first one.

"You've been away too long," Christopher said sadly, but no one heard him. Cannan had taken another step forward, and Karl had snapped out an order. The carbines blazed fire and thunder. Through the clouds of smoke Christopher could see Cannan writhing in shock as bullets shattered against the magically hardened skin of his face and arms, drawing blood despite his protection.

And then he was gone, ducking and weaving into the underbrush, disappearing in an instant. Without thinking Christopher charged after him.

"No!" Lalania called, but too late. Christopher was already into the brush. He could hear the red knight blundering through puddles and shrubs. The contest was unequal. The man was wearing armor. Christopher was not.

He caught Cannan in a hollow, a blank square of grass free of bushes. A building might have stood here once. Now the red knight stood waiting for him, his face ablaze in hatred.

"Man to man, then. Or as much of a man as a priest can be." Cannan, snarling and bleeding from a dozen wounds, was still a fearsome opponent. Christopher put his sword into a defensive position, and wondered if he could inflict even one more wound before Cannan cut him to pieces.

Before then, Christopher had to ask the question that had dragged him into this swamp in the first place, the mystery that had burned Niona's body and made a monster out of a good man.

"What happened, Cannan? Why did you change?"

"I came into my own. I gained a prize worthy of my power, and it made me too strong for your petty Kingdom and its mewling rules."

Reflexively Christopher's eyes were drawn to the gold and onyx ring around Cannan's finger. It glittered as brightly as it had the day they had torn it off Black Bart's corpse, untouched by the decay of the swamp and the man who wore it. Svengusta had said the ring was Dark, but no one took the old man seriously, least of all Cannan. They had warned the knight, but only in general terms that sounded like mere superstition.

And then Christopher had hired the man to fight for him, all but encouraged him to wear the ring in battle after battle, and helped him defend it against Black Bart's every attempt to regain it. This really was all his fault.

The Gold Curate Joadan had spoken of Black Bart as a servant of the Shadow. Now Christopher knew how that had come to pass. And with Bart's death, the ring had passed to another, who had then passed under the Shadow. And at every step, Christopher had helped it along.

His resolve melted like water, running down into the soggy swamp.

"It's not you speaking, Cannan. It's that damn ring. Just take it off. Please."

Cannan's lips twisted evilly. "That's what she said. The bitch. All through the woods she whined at me to take it off. She wouldn't shut the dark up about it. So one night I took her head off. And then I did things to her corpse. Fun things." He leered, running his tongue along his lips, and Christopher felt physically ill. His hands shared the crime as much as Cannan's; neither of them had known, but both of them had been careless in the face of danger.

Christopher heard someone behind him. Others were coming. They would kill Cannan without mercy. They would not be weakened by guilt or shame. They would not care that Cannan was innocent, and they would ignore any order Christopher gave in his current condition. Not that he could think of any other solution.

"The ring is controlling you, Cannan. If you can't remove it, you'll die, and I don't know how to save you."

Cannan's eyes glinted with cold malice. "Remove it? So you can have it? You want it for yourself. You always did. Here, then, old man. Come and take it." He held up his hand, fingers spread wide, and the ring shone in the sun. Both of them stared at the gold band, hard and ugly and refulgent with power.

With a deafening roar the ring disappeared, and Cannan's finger was replaced by a fountain of blood. The red knight stared at the gushing red liquid, and slowly crumpled to the ground. Christopher blinked, trying to recover from the stunning blast, and looked over his shoulder, where Karl was lowering his still-smoking rifle.

Karl had shot the ring off Cannan's finger. Or, more accurately, he had shot the finger off Cannan's hand.

Christopher sagged in relief. "Find that ring. But for gods' sake, don't touch it."

Karl pulled a dagger from his belt. "Even I have wit enough to know that."

The young veteran stepped over the body, searching the ground with his gaze. Christopher knelt next to Cannan. He still had his orisons. One of them would close the man's wounds and stop him from bleeding out, but without restoring him to consciousness. Christopher wanted the man bound hand and foot before that. There was the possibility that he was wrong. There was the possibility that it wasn't just the ring.

The cavalrymen dropped Cannan's body to the ground, none too gently. Carrying the barrel-chested man from the bushes to their camp had exhausted them.

"You'll have to heal him enough to walk," Lalania declared.

Nobody stated the obvious. Three of Christopher's men were going home in a sack hanging from Karl's belt, reduced to a mere finger. There was room in that sack for Cannan's head. It would seem to be the simplest solution.

"Tie his hands." Christopher wasn't going to take the easy path. He hadn't come into this swamp for a pocketful of tael. "Then we need to get moving."

"We need to burn these bodies first," Karl said. "We cannot leave them on this unholy ground."

Christopher remembered the last time he had brought dead men out of the Wild. Royal had carried them then. But now Royal was gone, lost to the swamp, and they did not even dare take time to look for him.

Tears spilled down his face.

"Dark damn it, Lala, what the hell is wrong with me?" His brain knew that crying over a lost horse in front of soldiers was a bad idea, especially when three of them had died so they could take a murderer alive. His emotions didn't seem to care what his brain knew, though.

Lalania was searching through a saddlebag, tossing the contents on the ground, and she didn't bother to slow down while she answered him. "The ghost has drained your mind, the way the others drained Gregor's strength. That you can still perform first-rank magic tells me you are not crippled, like Gregor is. So stop whining and make the best of it."

He would have said something cutting in return, but he couldn't think of anything. Instead, he put his mind through some paces. Mathematics, chess moves, lists of items they had brought with them. No problems there. In fact, he thought of something interesting.

"Those ghosts were intelligent. Doesn't that mean they had tael?"

Lalania stopped and looked at him, a coil of rope in her hand. She frowned as she said the three words she hated saying the most. "I don't know." She glanced out over the tangled weeds. "If they did, and assuming we actually destroyed any of them, how would you find it?"

"Tael is magic. And I can use magic to find magic. . . ." Christopher studied the landscape. The burned and blasted area where the grenade had gone off was a good place to start. Christopher waded through the bushes, concentrating on one of the little spells still left to him. He was surprised when two cavalrymen rushed to follow him.

"You can't see it," he told them. "Might as well go back."

"Begging your pardon, Colonel," one of them answered. "But we'd rather not send you into the bush alone."

Good point. Christopher's brain seemed capable of all the same abstract thinking it always had been, but his instincts were completely off. He kept doing impulsive things. Stupid things. The concept would have bothered him more, but then he saw a faint purple radiance emanating from the ground, and excitement washed away his concerns.

Twenty minutes later he was several thousand gold pieces richer. He was happy for an entire thirty seconds, until his still-logical brain calculated that after he raised the three dead men using the Saint's expensive fingernail spell, restored Torme's lost rank, and replaced the horses, plus the tack and armor they would have to leave behind, he would only be in the hole for twice as much. Roaming around the swamp and having hair-raising adventures didn't seem to be profitable.

Until he thought about it in a different way. He was only going to be in the red because he was replacing his men. Most nobles wouldn't even think of doing that. This explained why the nobility went on these little jaunts. It was a way of turning blood into tael.

Other people's blood, of course.

"Is he ready?" he asked Lalania, although he could see Cannan was. Lalania had bound the man's arms behind his back, from his wrists to his elbows. The woman had a knack for bondage. Christopher shook his head, trying to dislodge the stray and wildly inappropriate thought. He needed to get this ghost curse fixed, before it drove him to do something really, really stupid. Like crawling into Lalania's bedroll in the middle of the night.

"Yes," she said, watching him with a peculiar look on her face. Christopher stopped trying to guess what she was thinking. He couldn't trust any conclusions he reached in this condition.

Bending over Cannan, he reflected that this at least was something he could still fix.

"Wake up," he said, when his spells were done. "I know you're not dead."

Cannan opened his eyes, looking up at Christopher with a terrible emptiness. Earlier those eyes had been alive. Burning with psychotic rage, true, but at least there had been light in them. Now they were still and quiet, drowning in an unquenchable grief.

"I should be. I would curse you for your cruelty in keeping me alive, but I cannot. I am out of curses. I have taken them all on myself."

"Get up," Karl said. "We'll not carry you. Indeed, you may be carrying Ser Gregor before the day is done."

Thick black smoke rose from the funeral pyre, signaling that it was time to go. They left everything but the clothes on their backs, a loaf of bread each, and their weapons. Each cavalryman carried two carbines, and Karl carried two swords, his and Gregor's. Christopher had to carry Torme's katana. Karl cut the remnants of armor from Cannan's shoulders and left the pieces lying in the mud. They also left Cannan's sword. It wasn't magical. It could easily be replaced.

If only the damage it had done could as easily be left behind.

Cannan did not argue, complain, or even speak. He walked when they told him to walk, and stood when they told him to stand. His passivity unnerved Christopher even more than his manic hatred had. The raving creature he had been was just another monster. This broken, crushed man had once been Christopher's friend.

They stopped for lunch on a tuft of ground a few feet higher than the rest of the swamp. Christopher fought a losing battle to keep the flies off his bread while he ate it.

"Eat," Karl told Cannan, holding a loaf in front of the man's face. "Eat, or I'll shove it down your throat."

Cannan bit into the bread, chewed mechanically, and swallowed. It was like watching Karl feed a sick cow. Karl didn't bother to chase the flies away, and Cannan didn't bother to care. Christopher conquered his revulsion long enough to speak up.

"Don't let him eat flies. They might make him sick."

Karl nodded, and swept away the insects with his other hand.

Lalania wrapped half her bread in cheesecloth, and tucked it inside her lyre. She had refused to abandon the unwieldy instrument, saying, "It's already saved our lives once," to Karl's disapproving glance.

Christopher realized he probably shouldn't have eaten his entire loaf of bread.

They struggled on, the mud sucking at their steps. They covered ground as fast as they had with the horses, but only because they were carrying almost nothing. They were all tired, but Gregor was white with exhaustion. Christopher didn't think the man could do this for four more days. Without food, he wasn't sure he could.

When the sun was half covered by the horizon, Karl stopped. "We have to find a place to camp. Now." The rock-hard young man was only a shade less pale than Gregor.

"I wouldn't suggest here," a tree said. Its branches parted, and D'Kan leapt lightly to the ground. "There's a much drier spot a hundred yards farther on."

"Well met, Ser," Lalania said. "It is good to see you again."

"Indeed," D'Kan answered, but he wasn't talking to Lalania. He stared at Cannan, his face tight. The young Ranger stepped forward, his hands lightly touching the pommels of his twin swords.

"Ser D'Kan," Christopher said. "Take us to your camp. We are tired and in no mood for nonsense."

D'Kan did not reply, casually taking another step closer.

"Soldier," Karl said, stepping into his path, "that was an order."

The Ranger stopped, only because Karl was in the way.

"Do you have a sister?" he asked Karl, casually, as if in idle conversation.

"The Colonel gave you a *command.*"

D'Kan stared at Karl, as if seeing him for the first time. "Of course. This way." The Ranger turned around and walked off. Christopher took his hand off his own sword hilt and tried to ignore the blackness that swam at the edge of his vision.

It was dark by the time they reached the Ranger's camp, but the starlight was bright enough to reveal the identity of the creature that shoved its huge, hairy head into Christopher's shoulder, looking for an apple. Royal snuffled at him, like he did when Christopher stayed away from the stables for more than a day.

"He was doing a credible job of heading home," D'Kan said. "And keeping the herd together. I picketed the other horses, but Royal and Balance would not let me leash them. It is good that you came now. Another day and they would attract predators beyond my ability to deter."

Christopher put his hands in Royal's mane and sobbed. He wept for the loss of his horse, and for its miraculous restoration. He wept for his wife, and for the miracle he hoped would rejoin them. And he wept for Cannan, who could not even hope.

"The Vicar's mind was assaulted by a shadow. As was Gregor's body," Lalania explained to the staring Ranger, her voice tinged with a sharp edge. "Do you know anything of this?"

D'Kan shrugged, his focus still elsewhere. "They will heal on their own, or they will not. If he has not shown improvement in a few days, he never will."

Lalania frowned at the Ranger, and then turned away to face the rest of the group. "We need sleep. We can accomplish no more tonight."

Karl, swaying with fatigue, put his hand roughly on D'Kan's shoulder.

"If you think to disobey the Colonel during the night, then do not make the mistake of leaving any of us alive." The young soldier put his back to a tree and slid down to a sitting position. He was asleep before he reached the ground, his head pillowed on a low-hanging branch.

Christopher let Lalania lead him to his own earthen bower. Royal followed them and stood over his master. The sounds and smells of the great beast comforted Christopher, and he passed easily into darkness.

He awoke to brightness. The sun was dazzling, although it was barely over the tops of the trees. The beauty of it elated him, until he realized that such an emotional response to sunrise was proof that he was still impaired.

Breakfast crushed him, his spirits dropping like the downslope of a roller coaster. Strips of pale white meat, sickly sweet and bitter, smelling entirely too much like raw fish.

"D'Kan caught . . . something," Lalania said. "He says it is repayment for the porridge you gave him when he first came to you." She hovered over him, anxious and motherly. This was the first role Christopher had seen her perform badly. "How do you feel?"

"No," he said, "I'm not any better."

"Then we must call on your brethren for aid. I cannot bear to think of you like this . . . permanently."

The prospect was too daunting for him to consider. So he didn't.

"What about Karl and Gregor?" he asked.

"We are recovering," Karl said, joining them. "But now we can ride, so our weakness does not matter. We should turn north. We can reach Samerhaven in two days at most."

"Not likely," Lalania said. "If Christopher rides through Longvelt in this state, he might not ride out of it. The Marquis of Longvelt is no friend of the White."

"Give it a rest, you two." Christopher regretted the petty words as soon as he spoke them. He tried to smooth it over. "Let's ask D'Kan. He's our scout." Christopher was amazed at how readily he trusted the young man for answers, based almost solely on his gratitude for having had his horse returned.

D'Kan agreed with Lalania. "I have mapped the way to your fort, the lay of the land and the lairs of the predators. We will travel back in half the time we traveled here. I do not know the swamp-lands to the north, and would not ride readily into unknown danger with our principals in this state." With a sidelong look at Christopher, he added, "There is little cause for haste in any case."

Christopher looked up in alarm at this harsh diagnosis, but Lalania was already responding.

"Hush. He calls the greatest healer in the realm Brother; we shall not worry yet." The smile she flashed was as thin as paper, though.

This was the second time Christopher had been forced to ride Royal bareback, and he didn't like it any more than the first. He wondered just how many saddles he had to buy to always have one when he needed it.

True to his word, the Ranger led them on at a good speed, and by noon of the second day he announced their imminent arrival.

"Tonight will see us at the walls of your fort, my lord." He spoke only to Christopher, ignoring both Karl and Lalania. It was part of a general trend. The Ranger was so pointedly ignoring Cannan that it had spilled over to the rest of the patrol.

Such excess was wholly unnecessary. Cannan was easy to ignore. He moved slowly, like a man underwater, and made no sound. Karl treated him the same way he treated the horses, with due regard for his health and needs but without any notice of his emotions or thoughts. Christopher found that infuriating. He wanted to shout at Karl and make him recognize that Cannan had been a friend once. But some residual self-discipline held his tongue. Instead, he watched Cannan, waiting for the glacier to melt.

During lunch, Lalania picked leeches from Cannan's legs. The man paid neither the bloodsuckers nor the bard any attention.

Christopher followed her to the nearest pool of water where she washed her hands. "He might as well be a walking corpse," Christopher muttered, when they were safely out of earshot from the rest of the group.

"Have you ever seen one?" She made a face, spitting out tiny bone fragments of the stringy swamp-pheasant that had served for lunch. D'Kan's woodcraft was sufficient to keep them fed, as long as one's definition of food was generous to the point of absurdity. Lalania, whose definition tended toward the gourmet, was perforce in a bad mood, and Christopher decided not to argue with her on the topic of various species of soul-trapped abominations.

"Maybe Cannan was right," he said instead. "Maybe it would be a mercy to let him die."

"What makes you think Cannan deserves mercy?" Lalania's tone was acid on steel. "He is still ranked. He owes a debt to society. Let him find his death in defending those who cannot defend themselves."

"He can't fight like this. He can't be trusted with a sword." He couldn't even be trusted to feed himself.

"That is what atonement is for. Your Saint will take away his burden, and replace it with an obligation."

Christopher paused, surprised by the venomous accent on the last word.

Lalania tossed her hair defensively. "Did you think it was all daffodils and sunshine? The Saint will restore his mind, but nothing can restore his spirit. There was a time I envied Niona, but never again. Cannan has betrayed and broken his own inner nature, and all the Saint can do is put a Cannan-like puppet in its place. Not a soul-trapped. Something worse. A soulless being with the perfect imitation of a soul."

As always, he had to argue. "Cannan did not choose this. It was the ring. Cannan was only its instrument."

"Evil always lays a pretty snare. Good consists of not stepping into it, cinching the knot, and hoisting yourself into the air. Not one of us has walked a road without temptation. Only one of us fell. His hands are stained in darkness, and they will never be clean."

He had thought her world-wise; now he feared she was world-weary. Unable to restrain his tongue he blurted out exactly what he was thinking.

"You are too young not to believe in redemption," he said.

"And you are too old to still believe in fairy tales," she snapped back.

He put his hand on her shoulder, trying to reach her beyond mere speech.

"We are more than our deeds," he said. "Surely you must see that."

"Cannan is not," she answered. "He is a hero. He chose to be defined by his acts; he wrote his fate in blood across the world. A man does not pick up a sword and slaughter his way to rank without accepting responsibility for his *deeds*. Common men can seek refuge in mortal weakness, but heroes make their own fate, for good or ill."

Christopher shook his head in denial. "He's still human, Lala. No more or less than you and I."

She locked his gaze with her bright green eyes. "You can *fly*, and you still think you are no more than human?" She sighed, then, taking his hand from her shoulder and clasping it in both of hers. "But of course you do. That is why I love you so: your impervious innocence. It is an itch I cannot scratch, a perfect white wall begging for a muddy handprint."

Dropping his hand, she walked away to see to the horses and men. He was left to muddle over her words and her meaning on his own.

He had misjudged her. In this world, its hard edge of medieval poverty and cruelty honed into frightful sharpness by magic and monsters, there was little room for the generosity of wealth that he had grown up with. Not just material wealth, but cultural excess; in the swarming sea of humanity on Earth, no vice—and no valor—were unique. It had all been done before, and sung about, and studied, and made into an after-school TV special. Even heroism had been rendered banal by sheer quantity.

Struggling for balance on the naked horse and his raw emotions, he nonetheless recognized there was a value in that, a stupendous mediocrity that glorified by its very blandness. A nation of shopkeepers, Napoleon had sneered of England, and by extension her colonies who had taken bourgeois comfortability to heart. Hitler had sneered, too.

But Hitler and Napoleon had lost. Heroic men who had seized the future with their visions, only to be thwarted by the mundane and the ordinary. This was the history lesson that Lalania did not have. Dashing swordsmen were overrated. Statistics ruled the world, not personality and steel.

Unconsciously, automatically, he adjusted his katana so that the hilt was within easy reach as he rode.

6

LIKE A BAD PENNY

Under the brilliant starlight they came out onto the open marsh and in sight of the fort. It glowed in the distance, warm red and yellow light flickering from its walls. Christopher's spirits soared. This was the emotion the great castle in Kingsrock was supposed to inspire.

"Thank you, Ser," he told the young Ranger. "I don't know how you found it." They'd been traveling in the dark for over an hour.

"How could I miss it? You advertise your presence like a fishmonger. I fancy I could find the place by smell alone."

Christopher was trying to puzzle out whether D'Kan thought that was a good thing or a bad thing, when Karl answered for him.

"It is supposed to be easy to find, Ser. We would prefer the monsters attack us, rather than the peasantry."

D'Kan stiffened. "You think much of yourselves, then. Even the High Druid does not care to shout her name so loudly. There are worse things in the world than ulvenmen."

"It's true," Gregor said. "We do think much of ourselves."

The Ranger glared at the blue knight.

"It is also true," Lalania said, "that there are worse things in the world than I care to name at the moment. Nonetheless, men must live. We cannot all blend into the forest like elves. It is not our way."

"Only because you do not try."

"We are not theologians, Ser, to fritter our strength on mildewed disputations," she said. Christopher could not take offense at Lalania's terms. His was a completely practical style of religion. "The Vicar needs his mind restored to its full strength. This is our primary task. All else must wait."

"Agreed." Karl's tone left no room for dissension, either.

"Disa will be powerless against this, despite her rank," Gregor said. "We must press on to Samerhaven at first light."

Lalania cocked an eyebrow at him. "Since when have you shown so much interest in priestcraft?"

Gregor had the decency to blush before continuing. "The cavalry can suspend their patrols and lend us their horses. With double mounts we can make Samerhaven in a day and a half."

"Couldn't we ride faster if there were fewer of us?" Christopher was thinking of the time he, Gregor, and Vicar Rana had swept across half the Kingdom in a day.

"Yes, but you can't ride with fewer," Lalania said. "You made your men a promise. Your life is not yours to gamble with anymore."

"The Colonel will make the final decision." Karl didn't hesitate to correct Lalania. "Nonetheless, I agree with your advice. It would be a significant risk to expose the Colonel to danger in this state." He didn't hesitate to instruct Christopher, either. Christopher had thought he was acquiring a retinue of loyal servants, but instead it seemed he'd gained two babysitters.

"And the prisoner?" D'Kan asked, cool as an autumn breeze.

Karl answered with the finality of a hammer on an anvil. "He rides with the Colonel. From Samerhaven we go north to the Cathedral, where justice awaits."

Amazingly, D'Kan argued anyway. "What of my people's justice?"

"If your people wanted the right of justice, they should have captured him."

"Peace!" Lalania snapped. "Ser D'Kan, no one in the Kingdom disputes the even-handedness of the Saint. Your High Druid can appeal if she is not satisfied, and her arguments will carry as much weight as Christopher's. But this is not the time or place for this, either."

Royal added his own comments to the conversation. Smelling home, fresh hay, and the scent of the rest of his herd, he snorted and broke into a trot. The rest of the horses automatically matched him, except for Balance. Gregor made his mount drop behind, to take the rear of the column. The blue knight's strength had recovered enough that he carried his own sword again.

Riding in through the gates, Christopher saw Disa standing off to the side, silently watching. He tried to smile at her, to reassure her that Gregor was only last, not missing, but he was too busy not falling off his horse. The general mood of the men went from calm to alarm when they realized the horses had no saddles.

A sergeant stepped forward with a halter rope for Royal. Christopher slid off the horse and patted the animal on the shoulder. "Karl can explain it all," he said, suddenly weary to the core. "For now, we need food and rest."

Later, with a bowl of pleasingly bland porridge in his hands, Lalania's reforms having had a marked effect, he saw Gregor and Disa sitting discreetly together, her face a hooded beacon of relief and joy, his of comfort and happiness. It was pedestrian and familiar, and it sparked a pang of envy that Gregor and Lalania had never brought out in him.

The night was not long enough, yet it seemed unending. Karl woke him before dawn, while the sky was still a black velvet shroud studded with diamonds. Tired and disoriented, he followed the young man's instructions without questioning them.

In the flickering of the light-stones the party saddled up. This was the benefit of having an army: his losses were erased by equipment drawn from storehouses and fresh young faces drawn from the ranks.

Except the armor. Christopher, Gregor, and even Cannan had left a fortune in handcrafted metal to rot in the swamp. Christopher didn't miss it, but Gregor did.

"Gods but I feel naked. Nothing but cloth between me and the slings and arrows of outrageous fortune."

"Now you know how peasants feel, Ser." Karl might have been smiling, but it was too dark to tell.

"It doesn't matter," Christopher said. "Armor's useless now anyway. It just slows you down and makes you easier to hit."

"An opinion we share." D'Kan was already on his horse. He touched the pommels of his two light swords. "Skill and lively agility are better defenses than inert metal."

"Your fancy swordsmanship will not avail you any better, sonny. You can't parry bullets." Gregor was grinning at the young Ranger as he leapt into the saddle. "But consider, Christopher. Your foes do not wield rifles. You should armor your horsemen at least. Even a shirt of chain can turn an arrow and give your men a second chance."

"We can't afford armor," Christopher said automatically. But that wasn't really true anymore. To change the subject, he glared at D'Kan. "And why is he coming? I think we can find Samerhaven on our own."

D'Kan glared back. "I would see the murderer brought to justice, my lord."

Christopher looked back over the column of horsemen. In the middle he could see Cannan's gaunt figure, his hands bound to the pommel of his saddle.

"You'll do what the Colonel tells you to do," Karl was saying when Christopher interrupted him.

"Forget it. Let's just go." The sight of Cannan depressed him unbearably.

They rode out of the fort and onto the muddy streak that served as their road. Its only attraction was that it was free of brush and the stunted, gnarly little trees. The sky was beginning to lighten, and birds called and sang to each other. Christopher felt a bond of kinship stretching back to Cannan. They had both lost their wives to the unpredictable, uncontrollable power of magic. They had both lost their way.

D'Kan rode out in front again, his horse a silent ghost compared to the jingling, clodding steps of the others. The young man's back was straight, and his head was high. He knew exactly where he was going, and why. Or at least he thought he did. Christopher envied his absolute sense of purpose.

By the end of the day he envied D'Kan's youthful resiliency. They had ridden for countless hours, pausing only when the horses needed it. They had passed Carrhill without stopping, even though the gates were open and inviting. Christopher was exhausted, sore, and cranky. The only bright spot in his day was that he could see Lalania's patience with him visibly eroding. It seemed like a fair revenge for all the frustration she had caused him.

At least they got to sleep in an inn. There was one at the crossroads, a dilapidated, sad-looking structure that would have been picturesque and quaint if it wasn't so dirty. Christopher looked the other way while Karl spent more of his gold, but they had a hot meal and a soft, dry bed. It almost restored his spirits. But then morning came and spoiled everything, as it always did.

"Colonel, wake up." Karl's impatience at having to repeat himself leaked out in his tone. Christopher wondered what happened to ordinary soldiers who had to be told to wake up more than once.

"What now?" It was always something.

"Cannan is gone."

Well, of course. It was simply unthinkable that the villain would not escape at the first opportunity.

"Get D'Kan and track him down."

Karl lowered his eyebrows, his equivalent to Lalania's eye rolling at Christopher's perpetual stupidity.

"D'Kan is gone, too. Presumably the two incidents are related."

Christopher sat up, rubbing sleep out of his eyes.

"How many horses did they take?" he asked, remembering when he had chased Black Bart across the Kingdom.

"It doesn't matter," Lalania answered from the door. Karl stepped aside and let her into the tiny room. "Our path takes us to Samerhaven. That cannot be delayed."

"Are you nuts?" Christopher felt his blood rising. D'Kan had stolen from him. He would take the prisoner back to his bloodthirsty druids, and they would kill him, and everything Christopher had suffered would be for nothing. But that would not stir the merciless Lalania to pity. She didn't care about how much Christopher suffered, so he tried a different tack. "Cannan is a murderer. Gods know how many innocent people he'll kill." Come to think of it . . . "Wait a minute. What if he's already killed D'Kan?" Even unarmed, the Baronet was terribly dangerous.

"He hasn't, and he won't. Now get up. The sooner we reach Samerhaven the sooner we can catch Cannan."

"And you know this how?" Karl asked.

"My methods are of no concern of yours, as long as your lord is satisfied." Lalania's voice had ice in it, but the effect was wasted on Karl. He matched her glare with his steadfast gaze, until she looked to Christopher for help.

"So tell us how you know," he said. It was time that Lalania started treating Karl like more than a peasant. It was time that everybody started treating Karl like more than a peasant.

Lalania seemed disturbed by the tiredness in his voice, but she answered in a whisper. "They were seen, Christopher. Cannan rides unbound, following at D'Kan's lead. Their path can only end in druid lands and the jurisdiction of the Verdant Court. It is as I warned you: he goes to his death willingly."

"Seen how?" Karl demanded, but Lalania ignored him.

"Magic," Christopher answered for her. It was always bloody magic. "Lala, you have to teach Karl about scrying, too. He needs to know."

"Why don't I shout it from the rooftops?" she grumbled. "Oh, that's right, because arcane knowledge is dangerous, and sharing it with unranked men just makes them a target. An easy target."

"You've got some strange ideas about education," Christopher replied. Then he realized it was probably more accurate to say he had the strange ideas, from their perspective. He got out of bed and started getting dressed. Only when he had his trousers on did he realize Lalania was still in the doorway, waiting.

It was too late for modesty now. He kept dressing, and she kept talking.

"They make for Longwelt. A foolish risk on D'Kan's part; if Cannan were faking it, taking him through Gold Throne territory is only asking for trouble. No doubt the Ranger aims for the forest, where he expects his skills will render him safe from pursuit."

"Will they? Can't the Skald see him there?"

"She can, but you can hardly go tramping after him. Taking your retinue through those counties would only be inviting trouble. Taking your retinue through the Wild just over the border from those counties would be an engraved proposal for trouble. A chance to attack a Bright, in the Wild, and an insult to excuse it with? No, Christopher, I will not let you start a war."

"Another one, you mean," Karl said. "I believe Bart started the first one."

"To all of our loss." She glared at him.

"Then how will we get there?" Christopher asked, uncomfortable with her displeasure.

"First north, through the Undaals. From Tomestaad we can gain a welcome into Sandar, and then we can go south."

"That is many days out of our way," Karl said. "We might as well go to Kingsrock and catch the eastern road."

"Well, I thought we might chance the 'Nars. In Eastvale I could get a better read on the risk."

Christopher decided he was sorry he'd asked this question.

"You know what? I don't actually care. Let's just go." He strapped on his sword and pushed past them.

When he got to the bottom of the stairs, to the large open room that served as common sleeping hall by night and dining hall by day, he found another target for his anger. Four of his men were still sleeping, laid out on benches next to the fireplace.

"Get up, laggards, and tell me why you let Cannan escape." He kicked one of the benches, jolting the man lying on it, but to no effect.

"Begging your pardon, Colonel." A clean-faced boy in a private's uniform was at his shoulder, polite but insistent. "They can't get up. They was poisoned in the night by the Ranger."

Christopher wanted to scream. He wanted to pound his fist into somebody's face, and pour out all this rage and frustration. But on top of the pain of betrayal was the shame of kicking at a sick man.

"Will they live?" he asked. He regretted the tael he had spent restoring D'Kan to his nobility. He might need it back now.

"The Lady says yes," the private answered. It took Christopher a moment to realize the boy was talking about Lalania.

"Well, get the rest of the troop ready." Christopher looked around for something to eat. The innkeeper was cowering behind the door to the kitchen, peeking out like a man watching a bull in a china shop.

"They are getting ready, Colonel. Karl sent them outside twenty minutes ago."

"Right. Then you get me a bowl of porridge. With honey. And cream. I'll guard these men until you get back." Then he sat down next to the sleeping men and tried to salvage his pride.

They found the Vicar of Samerhaven in the main hall of his church. The room was full of miserable people, squabbling children, and crying babies. While Christopher was wondering if it would be rude to cut in line, Lalania swept to the head of the room, past the junior priests and priestesses, acolytes, and guardsmen.

"Lord Vicar," she said, going to one knee, "your Brother has need of your immediate aid."

The Vicar glanced at Christopher's party, frowned, and said, "Excuse me," to the mother he had been talking to. He turned and led the way through a door, deeper into the building.

Christopher followed, trying not to feel embarrassed. He could not detect any resentment in the stares of the others. These people were used to the privileges of rank. That only made him feel worse.

A few steps down a hall, and they entered a well-lit but plain room, remarkable only for its complete lack of decorations or furnishings. The room was painted white, from floor to ceiling, and Christopher cringed when he saw the muddy footprints his party left.

The Vicar faced them alone, without guards or assistants.

"You may speak freely," he said.

Lalania did so, relating their encounter with the shadows concisely with a candor that surprised Christopher.

The Vicar was reassuring. "Be at ease, Lady Minstrel. Your Ranger should leave the study of healing to more capable hands. There is no particular need for hurry."

Christopher frowned. "Did he lie to us about that, too?" How many lies had the Ranger told?

"Not necessarily. Druidic magic is all he knows. In any case my rank is sufficient that it can wait until tomorrow. I can give you a room in the church, Brother, but you must see to your men's quarter."

"No," Christopher, Lalania, and Gregor said simultaneously.

"We're trying to catch someone, Vicar," Gregor explained. "And he's got a half day's head start."

The Vicar shook his head in dismay. "Your kind are always in a hurry, from one ill-conceived enterprise to the next."

"It is truly urgent," Lalania said. "A man's life hangs in the balance."

"It always does," the Vicar said with a sigh. "The spell is not without cost, which I would have to charge you for in any case. However, if you require immediate assistance, I can provide it at a substantially greater price."

Lalania bit her lip, in a very fetching way. Christopher didn't think it would help, though.

"How much greater?" she asked.

"Sixteen pounds of gold," the Vicar said. His sad smile told them he knew it was ridiculous.

Christopher could bring a common man back to life for only ten pounds of gold. "Don't I get a discount?" Not that the Saint had ever given him one.

"I am afraid there is no precedent for that. Even though I call you Brother, you are a different Church. If Cardinal Faren were to instruct me otherwise, I would be happy to do so, but again your haste pre-empts such a discussion."

"And if I wasn't in a hurry?" Christopher asked, because he wanted to put a tangible figure on just how mad he should be at D'Kan.

"Only two pounds. Because you are of our faith can I waive all but the raw cost. There is precedent for that."

He'd spent over fifty pounds of gold raising D'Kan and restoring him to his rank. Another fourteen pounds didn't seem unreasonable, if it allowed him to catch D'Kan before the boy did something stupid and made Christopher mad enough to kill him.

"Do it," he said, fishing out the little silver vial that hung around his neck. As always, the answer to every problem was an insanely valuable purple pebble.

"As you wish. Please wait here for my return; it will be but a few moments." The Vicar left, closing the door softly.

"You should build a room like this," Lalania said to Christopher.

"To think you used to complain about my taste," Gregor muttered, but Karl was more direct.

"Why?"

"It's as effective of a defense against scrying as is possible without magic. There's nowhere for the telltale to hide."

Gregor and Karl looked around uneasily.

"I just *said* there was nothing to see," Lalania said in exasperation.

Christopher thought the room had another attraction. The lack of chairs would keep meetings short.

The door opened, and the Vicar came back in, carrying a plain wooden box. It was a few inches deep and wide and a foot long. When he opened it, dust fell off the lid, joining the dirt from their boots on the floor.

The Vicar removed a rolled-up sheet of paper, or more accurately vellum, as Christopher could tell by the leathery crackle it made when the Vicar unrolled it. The Vicar handed the empty box to Lalania and faced Christopher.

"You are certain you wish to consume this priceless relic for the sake of your immediate concerns?"

"It's not priceless," Gregor said. "We just paid you for it."

"Fair enough, Ser," the Vicar said. "Still, it has lain in the Church's possession for over fifty years, stored against need. If we use it today, we may need it even more tomorrow."

Christopher hesitated, but Lalania seemed to share Gregor's view. "For what we're paying you, Cardinal Faren can make two more."

The Vicar blew dust off the scroll. "Allow me some theatrics, Lady Minstrel. There is a point to our parsimony, after all."

Christopher opened his mouth to agree. After all, Lalania's College had gods-knew-what-all squirreled away in their dungeons. Lalania cut him off before he could speak.

"Fair enough, Lord Vicar. Now please, let us proceed."

The Vicar nodded politely and began to read from the scroll. The words were in Celestial, so Christopher could understand them, but he didn't really catch what they were. He was too preoccupied by the fact that the scroll was bursting into flame as the Vicar read from it, each word lighting up in fire. By the end of the text the paper was a burning ruin, and the Vicar let it drop from his hands. It turned to ash before it hit the floor.

Christopher felt the strength of his will settle over him, like an indrawn breath of fresh air. He sighed in relief.

"Thank you, Brother."

"I trust it worked?" The Vicar gazed at him piercingly.

"Yes," Christopher said. His anger at D'Kan was a righteous wrath now, not a petty rage. "Now if you will excuse us, we have a thief to catch."

"Oh thank the gods," he heard Lalania mutter as he marched toward the door.

"It would be more appropriate to thank just one, I think," the Vicar answered her. Christopher ignored them both. He didn't have time for theological debates.

"Tell me again why I can't ride through Gold counties," he demanded as they mounted their horses.

"He has a point," Gregor said. "He has the right to reclaim his stolen property, wherever the thief may flee."

Lalania wasn't happy. "It's still a risk. If they want to manufacture an excuse for a duel, you'll be giving them one."

"The Colonel rides without armor. We can delay any formal duel until that is replaced." Karl looked over the column of men. "And if they want an informal melee, then we have twenty carbines at our back. They will be no more prepared for them than the ulvenmen were."

"You would precipitate a slaughter?" Lalania raised her voice over the clop of hooves.

"On the contrary," Gregor said. "Christopher needs to act his strength, or others will think him weak. We fooled the ulvenmen by doing what they expected. Now we must do the same. No Black lord would hesitate to chase that cursed Ranger through a White county." Gregor seemed to have forgotten he wasn't wearing armor either. On the other hand, he did have a carbine strapped to his saddle.

"Then it's settled. We take the most direct route." Christopher called out the order. It felt good to be confident again.

"But not the woods," Lalania admonished. "We stay inside the Kingdom. On the road and in public inns, wherever possible. Let us not tempt them too much."

"Fair enough," he muttered. Stabling two dozen horses would cost a fortune at traveler's rates. He would just have to add it to D'Kan's bill.

7

THE KEEP AT THE
END OF THE LANE

Four days of hard riding left the horses spent. Christopher could feel Royal's weight loss every morning when he cinched the saddle on. But the animal sensed his mood and made no complaint.

Christopher struggled to match the horse's stoicism. Four days of riding through Gold lands left him with a jaw sore from the constant gritting of his teeth. If the White counties were an idyllic dream of pastoral life, the Gold ones were a nightmare. In the Green Undaals he had seen poverty and misery to match his preconceptions of the hard-scrabble life of a medieval peasant. But in these Shadowed lands the stench of fear was overwhelming. This wasn't medieval France, where peasants bowed and scraped to arrogant nobility. It was North Korea, where men and women cowered under the rule of capricious and incomprehensible tyrants.

The desire to confront the local nobility and explain the democratizing effect of firearms was a constant spur, applied directly to his spine. Only the abject deference of every person they met prevented him from boiling over into violence. Even the soldiers groveled when they recognized Christopher's rank. He could not gain any satisfaction by destroying them.

The nobility, the true target of his loathing, was careful to stay out of sight. Lalania assured him the only time he would see them was immediately *after* they launched an overwhelming assault. That was their preferred introduction.

"They swear that a man is a thousand times more polite and cooperative once he's hanging from a rack in your dungeon. So why bother with any other negotiations?" This time when she presented the Black's point of view, she did not try to hide her disgust. Christopher found it immensely more comforting than when she had worn a dark face to sneak them across the land. And that had only been in Feldspar, an outlier of the taint. In Balenar, riding under the shadow of the walls of the city that allegedly housed the Iron Throne itself, she had not had the courage to even speak. Silently they had paid a gate guard a gold for each horse and rider, and then skirted the city altogether, preferring the mud of the fields to the stinking misery of the town.

Only after it was a speck on the horizon, far behind them, could Christopher dare to think his own thoughts.

I'll be back, he thought, glaring at the distant city, like MacArthur abandoning the Philippines.

"The gods only know what your rashness will provoke now," Lalania warned him.

"They have no room to complain," Gregor argued. "Bart rode through our lands as freely as a bird. A carrion crow, no less, carrying his soul-trapped with him."

"They won't see it that way," Lalania said.

Christopher was deathly tired of caring how they would see it. But he understood Lalania's point. The difference was that he was secretly hoping to provoke a reaction, or at least was not appalled by the idea. Let them send an army against him. For all its terror and evil, the Iron Throne did not command anything worse than three thousand huge, hungry wolf-men.

And if they were truly the pawns of the *hjerne-spica*, then Karl's words from the swamp were doubly true. Let them throw their strength against Christopher's riflemen, instead of defenseless peasants. The mere fact that they had not already done so was proof that they knew they would lose.

At the end of the day the road ran down into a river and stopped. There was no bridge, no ferry, not even a rowboat tied up at the shore.

"Damn it," Christopher said. "Now what?"

"Now we go from the frying pan to the fire," Lalania said. She almost managed a laugh. "Keep your hands in the open, where they can be seen, and under no account draw a weapon." She spurred her horse forward, into the water.

The ford was shallow, only three feet deep. Christopher and the rest of the troop followed her, splashing in the cool water. The horses kept stopping to drink. Christopher felt exposed, sitting on a horse in the middle of a river. It was the perfect place for an ambush, and if his men had to dismount to fight, the water would likely render their weapons useless. Lalania didn't seem to care, taking her time in leading them across.

On the other side, as they came out of the water in a disorganized crowd, a voice finally greeted them.

"That's far enough, my lords."

An interesting greeting, both overly polite—they were not, in any sense, this fellow's lords—and subtly hostile. Despite the high title he had handed out, he wasn't exactly being deferential. In fact, he was issuing orders. Almost as if he didn't care what rank they were.

On the other hand, this was the first person to say so much as "boo" to Christopher in four days, and he was in no mood for it. He turned his horse to face the man, a plain-looking fellow standing in the middle of the path that passed for a road on this side of the river.

"I'm here to reclaim my property. You can either deliver it, or get out of the way."

"What property would that be, my lord?" The man wore faded green leather, and only one sword to the two D'Kan had worn, but his bow was as long and stout.

"The Baronet Cannan." Christopher was uncomfortable speaking of the man as property, but that was the only argument that would carry any force here.

"The kin-slayer, you mean. He is not yours anymore, my lord. He belongs to the Mother now."

"Not yet," Lalania interjected. "Not until the sun sets on the Verdant Court. And the court has not yet begun."

The man did not glare, exactly, but the look he gave Lalania would have frozen water. "No matter. The court starts and ends with the morrow, and until then the border is closed."

"The Vicar will lay his claim to the court, not to you." Lalania shot Christopher a glance that said, *That is the best I can get you.*

"Attendance to the court is by invitation only. And regrettably, the Vicar does not have an invitation."

"Oh, but I do," Christopher said. "I do have an invitation."

The green-clad man looked up at Christopher, a small smile of incredulity tugging at the corners of his mouth. "Then present it, my lord, and I shall not tarry you further."

Christopher jerked his thumb over his shoulder, at the men behind him.

"It's right there, behind me. On horseback."

"What, that lot?" The tone was almost amused. "They're not even armored. We only let them across the river out of kindness."

"They don't need armor," Christopher said. "They have rifles." Damn, but it was time he got some respect around here.

"I confess I do not know what that word means," the man said. "But I fail to see how it is relevant."

"Two excellent questions you should put to Ser D'Kan, as soon as you see him. But for now, I'm following that road to the court, and I'm saying my piece, and that's all there is to it. Is that clear?"

The man said nothing, staring up at Christopher as inscrutably as a stone gargoyle. Gritting his teeth again, Christopher pointed his horse forward. This display of recklessness was stupid and yet necessary. Gregor fell in on the left, and together they rode past the man, one on either side.

The fellow didn't flinch, standing as steadfast as a fencepost. But arrows didn't rain down from the forest. Apparently they had won this round.

As the column trotted down the faint track, Christopher asked Lalania, "This is the way to the court, right?"

"Yes," she said with a wry grin. "It's the path in, even if I am not certain it will lead us out again."

The land was different on this side of the river. Behind them the forest had been ravaged and beaten into submission; here, it stood all but untouched. The trail was starkly out of place, an unnatural artifact in a pristine wilderness. The illusion was strong enough that Christopher was surprised when they passed their first field.

Above the regular furrows of wheat nestled a stone farmhouse in a grove of trees, a hundred yards from the road. It looked sturdy and clean and wholly unlike a hovel.

"Apparently they are not elves after all. They find they cannot live without the plow any more than we." Lalania seemed more satisfied with this observation than she had with all her condemnations of the wickedness of the Iron Throne. Christopher could guess the reason. To condemn the unrelenting evil of the Black was the work of an instant. But the druids were Green. They were allies and friends. Their arguments would not be so easily dismissed.

"Don't underestimate them," Gregor cautioned. "They may not wear shiny armor and ride horses the size of mountains, but they have their own dangers. Not, I suppose, that I needed to tell you that. Dark take it, Christopher, all my life I thought the druids were the definition of different, and now you've gone and changed the meaning of the word."

Christopher wasn't sure he wanted to change this. It looked pretty good.

"These people don't seem so poor." Or as miserable, although since he hadn't actually seen anyone, it was hard to be sure.

"They're not," Lalania said. "They eat better than even your peasants, Christopher. They are free men, not bound to the land by law or custom. And they are not tenants."

"They own their land?" That seemed very non-feudal. Maybe he should have started his revolution here, instead of Knockford.

"No, they don't own it either. But neither do the lords. They all borrow it from the Mother. Not that the lords are poor farmers. They have the right to commandeer labor, for the common good, and the Lady of the land collects her fee for blessing the crops. It is a fine life, if you want to live in a farmhouse in the middle of a forest with nothing but trees for company."

"Lala likes towns," Gregor said with a wink. "And the things they produce, like lace and pastries and scented soap."

Christopher liked towns, too, and the things they produced, like rifles.

"How much farther is it?" The sky was getting dark. He started looking for another farmhouse. With luck it would have a barn big enough for his herd of horseflesh.

"A few miles. The road will lead us to Farmark Keep. I know this because it is a contentious issue amongst the druids. It is the only druidic keep one can find at the end of a road; indeed, this may be the only road in the entire Near Wild."

"How do they get around?"

"That's the point, Christopher. They don't."

He grinned in sympathy with Gregor. The exhibitionistic Lalania would find this life as bad as a prison sentence.

But for peasants, it would be an improvement. "Why don't the miserable, poor, starving wretches from back there come over here?"

"For a thousand reasons, not the least of which is that they are not welcome. They're dirty and smelly and have no idea how to live in harmony with the land. Nor do they hold the Mother to be absolute in her rule."

Neither did Christopher. That might be a bit of a sticking point.

"Indeed," Lalania said, guessing his concern. "But the druids are still Bright. They respect the Bright Lady, even if they do not revere her. To these people she is like a kindly aunt, obsessed with tea cozies and sweets, far removed from the gritty realities of life both wicked and good. They will not kill you out of hand, but neither can you expect them to accord your arguments very much weight."

He'd spent his entire career as an engineer making fun of the pointy-headed academics in their ivory towers, and now he was one of them.

"I do not know what words you can use to sway their course of justice, Christopher. I can get you into the court, and a chance to speak, but that is all."

"Nor can we shoot our way out." Gregor happily piled on the bad news. "Of all the foes your regiment would be ill-disposed to fight, they are the worst. They will snipe at your unarmored men from hiding places in the trees, and their high-ranks will use guile and stealth instead of overwhelming force. They'll not batter their faces against a stone wall until they die."

Why couldn't he have more allies like this? "What are my chances of recruiting them?" Although, given the disdain that D'Kan and D'Arcy had shown his guns, he could guess the answer was not good.

"Recruiting them for what?" Lalania asked him archly.

He could hardly say, *for a republican revolution*, and she knew that. That was why she'd asked him the question. To remind him that if he talked like that, other people might ask the same question.

"For scouts?" he asked, hoping it was an answer that would pass.

"Good enough," she said. "They'll only be disgusted by that. Although you already have a Ranger as a scout. It would be a grave insult to him to even suggest you need another."

"I'm not sure I have D'Kan," he said, although what he was thinking was, *I'm not sure I care about insulting D'Kan.*

"You do. You did not release him from your service. He is still yours to command, until you feel your bargain is done. Those were the original terms, and his own father will compel him to honor them. Indeed, if you release D'Kan for insubordination or incompetence, you may provoke a duel."

"And if I release him for stealing from me?"

"They won't—"

"I know," Christopher sighed. "They won't see it like that."

Farmark Keep was a disappointment, even in the dark. Christopher's rough fort out in the middle of the swamp, built in ten days by a wizard and pack of young men, was more imposing. The keep lay in so much darkness Christopher at first thought it was abandoned. He had become used to the flickering of light-stones bathing every significant building in importance, like the glow of neon back home.

The village that nestled in the woods around the keep was no better. The side streets were clean and neat, but gloomy, the windows of the houses shuttered against leaking light. The only sounds were the clomping of his horse's hooves and the short, sharp bark of a dog from every other house they passed. The dogs only barked once, though. Like the rest of the town, they were disciplined to obscurity.

The gates of the keep were shut, but a man was waiting to greet them. When Christopher pulled his horse to a stop, the man unhooded a lantern and raised it high.

"Greetings, Vicar. The keep is closed for the night, but with your permission, I will show you to a pasturage for your company."

"Your inn doesn't have a barn?" Not many of the establishments they had stayed in during this trip had a barn big enough for his troop, but for the clink of gold coins they had made arrangements for him with the locals.

"I'm sorry, Vicar."

"Okay. Whatever. But take us past the inn first, so we can unpack." No point in carrying the saddlebags back from the pasture.

The man froze, a statue of politeness. "I'm sorry, Vicar."

Christopher stared down at the man, perplexed. Royal sensed his mood and flattened his ears.

"You don't have an inn?" Lalania's tone was half in jest.

"I'm sorry, Minstrel. There are no inns in the Near Wild."

"Then where are we supposed to sleep?" She wasn't jesting now.

"With your permission, I will show you to a pasturage for your company," the man repeated like a clockwork doll.

Gregor laughed softly in the darkness. "Remind me not to visit in winter."

Lalania was not so easily put off. "Surely you do not expect the Vicar to sleep in a field?"

"Lord Einar and Lady Sigurane extend their regrets, but the keep is unable to accept guests at this time."

It was Christopher's turn to smile. He wouldn't let a high-rank of unknown disposition and a squadron of soldiers inside his house in the middle of the night, either. The rules of hospitality only extended so far, and then they became absurd.

"Lead on, Goodman."

"Ser, Vicar, though I assure you I take no offense."

Damn it, how were you supposed to know? Knights wore huge swords and clanking armor. They advertised their status with every swaggering step. This polite, middle-aged factotum did not match Christopher's preconceived notions, and he found it difficult to adapt.

While following the man and his lantern through the town, Christopher felt the sharp prod of irony. It was not comfortable.

The ranger left them in a pasture, which was to say, a round, flat plain devoid of anything but grass. After wishing them a good night, he hooded his lantern and disappeared into the dark.

"Enough of this nonsense," Christopher said, and pulled out his own light-stone. His company followed suit, and soon the field was glowing brightly.

Karl sent half the men into the bordering forest to collect fire-wood. Lalania objected, but Christopher overruled her, and then laughed at her frown.

"Make up your mind, woman. You're not happy telling me what to do, and you're not happy being told what to do."

Gregor laughed too, perhaps a little longer than was seemly.

"What I want," the minstrel said archly, "is for you not to be a jackass."

"Then you're doomed to disappointment." Christopher relaxed in the banter, missing for so many days. First his mental condition, and then the oppressive air of the Gold counties, had made everything unpleasant and creepy.

"He's coming here to force his ways on their Court, Lala," Gregor defended him. "He can hardly balk to enforce himself on a pasture."

"He's coming here to ask them to overturn one of their laws. The least he can do is respect the rest of them."

"I don't even know the rest of them. They put me in a field, with no more than a by-your-leave. What else can they expect me to do?" Niona's words came back to him then, how the druids had tried to control instead of influence, and how it had rendered them irrelevant in the long run. "If they want my cooperation, they have to at least ask."

"You would make a virtue of your ignorance?" Lalania shook her head in dismay.

"I'd rather call it innocence," he said. She had called it that, not too long ago. When she didn't reply right away, Gregor started laughing again.

"He's not a big, dumb warrior who thinks with his sword, Lala. He's a priest. Apparently they need to cover that distinction back at your College."

"Apparently," she said, and went to use her magic on their poor stores of dried meat and cold, hard bread. After heaping the rations for all the men onto a blanket, she dramatically passed her hand over the pile while speaking in that strange, lyrical tongue she had used to exterminate bedbugs when they had shared a filthy room, on the road to her College. When Christopher got his share, he was pleasantly surprised to find the bread warm and soft, and the meat hot and juicy. The woman was better than a microwave oven.

The company bedded down next to a crackling fire, tucking their light-stones under the saddles they were using for pillows. Wrapped in his greatcoat, crushed grass cushioning the ground underneath him, Christopher was as comfortable as he had been in many days.

Morning came too soon. Unfiltered by shutters, or windows, or a roof, the bright sun climbed over the treetops and poked Christopher in the face. Tired, cranky, and grungy, he sat by the embers of the fireplace as Lalania tried to make something out of breakfast without magic.

She was saving her magic for the day. Just in case. Christopher had been doing the same, reserving his spells in case of emergency since the moment he had gotten them back. It struck him as a colossal waste of power. Each night he went to sleep with spells still in his head that could have healed two people of terminal illness. He tried to imagine a system that would maximize the use of magic while not leaving him unprepared.

Then he could not help but remember a little girl, crying in her mother's arms until he touched her with his magic. He had not been prepared—could never have been prepared—for the price of that benevolence. The memory turned his mood black and sour, until Lalania chided him for being too used to soft beds.

He did not correct her. This was his burden to bear. There was plenty enough evil in this world to go around. Lalania had her own memories to suffer.

"When does this thing start?" he asked her.

"Technically, at sunrise. However, they cannot deny you your sacred hour."

He didn't need one, since he hadn't exhausted any of the spells he'd memorized days ago.

"Is there any chance of getting a bath?"

Gregor answered for her. "It's one thing to force your ways on them, Christopher. It's another thing to be *weird*. Your obsession with soap and water is not healthy for a man."

Lalania nodded in agreement. "I can take the dust off your clothes and out of your hair, but asking for a bath will just confuse them."

"Can't I pretend it's part of my priestly ritual?" That was something to bring up with Torme, when the man was able to talk again. If he was going to start a church, then he was going to include a rule that cleanliness was next to godliness.

Lalania frowned at him. "Praying is one thing. Performing sacred rites on the Mother's soil is—"

"Something different. I know." This final annoyance put him over the limit. Fully fed up with the arbitrary, insufferable, picayune details of religion, he stood up and adjusted his sword belt to hang comfortably. "I'm ready. Let's go."

Lalania picked up her lyre, and Gregor slung his shield over his back. Christopher looked across the dying fire to where Karl was brushing a horse.

Lalania spoke in a whisper. "As egalitarian as they are, he has no place there."

"Then they're idiots." This insult threatened to be too much.

"That's not—" She stopped herself and tried a different tack. "Christopher, they will blame *you* for not promoting him, when he is so obviously worthy."

"It's true," Gregor agreed. "As I did, at first."

"But—" Christopher started to object, but Lalania laid a finger across his lips.

"We know. We understand. But others will need time to see. And this is not the time."

He didn't want them to see. These druid lords were not allies in his revolution; the less they knew, the better, until it was too late. He understood this intellectually, but the unfairness of it dug into his shoulders like talons.

Something Lalania had said to him before rang in his mind. *They are Bright, but they are not your friends.* A good thing to be reminded of now.

8

A SURPRISING VERDICT

The gate of the keep was open, but they did not enter. Two guardsmen bade them wait, while a third went inside. After only moments he returned with their guide from the night before.

"Good morning to you, Vicar."

"Good morning, Ser." Christopher was prepared to argue his way through the gate, portcullis and all, but Lalania stilled him with a touch. The Ranger was leading them outside, not in.

"The court is held in the forest, not the keep," she explained as they followed the Ranger.

"Of course," the Ranger said, looking at Christopher with a little surprise. "Where the Mother wills it."

Christopher had gained in strength and power since he came to this world, but he still couldn't master his curiosity.

"How, exactly, does the Mother indicate her will in this matter?"

Lalania frowned, but the Ranger grinned and winked.

"She whispers it in the High Druid's ear the day before. Or close enough; perhaps a bird whistles, or a chipmunk chatters; and then the High Druid suddenly knows which patch of forest it must be. Since it's always a different patch, only those invited can find it before the affair is over and done."

Christopher nodded approvingly. If you were going to have ludicrous religious rituals, they should at least provide security. The whole point of secret knowledge was to confound outsiders.

They walked through pathless forest for an hour, their guide leading as confidently as a taxicab driver in downtown London. Christopher was sure the Ranger had taken them on the shortest, easiest route, and equally sure he had no idea where they were or even which way town was. He was surprised when they turned into a fallow field and found it occupied by dozens of green-clad men.

And one bound in iron. Cannan knelt in the middle of the field, an iron collar around his neck chained to a spike in the ground.

Christopher walked toward him, magnetically drawn to this spectacle of humiliation. Though Cannan was stripped half naked and trapped like a wild beast in the middle of his enemies, the knight did not seem to care. But when he saw Christopher, he was the first to speak.

"Get on, then. We're done, you and I."

Another man stepped into Christopher's path, blocking his way. "The court is for public justice, Ser, not private revenge. State your harm, but stay your sword."

Cannan laughed, a strange and hollow sound in the grave field of quiet. "He's not here to punish me, Lord Egil. He's here to save me."

An older man, standing behind Cannan, drew himself up in outrage. "Is this true, Ser? Do you think to redeem this beast after it has savaged my child?"

That was far too difficult a question to answer, so Christopher searched the crowd until he saw D'Kan's blushing face.

"Ser. I find you far from your assigned post."

D'Kan stiffened his shoulders manfully, but not convincingly.

"I crave your pardon, my lord, but family called. No man can hold his sworn word over blood and justice."

"Family?" Christopher barked. "Isn't that your brother-in-law chained to the ground?"

D'Kan opened his mouth, but nothing came out. His shoulders collapsed again, and Christopher, out of pity, was forced to turn his ire elsewhere.

There were plenty of targets. The crowd stared at him in distaste, and Lord Beric—for surely that must be whom the older man was—spat out a rebuttal.

"He is not kin to us. He never stood beneath the Mother's tree and made the vows. He took what I would not have given and fled like a thief."

"That's not true," Christopher said, and the field instantly sank into deadly silence.

"You name me false?" Beric challenged him in a voice strong, bitter, scratched with grief, and Christopher knew the wrong answer would end in violence. Perhaps any answer would.

"I say you are mistaken," Christopher said. "I know this, because I spoke to your daughter more recently than you."

With a piercing hiss a woman stalked forward from the sidelines, throwing off the green shawl that had helped her blend into the crowd of leather-clad men. Lady Io stared at him, and he fancied he knew what the mouse felt when the eagle gazed down from on high. "Dare you throw that in our face? Here and now, dare you?"

"I'm just saying," Christopher answered her, "that I know the truth. And I assume the truth matters here."

Excellent, he thought to himself. *You've gone from potentially insulting Lord Beric and his wife to potentially insulting the entire Court.*

"Forgive me," he said, before anyone else could recover enough to speak, "if my speech is indelicate. I am a soldier"—he'd almost said *engineer*, since that had been such a useful excuse back on Earth—"and I do not know your ways. But I knew your daughter. I knew her when she was with Cannan. I knew she went with him, of her own accord, and she came back with him, seeking your approval. I know she stood with him under a tree and exchanged her own vows, and they were every bit as real because she was in love."

"Shut up!" Cannan howled in fury. "Shut your dark damned foul mouth!" Rage-blind and maddened, he grabbed the chain that bound him, ripped it from the ground in a single pull, and charged Christopher, whirling the spike at the end of the chain over his head where it whistled like death. The sacrificial lamb had become a lion, and the Rangers were momentarily stunned. Apparently they had thought Cannan safely restrained.

Christopher raised his hand and spoke in Celestial, hoping to forestall this before it got undignified. Cannan froze, paralyzed by magic, the chain dying in its arc and wrapping around him with a dull clatter. Only the man's eyes were free, and in them one could see embers of fire drowning in sorrow.

A bit of luck, Christopher thought. The spell was by no means certain to work against Cannan's rank. A dramatic moment, courtesy of his god. Now he would have to make the most of it. He settled for the simple truth.

"You know as well as I that it was the ring. Yes, he was prideful; yes, he was foolish. But he is not a criminal. He is a victim, as much as any of us. More than any of us."

"More than Niona?" Of all the possible voices, D'Kan's was the last he had expected to hear, cracking with grief but still challenging.

"No." Christopher paused, searching for words. "But Cannan loved her more than you did, D'Kan. She was your sister, but she was his wife." He thought about wives, and the losing thereof to incomprehensible magic, brought on by foolish acts as simple as putting on a ring or stepping through an invisible doorway. "Maybe you don't understand, but I know there are men here who do. I know your father does."

"What do you know of a father's grief?" Beric's voice was not strong now. It was barely more than a whisper.

"Nothing," Christopher admitted. "But I know enough of a husband's."

"What is it you would have of us?" A different man, not as old as Beric, but ramrod straight with power and responsibility. By the tone of his voice, both measured and commanding, Christopher guessed this must be the Lord Ranger Einar. "Should we set him free, and bury our sorrow in an empty grave?"

"Not empty." Christopher slowly reached into his pocket and extracted a tiny wooden box. "I brought something to trade. The real villain." Opening the lid of the box, he let sunlight glitter on gold and sink into black stone.

Another woman of indeterminate age stepped forward, disgust written across her hard, sharp features. Her status was even less mistakable than Lord Einar's. "That abomination must be destroyed."

"I agree, Lady Sigurane. I brought it to you for that purpose. Take your vengeance on it."

The High Druid stared at him with her bright, birdlike eyes, and he wondered how he had ever thought of Lady Io as intimidating.

"You charge us with this task as well? Have we not trod under your yoke long enough? Have we not suffered enough on your behalf?"

He stood there, utterly mystified. She took pity on his stupidity.

"The ring was meant for you. Is this not clear? The Shadow reached out its hand once it found a fitter glove than Baron Bartholomew. It set out to capture you as its pawn. You shirked this fate, letting lesser men take the blow. And we paid the price. In precious blood."

Black Bart's incoherent last words came back to him. *I will show I am the stronger servant.* It had all been a ploy. His improbable victories, his temporary defeats, arranged by some hidden power to this end, that he should gain the ring and lose his soul.

At every turn he had placed the people around him into terrible danger. He had been a lightning rod, and it had been his friends and allies that suffered the strokes. He dropped the box, horrified. The ring rolled onto the grass, winking in the sunlight.

He turned to those who still stood with him. Gregor was white-faced with shock; Lalania had her hand over her mouth, fighting back tears.

"I should have . . ." she said, the words muffled through her hand. "I should have seen."

"There is much you should have seen," Lady Sigurane said. "There is much you have yet to see. The Shadow has espied you, and yet you are blind. You build up castles and ranks like a child stacking toys, thinking they will protect you. All they do is stoke the hunger of the Lords of Night, and trap their prey in a stone bowl."

She softened her voice, like a lioness growling to a cub.

"Your people are as thick as swine in a pen. Rank piles on rank until even the gods must be tempted by the tael-price of your great lords. Can you not see the wisdom of restraint? Can you not imagine that we might pass under the scythe by being too low for the harvest?"

Christopher could see. But it was not in his nature to cower, even in the face of the hurricane. And besides, there was the matter of the ring.

"Lady Sigurane, it appears the Shadow came for me when I was only first rank. How much lower can I stoop?"

"Then we should cast you off." Lady Sigurane had no mercy in her eyes.

Lord Einar had none for his wife. "And yet, honor remains. We are bound to Kingsrock by sworn oath and shared blood. When the harvest comes—if it comes in our lifetimes—we will do our duty."

It occurred to Christopher that this might be his true task. The battle for the fate of the entire Kingdom was being played out, even if few could see the score. It was, perhaps, too early to despair. The ring had failed. Having lost his head, he still lived; having breached every custom of the Kingdom, he still gained in power every day. He had a god on his side. Perhaps it counterbalanced the machinations of the Shadow. Perhaps the difference between ultimate victory and final defeat lay in how hard he could tip the scales.

That was a responsibility he did not want, a burden he was not sure he could bear. Knowing that he had already been carrying it unawares did not lighten it.

Cannan rejoined the conversation by collapsing in a heap as the spell ran its course and released him. The huge man lay on the ground, weeping silently.

Beric walked closer, like a man in a dream, his gaze locked onto the ring. "You bring me a blood-price in gold. But can you bring me blood? Can you restore my daughter to me?"

A rhetorical question, as everyone there would know.

"Strange priest of a foreign god, I beseech you. You returned my son. Can you return my daughter?"

Or perhaps not so rhetorical. Christopher hadn't known that they had known. He would not have guessed that they would care to reveal the fact of D'Kan's raising. But Beric's grief was overwhelming, and in his quavering voice Christopher heard only a heartbroken parent.

"Not without a miracle. But I am in the market for a miracle myself." It was the only way he would ever see his wife again. In the calculus of miracles, one seemed as likely as two. "Should I find another, I would gladly trade the second for Niona."

"Blasphemy," hissed Lady Sigurane.

"And the price of this succor?" Beric ignored the High Druid, his gaze lifting from the hated ring to bore into Christopher's eyes.

"We have a common foe. Cannan can still help us with that, maybe even more so now that he has passed through its grasp. Give him back to me, to continue the fight." Christopher could see that none of these perfectly rational arguments had any effect on Beric, so he launched his last and greatest bolt. If this did not save Cannan's life, he had nothing left. "I don't know much about death. I don't know where Niona is now, or what she is doing, or if she is anywhere at all. But I do know this. She will never return to this world if Cannan is not in it."

On the ground, Cannan clawed the earth in agony, tearing up clods of brown and black dirt that crumbled between his fingers.

"For the price of a cold and useless vengeance, my Lord Vicar will sell you hope." Lalania spoke up, entirely unexpected.

"Easy enough to promise what you may never have to pay," answered Lord Einar.

"Not so easy for the White, whose word is their bond. What ordinary men say in passing, the priests of the Bright Lady carve in adamantine. As you already know." Dimly Christopher was aware that Lalania had set this up, had lured Einar into questioning his integrity, solely so she could play this trump card.

"The Bright Lady has no authority here." Lady Sigurane bit off her words like pieces of meat.

"Nor do you, woman!" cried Beric in sudden fury. "Nor do you have power here. You talk at me of cycles and wonders, but my daughter is still dead. Your words are no comfort to an old man and an empty hearth."

"Blasphemies upon blasphemies!" Lady Sigurane met the old man, fire for fire. Christopher felt the situation slipping away, tilting crazily into some internecine conflict he did not understand.

"Peace, my lord brother, my lady wife." Lord Einar put out his hand and addressed the crowd. "Beric has the right of it. This is the Verdant Court, and we men are charged with enforcing justice. The fate of the murderer is in the court's hands, and the court will do as Beric chooses. Mercy or destruction, it is his call. We owe this much to a grieving father."

Christopher looked at Einar with respect. He'd been terrified of the hissing druid just because she was standing next to him, but Einar had to share a bed with the woman.

"I need not listen to the Mother insulted." Lady Sigurane turned the heat of her blaze on her husband, but the Lord Ranger was apparently made of asbestos.

"Then you may leave, if you wish. You are only here by courtesy in the first place."

Amazingly, astoundingly, Sigurane backed down. Christopher watched in fascination as she banked the flame in her face until it only smoked, and then retreated back a step.

Lord Einar now turned on Christopher.

"You will parole this man? If we release him, you will accept responsibility for his conduct, until such time as your charge is fulfilled?"

Christopher wasn't entirely sure what that meant, but he knew the only possible answer, so he said it. "Yes."

Now Lord Einar faced Beric. "Then the choice is yours, lord brother. Death, mercy, or if you cannot choose, you may submit it to a vote."

"I can choose. I am not so grieved that I cannot wield my will. Priest, I take you at your word. Take this wretched ring, and take this wretched villain, and return to me my daughter, should chance and miracle favor you."

Christopher knelt on the grass and closed the wooden box around the ring. It clicked with finality, the sound a seal to the contract they had just made. The box seemed heavier now that he understood what it truly contained. He put it back in his pocket as he stood up.

Lady Sigurane apparently felt she was still allowed to berate Christopher. "Niona will not return for you, priest. She was always true to her faith."

Christopher glanced around at Niona's family. Beric stood unchanged, as if he had not heard the High Druid's words, but Lady Io and Ser D'Kan wore a blush of the most shameful red. Now he began to comprehend the outlines of this rift, and how much D'Kan's revival had challenged the druids and their dogma. Lady Io worst of all, since she was trapped between a druid's faith and a mother's love.

"I'm not interested in faith," he said. "I just want what's best for Niona."

"And what of what she wants? How will you pluck her from eternal death and then reconcile this boon with her? What of all the others she has lost, aunts and uncles and cousins, who will not share in your generosity? How can you expect her to bear the burden of this special favor?"

Christopher had no answer. He hadn't even thought of the question yet. But Gregor had one that left the Rangers unconsciously nodding in agreement.

"Cannan will earn it for her."

Reflecting during the walk back, Christopher thought he understood why Gregor's words had ended the court on what seemed to be friendly terms—at least, from the men's point of view. This was the deal. This was the contract society made with heroes. They put their lives on the line, faced indescribable horrors in defense of the realm, and in exchange they got first pick of the rewards. That included miracles.

It seemed fair enough, from one perspective. Christopher admitted that. But at the same time, the question Sigurane had asked continued to bother him. Gregor's answer was good enough for everyone else, and probably as good as this world would ever have. To be honest, it was even good enough for Christopher. He'd seen what heroes were expected to face, and they did it with pointy bits of steel instead of rifles and artillery. They were due some compensation.

But Christopher wasn't sure it was *supposed* to be good enough for him. He wanted to discuss it with the Saint, although he was pretty sure that Krellyan would shrug and expect Christopher to solve his own moral quandaries.

All of this theorizing was a way to avoid the problem immediately at hand. Cannan walked behind him, clanking with every step, the chain still bound to his collar. The knight carried the links and the ground spike in his arms, a great bundle of weight, without complaint, although his arms trembled with fatigue. Christopher looked at Gregor, imploring him to help the other knight, but Gregor shook his head. This was something Cannan had to do on his own.

Sadly, Christopher knew it would be only the first of many trials that Cannan would have to do on his own. To accept help from anyone else would invalidate Cannan's right to claim his miracle. The red knight would have to endure, suffer, and succeed at every task from now until he died, knowing that a single failure would doom not only himself but all hope of Niona's resurrection.

A cruel hope that had sprung from Christopher's lips. Promising what he might never have to pay had become a bad habit.

Gregor, in his simple strength, spoke as if everything were normal.

"Gods preserve me, Christopher, but I thought your days were done. I thought the High Druid was going to turn into a dragon and bite your head off, then and there."

"Ha," muttered their guide. "Dragons wish they could turn into High Druids."

"How does—" Christopher realized it might be an indelicate question, but he couldn't help himself. "How does Lord Einar . . . cope?"

"It's a poor knight who can't master his horse. You have that saying in your lands, yes? Well, a Ranger is expected to master all beasts, tame and wild and fey to boot, and a Lord Ranger is a master of men as well. She may fly off in a huff, but she'll come to his whistle when he calls her. He wouldn't be a Lord Ranger if he couldn't tame one hot-blooded woman, for all her Mother's power."

Christopher gaped in awe at hearing so many words from their previously laconic guide. Perhaps they'd finally found a topic the man felt worth discussing.

Lalania couldn't resist the bait, though. "I imagine your womenfolk have a different take on the matter."

"I imagine they do, Lady. As well they should. Men and women were made by the Mother to be different. And thank the Mother for that!" The guide turned to wink at Lalania, crudely suggestive, but juvenile enough that Christopher couldn't imagine taking offense.

When Lalania stuck her tongue out, Christopher started worrying about the situation resolving itself in an entirely different way. Then he had to remind himself it wasn't his place to object.

When they finally reached the pasture, D'Kan was already waiting for him. The young Ranger knelt at his feet silently. Christopher was exhausted with protocol, with judging and punishing and forgiving, and so he decided to skip it all and get on with things.

"Can we make the border by nightfall?" he asked.

"With hard riding, my lord, we can reach Palar, where you can find accommodations for the night." D'Kan spoke without looking up.

"The north road to Kingsrock, after all?" Karl said.

Christopher and Cannan both needed to see the Saint, one for questions and the other for atonement. Lalania may have made Christopher uneasy with the process, but Cannan in his current state was useless to anyone. Something had to be done, and Krellyan was the man to do it.

Instinctively Christopher knew Krellyan would never let him pass off his responsibility for the red knight, but right now he needed a destination. Kingsrock was as good as any.

"The north road," he said, and swung into the saddle.

9

APPEAL TO BETTER NATURE

They couldn't buy a horse for Cannan, not for love or money. Not that there was any love lost between the druids and Cannan. One farmer went so far as to suggest that Christopher tie the knight to his horse and drag him.

Karl fared no better. The peasantry loved their horses too much to sell them "across the river," which apparently was a fate worse than death. They made it clear they would rather *eat* their animals than sell them to heartless brutes who would think of nothing but how much value they could get out of the beast before it died. When Karl, in exasperation, complained that a farmer was valuing his horse as if it were his sister, the man looked at Karl with complete seriousness and said, "Well now, she very well might be."

Now Christopher had Lalania behind him, clinging to him for dear life, as he had once clung to her when paralyzed. It was intensely uncomfortable for him. But the destriers were the only horses strong enough to bear two, and Christopher couldn't inflict Lalania on Gregor. Not if he wanted to be able to look Disa in the eye again.

Cannan rode Lalania's horse like a sack of potatoes. The druids had at least removed the collar and chain, but only because the metal was too valuable to give away.

They rode into Palar well after dark. It was a pretty town, set on a hill that gazed out over fields to the west and forest to the east. Lalania said they were half druid here, but they had an inn, so Christopher forgave them for their injudicious choice of parenthood.

In the morning he haggled with the innkeeper over the bill while

Karl raided the town for horses. The innkeeper smiled and told jokes and adamantly refused to charge less than three times the normal rate for the rooms he had let. The steep price annoyed Christopher until Karl presented him with the staggering bill for the train of animals he'd picked out. Karl was, as always, unsympathetic.

"Your cavalry has an inexhaustible appetite for fresh horses, and these are the best in the Kingdom. You'd eventually buy them anyway, at twice the price, once they'd made it to the market in Kingsrock."

At least now they made good time, changing mounts every few hours to give all of the horses a break. Christopher felt a little strange riding a horse other than Royal. It felt like infidelity. Royal didn't seem to care, though.

When they finally climbed the winding road to the gates of Kingsrock, Christopher detected a change in the gate guards. They forewent giving him a hard time, concentrating all of their hostile stares on Cannan.

Inside the city, the reception was more subtle but no less dismaying. People glanced their way, and then casually disappeared, entering the nearest shop or turning down a side street.

Gregor unlimbered his shield from its normal resting place on his saddle, and let it hang from his left arm instead. Christopher had been here long enough to see that the simple act transformed the blue knight from road-weary traveler to combat-ready soldier.

Lalania followed suit in her own way, shaking her hair loose and taking her lute out from its case. The destriers, ever alert to the moods of their masters, flattened their ears and stepped a little higher.

"What the dark is going on?" Christopher asked.

Cannan answered, the first time he had spoken since the court.

"What did you expect? You bring a demon-possessed monster into town, and you don't even have the decency to chain him up."

Christopher had replaced Cannan's clothes in Palar, plain, simple garb fit for peasants, trying to make the man look civilized again. He hadn't replaced the druids' chains. Cannan wasn't going to run away now.

He'd also tried to get Cannan a shave and a haircut, but the local barber had taken one look, turned white, and walked away without another word.

Gregor ignored Cannan and offered his own answer.

"Being ready for trouble often averts it. Or at least, appearing to be ready. The townspeople will be reassured to know that we are prepared to act should anything untoward happen."

"It might also discourage any unwelcoming parties," Lalania said. "Cannan left many memories here, but few of them are fond ones."

"None," Cannan growled in correction. The word stuck in his throat, deep and bitter. After that he was silent again, remote and inert as he had been throughout the journey.

Christopher's nerves were jangling by the time they turned into the stable behind the Cathedral. Captain Steuben wasn't there to greet them. In his place was one of the handful of young knights who served as honor guard to the Saint. The young man gulped at his first sight of Cannan, but he stiffened his spine and put on a brave face. He even went so far as to speak to the dreaded monster.

"You cost me a purse of gold, Ser."

Cannan blinked, like a man suddenly awakened in strange place. "Then you shouldn't have bet against me," he said. Cannan-enough sounding words, but his voice was tired and uncertain.

"I didn't, Ser. I gambled for you to win. Then the Saint asked me if it was proper to gain from no labor, and another's suffering to boot. In the end I wound up distributing two pounds of gold to the poor."

Lalania rolled her eyes, but Gregor laughed. "I never thought of it like that before."

Christopher sighed, and resolved to ask Torme if gambling were against Church rules. Not that he'd done any gambling. Other than with his life, of course, but that was an occupational hazard.

"Is Pater Torme here?" he asked.

"Yes, Vicar, and in rather better shape than when you sent him to us. Shall I fetch him?"

"Please," Christopher said, relieved of a worry he had forgotten to worry about. "And let the Saint know I need to speak to him as well."

The knight bowed his head and left. Christopher dismounted, and then stood around uselessly while Karl and D'Kan settled the herd of horses in stalls. A young groom stepped up to expertly unsaddle Royal, and began brushing him down.

"Never you mind him," the boy said, flashing a grin. "Your Ser made me three weeks' pay in one afternoon, and a right good show it was."

"Don't tell the Saint," Christopher said, trying to match the boy's grin, but failing. He wasn't looking forward to telling the Saint about the gambles he had taken, either.

"Let's go," Gregor said from the doorway of the stable. Cannan stood next to him, looking lost, which was an improvement. Lately he hadn't looked as if he cared where he was enough to be discomfited by being lost.

Lalania fell in behind him as they made the short trip through the courtyard to the rear entrance of the Cathedral. Mounting the short marble steps up to the door, Cannan finally balked.

Gregor instantly turned and watched the red knight warily. Through the barn door Christopher could see Karl calmly set aside his horse brush and put his hand to the wall, as if reaching for something leaning just out of sight.

"Not that I care," Cannan said, looking askance at the entranceway. "But you might. You've ridden a long road just to watch me blasted to ashes."

Christopher started to ask what he meant, but decided not to. By now people should just know that they had to explain everything to him.

"We do not command magic so potent, Ser," the Saint said from the doorway. "Nor would we obliterate you merely for being guilty, even if we could."

"My lord," Christopher said, a sigh of relief spilling out.

"Only under the most legalistic interpretation, Brother." Saint

Krellyan smiled at him, and Christopher felt the weight of his recent tension and anxiety only by its sudden departure. "But please, come inside. You must be weary from riding."

"I—" Cannan stuttered, and tried again. "I do not wish to profane your sacred ground." His voice was low, without the hard edge of bitterness it had worn for so long. Forever, even: before the ring Cannan had been as hard as nails too, if not quite so depressing.

The Saint shook his head gently. "Shame cannot profane us, Ser. Only lack of it." He moved away, leading them inside. Cannan climbed the short steps with more visible effort than he had shown while carrying a hundred pounds of iron chain.

Christopher followed, with plenty of effort of his own. Despite the relief of having someone wiser to talk to, he wasn't looking forward to the conversation.

Sitting in a stuffed leather easy chair, with a cool light ale in one hand and a plate of tiny slices of colored cheeses in the other, Christopher was once again reminded that army life left some things to be desired.

"Those aren't all for you, Christopher," Lalania said, helping herself to several of the blue-green slices.

"We should get some of this shipped out to the fort," he told her. "Especially the red." Red cheese was a novelty for him, but the taste was as close to Cheddar as he'd found here.

"It would be wasted on your peasants." Sometimes Lalania forgot to play the part of champion of the common people. Christopher let it slide; back on Earth she would be a movie star, swaddled in luxury a thousand times greater than a few slices of cheese. And no doubt still jetting off to impoverished countries to do what she could. "Until you decide to set your own table, you'll have to live with porridge. Something you'll have to take up with Karl."

He grimaced, knowing how that discussion would end. "I'm sorry, Lala."

"Don't be sorry for me," she said. "I'm taking two wheels of this, along with several saddlebags' worth of other pleasantries. I'll be fine. But as they'll never leave my tent, and as you'll never enter it, you're the one who will do the suffering."

Saint Krellyan came into the room on the tail end of her words. "If all suffering could be alleviated by the provision of cheese, we would live in a much happier world."

"I don't know about that," Lalania said. "Have you seen the cost of this stuff? You'd think they put the blue in there with tael."

"Perhaps they do," the Saint mused aloud. "It would explain the shortage of tael on the open market, if gourmands have resorted to eating it. But I confess I know little of cheese-making."

Both of them looked at Christopher.

"No," he said. "I don't do cheeses."

"A pity." Saint Krellyan smiled wryly. "You've made paper plentiful enough that my clerks no longer panic over an inkblot. It would have been pleasant to see how much good could be wrought by an abundance of dairy products."

"Speaking of good—how's Cannan?" Christopher blurted out the question that had been burning him for the last half hour.

"As well as can be expected. His affiliation is improved, if I am to understand previous reports. He flickers on the border of Blue, well above the ordinary shade of Green. Though of course his deeds weigh heavy on his mind."

Lalania looked dubious, so Krellyan offered an explanation.

"Brother Christopher has extended mercy to him far beyond the bounds of kin or friendship. I believe this has shown Cannan, in a personally compelling manner, the value of a moral code that exceeds mere honor."

Lalania bit her lip in a terribly fetching way. "Now, Christopher, we are in the presence of a theologian."

Krellyan winked at her. "'Even the Void ends before the arguments of theologians,'" he quipped. "I know our fine distinctions have little practical value to men and women of action, but someone has to worry about them. Better myself than those doing useful work."

Lalania had been growing redder and redder as Krellyan spoke. He wasn't mocking her; he was mocking himself in Lalania's language. Christopher would have thought it hilarious if he wasn't so concerned about when it would be his turn.

Torme joined them, looking terribly serious, and Lalania jumped at the escape.

"I can see you gentlemen wish to discuss professional matters, so with your permission, I shall withdraw."

Christopher didn't particularly want her to leave. He relied on her for magical advice, and he wanted to bring up her allegations about atonement. But Krellyan let her go with a polite, "As it please you, Lady."

After she was gone, Krellyan glanced at his troubled face. "Do not push her too hard, Brother. You present enough dilemmas for a seven-headed hydra. Let her come to her own decisions in her own time."

"No, I— What?" Christopher realized he had no idea what Krellyan was talking about.

Torme did. "You challenge her, Brother Christopher, to the very core of her beliefs about the world. As you challenged me. It can be a difficult experience."

"I— How?"

"Forgive me," Torme apologized to Krellyan for what he was about to say, "but as you must already know, many consider the White to be soft and weak. When I lived under Black Bart, it was a tried and trusty joke. Pig iron, we called it: the right color, but of no use to anyone."

"I can hardly take offense at a claim so close to the truth." Krellyan smiled wryly.

Torme turned back to Christopher. "But then you show up, guns blazing, and it becomes apparent that strength wears more than one face. To ask politely, and then to back it up with sky-fire, is a compelling argument. One most people are wholly unprepared for."

Speak softly and carry a big stick, Christopher thought. That's not what he said, though.

"But guns don't care about morality. Anybody can use gunpowder."

"No," Torme said, "they can't. Black Bart ruled by fear of his personal prowess. I and all his soldiers lived in utter terror of the day he would turn on us, cut us down like a weed for some imagined slight or merely for his momentary amusement. If Bart had armed his men with weapons powerful enough to kill even him, he would not have survived his first battle."

Christopher thought of another, less pleasant phrase from Earth. In Vietnam they had called it "fragging."

"That's no guarantee," he said. "Evil men can still field an army of rifles." The democratizing effect of firearms hadn't hindered Hitler or Stalin.

"But not through personal strength alone. I do not know if the Iron Throne can adapt to your methods, Brother Christopher, but at least the Bartholomews of the world cannot."

"It is true," Krellyan said. "Your continuing adventures raise many eyebrows. We have been healers so long that many have forgotten we *chose* healing. It was what the Kingdom needed. The blessed Prophet Bodecia believed that greater strength lay in unity than in ceaseless wrestling for power. Since no others would give up personal gain for the sake of the realm, she chose to. And we followed her example. For generations now we have bound the wounds of the Kingdom, trying to hold it together."

Christopher felt his own face growing red.

"It has been hard." Krellyan spoke simply, without blame or complaint. Those were qualities his audience would have to supply on its own, if it chose to. "We have had to make common cause with wickedness, for the sake of a nebulous vision. We have had to choose the lesser of two evils for so long that we no longer seem to be striving for good."

"But you've been expanding," Christopher argued. Cardinal Faren had made the strategy sound successful, back when he'd first lectured Christopher on the follies of warmongering.

"The King favors us. I believe he thinks a realm administered by passive churchmen will enhance royal power at the expense of baronial privilege. But he does not intend to share that power with us. Nor does he intend to do away with the peerage. In his view supreme heroes must still take up the sword to tame the Wild. Only the ranked strength of the nobility can defeat monsters, and thus the nobility is necessary to the safety of the realm."

Torme's face was undergoing its own difficulties as he absorbed the Saint's words, and what they inevitably implied. Christopher watched Torme's eyebrows rise, then lower, and then beetle up into a frown. Torme opened his mouth, changed his mind, and bit his lip instead.

"Indeed," Krellyan said softly, also watching the young priest, who had once been a knight, piece together the realization that his boss was intent on obliterating not just a few bad nobles, but the entire institution of nobility itself.

"If it's any consolation," Christopher offered, "I couldn't do it without you. The peasants of your counties have lived with justice and dignity long enough to assume they deserve it. They have money to spare, a strong spirit, and faith in the power of collective action."

"The consolation lies in the fact that Marcius sent you. Were you one of my own priests, I would let Faren drub some sense into you. But you come with the sanction of a god. That allows me to preserve some shreds of my self-esteem."

It wasn't so much a sanction as a deal. Christopher wasn't positive that was worth betting a kingdom on.

"In any case it is too late for second thoughts. We must continue to act as neutrally as possible, but only to buy you time. Nothing we can do now, short of hanging you from the bell tower tonight, will distance us from your actions. Should you perish or fail, our Church will inevitably pay the price as well. In the minds of the rest of the realm, one is either innocent or guilty, nothing in between. Having failed to denounce you at the outset, we have become tarred with your sins."

"You can always say I took advantage of you. The King will like that; he'll think he can take advantage of you, too."

Krellyan gave him a sad smile. "I fear if we play the role of patsy that well, we will become it. Our faith will wither and shrink, and we will be eclipsed by some stronger, more vibrant color."

Christopher sat back, troubled by the Saint's pessimism. He had enough to worry about. He didn't need to be charged with the fate of all that was good and pure as well.

Krellyan, apparently incapable of not being helpful, offered him solace. "Cardinal Faren does not share my dismal view. He believes that with appropriate caution, we can survive your destruction and suffer only a temporary setback."

"Then by all means, be cautious." Christopher jumped at the escape. It took him a few moments to realize he'd fallen into the same trap Lalania had: volunteering to do what the Saint wanted him to do. In this case, to accept as little help as possible.

"Then you understand why I must charge you full price for this," Krellyan said, indicating the long, thin box Torme had brought with him. As if gold had been all they were discussing.

"Another priceless relic?" Christopher regretted it instantly, but consoled himself by pretending it was what he would have said if they really had been discussing money.

"Not exactly. More of an evasion of my responsibilities, though a necessary one. I cannot atone Cannan. The process must be voluntary, and he does not look to me for absolution."

"About that," Christopher said uncomfortably. "I had some questions. . . ."

"No doubt. It is poorly understood by most, and any number of ridiculous superstitions cloud around it." Krellyan spoke with the slightest tint of exasperation, as if he was tired of making this particular argument. "However, you will receive your answers in the most direct manner possible."

Torme held the box open, and Krellyan carefully withdrew a scroll. This one was new, on clean, bright parchment that was still soft and white.

"My apologies, Brother, but I did not care to risk so much on the quality of your paper."

"That's okay," Christopher said. The market for scrolls was pretty small. He'd only seen two in the last year. His industry could sustain a loss of sales on that scale.

He took the scroll gingerly, opening the first few inches of it. In plain language it stated the name of the spell it contained, and then a line that said, "Read no further." So he didn't.

"I don't know how to do this." Surely there was more to it than casting a spell. Psychological counseling or something.

Krellyan looked at him earnestly. "You brought Cannan here, alive, when he had bent all his power on self-destruction. You need only bring him a step further."

"But what's going to happen?" How would Christopher even know if the magic replaced Cannan with a Cannan-bot? He had no idea what such a process would look like, or how to tell the difference afterward.

"Cannan is tainted with a rank of something foul and dark. I would think the first step would be to remove that. Then the two of you must decide how much pain he can bear. The spell will let you remove anger, grief, shame, or even knowledge. I do not advise the latter, however. The truth of his acts are publicly known, so eventually he must become aware of them again."

Torme spoke, from his perspective of firsthand experience. "I recall the evil I did when I served Bart. But the memories no longer poison me. It is as if someone else did those things while I only watched. Someone who was once me, but is no longer."

Krellyan nodded in agreement. "Cannan's cause is just. He did not choose his evil willingly, and he repents of it. In time he might well make his peace on his own. Assuming he survived that long, which we must admit seems unlikely. So we are justified in this act. Or at least I believe so; you will have to make the final decision while in the spell. Cannan will not be able to deceive you, nor will you be able to deceive him. As long as the spell lasts, you will share his knowledge and his pain, as if through his eyes."

Christopher paused. Was he about to Vulcan mind meld with a man who'd murdered his wife and burned her corpse? Wouldn't *he* need some psychotropic medication after that?

Looking up from the scroll, he could not help but stare at Saint Krellyan. The man had done this a dozen times, for all manner of thugs and criminals. And those were just the ones Christopher had sent him. Who knew how many other wicked nightmares Krellyan had sat through, trying to bring someone into the light?

"If people knew what you did, they wouldn't think you were weak," Christopher said, thinking of how difficult it was going to be for himself.

"My hands have never held a sword. I have slain no monsters, suffered no fangs to bite or claws to rend me. Few in this world think of that as strength."

Christopher didn't kill very many monsters, either. His men did, and they suffered the biting and rending—and dying—for him. That fact nipped any sense of superiority in the bud.

"Okay. Let's get this over with."

"Are you sure you wish to proceed, Brother?"

"No," Christopher said quite honestly. "I absolutely do not wish to do this. But my only other choice is letting Cannan die, right?"

The Saint nodded in sad agreement.

Christopher shrugged. "Then let's go."

10

ATONEMENT

Christopher hadn't expected the Cathedral to have a dungeon. It was the nicest possible dungeon—clean, neat, and tastefully appointed in cheap but serviceable furniture, with paneled walls and heavy oaken doors—but it was still a dungeon. A place to store prisoners until they were ready to be dealt with.

Light-stones on the walls tried to keep the place well lit and bright, but they could not overcome the sheer fact of the dungeon's nature. That such a thing existed at all, underneath the White Cathedral, was a sad and somber fact that would not be dispelled.

That Christopher had sent at least a dozen men here to spend their last days in relative comfort before Captain Steuben draped a noose around their necks and let them fall was another fact that refused to be banished. The thought kept peering out at him from behind every closed door they passed.

When they turned into a room at last, Christopher slipped into the relative gloom with a sense of escape. Only a single flickering light-stone kept the underground room from total darkness.

"It helps a man think," Torme said. "It's odd, but in the shadows you can't focus on anything else but why you're here."

Torme had once been in one of these cells.

Steuben blocked the doorway, a mere formality since the only escape led past Saint Krellyan. Krellyan's magic was far more potent than the Captain's sword. In this case they had nothing to worry about. The victim, Cannan, sat on a plain wooden chair, his head in his hands, passively waiting to die.

"If you want him chained, I'll have to send out." Steuben sounded apologetic.

"No, of course not," Christopher said automatically. What a hideous idea that was: to bring chains into this building.

"Normally we don't bother, on account of the Saint's high rank, and the prisoners being of no account."

Christopher was only a few ranks higher than Cannan. He might possibly be in danger if the red knight went berserk again. Christopher hoped the furniture was as cheap as it looked. If a chair was going to be smashed over his head at any point, he would prefer it was a shoddily constructed one.

Chains, on the other hand, were simply out of the question.

"No," Christopher repeated.

"I'll need your blade, Vicar. I can't leave it in his reach."

Steuben was a knight of some rank himself. He didn't fear Cannan wielding a chair. But everyone with a lick of sense feared the huge man armed with steel.

Silently, Christopher unlooped his baldric and held out the sword. Torme took it gravely.

"We will be right outside, Brother Vicar. You need but call."

The two other men stepped outside, or, rather, Torme did. Steuben had never really entered the room. Now he swung the heavy wooden door shut, leaving the room in semi-darkness. The solid thunk of the exterior bolt being thrown home settled uncomfortably in Christopher's stomach.

Cannan did not move, had not moved at all. Christopher sat down on the narrow bed and tried to think of something to say.

Cannan spoke first. "It would be a mercy to let me hang."

"You can still choose that. But if you do, then Niona will stay dead. Forever."

"Can you make such a promise, little priest? When not even your Saint will pretend such a thing is in his power, can you promise me there is a way to restore life to ashes?"

Saint Krellyan didn't have the power to send Christopher home, either. But Christopher knew it was possible. He knew it had to be possible.

"Yes, I can promise you, there are miracles. I don't know how, or when, or where, but there are miracles in this world. But they only come to people who don't give up."

Cannan should have snorted, made a little laugh of derision. He didn't. He spoke simply, without adornment.

"You do not know of what you speak."

Christopher watched the shadows dance across Cannan's dark and craggy face, the valleys of its sunken cheeks, cracked lips, and unmoving mouth. That was the most disconcerting thing. Cannan's mouth no longer betrayed emotion. He did not snarl or leer. The lips did not curve up in wry smiles, sink down in thunderous frowns, or open in uproarious laughter. Cannan wore the mouth of a corpse.

"Maybe not. But I know that if it were my life in the balance, you would risk yours to save it. Not because you owed me, but simply because you could."

In the silence that followed, Christopher rolled open the scroll. Below the warning line was a single word of many syllables, written in huge, flowing letters of Celestial. He read the word out loud.

The letters came to life in white flames, burning the parchment with cold, holy fire. Sensations swelled out of the light: the crackling of flames, green wood hissing and spitting as it popped, heat beating on his face, the sting of smoke in his eyes. Christopher stared across a campfire into Cannan's face. Cannan was now wreathed in an aura of blue, shot through with sparks of green and red, but it was blotched and sickly. Blackness lay over the flickering colors like crude oil on water. Christopher felt himself falling, as if diving from a great height into a pool. But this water was foul and unclean, and he would sink in it like a stone.

"No," Christopher said. "I changed my mind. I don't want to do this." But it was too late.

"Husband. What have I done to displease you so?"

Niona's voice had always made Christopher think of bells, bright and moving in the wind. Now her voice grated at his skin like broken glass, sharp and shrill and merciless, a bag of metal jangling in his face, a biting fly that harassed him day and night.

"Leave it be, woman."

Christopher was startled at the harshness of his words. He glanced across the fire, which was banked low to make little smoke and less light. Niona sat with her arms around her knees and her hair hanging loose, her dark eyes watching him warily. Once he had found that fey look unbearably interesting, like a wild creature that might be tamed with great patience. Now the burden of her vulnerability weighed on him like a stone.

"It is only a mood. It will pass in the morning." His huge hands idly snapped a twig, and he threw the broken parts in the fire.

"It has been a mood for many days." She spoke in the druid's way, careful not to sound reproachful. Merely stating a fact, without bias or judgment. It infuriated him. A constant reminder that his emotions were played out in public, like a child's tantrum.

With a supreme effort of will, he did not snap back at her.

"I have been dueling for many days. Something about entering the field of death every day makes a man moody. That's why we left, remember? A break, to soften my mood."

No, we left because of the ring. She didn't say it, but he knew she was thinking it.

Deep inside the core of his being, he felt a dizzying flutter. It came more and more of late. Always, when he thought of Black Bart coming to get his ring. That was to be expected. Bart was a creature of darkness; his demonic aura created fear in the bravest of men.

But even now, when they were deep in the Wild, untraceable and untrackable by dint of Niona's druidic lore, the fluttering came again and again. He suspected it was fear. The suspicion unnerved him, because he had never before felt fear. Apprehension, perhaps, or even doubt, but never this sickening, weakening hollowness.

Her silent reproach had brought on this fit, as it did night after night. She no longer mentioned the ring directly, knowing that it would make him angry, but she still thought of it. He could feel her thinking of it, feel her black glances at the tiny band of gold on his finger, stabbing him with hatred, or resentment, or perhaps envy. It did not matter. All that mattered was that the ring was his.

He forced himself to smile.

"You had the right of it. We spent too long in that stinking city. I needed fresh air and open skies. Let me breathe a little longer, wife, and I will be better in the morning."

It was a lie, a patent, obvious lie. He had never told such a poor lie in all his life. And yet she believed it. She lay down next to their fire, stretched out like a feral cat in front of a stranger's hearth, and closed her eyes. She believed it because she wanted to, because she could not bear to imagine not believing.

He should have pitied her, but he could not. Her unrelenting need for him was revolting, rendering her a pathetic clinging parasite, like a tick burrowed under the scalp.

A tick whose fangs were in deep. Mere words would never drive her away, no matter how harsh. She had laid claim to his body and soul through the ritual of marriage, and like every brainless woman, she took the words they had exchanged seriously. He could not chase her away.

Nor could he escape her. The cursed woman could follow a mouse over a mountain with her eyes closed. And if by chance he did shake her from his trail, she would just run crying home to her parents. Then he would have druids and rangers stalking him. There would be no end to it.

As he sat by the dwindling fire, listening to her sleep, his hatred blossomed in the growing dark. The depth of her trust was cloying, sickly sweet and foul. It was shameful. He was a warrior, a professional duelist, a freelance killer who survived off the ransoms he won on the field of honor. He was far too dangerous to be treated like a tamed cat. It was *disrespectful*.

When he acted, it was without conscious thought—a sudden and instantaneous movement. Or so he lied to himself. In truth his first act was as premeditated as it was possible to be. An enraged man might have wrapped his hands around her pretty white throat and squeezed the sweetness out of her, or struck at her smooth neck with the great two-handed sword that never left his side these days. What he did was altogether different, and cruelly aware.

Walking casually, as if he intended nothing more than to cross to where she lay, he felt as solid as ice. No tremble belied him. Had she been awake, she would have known his falseness by the exaggerated calm that gripped his limbs, but she was not awake. She was not pretending sleep. She did not fear him, and he could not stand it.

With one smooth motion he thrust his great sword down, through her belly, deep into the earth, pinning her to the ground. Let her try her druid tricks now. Let her change shape and form as she willed; it would not free her from his iron anchor.

Blood welled out from where the blade disappeared into her flesh. A memory sprang into his mind, unbidden, of the smoothness of the belly under her robe, of the contrast of white oval and black triangle that would now be marred by red. He had loved the sight of her naked. It had driven him mad with desire, robbing him of will and power even more than the fluttering fear. No more.

"Husband," she cried, opening her eyes in shock and pain. Her tael was too great to let one blow still her, and so she flopped on the end of his sword like a hooked fish, her small hands futilely pawing at the leather-wrapped hilt.

She looked up at him and still did not believe. He knelt by her side, the better for her to look into his eyes and know what he truly was, and still she would not see. In the reflection of her wet, shining eyes, he saw only the weak, foolish thing she wanted him to be.

Revolted beyond reason, he lifted a heavy rock in both hands and brought it down. The dry crunch of bone and wet tearing of skin rushed into his ears, a river of noise that deafened him.

"Husband," she whispered through her broken mouth, white teeth like pebbles spilling out on a tide of red.

Howling with rage, he brought the stone down again and again, until there was nothing left to remind him of what he had once been, or what she had once been to him. Through the red haze of his vision, he recognized the purple glint of tael mixed in with the gray, white, and red that flecked the ground. The beast inside him took complete control, then, and he fell on the feast of power, shoveling bloody lumps into his mouth until the rage abandoned him. The fire rushed out of him like water from a spilled barrel, leaving him light and fuzzy and hollow in its wake.

Staggering to his feet, unable to tell which way was up and which was down, he stumbled only a few steps before he fell again, this time into merciful blackness.

In the cold light of morning he cut wood, stacking a funeral pyre fit for a king. His hands worked automatically, without conscious effort. His mind was focused on other things, trivial distractions like the song of a robin or the glint of sunlight on dewy leaves. Somehow he picked up the body, wrapping its ruined part in its cloak, without ever really noticing what he was doing. When the fire leapt above the pyre, hiding everything in a blaze of destroying flame, he began to walk in a random direction, leading his great destrier by the halter. He dared not mount it, not while her blood was still fresh on him. The animal would rebel, and he would have to kill it, and he still needed it for a little while yet. Already her mount had fled in the night, having been hobbled only by cloying sentiment instead of strong rope.

At a stream, late in the afternoon, he paused to let the horse drink. Stumbling forward, he immersed himself in the cold water and let it wash him clean.

Only then did he recognize what he had done. Only when it was too late. A part of him marveled that madness could be so pure, so methodical, and so complete. Another part of him called it freedom, escape from the pitiful sham of hypocrisies that mewling sheep called law and goodness. Both parts spoke in his head, each pretending to be unheedful of the other, each pretending it was the whole of him. But only one part could be the whole.

Forcing the horse to stillness, he swung into the saddle. When the animal snorted, flattening its ears in displeasure, he cuffed it with a powerful blow to the side of the head. Then he turned the horse south.

The ring clung to his finger, heavy and burning with cold. Only one part could be the whole. Dull and black inside, he rode, and after a while there was only one part left.

Christopher fell to his knees, sick and disoriented. The hard stone of the floor told him that he was here, in the Cathedral, even while his vision swam with images from someone else's nightmare.

He put out a hand to steady himself, and Cannan caught it in a powerful grasp undiminished by the stub of a missing finger. The huge man was trapped in the images, too, all the more disorienting because they were from his own past.

"Do you see, priest? It was me. All me."

Christopher shook his head. "Part of you, Cannan. Most of you, even, but not all you." He struggled in confusion, still bound to Cannan through the spell. He could hear his own voice in Cannan's head and feel Cannan's reaction, like an echo. "The ring took part of your mind. It's like . . ." A lifetime of casual reading in neuroscience deserted him. This language had no words for the structure of the brain. This culture had no notion of mental illness as a consequence of crossed wires and procedural malfunctions. An image came to him, of a computer screen spewing random characters after a hard crash brought on by the tiniest of errors and the omnipotent law of unintended consequences. It was an image he could never hope to explain to Cannan.

"Do not tell me it is like being drunk. I have been drunk to the point of foolishness before and since. Never have I desired evil so fully as I desired it that night."

Christopher racked his memory for some metaphor that would make sense. The concentration left him reeling, and he would have collapsed on the floor if it weren't for Cannan's steadying hand. Inspiration came to him in a flash, sparked by the unthinking strength of Cannan's grip.

"It's like herding sheep, Cannan. Have you ever seen a shepherd move his flock? Now have you ever seen one try it without his dogs?"

Obediently the spell created the hallucination for them, a baa-ing giant pillow of fluffy white and brown bumping through a green pasture. A hooded man with a crook strolled behind them, while dogs ran and barked at the fringes. On an invisible cue the dogs silently faded out of existence, and within seconds the organized mass began to disintegrate into tiny bits of fluff that scattered across the field, while the shepherd called and whistled futilely, waving his useless stick in the air.

"They're still the same sheep. He's still the same shepherd. But the flock will never make it to market. They took your dogs, Cannan. The sheepdogs of your mind, the part that keeps you on track."

In the vision, the sheepdogs came slinking back, whining in shame. The shepherd raised his stick in furious anger, and the dogs cowered at his feet, terrified. For a moment Cannan's white-hot rage burned through all of them, Cannan and Christopher and the hooded man in the vision. Christopher trembled, as afraid as the dogs of what might happen next.

But then the shepherd lowered his staff. With stalwart resignation he whistled commands. The dogs leapt into action, darting out across the field, and the vision faded away.

"Heroism isn't being too tough to fall. It's about getting up after you've fallen. It's a choice, Cannan, one you make day after day. And it never gets any easier."

The words sounded vapid even as Christopher said them. This wasn't a Little League player who had struck out at the homecoming game.

The smell of wood smoke filtered into the room, the nightmare leaking in from the dark corners around them. The vision pushed at the edge of their sight, threatening to overwhelm them again, and Cannan shuddered. Christopher instinctively reached out with his free hand, gathering the images in spider-web tendrils in his fist. As the strands swirled in on themselves, Cannan whispered a plea.

"Don't take her from me completely."

In the gaps left by the strands of the vision, another hallucination took shape. One of Christopher's choosing: a homey attic, full of unused junk that was too valuable to discard but too old to be of any real use. Christopher wrapped the memories in a frosted glass box with brass hinges, and set the box on a shelf, where Cannan could open it and look at it any time he wanted to. Any time he needed to. The box held the scene like a diorama, two tiny people around a spark of fire, and you could smell the wood smoke when the lid was open.

Christopher shut the lid. He walked back to the stairs and turned out the overhead light. The box glowed dimly in the dark, waiting for him, safe and sound and treasured. He went down the stairs, closed the door, and found himself back in the dungeon.

Kneeling on the stone of the cell floor, bathed in the flickering of the light-stone, Christopher realized the spell was done. He climbed back onto the edge of the bed and watched Cannan. The man sat with his head in his hands, breathing gently, for several minutes before he spoke again.

"Now what?" Cannan's voice, laden with grief, was still more alive than it had been in many days.

"Now we go to work. I have a job to do, Cannan, and when I'm done, a god will owe me a favor. Your job is to keep me alive while I do my job." It wasn't much, but it was the best Christopher had to offer.

"So once again I am your champion?" Cannan's mouth twisted so wryly that it was bitter. Christopher watched in fascination, curious that such a small thing could be so significant.

"Not so much with the dueling, though." Christopher winced as soon as the graceless words left his mouth. "Mostly it's assassins. And ulvenmen."

Cannan shook his head. "You have more enemies than you know. I remember people asking questions, when we were still in the city. Strange people, and strange questions, and they paid for as much ale as I could drink. I do not remember their names, or what they looked like, or what I told them."

Christopher shrugged reassuringly. "It doesn't matter." Cannan hadn't known about his revolutionary plans then, so he couldn't have told them anything important.

"I will do what I can. I shall not fail you from lack of trying. But you should know I am only third rank again." Cannan opened his fist and offered Christopher a bright purple stone.

"How's that?" Christopher said, confused. Usually it was him giving other people tael.

"The rank I gained from . . ." He paused for the space of several unspoken words. "I shed it. It clung to me like a rancid second skin, but when your spell ended, it was gone, and this was in my hand. It belongs to you now."

It wasn't enough to restore a fourth rank, due to the criminal calculus of tael, but it was a healthy lump. Christopher took it, because he was expected to, but he didn't know what to do with it.

"I will need a sword," Cannan said. "After that, you will give me whatever you think I require, and I will not complain. I no longer live for myself, but only for the hope you represent. Should you have to choose between my life and yours, you will choose yours, for Niona's sake. Is that clear?" Cannan spoke with more earnestness than Christopher had ever seen him use before.

"Yes, of course." It felt strange to promise he would look after his own life before that of another's.

Cannan left the chair to go to one knee in front of Christopher. He turned his palms up, like a supplicant, but he spoke with calm conviction.

"Then I am your dog, shepherd, until I am rejoined with Niona. I ask only one mercy: should you change your mind, do not tell me. Simply put me down in my sleep."

"I can't do that," Christopher said. "I made you a promise. I have to keep it."

Cannan shrugged, not disputing him but not agreeing. In one eloquent lift and fall of his shoulders he seemed to say, *The world is perpetually surprising.* But of course Cannan would never use a word like *perpetually.*

Christopher stood, trying to shake the sympathetic bond that still lingered. He wanted to be friends with Cannan, but he didn't want to be in the man's head anymore. His own head, with its own problems and pledges, was enough.

Torme and Steuben were sitting at the end of the hall, waiting. They stood when they saw Christopher and Cannan walk out of the cell. Torme immediately passed his hand in front of his eyes and cast a spell.

He stared intently at Cannan for a moment. The red knight endured the scrutiny, but Christopher was unbearably relieved to see that Cannan endured it with a carefully buried touch of resentment. It was inevitable; Cannan would undergo many such examinations in the immediate future, and perhaps for the rest of his life, and he knew it. But that he could still be annoyed by it was proof that the old Cannan had returned.

That he didn't immediately murder Torme was proof that the new Cannan was gone, too.

"My apologies, Ser," Torme said.

Steuben wasn't ready to apologize yet. "Well?" he asked Torme.

"Blue, Captain. And no taint."

Christopher winced. To hear a man's moral nature discussed in such frank terms was uncomfortable; to talk about it in front of others was insulting.

"Good enough." Steuben strode forward and handed Christopher's sword back. "For me, at least," he said to Cannan, addressing the man directly for the first time. "But not perhaps for others. You left many enemies on both sides of the aisle."

Cannan shrugged.

"He's under my protection," Christopher said.

"Well, then, you can face your enemies together. But not your friends: the Bright who have cause to dislike Cannan will now dislike you, and those that disliked you will now hold him in the same regard."

"That doesn't seem fair," Christopher said.

Steuben glared at him. "Indeed. But when you take a friendless wolf under your banner, what else do you expect?"

Cannan shrugged tiredly. "My enemies are petty knights, whose chief complaint is that they lost against a ring I defeated. If they seek satisfaction in the dueling ring, then they can apply to the Vicar. For my part, I will fight or befriend whoever he directs me to."

Christopher thought he could detect a slim smile hiding under Steuben's beard.

"Fair words, Ser," Steuben said, "if not fair-faced. But then, we are knights, not priests. No doubt your Vicar can put honey on them."

"That's why I have Lala," Christopher said. "She writes my speeches."

"Is that what you use her for? Well, that explains a lot." Steuben seemed to decide the conversation had gone on long enough, and he led the way out of the dungeon, and up the stairs to the Saint's office.

Krellyan looked up from his paperwork and asked, "I trust all went well?"

Steuben answered. "Pater Torme reports Blue and clear."

"Welcome back," Krellyan said to Cannan.

Cannan bit his lip and said nothing. Christopher could feel the tension in the man, twisting him like a wet towel. To be so completely accepted, when only an hour ago he had been feared as a dangerous beast, had to be disorienting. It was making Christopher dizzy, in no small part because he found himself treating Cannan without reservations too. For the big, hard man, who had never shared any emotion but sardonic irony, who had lived without hope for so many months, it would be exhausting.

"What will you do now?" Krellyan asked Christopher.

"Go back to my post."

Krellyan smiled and shook his head. "I meant in a more general sense."

Christopher thought about it for a moment.

"The answer's still the same. I know my duty, and I will return to it."

"And the regiment you are training in Knockford? You will turn it over to whatever lord the King assigns it to?"

He was planning on turning it over to Karl. All he had to do was convince Karl to become a noble. Given the miracle he had just witnessed, that was surely possible. But then Karl's choice was a principled one, not an act of madness brought on by mind-breaking sorcery. No magic would avail against that.

"If it comes to that, sure." It would be like free advertising. Once the other lords saw firsthand what guns could do, they'd buy them like mad. "But I'd like some influence over the choice, if it's possible."

"It may be. You are in high favor, thanks to your recent success. You have been invited to the Concord of Peers. Only as a guest, understand; you do not hold any land. But it is not uncommon for those of your rank to attend."

"Concord? Like a political meeting?" He might actually have a chance to affect state policy.

"In the beginning, perhaps. Now it is merely excuse for the ladies to glitter and the men to brag. Still, you will meet the King face-to-face, and if you have a candidate in mind, that would be the time to bring it up."

"When does this happen?" How much time did he have to work on Karl?

"Not until midwinter. You have half a season to prepare, and what is left of this one."

"Then I better get cracking."

"Indeed." The Saint smiled at him, perhaps thinking of how hard it would be to crack Karl. After all, the Saint had offered the man a rank, and was turned down. How could Christopher hope to succeed?

But Christopher had more than rank to offer. He had an army to give away.

While they were preparing to leave, a rather involved affair considering the number of horses they were leading, Gregor stood in the yard and frowned at Cannan. For his part the red knight bore the scrutiny without comment.

Christopher, feeling like a motherly hen, intervened anyway.

"The Saint declared him atoned. Isn't that good enough?"

"Oh, it is for me," Gregor said. "But unless you want to repeat that phrase to every single person we pass, you need to dress him like something other than a prisoner."

Cannan still wore the peasant clothes they had bought in Palar. They had tried to give him spares from the cavalry troop's supply of uniforms, but nothing fit. The man was absurdly broad across the shoulders.

"Lala said there was a tailor down the street," Christopher mused. Glancing to where she was trying to stuff too many parcels into her saddlebags, he bit his tongue. The new brown leathers she wore were a mockery of his army uniform, skintight, sleek, and sexy.

Gregor snorted. "I'm not talking about clothes. A rehabilitated man would be an armed man."

Lalania wandered over to them with a large sack and began tying it to the back of Gregor's saddle.

"I agree," she said. Christopher hadn't realized she had heard the conversation. "Until you trust him with a blade, no one else will trust him at all."

"Well, let's find a smithy and buy him one."

"Off the rack? For a man of his rank?" Lalania was shocked. "If you gave me fifty pounds of gold and a season to search, I might be able to find something suitable."

Karl, walking past on his way to another task, stopped to shake his head. "You must learn to make do with what we have." Karl unclipped his baldric and removed it from his shoulder.

"Giving away my sword again?" Christopher had lost count of how many expensive swords he'd given Karl, only to see the young man hand them off to someone else.

"I told you in the beginning, Christopher." Karl had said he could not accept a sword from Christopher's hand. But Christopher had stopped being upset by it, once he noticed that Karl never offered to give away his carbine.

"Fair enough. Cannan, is this suitable?" Swords, like suits, worked best when they were custom-made. Christopher's sword had been made specifically for him, to a god's specifications. He owed Cannan at least a chance to turn down a weapon the knight couldn't excel with.

Cannan took the weapon and drew it partially out of the scabbard. The black blade gleamed dully in the sunlight.

"Gods, Karl. . . ." Lalania looked at the ugly weapon in disgust. "That's Black Bart's sword." Christopher caught his breath. Karl had worn it so long Christopher had forgotten where it came from.

"I have borne it many months, to no ill effect. Just as Christopher has worn his armor."

Cannan held the weapon, half drawn, and stared at Karl.

"Also," Karl confessed, "I asked the Saint. He declared the weapon untainted."

"You place great trust in the Saint's magic," Cannan said, though whether he was referring to the sword or his redemption was unclear.

Karl shrugged. "I trust the Colonel's carbines more."

From a lesser man it might have sounded like boasting, the commoner reminding the knight of how he had been laid low. But Cannan slid the sword back into the scabbard with the ghost of an approving smile.

"It is sufficient," he said. Slinging the baldric over his shoulder, he turned to his horse, and Karl marched off to his tasks. Christopher, Lalania, and Gregor were left standing there, to share stunned looks.

Gregor smiled ruefully. "Karl is right. If the man were going to break, better we should know now than later. If he lacks the strength to grasp evil and turn it to good, then he is not worthy of the trust you have placed in him."

"Still . . ." It was unbearably rude, as if calculated to maximize Cannan's pain.

"Gregor is right." Lalania seemed unhappy to admit it. "He will face this issue many times. If he can't handle it in a stable, then we can't risk him on a battlefield. Whatever pain it causes, he must be able to deal with."

"He'll need to work on that, then," Gregor said. "It's generally not considered proper form to accept a magic sword and not even say thank you."

Lalania frowned. "I don't imagine he was feeling very thankful."

"I don't imagine Karl expected thanks," Christopher said.

They went to their own horses. Christopher mounted, and watched Lalania watching Cannan. He suspected he knew why she was so unhappy. Cannan's actions were not those of a Cannan-bot. They were the deeds of a hero. The woman hated being wrong.

11

JUST LIKE OLD TIMES

He didn't go back to his post. He went to Burseberry instead, dismounting in the chapel yard while its last master came out to greet him.

"You just left, and you're already back?" Svengusta said. "If you'd only ridden a little faster, you could have arrived before you left, and saved yourself the trouble of going in the first place."

Gregor laughed out loud. "It's good to see you, too, you old rascal."

"Ser Gregor, well met again! And is that Ser Cannan? Come to escort the Pater home from his latest misadventure, no doubt. Just like old times. I tell you, the things that boy gets up to."

It wasn't even remotely like old times. The chapel had been expanded half a dozen times, the village was drowning in a sea of young men, and the sound of gunfire from the rifle range was almost constant.

Cannan stood silently, scanning the chapel grounds. At first Christopher thought he was looking for Niona, and instinctively he glanced around for her. But she was not here, of course.

Not like old times, at all.

"All this greeting and well meeting has left me dry," Svengusta said. "Let us repair to the tavern for some restorative elixir."

"Maybe later, Sven. I've got work to do." Christopher's assault on the mound of paperwork had been interrupted ages ago, and the pile had taken advantage of his absence to advance across the entire surface of the table. It was times like these that he regretted making paper cheap. "Where's Helga?"

"Hiding in her kitchen," Svengusta said. "She's got so many pots and pans now she's better armored than a knight."

"Speaking of which," Gregor mused aloud, "we've none ourselves. I was thinking of visiting your smithy and seeing what they could do."

"There's an armorer in town." Christopher waved in the general direction of Knockford. "Senior Palek. He can do good work, but it will be expensive."

"If I wanted to pay for it, I would have bought it in Kingsrock. Let's see what your own men can make first." Apparently Gregor was taking Karl's economy lesson to heart.

Another reason for Palek to hate him, but Christopher kept his mouth shut. He probably owed Gregor a suit of armor, having made him leave his own in the swamp. If the blue knight would be happy with something homemade, that would save Christopher a lot of money.

When Christopher went into his office, Torme and Cannan followed him.

"You can go get a drink or something," Christopher said to Cannan. "Torme and I can handle this." Christopher wasn't even sure if Cannan could read.

Cannan didn't answer, unless his grunt counted. The red knight sat down on a chair next to the door, drew out and planted his sword between his knees, half closed his eyes, and settled in, like a lizard basking in the sun.

Torme glanced at the red knight once, and then went about his business.

Christopher realized that he'd just added another layer to the shell of people that surrounded him. Cannan would sit there all day, rather than leave Christopher alone for even an instant. This could prove embarrassing when it came time to visit the outhouse.

And outhouse it still was. He might have introduced assembly lines and power tools, but modern sanitation would take more time and money than he had to waste.

Dinner was the first time he got to see Helga. She served them at the officer's table but did not take a seat. Christopher missed his little family gatherings. Dinner had become a formal affair. His table was in the same room as the rest of the mess hall, which struck him as a classic medieval arrangement. At least it matched what he had seen in the movies. Lalania assured him it was unusual here, however. Lords ate, drank, and lived with their retinues, their peers in class if not necessarily in rank. To have a rank was to be separate from the ordinary. The gulf between aristocrat and commoner was larger here than it ever had been on Earth.

It was also unusual to eat from the same dish as his men, but that was purposeful. He wanted his men to be fed decently, since his strength depended on them. For the farm boys, army food was often a step up in quality. The original reason—fear of being poisoned—had gone away, replaced by the habit of saying a blessing over his food at every meal. Magic had become so integrated into his life he didn't even notice it half the time.

Helga kept running off every time he tried to talk to her. He would have been annoyed except he noticed she was giving Karl the same treatment. The young soldier didn't show it, of course, but Christopher was sure he was also bothered by it. Not that he should be; Christopher was pretty sure his conduct in Helga's absence would not meet with her approval.

Lalania was bright and cheery, steering the conversation to light laughter and easy banter, smoothing over Cannan's silence. Though Cannan had been persuaded to take a seat and forgo taste testing every bit of Christopher's food, he brought his sword and his surly suspicion to the table. D'Kan treated the man without any special deference, as did everyone else. Christopher was worried about the potential for conflict there, but D'Kan had made no argument or objection since the atonement.

No one had. The strength of the Saint's reputation was so great that Cannan was accepted as a redeemed man, solely by virtue of having walked out of the Cathedral in one piece.

"I tried to talk to your armorers," Gregor said through a mouthful of mashed yams. They were like mashed potatoes, aside from being yellow, sweet as grapes, and as stiff as meringue. "But they don't know anything about armor."

The men who ran his armory here in Burseberry maintained the rifles and cannons. "Sorry," Christopher said, "we'll have to go back to Knockford for that."

"There are other things in Knockford you should be checking up on," Svengusta said with a leer. That look was the one the old man used whenever he talked about Fae. Christopher sighed and wondered what trouble Tom had been up to now.

"Tomorrow, then?" Gregor seemed unusually eager to get moving again, until Christopher realized the knight wasn't relaxing at home like he was. Then he remembered it wasn't his home anymore, either.

He'd left the swamp fort under the command of a mercenary sergeant and a young priestess. At the time, escorting Cannan had seemed the greatest danger. Now he was having panic attacks about leaving the men so stripped of rank.

"Have we received any reports from the fort?" Christopher asked, despite the fact he'd never sent one back while he was in charge.

"It's still there, at least as of yesterday," Lalania assured him. No one thought to question her ability to know this. They just accepted it if Christopher accepted it. This aggravated him, but he didn't know how to instill professional-grade skepticism into an army that depended on magic to function.

"And Disa?" Gregor asked the bard.

"Your precious flower is safe, Ser." Lalania was more gracious than the words sounded.

"I left instructions," Karl said. "Should the fort fall, Kennet is charged with cutting a finger from the Prelate's hand and hiding it in a prepared safe hole in the walls. Even if the fort is destroyed, the Prelate at least should return."

"What about Kennet?" Christopher asked. For that matter, what about the rest of the men? "Can he throw one of his own fingers in afterwards?"

"No, Vicar," Torme corrected him. "One must already be dead before the sympathetic token is harvested. Even if he could save everyone else, he could not save himself."

"Nor would he try," Karl said. "Hiding a single finger has a hope of success. Hiding a bushel of them would reveal the plan to the enemy, thus negating it. Prelate Disa belongs to the Church of the Bright Lady. We have a duty to return her. The men, however, belong to the Colonel. It is their duty to die in service to his cause."

"Wait," Christopher said. "That means Disa would have to be dead before . . ."

Karl did not even shrug. "Kennet has a carbine. Should worst come to worst, he will do what is necessary."

Strangely, Gregor looked relieved. Christopher shook his head in confused dismay.

"Let's see that it doesn't come to that," he said. "Karl, figure out how soon we can march again."

Karl paused, as if thinking. "Three days, without undue effort."

Christopher realized the pause was for him to do the thinking. Karl had just explained why there was no need for haste.

"That will give us time to talk some sense into your smiths in town," Gregor said.

"It's not them you need to sensify," Svengusta objected. "It's your Vicar here. He likes wearing soft clothes. Why, it's almost like he's a priest instead of a warrior."

"Plenty of priests wear armor, too," Gregor said. "At least where I come from. And in any case, I'm not a priest."

"Not yet," Lalania muttered, and Gregor laughed at her.

Christopher delayed another day, sending Gregor off to harass the recruits and abandoning the paperwork to Torme. He'd had another idea.

Now Jhom stared at Christopher's blueprints, in total silence, for a full fifteen minutes. When he finally spoke, he seemed distracted and bemused.

"Pulling wire used to be the work of apprentices. Now you will make a machine to do it?"

Christopher shrugged. "It's not like the apprentices will complain." Making wire was more tedious and less interesting than making nails. "It will take plenty of apprentices to run the machine, anyway." It would also take a water mill, and rolling parts made smooth by the senior smith's magical precision.

"What are you going to do with such a profundity of wire, my lord?"

What Christopher wanted to do was find some insulating rubber and run a telegraph line across the Kingdom. But copper was too expensive to leave hanging around in trees. He could only afford steel wire right now.

"Chain mail. Apparently the army needs some." It wasn't just Gregor anymore. Karl had changed sides, too. Originally the young veteran had considered armor not just a waste of money, but a pernicious liability, since it meant the peasants couldn't even run away once they started dying. But somewhere along the way Karl had noticed that Christopher's men didn't run.

"You would not let us put our boys in studs and leather, yet now you will coat them in mail?" Jhom stared at him.

"We couldn't afford it then. We can only afford it now, if you can make this machine work." It seemed absurd that it would normally take a smith an entire year to make a suit of chain mail, until you remembered the smith had to make his own steel wire. And his own steel. At that rate his troops would die of old age before his smiths could armor them all.

"And when you make machines to do the work of senior smiths, what can we afford then?" Jhom asked. "That is, if we smiths still have jobs to earn our bread with."

"Don't worry, Jhom. We'll always need someone to make the machines." Christopher tried to frame it as a joke, but the truth was that most of his apprentices would never become smiths. They would become factory workers. He wasn't sure they would thank him for that. Did the early factories improve the lives of the common people, or make them worse? Was the squalor of the industrial revolution a result of economic necessity or merely social indifference?

"Well, my lord, I will bend my every effort to birthing your new machine. But I warn you, should you ask me to make a machine to plow our fields and our wives, I will have to rebel."

Christopher was about to ask Jhom what he had against tractors, but decided he really didn't want to pursue this conversation any further down the strange path it seemed to be taking.

He went off to see Fae, which, sadly, promised to be no less difficult a conversation. Once again he had to ask for her help.

Fae was dressed more modestly than he had ever seen her, which was a relief. Before he could work around to the topic at hand, she called three young women into the office. They had a different air about them than the usual peasant women who worked for Fae as cartridge-rollers and paper-cutters. He would have thought them troubadours from their daring clothes and the sly looks they gave him, except for their poor fashion sense.

Fae spoke with prim authority. "As Flayn once held my apprenticeship, I am entitled to hold another's. I have judged any of these three worthy, but I leave the final choice up to you."

Christopher thought about the things Fae had been willing to do to become a wizard. That explained the girls' rather forward demeanor.

He also thought about Fae's demeanor, and how she had gone from exploited shopgirl to town gentry in a very short amount of time. That might explain the girls' eagerness.

"Why not hire all three?"

Fae stared at him. "I did not think I could spend your tael so freely, my lord."

That was nonsense. She always assumed she could spend his money. Probably she had lectured the girls on how hard they would have to strive to be chosen, and she was just annoyed at him for proving her wrong.

He smiled at the girls. Annoying Fae was enough to put him in a good mood.

"I think it would be a wise investment." Come to think of it, it would be. Having three more sources of sulfur would weaken Fae's lock on him. He decided he needed to throw her a bone. "I'll make them first Apprentice rank, but I'll leave it up to you to say when they are ready for more. And I'll promise to make them a full-fledged first-rank wizard in four years, if you say they are ready."

"Ten years, my lord," Fae corrected him. "If they have not been promoted in a decade, then they are surely not worthy. But any time less than that is purely up to your discretion."

"Fair enough. Now if you ladies would excuse us, Mistress Fae and I need to talk shop."

The girls curtsied low and swept out of the room, not without a few doe-eyed looks of gratitude. Then they were gone, and the only feminine presence in the room was Fae's oddly muted, almost matronly air. It made him take her more seriously, which after a few minutes he realized was worse. He was starting to think of Fae as a person, not as a witch in black leather. Perversely it made her more attractive.

He set a book and a tiny wooden box on the table. Fae went for the box first.

He could not stay his hand from precaution. It strayed to his sword hilt of its own accord. But Fae set the box down again, the lid open but the contents undisturbed.

"I must warn you," she said, "the identification of enchantments can be perilous. I would be of little value to you as a corpse, or worse."

"I don't want it identified. I already know what it does. I want it destroyed."

Despite her words, she looked unhappy at this. Apparently the lure of magic was stronger than her fear.

"You must tell me what it does before I can offer advice."

He sighed and looked out the glass-paneled door, where Cannan stood on guard. Lowering his voice, he said, "It breaks minds. It turned Cannan evil, and before him, Bart. Well, eviler, I guess. It also protects against damage. Bart was almost immune to mundane weapons."

She looked at the ring with avarice, which was her version of respect.

"That is a rare and powerful item. Are you sure you wish to destroy it? There might be a way to avoid or reverse the undesirable effect."

This from the woman who couldn't say the word *experiment* without sniffing?

"Yes, I am sure. It is far too dangerous to fool around with."

"As you wish. What have you tried so far?"

Now he had to blush. She knew him too well.

"The Saint used a spell on it. Captain Steuben used a chisel. Neither of them worked." The chisel hadn't even scratched the ring before breaking.

"Of course the chisel failed. If it protects flesh from harm, how much more so would it protect itself? You cannot defeat it by attacking its strength."

He started to speak, but she held up her finger imperiously. She did not hesitate to boss him around when she thought she could get away with it. It would have been refreshing if it wasn't so aggravating.

Casting her detection spell, she studied the ring carefully through her circled thumb and finger.

"What is the weakness of gold?" she asked him, like a lecturer examining a pupil.

"Other than its softness, you mean? Um. Low melting point?"

She pinched her lips together, a tiny sign of disappointment. "I was going to say *aqua regia*, but yes, I suppose heat as well."

He didn't know what *aqua regia* was, but it sounded expensive. Heat, on the other hand, he manufactured on an industrial scale.

"It won't . . . explode? Or release some kind of curse?"

She shook her head, her superiority restored. "If it were powerful enough to do that, it wouldn't melt in the first place."

After closing the lid, he put the box back in his pocket, and found himself breathing normally again. Fae picked up the book, a dubious second prize, and leafed through it.

"That stuff will explode," he said, "so be careful. And worse, I have to show you how to handle quicksilver. If you touch it, or even merely heat it up in an enclosed room, it will make you sick." Mercury was nasty stuff, the origin of the phrase, "mad as a hatter."

"Could you not undo that sickness?" she asked. "Nonetheless, I will abide by your restrictions, and I appreciate your concern."

He was pretty sure it wouldn't have been her getting sick anyway. That was what apprentices were for.

At the end of the day Christopher stood in front of a hot forge, flanked by the members of his retinue. Dereth had stoked the forge high before sensibly fleeing, and waves of heat beat at him. The forge contained only slag, having done its productive work for the day. It still retained the power to destroy, which suited his purpose now.

He stepped forward and took the tiny wooden box out of his pocket. Briefly he considered how to best empty it over the glowing crucible without frying himself. Then he just tossed the box, unopened, into the crucible.

The wood flared into a jet of flame three feet high, consumed by the intense heat. The walls of the box turned to ash, which took flight on a wing of convection, leaving the bright gold ring lying on boiling gray slag in the crucible. For a moment it sat there, defiant, the black stones fantastically dark against the incandescence. Then the ring lost its shape, all in an instant, and gold puddled across the surface of the slag before sinking out of sight. The stones, freed from their golden bezels, cracked and turned gray. Christopher dipped a ladle into the thick liquid and lifted it a few inches. When he tipped the ladle and let the liquid spill back into the crucible, streaks of purple ran with it.

With his other hand he cast an orison. The purple streamed to his grasp, forming a pellet between his fingers.

"So little reward for such potent evil," Lalania said, frowning at the pellet. Her definition of *little* was relative; the tael was easily worth a hundred pounds of gold.

On the other hand, the damage it had wrought was vastly greater, so perhaps her evaluation was accurate.

"This is why artifacts are not normally reduced," Fae said, apparently not having heard the last word. "It is no better reward than from a moderately ranked noble, and yet the artifact would have cast its power across the ages, undiminished by the passage of time."

"Then why aren't we drowning in the things?" Christopher asked. "If they're permanent, and each generation makes a few, then after enough time the place should be littered with magic doodads."

Everyone looked at him.

"I presume," Lalania said, "that every generation makes the same decision we just made. Power we can use today, however small, is worth more than power that will only aid some distant future."

Christopher could tell she didn't believe that. She was just covering up one of his gaffes again. The Skald had given him a perfectly good reason why they weren't drowning in historical artifacts: they didn't have countless generations behind them.

"This was a power we did not want cast across the ages," Torme said. "Although I wonder at its wisdom. Could the White make such a ring that improved minds? Could we recruit to our color through sheer artifice?"

"When you put it like that," Christopher said, "I think the answer is obvious."

Strolling back through the darkening town, the path illuminated by flickering light-stones, he considered his advantages. Magic required tael, which was always in short supply. No matter how much the enemy had, they were unlikely to get more anytime soon. But technology just required labor, and ironically it increased the productivity of labor. If he could get an industrial revolution started, maybe he could grow it faster than the enemy could adapt. He resolved to keep his head down, stay out of trouble, fan the flames of change from his forges, and let the politics take care of itself.

12

A SOCIAL CALL

The politics came in search of him the very next day. He would have thought it a consequence of breaking the ring, some latent curse leaking out, but it was too soon. The Gold Curate Joadan had to have been already on the road from the day before.

Christopher stood on his chapel steps, looking out over the field where Joadan sat astride a beautiful bay stallion. The horse was armored in the same elaborate gold filigree style as the Curate. Twenty more horsemen followed. Although their armor was plain, it was no less serviceable. The yellow tabards and cloaks marked them as Joadan's men; the discipline with which they held their places and their mounts marked them as professionals.

All in all, an intimidating, if elegant, display.

"What do you want?" Christopher said.

"And good day to you, too, my Lord Vicar." Joadan smiled at him. It appeared to be a genuine smile, which was even more disconcerting than the army at his back.

Christopher's own army stood around with rather less military dispatch. Uncertain and mostly unarmed, they looked more like indolent peasants than soldiers. How Joadan had ridden into the village with so little warning was a real concern. Christopher had become so used to his military traffic dominating the road that he had forgotten other people could use it too.

"But as for what I want," Joadan continued, "we for once have common cause. I have come seeking justice."

"That seems," Christopher said, "highly disputable."

"What is not disputed is that a known murderer shelters under your wing. My purpose today is to lay claim to him, and escort him to the judgment of the Gold Throne. Please forgive my presumption, but you have given us leave to assume you will be sympathetic to such a mission."

So his trip across the southern half of the Kingdom was now bearing rotten fruit. Nonetheless, Joadan was going to find the trip fruitless. He hadn't turned Cannan over to the druids; he sure as hell wasn't going to turn him over to the Gold Throne.

"Justice has already been served," Christopher said. Cannan, standing at the foot of the steps, physically blocking any access to Christopher, didn't bother to react to the discussion. He stood like a statue, the black sword resting point-first on the ground. "He atoned at the Cathedral."

"Him?" Joadan shook his head, still smiling. "We have no interest in him. He has done no harm to us, however much he may have annoyed those thrice-damned druids."

Christopher, hell-bent on defending Cannan, was thrown off-balance. "Then who?"

"A man who commits murder in cold blood. One who does not respect the laws of the land, or the wishes of his host. One who has killed a priest of our faith, and so far escaped retribution."

Before Christopher could puzzle out whom he meant, Gregor stepped out from the chapel doors to stand next to Christopher on the steps.

"That rat's death was an act of war."

"He was a prisoner, and his death was illegal, as you knew at the time. But I have not come to banter words with you, Ser Gregor. I have come to speak to the noble and virtuous Vicar Christopher. Once it was not in your power to bring this rogue knight to heel, my lord, but now it is. Will you bind him over to those he has wronged? Does your White law have any hold over those you call friends?"

Christopher took a step down before he caught himself. Every fiber of his being wanted to stride across the ground, grab that smarmy bastard by the throat, and bounce his grinning head off the cobble-stones until something broke.

Not mere civility stopped him. There was also the consideration that Joadan was in armor, and Christopher was not. And Joadan had already won their first duel under far more equal terms.

"You have no place to condemn me," Christopher said. He managed not to spit the words. The hypocrisy was enough to make him gag. He knew full well that Joadan would have done the same thing. Black Bart's priest had been a secret servant of the Shadow, and an enemy to both of them.

Another part of his mind reflected on the white-hot anger he was feeling. If he were still crippled by the ghost, he would have already attacked, Joadan's apparent diplomatic status notwithstanding. He would have already started a battle. For surely this was the point of this tawdry exercise: to provoke open war between his little chapel and the full might of the Gold Throne.

The realization cooled him off enough to think. How could they even know these facts? Only Christopher and his people had been left alive after Bart's failed attack in the woods.

And Cannan. Cannan, who had drunk too much and said too much to people he could not recall.

"No," Christopher said. "I will not turn him over to you. If you want justice, you must apply to the Cathedral. I will send Gregor to atone; I will pay a ransom for your loss, but I will not commit a second wrong by putting a good man in your grasp."

"Yet you did not hesitate to pull a bad man out from under the druid's."

Cannan spoke, his voice flat and hard.

"They let me go by choice. The Vicar's words were sweeter than any wine you've ever poured. Now we will see if your golden tongue is sufficient to save yourself."

"Aye," Gregor said with a growl. "One dead priest deserves

another. Putting you in the fire will brighten a thousand days." He took a small step forward.

Joadan did not stop smiling. "Strong words from naked men. Not even a scrap of mail covers you. Perhaps you think your virtue will turn the edge of a sword?" His men leaned forward in their saddles.

Some of Christopher's soldiers in the crowd had rifles with them. They began to filter to the front, while men in the back slipped way, running toward their barracks and the armory. The situation was escalating dangerously. He was pretty sure his men would win this fight, but not certain, and in any case the cost afterward would be staggering.

Karl's cavalry came to the rescue. The troop was returning early from its patrol, with Lalania riding next to him at the head of the column. She must have gone after them the instant Joadan had been seen. The horsemen were green recruits, and their rifles were empty. Still, their appearance restored order. The other soldiers fell back, sorting themselves into platoons at parade rest, which was the only safe and natural thing to do in Karl's presence.

Karl split his troop, flanking Joadan's men on either side. They brought their horses to a halt. Joadan's knights leaned back now that they were faced with mounted foes.

Christopher spoke with a little more confidence. "When I took Cannan from the druids, I took him to the Cathedral. I will take Gregor there as well. He will serve whatever penance the Saint assigns. I will pay whatever ransom the law demands. You will have to content yourself with that."

"Would you deny us the right to choose our own jurisdiction, as you have chosen yours?"

"The Saint will be fair. You know that."

"Krellyan will be fair to the victim, and even to the accused. But he will not consider the law to be a party worth fairness. Yet we put great store by fairness to the *idea* of law, and serve its cause even when it causes us pain. How shall the Saint's ruling be fair to us, then?"

Christopher's opinion of bloody theologians was, at the moment, even lower than Lalania's.

"If your law wanted jurisdiction, you should have kept Bart on your own land. Give it up, Joadan. I am not going to be talked out of this."

"So now you inveigh us to keep to our own domain. Should you ever venture into our lands again, be prepared for a similar argument."

Christopher shook his head. "Joadan, believe me, if I ever come to your lands again, I will be seeking it."

Joadan stopped smirking. His easy smile was one of satisfaction now. He had paid Christopher back with interest. Christopher had chased him out of Carrhill. Now Joadan had effectively banished Christopher from half the Kingdom.

If only that were the end of it, Christopher might have welcomed it. But Joadan was not a man to sell his grudges cheaply. Christopher watched the yellow troop ride slowly down the road, escorted by his own brown-clad cavalry, and wondered what wicked plots were roiling in that golden-clad head. A shooting match might have ultimately been the less painful path.

Lalania slipped from her saddle and came over to the steps, shaking her blonde hair.

"That was not wise, Christopher. You've gone from trading in promises to dealing in threats."

"I wasn't going to give them Gregor. That was never going to happen."

"Of course not. Yet you gave them a pretense for war, should you ever trespass on their lands again."

"I cannot accept this," Gregor said, his face strangely white. "I can't let my presence put you in danger. You should have thrown me to the jackals."

Lalania stared at him, shocked. Christopher was surprised, too.

"I still could have claimed the protection of the Saint," Gregor added, almost as an afterthought.

"The Saint wouldn't have thanked me for that," Christopher said. "I'm pretty sure you're my problem, not his. And anyway, Gregor, they're just wrong. They're just baiting us."

"They're not entirely wrong. The rat had surrendered; you had asked me to stop. And I didn't. I cared more for my own vengeance than I cared for how it would affect you, or anyone else."

Christopher frowned. "Gregor, get real. I wanted the rat dead as much as you did." The thought of turning the foul little priest over to the Saint, who would have had to let him go, still sickened him.

"No." Gregor shook his head. "Even then you were swayed by his claim to immunity. Even then you saw the bigger picture."

"It doesn't matter." Christopher waved his hands in dismissal. "I'll pay them a ransom. That's all they want, anyway."

"And a story," Lalania said sourly. "They will make a fine tale out of this. They will say that the only difference between Bright and Dark is that one is honest about their crimes."

Christopher folded his arms in satisfaction. "Good."

Lalania frowned at him. "How do you figure?"

"At least they'll stop thinking of us as weak."

"The Vicar speaks truly," Torme said from the chapel doorway, his carbine on his shoulder. "The Iron Throne respects only strength. That Joadan rode away empty-handed will say more than any tune they can whistle."

"Joadan used to think of you as weak," Lalania said to Christopher. "Now he takes you as a serious threat. Do you find the alteration preferable?"

"No," Christopher answered honestly. "But it was always inevitable."

Somehow he rode out of Burseberry without seeing Helga again. The girl had been all but hiding from him and Karl. Obviously Karl couldn't deign to notice, but it bothered Christopher. All of his girls seemed to be deserting him. Even Lalania had given it a rest.

But the swampland called to him. It was his duty to share the biting flies and sweating humidity with his men. Lounging around the village and drinking cold lager was making him feel guilty. Worse, it was making him feel like a feudal lord. When he finally got around to asking Big Bob where the barkeeper had found ice this time of year, the man had confessed that Fae's apprentices had delivered several blocks of the stuff as proof of their newfound abilities. Now every sip of cool beer made him feel privileged.

On the other hand, the ice was just going to melt anyway, so he didn't stop drinking cold brews. He just felt bad about it, until Karl finally gave the order and he and his cavalry troop set off once again, riding south.

He also felt bad about abandoning Gregor. The knight was going to Kingsrock, to see the Saint and undergo the atonement spell, at Lalania's insistence.

"You promised," she had told him. "Gregor has to go now or forfeit your protection. And you'll need to give him tael, to pay for the spell, and to pay a ransom for the dead priest."

"But we can't send Gregor out alone, now that he's a marked target."

Lalania sighed at him. "We are all marked targets, merely for standing in your shadow. But we can't hide under your wings all the time. Then we'd stop being targets, and become liabilities."

"The girl is right," Gregor said sourly. He'd been in a surprisingly bad mood for the last few days. "I'm not afraid of the Dark. It's not like we were on friendly terms before, and yet I managed to survive."

"Only thanks to me," Lalania said.

"And armor." Christopher was feeling guilty about sending Cannan out alone and naked. "But you lost your armor, because of me." The blue knight had spent his entire professional career in armor, had been defined, in part, by the quality of armor he had worn. And for Christopher's sake, he had left his lying in a swamp.

"I gained a rank," Gregor answered. "It's a fair trade, for me. Not so much for you."

"At least let me send a squad of cavalry with you."

Gregor frowned. "If you make me appear weak, that will only encourage them to attack."

"Then we'll make the Vicar look strong instead," Lalania said. "I'll ride with you, and you'll surrender your sword to me. It will look as if you are being sent in under arrest. I need to visit Kingsrock, anyway."

"What? We just got back from there," Christopher objected.

"Yes, well, I'm already out of blue cheese. Gregor and I will rejoin you at your blasted swamp as soon as possible."

Lalania agreed to take four of his mercenaries, after Karl agreed he could spare that many from protecting the supply column.

So now Christopher crawled south at the pace of wagons, without music or pretty girls accompanying him. It was enough to cure him of feudal lordliness, and he started to feel better.

Two days later he was forced back into the role of lord while the Vicar of Samerhaven grilled him on his plans for the future. Christopher had only stopped by on his way through as a courtesy call, and now he was facing the Spanish Inquisition. He sat in front of the Vicar's desk, feeling like a schoolboy called to the principal's office.

"You have instilled a ridiculous sense of pride in our young men. While that is well enough for those under your command, what about those who train for the next draft? How will they reconcile this spirit with the realities of life as an ordinary soldier in an ordinary lord's army?"

Christopher was pretty sure the real question was, *Are you going to give them rifles?* But the Vicar was too politically astute to come right out and ask.

"I am hoping that they are assigned to someone . . . friendly."

The Vicar frowned. "The King assigns our draft levies where he thinks best. We cannot interfere with that."

"It doesn't hurt to ask," Christopher said. "I'm trying to come up with a short list of names for the King. People who would be able to properly employ our draftees' unique training."

"A short list it must be, by necessity. To command a regiment requires at least the fifth rank."

Christopher grinned. "Well, then, I can put your name down."

"An ill-formed jest. I am not capable of leading an army. Nor is any other priest of the Bright Lady."

That wasn't true. Cardinal Faren would make an excellent *strategos*. Then Christopher remembered that generalship in this world was still coterminous with swordsmanship.

"Then perhaps you could help me by suggesting some names."

"The Baron of Parnar is a good man, and old enough that he is unlikely to engage in foolish adventures. However, for that very reason, the King is unlikely to favor him. There is another, more obvious choice. A man who is righteous, generous, careful, ambitious, and wildly successful."

"Really? Who?" Christopher liked the sound of this fellow. He could use a dozen of them, starting yesterday.

The Vicar looked at him without pity. "Lord Duke Nordland."

Christopher drummed his fingers on the Vicar's desk. "Like I said, it's going to be a *short* list. Really short." The Blue Duke might be everything the Church wanted in a lord, but he lacked the creativity that Christopher needed. Trying to teach the Duke a new way to fight would have been hard enough in the best of circumstances. After the goblin debacle, it would be impossible.

"You must learn to set aside your personal differences for the sake of the Kingdom." The Vicar was lecturing him like a headmaster talking to a bright but difficult student. Christopher found it very galling, particularly since it was exactly the sort of thing he might say.

"It's not just me, Brother. I can't put my men under him. Half their spirit comes from standing fast where he fled. Can you imagine him looking into their faces and seeing that every day? He'd be hanging them for insubordination on an hourly basis."

"True enough," the Vicar agreed, shaking his head sadly. "But Nordland is a force for good. You must find some way of healing this rift and putting it behind you."

Christopher knew exactly what it would take to resolve the issue. It would take Nordland admitting his way was wrong. And since Nordland's way was the King's way, that admission wasn't going to happen anytime soon. But heretical treason probably wasn't the solution the Vicar was looking for.

"I'm already over it. I'll meet Nordland halfway to anywhere. But he needs to learn from his mistakes, and I can't help him with that. Maybe you can." That was a good idea. Sic these lecturing moralists on the Duke for a while, and maybe they'd give him a break.

The Vicar grimaced. "I am afraid there is little one of my station can say to a Lord Duke that would carry any weight. Why, I routinely fail to talk sense into my own Church brothers."

Carrhill wasn't any less wearying, but in a different way. With the wizard, Christopher had to be careful not to offend him, while concealing the fact that he was being careful. If the wizard suspected he was being patronized or played, he would likely become unpleasant, and Christopher had a healthy respect for how unpleasant a wizard who pretended to be an undead monster could be.

He settled on honesty, combined with focusing on the wizard's good points, which were admittedly few and far between. The wine the man served was one of them. Christopher had no idea where the stuff came from, but it was light and fragrant and very, very potent.

"How goes the flying?" the wizard asked. Talking shop was about all they had in common. Since it was unlikely to lead to thorny moral discussions, Christopher didn't mind.

"I hardly get to do it anymore. My security detail says it's too risky."

The wizard chuckled. "I used to only fly while invisible. Then I realized that zooming around without being seen meant that the only things that would attack me would be things that could see me. And since anything that can see an invisible wizard is ten times worse than anything that can't, I just stopped leaving the city."

"You can turn invisible?" Christopher wondered if assassins could do that. It would make catching one a thousand times harder. He started to ask and then stopped. This was another question that, once phrased, was already answered.

"Some wizards spent all their time that way," the wizard said. "I don't know how. It's a bloody annoyance when you can't see your own hands. And soon as you pick something up, it disappears too. Do you have any idea how hard it is to fill a wine glass when you can't see the wine or the glass?"

"No," Christopher said, suspecting that it was twice as hard if one was half as drunk as the wizard usually seemed to be.

"I should make you invisible someday, and then you could find out. Wait, there's an easier way. Close your eyes."

Christopher contained his sigh and held out a hand for the bottle.

In a stroke of inspiration, he remembered how blind people did it. He tipped his thumb in the glass, so he could feel when it was full, and he held the bottle by the neck, with his other thumb protruding slightly. Now it was just a matter of moving his hands together slowly.

"Huh," the wizard said. "Pretty clever."

"Thanks, but I can't take the credit. Someone else taught it to me, long ago." Christopher looked at the very full glass, and decided he'd earned the whole thing.

"Erm." The wizard stared at Christopher, and he was reminded that the man was, technically, a genius. Lalania had sworn that wizardry required a phenomenal mind to master, especially the higher ranks. "I did some research. Cast your horoscope, that sort of thing. Might have even consulted with a demon. Or not." He scratched his beard, which for the wizard was a sure tell. Genius or not, the man should never let himself be suckered into a poker game. "I came up with nothing. It's like you didn't even exist until a year ago."

"Is that possible? That I didn't exist, I mean."

The wizard grunted in amusement. "Yes, it's possible. You could be a construct. It's even possible for it to be true and for you to not know it."

Christopher gripped the arm of the chair to stop from falling out of it.

"I am," he said. "I am a construct. The Saint said he raised me from an empty skull. That means my entire body is made out of . . . magic." He lifted his glass and drained it, trying to find an anchor to reality. The wine burned his throat, blocking out everything else for a few blessed seconds.

"This just now occurred to you?" the wizard asked.

"I didn't think about it before." Why would he? Who would ever think about such a thing, if they didn't have to? Who on Earth had ever been destroyed and resurrected, to be in a position to have to think about it? He set the empty glass down and tried to pretend his dizziness was from the rush of alcohol.

"Well, you can relax," the wizard said. Reassurance from him was so uncharacteristic that it rang true. "Revivification magic doesn't work that way. It reaches into the past, to the instant just before your death, and pulls you into the now."

Christopher sagged with relief. "So I'm . . . me?" He realized it had to be true. When the Saint had brought him back, his legs had still been mangled from the torture. He had awoken in the same old broken body he had died in, not a nice fresh new one. "But what about the past? Wouldn't they notice my body was suddenly missing?" How could there have been a skull left, if he had been pulled back into the future?

"Well, they didn't, did they? So no, they must not have. I'm not sure how it works; it's not really my specialty. I know it's not a copy, though. Otherwise you could do it again. Imagine that—they revive you half a dozen times, and now there's not enough room in your sock drawer to last the week. Though you raise a good point. Normally constructs are immune to revivification magic."

There was still room for doubt. In his memory the transition from Earth to here was instantaneous; he had been in the desert for one footstep and in the snow for the next. He had always assumed that was because he wasn't paying attention to where he was walking, a common enough occurrence for him, but what if it was because this body had only begun existing *here*, with the memories of *there* somehow copied over?

Why even assume the memories were real? The Saint had openly doubted Christopher's claim to be from Earth, or even that such a place existed. What proof did he have that Earth was real?

He put his hand to his pocket, but his pickup truck key was not there, misplaced or lost some time ago since it had no value here. Assuming it had ever existed, and wasn't just a false memory itself.

But he could rely on other people's memories. He and the wizard Flayn had first quarreled over that key, setting into motion a sequence of events that had ended in violent death. Fae had witnessed it all from start to finish.

That left only his miraculous appearance on Prime, and the Saint had found the notion of a random portal hardly worthy of a raised eyebrow. The simplest solution still pointed to his being really him. Thus the key had really existed, and by extension, the whole of Earth was saved.

"So the Saint proved I'm real." He leaned back, as empty as the wine bottle.

"Not necessarily. You could be a god's avatar. I'm guessing divine magic works differently on them."

Christopher thought back to his conversation with the demi-god Marcius. That was unequivocal; one did not make ambiguous deals with one's own avatars.

"No," he said, "I'm afraid not. I'm just a middle-aged man with a good education."

"Sure you are." The wizard was grinning now. "And I'm a cheese-maker's apprentice. Go ahead and keep your secrets—we've all got 'em. But if you're planning anything big, I'd like a chance to choose sides first."

Winning friends and influencing people—that was exactly what he was supposed to be doing. But his so-called friends kept torturing him with terrifying revelations, while requiring him to conceal his own truths.

"I'm not planning anything," he said automatically. The wizard stared at him with sardonic amusement until his conscience forced him to retract the lie.

"I mean . . ." He couldn't think of anything clever to say, so he had to surrender the truth. "Fine. If or when I do something—big— I'll let you know."

"Good enough for me. In the meantime, try to keep your head down. The less attention you attract, the less shares of the pie you'll have to give out."

That would be hard, given that the wizard had ferreted this much out with magic. "Won't other wizards ask the same questions you did?"

"I don't think any others can. It may surprise you to learn that I am the ranking wizard in the realm. It's not a popular profession. Dealing with demons and all tends to be fatal if you're the careless type. And most people are careless."

Fae hadn't said anything about demons. Well, she hadn't actually told him anything about how her magic worked.

The wizard was musing over the competition. "There's that hack that works for the King. And that tyro over in Dalenar, and of course the bloody Witch of the Moors. A few lackeys playing court jester for barons. A couple of dozen first-rankers making a living as shopkeepers. I wouldn't trade a bucket of piss for the lot of them."

And to think Christopher had spent all that time worrying about the fearful Wizard's Guild.

The wizard corrected himself. "Well, maybe the witch. Anyway, your real problem is other priests. But if they divine you and come up with nothing, they'll just assume your patron is blocking them. It's not unheard of for some new hero to pop up out of obscurity, with a prophesied destiny and enough luck to pull it off. Although . . . usually they're a lot younger."

"Cheers to you, too," Christopher said, raising his glass. The wizard laughed, and after only two more bottles, Christopher got to go home.

Cannan was waiting for him at the foot of the tower, exchanging baleful looks with the wizard's doorman. A squad of his cavalrymen lounged around as well, looking positively insolent. Christopher let them. He didn't want any of the townspeople getting too friendly with his forces. He couldn't protect them from his assassin. The only way he was safe was hiding in the vast stone barracks, now occupied only by his cavalry escort.

In the morning he rode out with a foggy head but a clear conscience. Finally he was going where choices were easy, where the good guys were on his side and the bad guys had fangs. And where idle conversations over a bottle of wine didn't make him question his sanity.

Gregor and Lalania caught up with them on the road south. The knight seemed different somehow. Less reserved, or perhaps just more relaxed.

"It went well?" Christopher asked.

"No," Lalania complained. "Your Saint did not merely make a show of it, as I had hoped. He cast the spell for real, and now that grinning idiot is insufferably cheerful."

Christopher cocked an eyebrow at Gregor.

"It's true," the knight said. "I feel like a new man. Or more accurately, like a man who has been given a second chance."

"I didn't think you'd actually done anything terribly wrong," Christopher said.

"Neither did I, or so I told myself. But it adds up. All the little compromises you make, all the times you give yourself a pass without meaning to. Without realizing it. All the things you put in a box to be dealt with later. It feels good to just throw the damn box out and start over."

Christopher glanced at Lalania, thinking about her previous comments on the process of atonement.

"Don't even get me started," she warned him with a glare.

"And the ransom?" he asked, changing the subject for her.

"Your Saint made Gregor hand it to the Gold Apostle *personally*. He got down on one knee and asked forgiveness. From that monster! I swear to the gods, Christopher, I nearly vomited to see that. I cannot imagine how the Dark crowed about it. I cannot imagine how the Bright went home early from the taverns, rather than listen to the talk of their shame."

Christopher looked at Gregor with concern.

"It was hard," Gregor admitted. "But it was a good bargain."

"How in the nine hells was it good?" Lalania exploded.

"They're down a priest," Christopher said. "All we're out of is a handful of tael. If we do that another hundred times, we'll be broke, but they'll all be *dead*."

The minstrel stared at him, while Cannan chuckled. Well, as much as an angry bear could be said to chuckle.

"We're Bright," Gregor said. "Not stupid."

Lalania was silent, thinking under creased brows. Today her hair was auburn, radiant in the sun and full of curls. "How, exactly, do you square that with your vaunted fairness?"

Christopher shrugged. "If the Gold Apostle asked me, I'd tell him exactly what our strategy is. But he won't ask, and he wouldn't understand the answer if he did. The reason he accepted a public humiliation and a ransom in exchange for the life of one of his people is because that's all he values it at. To recognize that it was a bad deal requires him to understand that people are worth more than tael. And that, I'm guessing, is not a realization he can make."

"If he valued the life of his servants over what they could do for him, then he wouldn't be Black," Torme explained. "Bartholomew never looked at us as anything but animated swords, to do his bidding or die trying. In return, we never viewed him as aught but a thunderstorm, to be endured while hoping the lighting struck elsewhere."

Gregor was nodding in agreement.

"Gods," Lalania said, "you've all become theologians. Pray tell me the Ranger is still sensible, or have you ruined him as well?"

"He's what he always was," Christopher said. In his eyes that wasn't a compliment. The boy should have learned or grown or something from all the tragedy he'd been through. He hardly seemed any different than before he had died.

Lalania galloped ahead of the column, where D'Kan was doing his alleged scouting. Torme watched her go.

"Should someone warn the boy?" he asked. It was a rhetorical question; the young Ranger would never take such counsel from the older men. What young man ever had?

Riding into the fort, Christopher felt a weight being lifted from his shoulders. At first he thought it was the welcome he got from his men, but then he understood that it was that his men were still fit to welcome him. He had left them in the Wild, and in his absence they had tamed it. The road was lined with gravel, the ring of clear ground had been expanded around the walls, and the buildings inside were now solid logs instead of hastily assembled branches and twigs.

Disa embraced Gregor fervently, and he returned it, but only for a moment. Then both of them came to listen to the officer's report.

"Aside from crocodiles, we have seen nothing worth shooting since you left. Though we rode only close patrols."

Christopher nodded in satisfaction before realizing what the good news implied. "I guess we'll have to expand the range of our patrols. And," he sighed, "put myself and Gregor in the random rotation. D'Kan and Torme, too." As miserable as the duty sounded, Christopher knew he'd get soft and useless if he didn't carry his share of the load.

"I ride with the Vicar," Cannan said.

Christopher nodded, accepting the limitation. "We'll wear regular uniforms, and ride with different men each time. Hopefully they won't be able to pick us out."

"Then you won't be riding Royal or Balance," Karl said. "Just as well; we'll save their strength for the real battles."

"And when will those be?" Christopher asked.

Karl shook his head. "The enemy has been soundly beaten. They will not return without overwhelming force."

Christopher was pretty sure that was exactly what several thousand ulvenmen were supposed to have been.

Torme nodded in agreement. "Then we must take the fight to them, before they build that strength. Our patrols must go deep, to harry them and provoke a response before they wish to give it."

Lalania was wrong. He wasn't surrounded by theologians; he was surrounded by strategists. He felt like he should tell her that. She would probably find it comforting.

13

PARTY DRESS

Christopher slapped his face, and his hand came away wet with sweat and condensation and bug juice. Staring at his palm, he did not recognize it. Calluses mixed with dirt, and the remains of a huge black horsefly, obscured the flesh underneath. He wiped it off on his pants leg.

He had told Karl not to spare him, and the young man had taken him at his word. Christopher's first season of training in Burseberry had made him strong. This sojourn had made him tough. Karl had pushed, and he had responded in ways he had forgotten were possible. His regenerated body had no weak points, no lingering injuries, no excuses.

Nor was he bound by mundane limitations. Bodybuilders had to wait a week for their torn muscle fibers to regrow before they could tear them again. Christopher healed himself every night. Between magic and Karl, Christopher had gained hard and bulging muscles he couldn't even name. He was unquestionably in the best shape of his life.

And yet both Gregor and Cannan easily put him to shame. Their strength and precision showed every time they sparred with him. He could only compete with them because of the imbalance of tael. It was strange, perhaps, that he should practice swordsmanship in a camp full of rifles. But the ranked men were not there to carry guns. Their job was to kill things that couldn't be shot.

He never sparred with Karl anymore. The last time he had tried had left him utterly depressed. Karl was still harder and leaner than Christopher, but the young man had no tael. Karl's cynical prediction about the perquisites of rank had proven correct: sparring with the unranked was like sparring with the blind.

That so much skill and spirit should be trumped by what amounted to no more than money had to be soul crushing. Christopher knew he could only guess at how badly. The world he had come from had long ago come to terms with the unfair advantage of wealth. Even the Olympics, once the ultimate amateur competition, had thrown in the towel. But this world had no such social protections. A man was judged only by his physical power, and tael gave the knights unquestionable supremacy. Strength was its own virtue, however a man came by it.

Christopher glanced over the training yard, where Karl was leading a bayonet drill. Every night he resolved to confront his best officer and order him to accept a promotion to rank, so that he might lead an army instead of a squad. Every day he watched Karl lead the men with only the strength nature had given him, and held his tongue.

Lalania didn't hold hers, however. "The Concord will not wait for your conscience, Christopher. Nor will the fate of your soldiers wait for Karl's prickly pride. You must act now."

He started to make an excuse, but she cut him off.

"Today I actually mean it. We have only a few weeks left, and there is much to be done besides spending your fortune. Karl's promotion will need a public witnessing. Then he will need equipping: arms and armor, a horse, and magic befitting his rank."

"Isn't that just more spending?"

"Yes, but it takes time to arrange. We should have started long ago. Going from commoner to baron in a single step is already pushing the limits of credulity. Your fabulous wealth will make it believable, but no man wants to owe the respect of his rank solely to another's reputation."

That would go double for a man like Karl.

Lalania scowled. "At least one duel is inevitable."

Again, something likely to go double with a man like Karl.

"Maybe that will work in our favor," Christopher mused. "If we tell him he can knock down a few lordlings, perhaps Karl will go for it."

Lalania scowled harder, this time at him.

"Don't be stupid. Once you unleash Karl on the nobility, how will you call him off before they are all dead?"

She shook her head sadly, and went back to scowling at the world.

"Also, you are assuming he will win. Though I love the man as much as you do, he will be newly minted, without the time to learn how best to use his rank."

Christopher winced in sympathy. "Can't Gregor and Cannan teach him what he needs to know?"

"I'm sure they could. If they had time." With a final minatory glare, she flounced off to do whatever it was she did when she wasn't haranguing him.

A trumpet blew, and the fort's gates opened. A mounted patrol was returning. Christopher watched them troop into the main yard with only a little anxiety. They had suffered no casualties since he had returned, but the worry never went away completely.

Christopher sighed and went to find his adjutant.

"Kennet . . . call a staff meeting."

"Sir." The young man snapped out a salute and trotted off to arrange it. Christopher went to his cabin to array his arguments for battle. Briefly he considered just holding Karl down and force-feeding him a lump of tael. It might be easier.

"So that's the situation," Christopher finished. "I've no idea who to put forward to lead the next regiment. All of you have been here longer than I have, so I'm going to ask you for suggestions. Each of you must give me the name of a suitable candidate."

He'd set it up this way on Lalania's advice. Once Karl saw how short the list was, and how likely the new regiment was to go to someone unacceptable, he would be pressured to accept it for himself. The list of nobles would be whittled down until none remained, and adding a new one would be the only answer. Their clever plan, like so many plans, did not survive contact with the enemy.

"I have a name at hand, Brother," Disa said immediately. "I nominate Ser Gregor."

"Wait, what?" Gregor said, but Disa plowed on.

"He is intimately acquainted with your arms, holds the respect of your men, and has earned your trust a thousand times."

Lalania tried to steer the conversation back on track. "No one doubts Ser Gregor's qualities, Prelate, only his rank. King's law requires the regiment be captained by no less than fifth, and Ser Gregor is but fourth."

"I know this." Disa was adamant. "But I also know you intend to promote a candidate if none suitable can be found. Promoting Ser Gregor would cost half as much as promoting anyone else."

Christopher bit his lip and glanced around the room. Who had betrayed his secret? Surely not Lalania, since it was her plan too. Not Gregor, who seemed genuinely surprised by Disa's argument, and in any case how would he have known? Cannan's face was unreadable; Christopher wasn't even sure he was paying attention to the conversation. Torme was also carefully inscrutable, but he always was. D'Kan was too obviously shocked by the mere suggestion to have had wind of it before.

Only in Karl's eyes did he see anything amiss. Behind the ordinary serene indifference was the spark of triumph. The boy had outflanked him.

"Gregor is not mine to promote," Christopher said.

"He can be," Disa shot back. "He always intended to take a rank of priest next. Now that the White fields a war god, he can take your colors as easily as he can take the Blue."

"He would be a poor priest with only a single rank of it," Lalania said. An undiplomatic comment; the woman must be quite flustered.

"My lord," Disa said, addressing her response to him rather than Lalania. "You have already bought the powers of a Curate, when you promoted me. For the mere price of the first rank the Church gave me, you can buy my freedom. For the price of promoting Ser Gregor, you can buy my fealty. I will serve him, as long as he serves you. And he will serve you as long as your new Church serves the realm."

"Woman, hush," Gregor said with a growl. "You embarrass me."

She blushed, but she didn't hush. "I embarrass myself, but only because it must be done."

Torme leaned forward. "How will you serve us, Sister? Priests of the Bright Lady cannot join Marcius's Church. Cardinal Faren would never allow such a commingling."

"I will not serve you," Disa said. "I will serve Ser Gregor. I owe Krellyan only the price of my first rank. I owe no one the price of my next three, as Brother Christopher named that a gift when he gave it. So for a trivial price I will be a free agent, and no one will think it unseemly that a wife cleaves to her husband."

"A wife?" Lalania said, perhaps more sharply than she intended.

"Yes. We are already betrothed, though we set our wedding date for after my release from the draft."

Everyone looked at Gregor.

"I should have told you earlier," the knight said, "but I did not want to influence your decisions, Christopher. She is still yours to command for two more years."

Christopher rubbed his face with both hands. "This is not what I had in mind."

"Perhaps not, my lord, but it is wisdom nonetheless," Disa said.

"Will you truly turn from your family's gods and serve Marcius?" Torme asked Gregor.

"Aye," the blue knight said, "and for much the same reason as you."

"With your permission?" Torme asked, and waited until Gregor nodded. He cast a spell and stared intently at Gregor for a moment. Then he turned to Christopher and spoke, with his face fixed in that hard way when he was going to say something Christopher might not want to hear.

"If you would have my counsel, I would give it."

Christopher sighed, a mixture of exasperation and relief. "Of course, Torme. That's what Faren sent you to do."

"I, for one, would welcome Ser Gregor as our Brother."

"Well," Christopher said to Gregor, "as Torme comprises half of the Church of Marcius, and I comprise the other half, it appears that decision is unanimous. But will it work? Can we convince the King to give you the regiment?"

"The law is on our side," Lalania said. "Still, with kings, that is not always enough. We will need to go to the Concord and beg his permission."

Christopher took out his silver vial and split his remaining tael in half, handing one of the lumps to Gregor. "The final decision is up to Marcius. I can give you the tael, but I can't give you the god's blessing."

"I do not expect that will be a problem," Torme said.

Christopher would have to face the Concord alone. Lalania explained that retinues weren't allowed; this was a gathering of peers only. Yet the party that rode the highway to Kingsrock was substantial. In addition to the score of cavalry that seemed to accompany him everywhere these days, Gregor had come along for the trip in case the King wanted to meet with him afterward. Cannan would not leave Christopher's side until he was forced to, and was prepared to spend the entire evening in front of the castle gate. A shameless display of loyalty,

Lalania said, that would only cause jealousy, but Cannan ignored her. And of course Lalania was there; she was even going to the party, though not with Christopher.

"We bards always have a standing invitation," she said, smiling sweetly. "It's the only event we play for free, and only if we are allowed free access."

"Will Uma be there?" he asked.

"Of course. But you may not recognize her, and if even you do, it would probably be best not to say anything. She may be playing a role. The Skald, on the other hand, you may greet freely. She attends as a guest, not as a servant. If at all possible, seat yourself at her table. She may be able to protect you from your worst enemy—that is, to say, yourself."

It was a true statement. Christopher was extremely uncomfortable with the coming ordeal. He would be completely alone with virtually the entire nobility of the realm. He could do no more than acknowledge the Saint, lest he appear too close. None of the other members of the Church would be attending.

"Wait," he said, "why isn't the Cardinal going? Surely it's safe enough." Normally the Saint and the Cardinal were never together outside of the Cathedral, for the same reason that airline pilots and copilots never ate the same meal. But if it were possible to assassinate the entire Concord, then the realm was as good as toast. Anything that could defeat that much massed power could surely defeat it in detail.

"Your Cardinal suspects the peerage of stupidity. Namely, that if they do not see White robes, they will forget how many counties are governed by the White. In this, as in most things, your Cardinal appears astute. So he sends the Saint alone into that den of liars, and hopes for the best. Your best hope is to say as little as possible, as often as possible."

The only bright spot was that Lalania was letting him off easily in the wardrobe department. She had conceded that wearing his uniform would strike the right tone, marking him as a servant to the King regardless of his rank.

"Most lords don't want to look like working men, but you do. Let them think you a buffoon, if you can," she had said. She had also seemed surprised when he nodded in agreement. "How is it you have so little pride?"

Cannan had answered for him. "It's not that. It's that his pride is so great he takes no heed of what those popinjays think."

Gregor had laughed himself into a coughing fit while Lalania frowned. Christopher tried to reassure her, but she would have none of it.

"We can only hope they are not as perceptive as your guard dog. For all our sakes, Christopher, try to be *normal* for once." Then she cleaned his clothes, hair, and face with magic, kissed him on the cheek for luck, and sent him off.

So now he was walking over the drawbridge to go to a fancy ball. But the glittering royalty held no attraction for him. He did not see shining knights and charming princesses. All he saw were dangerous men and women, unbound from the rule of law or even reason by the possession of unnatural powers. Realizing he was one of them—even gravity now surrendered its grasp at his command—was not in any way comforting.

He had counted on his earthly experience to inure him to spectacle. What could these people do that Hollywood's special effects had not already prepared him for? As it turned out, plenty.

The main room was a clean, neat pasture with a stream running through it and the bright starry night sky above. The effect was so perfect he could not tell if it were mere illusion or if walking through the doorway had transported him to a new place. When he bent down next to the stream and put his finger in it, he realized it was wine instead of water. A crystal goblet floated up out of the wine to hover in front of him. Stupefied, he reached for it as if it were a phantasm, and almost dropped it when the weight became real in his hand.

From somewhere came gentle music. He looked around, hoping to locate a bard or two. Instead, a handsome man in blue-and-white silks found him.

"You need not kneel," he said. "The glass will rise to your hand."

"Ah," Christopher said, standing up. Small groups of well-dressed people stood throughout the grassy field, like any cocktail party. Except for the swords. His new companion had a sword, too, a long straight blade with a blue gem the size of a tangerine for the pommel.

The man had been looking at Christopher's sword, too. "I take it from the shape of your blade that you are the new priest everyone is talking about."

"Yes. Ah, I am Christopher, Vicar of Marcius." The urge to hold out his hand was overwhelming, so he hooked his right thumb in his belt.

"I have the privilege of being the Earl of Istvar, but I am also a servant of Eldir. Thus we have something in common, you see."

Christopher put his left hand to good use, taking a sip of wine. It was surprisingly flowery.

"I'm sorry, Lord Earl, but I'm not sure what you're getting at."

The Earl looked surprised. "I just meant we are both priests. Though I confess, the idea of a White war priest is hard to credit."

"I agree, Lord Earl." It was hard to credit, and getting harder every day.

"I see you take after your Saint." The Earl apologized. "We shall have no theological squabbles here. If we started, there would be no end of it."

Christopher nodded distractedly, looking around the room. The Earl watched him for a moment.

"Who might you be looking for?"

"The King," Christopher said. "I want to talk to him."

The Earl made a noncommittal sound. "I begin to perceive why my cousin has such harsh words of you. You set your station high. Tell me, is not the company of an Earl sufficient?"

Christopher turned his attention back to the Earl. "Did you say cousin?"

"Yes," the Earl replied, "I did. The Duke of Nordland is my cousin, by marriage."

"I'm sorry," Christopher said.

The Earl raised his eyebrows.

"I mean, I'm sorry about Lord Nordland. I didn't intend to offend him."

"And yet you managed, all the same."

"I'm good at accidents," Christopher said. "It's one of my specialties."

"I take it back," the Earl replied. "You're not very much like your Saint at all. Your tongue is sharper than your sword."

Christopher found himself nettled by the remark. "My sword is plenty sharp enough, I think."

The Earl stared at Christopher intently, his hands lowering to his waist. Christopher could feel the menace under the man's elegant, graceful stance. He raised his own hand, palm out, in surrender.

"I'm sorry, Lord Earl. I seemed to have done it again."

"Indeed," the Earl said. "I came to tell you that my cousin intends a duel, and almost challenged you myself. I confess I am truly astonished at your talent for fatal accidents."

I told you so didn't seem like the best response. Instead, Christopher said, "I don't want to duel anybody. Least of all the Duke. For the sake of peace, Lord Earl, tell me how I can appease him without fighting."

"For the sake of honor, you cannot. However, you need not

tremble yet. My cousin has considered that you are not of an equal rank. Therefore, he delays his satisfaction until such time as you are. Should that day come, which admittedly seems unlikely for a man of your advanced years, you will have to face the Duke in single combat. Although the strength of your rank and your magic should render your chances of surviving reasonably high, do not fail to have your ransom in hand. My cousin does believe you have lightened his purse, and many are inclined to agree."

Christopher sighed. It was always about money. In this case honor and bloodshed were mixed in, but only to spice the wine. At the bottom of the cup was tael.

He almost offered to pay on the spot, until he realized the ransom for an eighth rank was more than he had left. Gregor's promotion had rendered him almost poor.

"Please let your cousin know I am grateful for his forbearance."

The Earl nodded. "To say nothing of mine. Still, honor is served, and we should not quarrel amongst ourselves. There are plenty enough deserving of our ire. And you are not without your qualities. Sparing us the presence of the Baron of Baria is a true boon."

Judging by the quality of his grin, the Earl didn't seem to have any of Lalania's reservations on that matter.

"Nonetheless, it would be wise if you spared my cousin the pleasure of your company this day. Or any day; I do not think he can tolerate any more accidents on your part."

Christopher nodded in agreement again, and kept a silent smile plastered on his face until the Earl was safely gone. Then he turned and walked the other way.

He wandered across the lawn, looking for the King or at least someone he knew, when he spotted a handsome woman in blue taffeta and white hair standing among a small group of elegant ladies. The Skald wore no magic here to disguise her age. He joined them with relief.

"Lady Freia," he said. He was trying to figure out how to address the other women when he recognized one of them.

"Lady Nordland," he said. Unable to bear her cold blue eyes, he bowed low, but eventually he had to stand up again.

"If you could have bowed to my lord husband, it would have saved us all much grief." The sorrow in her voice was more painful to him than the glare in her eyes. "Why did you not tell us you had a guardian that would snatch victory from certain defeat?"

Christopher managed to quell his immediate impulse to explain, using charts and diagrams if necessary. It wouldn't be of any help now. He swallowed his retort, too. That wouldn't help either.

"I tried, my lady," he said. "I am sorry I failed."

She looked at him without speaking. Turning to the other women, she tipped her head. "I beg your leave, Lady Ariane, Lady Friea. If you will excuse me?"

"Of course, my dear." The Skald smiled graciously while Lady Nordland left, her smile turning to amusement as she watched Christopher watching the Lady leave.

"You have a way with the ladies, Christopher. A way worth remarking on, although I don't know many men would care to follow it."

"Humph," Christopher said. "You should see me with druids."

The other woman laughed at him, which he found strangely comforting.

As if summoned by some invisible signal, a pretty girl in a painted-on green dress and long blonde hair hung herself off Christopher's arm, relieving him of his half-empty glass.

"I, for one, find it a great relief," Lalania said. "The Vicar is perhaps the only man in this room who can talk to a woman without turning the conversation to romance."

"Our burden and our blessing," the Skald said. "Every hour they spend between the sheets is an hour they aren't killing each other."

"True enough," said the Lady Ariane. "A man only has two uses, and both of them involve his sword." She eyed Christopher appraisingly. "Sadly, skill in both is rarely encountered."

"A deficiency I have not yet found rectified," Lalania said. "Despite long and professional inquiry. But if you will excuse the Vicar, duty calls. He needs must speak with our King." She finished the wine and let go of the glass. It floated off under its own power.

Christopher was distracted by Lalania's outfit as she led him away. She was scantily wreathed in leaves that hung loosely, threatening to reveal intimate details with every movement she made. He could not see any fabric under the ivy.

"Lala," he asked, "how does that thing stay on?"

"It doesn't," she said. "There's nothing to stay. The dress is pure illusion."

"You mean you're naked—"

"Indeed. It's one of the rules of the Concord—can't have the working girls outdressing the nobility. You can imagine the men who run things find it quite amusing."

Christopher wasn't that naïve anymore. He could guess that the bards found it amusing, too, since they could cloak themselves in magic. There wouldn't be any common woman out-spying the bards. It wouldn't surprise him if the Skald had made up the rule in the first place.

"Are we really going to talk to the King?" he asked.

"Only after you promise not to be stupid. The King may ask me to stay with him. If he does, it will almost certainly be intended to provoke you. You must promise me you will offer the King the use of your servant without hesitation."

Christopher stopped walking, pulling the woman to a stop in front of him.

"I mean it," she said, staring up into his face earnestly. "You cannot be stupid. I have asked little of you and given much, but now, I ask this. Please, for my sake, do not be stupid tonight."

In answer, he let her lead him onward.

Lalania steered him through the glade, past little knots of well-dressed and glamorous nobility. Treywan was in the center of all things, as expected. He was speaking with three cloaked men, one in yellow, one in white, and one in purple. The yellow cloak glittered like solid gold, although it hung like cloth. The purple was studded with sapphires and rubies, and shot through with silver thread. Treywan's own outfit shifted hue as Christopher stared at it, rippling through the entire visible spectrum. The white cloak was the only one that was simple and unadorned.

As he and Lalania approached, Christopher caught the tail end of the man in gold's joke, delivered with a self-deprecating bow.

". . . we loyal servants of the King."

Ice ran through his veins even as his heart pounded. Unwilled, he was pulled into the circle of conversation by Lalania. She curtsied while still on his arm, but Christopher was unable to take any action. All that remained of his fragmented attention was dedicated to not drawing his sword.

He knew that voice, though he had never laid eyes on the face it emanated from. The last time he had heard that voice, his eyes had been nailed shut.

"Your Majesty," Saint Krellyan said, "allow me to present my brother in faith, the Lord Vicar Christopher."

The man in gold gave no visible reaction, no sign of surprise or distress. Christopher, in his heightened state of awareness, saw it anyway.

"Lord of where?" Treywan said. "Has he pulled a county out of his pocket? Or are you telling me he has broken the ulvenmen to the plow, and intends to claim that blasted swamp as his fief?"

Christopher stared at the side of the golden man's head, willing him to turn and face him.

"Neither, I am afraid," Krellyan said. "He holds only the village of Burseberry. Still, it is sufficient for the technicalities."

Treywan looked Lalania up and down with frank admiration. "That's not the thing he holds that interests me. A personal troubadour bought for paper? What kind of magic is that, Master Sigrath, and why haven't you worked it for me?"

"A thousand apologies, my Lord King." The man in purple made a subtle bow. "But Your Majesty has no need to purchase bards by the piece. You have command of the whole of them simply by your royal voice."

Treywan turned his attention to the man in gold, as if sharing a private joke. "What do you get when you breed a demon-calling, soul-sucking wizard with a lawyer? That's right, a *lawyer*."

The golden man tittered. "Insightful, Your Majesty, as always."

"Pardon me," the King said, "I have failed to make introductions. Lord Christopher, this is the Lord of Balenar, Apostle of the Golden Throne."

Treywan smiled like a boy lighting a firecracker and waiting for the sparks to fly.

The golden man, the apostle of darkness, whose cruelty Christopher had seen in broken peasants and felt in broken limbs, turned to him and tipped his head. Whatever he was about to say withered into silence under Christopher's unflinching gaze.

"We've met," Christopher said.

"Your Majesty," Lalania said with a bow that tested the limits of her illusionary dress, "my lord begs a favor of you."

"Does he now?" the King said absently, watching Christopher watching the Apostle.

"As you know, the Church of the Bright Lady sends forth another regiment with the new year. The Church of Marcius has sent forth a new champion to lead it. Baron Gregor has always been your faithful servant, and now he seeks to serve the Kingdom best. We ask that you let Saint Krellyan assign the regiment to the Baron, should the Saint deem it appropriate to do so." Lalania was flirting with all steam ahead, trying to drown out the palpable tension between Christopher and the Apostle.

"I am surrounded by faithful servants," the King said to Lalania, his gaze raking down her dress of foliage as if seeking a weakness in a besieged fortification. "But are they willing?"

"Without reservation, my lord," Lalania answered with the perfect imitation of a chaste blush.

The King looked back up at Christopher, who still stared unblinking. "Let me have your bard for a night, and I'll let you have my regiment for a draft. What do you say, Lord Vicar?"

Christopher had no distaste left for Treywan's petty crudities. Every fiber of his being was already consumed with shuddering contempt. He spoke without turning away from the Apostle. "As long as I get her back in one piece."

Treywan snickered, then guffawed, his beery, dangerous laughter washing over everyone. "You would be insolent, priest, if you weren't so entertaining."

The Apostle's lip had finally curdled into a sneer. "Your Majesty is more discerning than I."

Christopher didn't say anything.

Lalania bowed again. "A favor for myself, Your Majesty. If I could but fetch my lyre, I would sing such a song for you. Though I fear Lord Christopher will perforce miss the play, as he must be off to see to his regiments."

"Fair enough, girl," the King said with a disappointed growl. "Fetch your strings and take your sourpuss puppet away before he spoils our little party."

She bowed so low her golden locks touched the grass. Standing, she put her shoulder into Christopher's chest and forced him to step back and turn away. With an arm around his waist she propelled him back across the glade. He moved liked an automaton, his breath slow and deep. When they were safely out of earshot, she whispered forcefully.

"Control yourself, Christopher. He is an Apostle. He could destroy you with a syllable."

"I am under control," Christopher said. The proof was self-evident. He had not killed the Apostle yet.

"Priest," Treywan called across the field, his voice angry and blustering. "You take those regiments and put a stop to the ulvenmen. Do you hear me? I want an end to it, once and for all."

Christopher turned to face the King's group. From here their faces were indistinct. All he could see were their cloaks, yellow and purple and white and shifting rainbow. He bowed, deeply, one hand at his waist and the other outstretched, palm up. Then he turned and strode purposefully away, Lalania skipping to keep up with him.

Stepping through the vine-entangled archway left him back inside the castle, where his steam-fueled determination deserted him. Lalania took over again, leading him with purpose down a hallway he did not recognize. Suddenly she pulled him into a side room and shut the door.

A beefy, bearded man dressed as a wealthy knight was waiting for them.

"Ser Morrison," Lalania said with a minimal curtsey.

"Ivy?" Ser Morrison said, frowning at Lalania's dress. "What were you thinking?"

"Oh hush," Lalania said, and stepped forward to kiss the knight.

Christopher blinked. Somehow Lalania and the knight had switched places. The woman stood on the right instead of the left, wearing the knight's elaborate tunic and hose. Ser Morrison now stood on the other side, wearing Lalania's ivy dress, which covered him no better than it had her.

The woman began stripping off her outfit, handing the pieces to the knight who put them on as quickly as they came off.

"You look terrible in green," the new Lalania said, but in Ser Morrison's voice.

"Voice," Ser Morrison hissed. "Get on cue, Nila. Don't spoil this for me."

"Simple for you to say," the new Lalania said, this time in Lalania's voice. "You've got the easier task. But if you want, just say the word, and we'll switch again."

"It's an easy way to lose my head." Ser Morrison was exasperated, in the way Lalania was often exasperated. "All you have to do is get drunk."

"That's not all," the new Lalania said. "Hardly all." By now she was stark naked. Christopher, still confused, did not have time to react before she spoke a word and green ivy shot out from her hands to cloak her as it had cloaked Lalania.

She picked up one of two golden lyres sitting on a table, strummed it experimentally, gave Christopher a salacious wink, and slipped out of the room.

Christopher tried to remember how many glasses of wine he had consumed.

"You remember that the King told me to fetch my lyre, right?" Ser Morrison was looking at Christopher earnestly, the way the real Lalania often did. "Well, I'm going to obey that royal command. This disguise will just make it easier." He picked up the other lyre and stuffed it inside his doublet. Somehow it fit without leaving any unsightly bulges.

Ser Morrison led him out and down the hallway. They passed a serving woman, who stepped quickly out of their way and kept her head down. When they turned the next corner, he spoke over his shoulder. The voice was Ser Morrison's, but the question was pure Lalania.

"When did you meet the Apostle?"

All of the tension in Christopher's body contracted into his stomach in a gut-wrenching punch. He fell to his knees, heaving, and threw up on the floor. All that came out was sour, stale wine.

"Lord Vicar! Are you poisoned?" Even in this extremis, Lalania did not slip back into her own voice.

He wiped his mouth with the back of his hand. "The Apostle was my torturer."

She frowned through Morrison's bearded face. "That seems unlikely. Why would he stoop to such a thing?"

"Maybe he likes it." Christopher stood up, weak and light-headed. He looked down helplessly at the mess on the floor.

"Leave it," she said. "They'll just assume someone had too much of a good time. But are you well? Can you continue? I promise you we will not meet the Apostle again tonight."

The pulse of blood rushing through his veins was gone, replaced by a terrible itching in the palms of his hands. They ached to wield his sword, to feel the peculiar sensation of holding steel as it sliced through meat and bone. His forearms twitched in anticipation of strike after strike, his diaphragm seizing with each imaginary blow.

"I'm fine," he said.

Morrison stared at him intensely for a brief second, a look of such personal concern that he could almost see Lalania through it. Then she threw herself back into her role. With a short bow, Ser Morrison said, "If we may continue, Lord Vicar, please follow me."

Servants and soldiers got out of their way with bowed heads and cautious greetings. "If it please you, Ser Morrison," they said, if they said anything at all. The fake Morrison led him through bewildering halls, stairs, and rooms, going up and up, until they came to a massive double door bound in iron and flanked by two guards.

"Open it," Ser Morrison said, in a tone that brooked no argument. The guards glanced at Christopher, but they obeyed Morrison, both of them struggling to lift a massive beam from its brackets. When they dropped it to the floor, Morrison pushed one of the doors open and stepped over the beam. Christopher followed him inside.

The room was smaller than he had expected, and although there weren't piles of gold coins lying around everywhere, it was clearly a treasure vault. Wooden chests lined the walls, stacked three deep. In one corner several suits of armor hung from stands, some plain, some studded with jewels. Against the far wall a rack was crowded with dozens of swords, and a few odd weapons like maces or morning stars.

Morrison shut the door behind Christopher. Silently he pointed up, toward the ceiling. In the wavering light of magic stones Christopher saw three crude, ugly shapes, deformed humanoids with stubby wings and fanged faces. They perched on a ledge above the door and glared down with sightless stone eyes. Notre Dame's gargoyles seemed friendly compared to this lot.

While Christopher stared up, fascinated by the intricate details, Morrison crossed the small room to a sheet-covered pedestal. Whispering and moving his hands in a complex pattern, he raised the sheet without touching it, lifting it into the air, folds and all. Underneath was a gold-painted lyre.

From inside his voluminous doublet he extracted the other lyre, a perfect match for the one on the pedestal. Quickly he swapped them, making the vault's lyre disappear back into his doublet and carefully arranging the new one to replace it. Then he lowered the sheet, apparently through sheer concentration, and only relaxed when the spell was spent. After that he took a pouch of dust out of his pocket, and artfully replaced the specks that had fallen away.

Christopher was impressed. He didn't think a CSI unit would be able to tell the sheet had been touched.

"What did you need me for?" he asked.

"Access. Your presence provides a plausible excuse for entering in the first place. Now hush, and do nothing. Do you understand? No matter what happens next, do not react."

Morrison went to the door and reached for the handle with some hesitation. Just before he touched it, the gargoyles moved.

They shifted and preened, like great birds of prey, the sound of stone on stone grating on Christopher's nerves. One lolled out a long, gray tongue. All of them leered down at the fake Ser Morrison. Christopher felt hairs on his neck rise, and not just from shock at the terrifying sight. Someone—or something—had cast a truth spell.

"I take only what I may by King's Right," Ser Morrison said, in Lalania's voice, though quiet enough that the sound would not carry through the door.

The gargoyles stopped moving, sitting perfectly still, though still watching. Morrison forced his hand to clasp the door handle and pull.

The door swung open, and the gargoyles remained as still as stones. Morrison stepped out into the hallway. "If you are finished, Lord Vicar, may we go?"

He had been told to hush, so without speaking he stepped forward. The gargoyles let him pass under them and through the door without reaction. The guards closed the door behind, grumbling as they struggled to restore the huge oaken crossbar to its iron brackets. Morrison and Christopher walked silently but quickly through the halls, returning the way they had come.

In the room where Lalania had first turned into Morrison, the knight stripped off his clothes and tossed them into a basket in the corner. This time Christopher turned his head away, in anticipation of the resumption of her true and necessarily naked form.

"Very sweet, Christopher, but wholly unnecessary. I have learned my lesson." When he looked back she had turned into a different bard, one with dark hair and a terribly risqué lace gown. "However, you must let me play the part of a companion, at least until we return to the Cathedral. You can hardly be seen to be leaving with the Minstrel Lalania, as she is currently entertaining the King."

She picked up the lyre carefully, covetously, and for a moment triumph sparkled through her mascara-painted eyes. Stepping close to Christopher, leaning into his arms as she guided him out of the room, she whispered, "I will play such a song for you, my lord. But not here."

14

FOUR WEDDINGS

Freed from the Concord by days and distance, Christopher rode comfortably past snow-covered fields and pastures, traveling up the same road he had once fled down. Then, he had been dressed in rags and frightened for his life. Now, he was warmly cloaked in furs, but not particularly safer. His enemies bred faster than he could bury them, and he suspected burying the worst ones wouldn't even slow them down.

A year ago he had feared what lordship would do to him. Now he feared what it would do to the people around him. By being his friend, taking his gold, or simply living near him, they had gained his enemies. He wondered if what he had given them in return was enough.

The villagers did not seem to question the bargain. They turned out en masse to greet their new lord. They cheered him as loudly as his own soldiers, lining the road and crowding around the chapel. Christopher had come to collect his troops, but when he saw Faren's carriage on the village green, he went in search of answers first.

"We didn't tell you because we weren't sure we were going to do it. I drew up the papers in advance, so Krellyan could choose to name you lord or not, depending on how the conversation went. Apparently he felt you needed the help." Faren sat in Christopher's chapel, comfortably warm and less crabby than usual.

"And now you are master of Burseberry," Svengusta said. "Had I known you would become my lord, I might have treated you better in the beginning." This was a lie, of course. Svengusta had treated him like a son from the start.

"It's more than just a title," Faren said. "It's two thousand gold a year." A year ago Christopher would have boggled at the amount. Now it was only worth a nod. The Cardinal had already given him ten thousand to equip and feed the regiment for the next three years. "It is money we can give you without making it look like charity. As the head priest of Marcius, with the rank of a peer, you had a solid legal claim to the village anyway."

"It is a cheap price for what you give them in return, Christopher." Lalania was holding her new lyre, something she did a lot of these days. She never let the thing out of her sight anymore. Christopher was pretty sure she slept with it.

"And what is that?" he asked.

"Immunity," she said. "This is your land now. If another Bart comes to make war, they need take no action."

"Yes, that too," Faren said. "We no longer need be responsible for the trouble you cause."

"How does the village make so much gold?" Christopher wondered aloud. In the year he'd lived here, he had seen hardly any coinage.

"It's not gold, but wheat and barley you'll be paid in," Svengusta explained. "You'll need a bigger purse if you expect to take your money shopping."

That was all right. Grain was something he needed now. In sheer point of fact, it would be the same grain he'd been buying from Vicar Rana.

"Wait . . . didn't those taxes used to go to Knockford?"

"Indeed," Svengusta said. "You've picked the Vicar's pocket. No doubt she would like to hang you for a thief, but now you're her equal in rank. She can't boss you around anymore."

"Like she ever could," grumbled Faren. "Still, you need not fear her vexation. She is as happy to be rid of the responsibility for you as any of us."

Gregor leaned forward earnestly. "You don't happen to have another village to spare, do you? We've got another regiment to feed."

Gregor was earnest a lot these days. Christopher kind of missed the old happy-go-lucky errant knight he had been.

"I would sooner give you my left foot," Faren said. "You were never our burden. We need not buy your release."

Gregor chuckled, and well he should. The Saint would be giving him ten thousand gold for the new regiment. More money than one man could carry, no matter how big his purse, though Christopher knew it would not be enough.

"I'll have to sell more bonds." Christopher wondered how many times he could do this before the people stopped falling for it.

"Isn't iron making you plenty of gold?" Svengusta asked. "You've drained the country of roustabouts and farm hands. Every peasant who doesn't own a plow seems to be working for you."

Christopher didn't know how his businesses were doing. He'd ridden past Knockford without stopping, unwilling to face the Vicar on an empty stomach.

A problem solved when Helga finally emerged from the kitchen, followed by two girls bearing dishes of food. Christopher wondered why she wasn't carrying one herself—it wasn't like her to merely oversee work instead of doing it—until he saw that she was carrying enough as it was.

"Oh my gods," he said. "You're pregnant."

"A brilliant diagnosis," Svengusta said, bursting with laughter. "And I was afraid all those hours spent teaching you medicine were wasted."

"You didn't know?" Lalania asked Christopher, surprised.

"Congratulations," Faren said. "When are we to be blessed? Though from the look of it, it must be soon."

"Next week," Helga confirmed. "The midwife says it will be a boy. But Pater says she is full of old wives' tales, and no real magic. Can you tell, Christopher?"

"I don't know," Christopher said. Did he have a spell for that?

"A foolish waste of power, if he could." Faren dismissed the idea. "In any case, you'll know soon enough."

Christopher thought of something that would be far more useful than a sonogram. A blood test. "Who is the father?" he asked.

The room went silent. Helga blushed, on the verge of tears, and Lalania shook her head in dismay.

"You wisely built a barn to hold your horses. You should have built a fortress to hold your tongue," she chided Christopher. "She cannot name the father to you until she names it to him, and clearly she has not done so, or she would have already told us who the father was."

"Oh." Christopher belatedly realized it had to be Karl. He started to ask, but stopped when he discovered he wouldn't know what to say if it wasn't.

"Ser Gregor," Lalania said. "Disa is now released from the draft. This implies your wedding is imminent. Have you considered the guest list? If you wish to invite your friend Karl, you will need to do so soon. He has a long trip to make." She watched Helga's face while she said this. Helga blushed a color of a different character, and even Christopher could read the answer.

"We should probably invite the bride, too," Gregor said.

"Then I must get to work." Lalania stood up from the table, apparently ready to begin at once. "We cannot give you a peer's wedding, but we must come close. This bond must be seen to eclipse her old one. And she deserves it—both of you do." Lalania seemed almost wistful, so she turned to Christopher and changed the subject. "Who will you leave in charge of the fort?"

It was really a question about who would not get to come to the wedding. "Torme, I guess."

"You should promote another Pater," Faren said. "One priest is not enough for so many, and you spend perilous little time at your post."

It was worse than that. Torme and Christopher did not have the extraordinary healing power of the priests of the Bright Lady.

"About that. . . . My regiment is supposed to have two healers. I need replacements."

"Only because you keep promoting them out of the position!" Faren exclaimed. "How is it we must bear the price of your profligacy?" It was just for show, though. The old man always enjoyed haggling.

"Careful," Svengusta warned. "He may wind up being your lord soon enough, and then you'll have reason to regret your hard words."

"Gods preserve us," Faren said, passing his hand over his eyes. "I'll have nightmares for a week now."

Armed with assurances of Vicar Rana's peaceableness, Christopher risked a trip into Knockford. Guards waved him through the new gate into a town he hardly recognized.

Buildings were going up, and only some of them were his. People he didn't know were choking the streets, and some of them didn't seem to know whom he was. Only the church stood unchanged.

His fellow clergy gave him a warm welcome, helped no doubt by Cannan's remaining outside. A young acolyte, Sister Mariche, went so far as to hug him with tears in her eyes.

"I am to be promoted for the draft," she told him. "I was so scared, but then they said it would be with you."

"We'll take care of you," he reassured her, but privately he was concerned. The girl seemed too soft and clean to go to war. Not to mention young. He sought out Vicar Rana with the intention of changing her mind, forgetting that he was supposed to be placating her.

It didn't matter either way. Rana was as immobile as always.

"Mariche is the same age that Disa was for her draft. A foolish girl now, but you will make a priestess of her. Both she and the Church will profit from the experience." Rana sat behind her desk and eyed him like a toad staring down a particularly fat housefly. "We are to make four healers for you this year, and beggars can't be choosers."

"Disa volunteered," he said. At least he thought that was the story she'd told.

"And so did Mariche. She accepted promotion knowing the cost. Speaking of promotions, don't you owe us a fee for the priestess you stole? And do not even think to offer in gold; we are uncommonly short on tael as it is."

Christopher wondered if she would ever let that particular mistake die. He tried to hand over the small purple lump for Disa's release, but Rana wouldn't take it.

"You might as well give it directly to Mariche," she said.

He drummed his fingers on the table, annoyed. "I don't want her to think she is bound to me."

Rana smiled sweetly at him. "You need not worry on that score. She will not forget who trained and raised her."

Implying, of course, that *he* had forgotten. Rana wasn't trying to bind Mariche to Christopher; she was trying to bind him to the girl. Christopher could see her conniving as clearly as he could see that it would work. Handing people their life's dream was addictive. Once you started, it was hard to stop.

"Who else am I getting?" he asked.

"One from each of our counties. All women, I am afraid."

Clearly the Vicars felt service in one of his regiments was the easiest duty a woman could ever hope for. And the safest. He didn't know how he was going to deal with a gaggle of young women in an army of teenage boys, but then he realized he didn't have to. He could put Lalania in charge of that. Not that she would make the chastest chaperone, but at least anything that happened would be consensual.

"I also wanted to apologize for Burseberry. I didn't know they were going to do that."

"If I let you start apologizing for all the trouble you've caused me, we would both die of age before the end. Save your breath for my son. He has need to speak with you. Now begone, and let me work."

There were papers piled all over her desk, but he was pretty sure she actually enjoyed dealing with problems like that. He could relate. The time he spent with his drawings was the only vacation he got anymore.

The interview with Rana went so well he decided to tackle Fae next. Going out the back door of the church, he found Cannan engaged in a silent staring match with one of Rana's police. As they walked through the streets he asked about it.

"Just passing the time. Better than being mewled to death by your church kittens," the knight said.

"Well, we're about to deal with the queen of cattery," Christopher warned him.

At the door to Fae's office, he reached for the handle, convincing himself that he didn't need to knock first. He owned the place, after all. Cannan leapt in front of him.

"You must let me open strange doors, and enter first into new rooms," Cannan said. "The tart claims portals of all kinds can be rendered dangerous by magic or craft." By "tart" Christopher knew he meant Lalania, which was one of the nicer terms he used for her.

Christopher followed the big man inside. One of Fae's apprentices greeted them with the faintest touch of superciliousness. Normally girls, especially young and attractive ones, fluttered in Cannan's presence. This one, however, was as fresh as lemonade on a summer's day. Christopher wondered if the cause was arcane power or merely Fae's tutelage.

Cannan took no notice of it, scanning the room for danger.

"Is your mistress about?" Christopher asked.

"Of course, my Lord Vicar. If you will but wait a moment." The apprentice bowed and slipped out of the room. Christopher was amazed to be left to cool his heels in his own building.

When Fae waddled into the room, he redefined amazement in context of the unexpected sight before him.

"Oh my gods," he said. "You're pregnant."

"As you say, my lord." Fae was serenely self-confident, leaning on her apprentice for support as she sank into a chair. "Yet I assure you we will meet your production quotas."

Flustered, he stuck to business. "I was going to ask you to double them. And do some experiments, for next year." He'd been making drawings for the future. Nothing that would be ready for this campaign, but it was time to start looking toward the next one. He handed Fae a sheaf of diagrams and notes.

She pretended to look at them before saying the inevitable. "If you would have more magic, you must have more rank. I believe my apprentices are ready for their second grade, which will not incidentally double our capacity."

He handed her a small purple stone from his silver vial. She crossed her hands and then opened them to show empty palms, an act of either magic or sleight of hand. It was hard to tell the difference. Watching her he noticed she was wearing a lot of jewelry.

"Business has been very good, my lord. Your books are in order, and your account at the church is up to date."

Rana charged him interest for storing his gold. That might explain the Vicar's recent good mood.

He wanted to ask the obvious question, but the experience with Helga had convinced him he didn't know how to do it politely. He looked around the room, but no one here was going to help him. Lalania would have known how to ask, but then, Lalania probably already knew the answer.

"Do you need anything? Can I help?" he asked instead.

She looked at him disparagingly. "I was a woman before I was a wizard, my lord. I know how to do this."

"Cat's claws indeed," Cannan said dryly.

Christopher had to take his leave then, before he ruined everything by laughing.

Outside he promised Cannan the rest of the day would be easier, because they would only be talking to men. Cannan was unimpressed.

"They are your servants. Therefore they will always seek to mislead you to their own gain. It is the nature of servitude and rank."

"They're really more like partners," Christopher said.

Not that anyone could tell from the way Jhom bowed and scraped when they entered the factory. The man was being obsequious, which was a sure sign he wanted something. Cannan was indifferent enough not to smirk, for which Christopher was duly grateful.

After a mildly self-aggrandizing speech Jhom presented his latest accomplishment, a tunic of finely meshed chain mail. Christopher was impressed, but Cannan held it up in one hand and complained.

"It is too light."

"The weight is misleading," Jhom said. "This is steel, not iron. Tests show my mail is stronger than the ordinary grade, if not quite so good as a Master's. But it has another virtue that no Master can ever hope to match. I can sell that tunic for a quarter of the current market price and still show a profit."

No more "Ser" or "my lord" now. Jhom's servility was only skin deep; it evaporated once objective evidence of his skill was on display. Even Cannan was impressed.

"Twenty-five gold for such a piece? You will beggar the armorers of the Kingdom."

"I was thinking fifty," Jhom said. "They'll beggar half as fast with twice as much profit to us."

Christopher grinned. "I read the law books in the Cathedral, and they say I can sell any goods to any county." It would be a double play.

He would be taking money out of the pockets of the lords, selling them armor that was useless against his guns. "But I wanted to ask you first, in case you think there will be complaints." He had gotten lucky with the wizard's guild and paper. This time he would look before he leaped.

"None," Jhom said, his hands spread in grandiose expanse. "The Masters will sniff and make plate. The Journeymen will complain and make nails. The realm will be better armed, which will please the King, and the soldiers will bless your name for lightening their load."

There was always a catch. Christopher knew that, and he knew Jhom knew it too.

"What are you not telling me?" he asked.

Jhom shrugged. "There may be some baseless whining about the manufacturing process. It is, after all, wholly untraditional. But soldiers are not superstitious wizardlings. Steel is steel, and the armor will prove itself in their hands."

Christopher grinned again, of a somewhat different nature. "Show me what you mean by untraditional." That Jhom had not mentioned it up front meant it must be pretty bad.

Jhom raised his eyebrows. "But it was your design. Here, come and see."

A new room in a new building contained new things. Christopher's wire-pulling machines, manned by half a dozen laboring young men. Jhom had taken the concept of division of labor and run with it.

"This is the heart of the operation," Jhom said. "We produce wire in such a profundity that we scarce know what to do with it all. I will sell the raw wire, too, to any who want it. And if we thicken the strand here, and leave out that step there, we can make nails by the barrelful."

Christopher stood on the factory floor, listening to the sounds of turning gears, smelling the heat of iron, feeling the bustle of activity from man and machine. It was as close to home as he had ever been in this world.

"They'll get used to it," Christopher said. "They'll have to." Adopting new manufacturing techniques would only annoy the smiths who had to compete against them. The soldiers wouldn't care how their armor was made.

"Well," Jhom said, "there's also this." He opened another door. In this room a dozen young women sat around half-finished chain mail tunics, with curious tools in their hands.

"The last step is like weaving, though it's steel instead of cloth. I made a special clamp and plier, so that even a girl can link the rings. I figured they already know how to weave, and your witch already employs women in your name, so you would think it all right. The girls need something to do part-time, and they can always use the money."

Christopher could already guess Jhom was saving money, too. He certainly wouldn't be paying the women as much as he would have to pay a man. That hardly explained this radical step, though.

"I do approve, Jhom, though you're going to have to give them a raise. I won't let your apprentices get out of work that easily."

"It's not a matter of money, but muscle," Jhom said. "Every man has a hammer or a shovel in his hands these days. If women don't do this, it won't get done."

Christopher laughed, long and hard. Jhom stared at him askance, clearly not getting the joke, but Christopher couldn't help it. He'd been worried about creating change, about starting the industrial revolution in a feudal economy, and Jhom had gone and given birth to Rosie the Riveter.

"Make sure you pay them what any weaver would be paid," he told Jhom. The rest would take care of itself, eventually.

Cannan had been examining the tunic closely. "Do you have more of these?" he asked Jhom.

"Dozens," Jhom answered. "For the Vicar's cavalry, first. Only then for other customers."

Cannan had stopped listening after the first word, draping the tunic over a thick wooden table. With one smooth motion he drew the huge black sword he wore, cutting a terrible arc through the air and into the table.

Sparks and bits of steel flew as the chain mail squealed under his blade. Cannan brushed the tunic aside and examined the table. The wood was dented but not scored.

"It is good," Cannan said. "Get me another one, and one for the Vicar."

"And Gregor," Christopher said. Hadn't he promised the man armor ages ago? "And Karl, and . . . well, everybody, really. Get one for everybody."

He gave Dereth a stack of drawings, some of which matched the ones he'd given Fae and some of which didn't.

"The cannon I understand," Dereth said, "though I hope you understand a gun of these dimensions will weigh several tons." Christopher had sketched a rifled cannon, intended for the day when he would need to knock down stone walls. Although its muzzle was only the same five inches across as the Napoleons, the barrel was longer and much thicker to allow for a truly massive charge of powder. "But these other tubes are too thin to hold a charge, even though you've stacked them together like organ pipes."

"Those are rocket tubes," Christopher said. "They only need to guide the rocket, not propel it. Just make a single tube for now, so Fae can practice." The one drawback of his cannons was the slow rate of fire. The rocket tubes would let him shoot three dozen missiles at once. The massed charges of the ulvenmen had been terrifying; outside of his fort they would have been terminal. He really wanted machine guns, but while his craftsmen were doing surprisingly well at making machines and guns, they were not up to combining them.

He went looking for Lalania, but only found her when she came looking for him. As usual, she wanted something.

"I need command of your chapel. It is necessary that we have the wedding there, in the god's hall, but your soldiers will not leave off their drills."

They used the chapel as a lecture room, having noticed that the boys paid more attention inside the stone walls. The officers claimed religion was due the credit, saying the wooden gaze of the frieze of the god Marcius staring serenely down made the boys respectful. Christopher suspected it was the history of the building. His original crop of draftees had fought a desperate battle there against walking corpses and the evil Black Bart. In a night they had gone from village boys to victorious warriors, a journey that all of these young, beardless men were desperately eager to make.

"How long do you need it for?"

Lalania calculated, looking at her lyre for some reason. "One day will suffice, I suppose. You were going to give them all that day off anyway, weren't you?"

"Sure," Christopher agreed. At least she wasn't asking for money. "I'll declare a holiday." Maybe it would make Gregor more popular with the troops he was going to be leading.

"Also," she said, as she was leaving, "I need money. At least a hundred gold. Even cheap weddings are expensive, and this one should not be too cheap. Remember, Christopher, this will be our last taste of civilization for a while."

Not too many days later Disa, Karl, and two dozen horsemen rode into town. Karl had brought all of the cavalry. Protecting the Lady Disa was more important than running patrols through the quiescent swamp.

"I've got wedding presents for you," Christopher told them with a grin. He, Gregor, and Cannan were already wearing the new chain mail. Even though it was lighter, it was still a shirt woven out of steel. It turned every stairstep into an exercise machine. The two knights didn't seem to notice it, so Christopher was gratified to have mortal company for his misery.

Gregor waded into the knot of horses and lifted Disa bodily out of her saddle, carrying her like a china doll. She giggled and blushed in ways Christopher had not thought to associate with the dedicated professional healer he had known in the swamp. Gregor, too, seemed a different man today. These people were used to mixing their martial discipline with their ordinary lives, stirring moments of personal expression into campaigns of war. They had to be. In a world where horror could attack from the grave, there was never any time off from fighting. Only Christopher found solace in the unrelenting rigor of military life, using its strictures to drown out every remembrance of the past, focusing solely on the now and the future.

Not only Christopher. Cannan stood by him silently, ignoring the loving couple.

Instinctively Christopher looked to see what Karl was looking at, and found the man wearing an unusual expression, a sort of bemused and sly smile. Christopher followed his gaze, to where a blushing Helga was waddling down the chapel steps.

"Go on," Christopher told him. "You can report later. I'm not ready to hear it, anyway."

"Very well, Colonel." Karl saluted and led his men and horses to the stables.

Christopher almost stopped him. He almost suggested that Karl could have someone else see to his horse. But he didn't. Karl had rejected the life of privilege and rank.

Sighing, Christopher stopped fiddling with the ties on his chain mail, quietly surrendering the idea of ditching it for the day even before the thought had been fully formed.

The next day dawned clear and cold, and Christopher proclaimed his holiday from his chapel steps to a general cheer. Of course, it was a vacation only for the men; the women still had their daily work to do, cooking and cleaning so that life could continue, and on top of that they had a wedding to put on. Nonetheless, they cheered as loudly as the men.

After that he felt singularly useless. There was nothing he could do to prepare for the wedding because the women wouldn't let him, and there was nothing he could do for work because his men were off drinking, gambling, and having snowball fights. It was sometimes hard to remember how young they were.

He assigned himself the job of overseeing the deliveries that Finn's drayers were bringing for the event. Barrels of beer and sacks of flour he expected; twenty yards of white-and-gold bunting he didn't. When he found himself frowning at the cost, he fired himself from the position. Nobody noticed his absence, which only reinforced his uselessness.

He went looking for Karl and found him in the armory, meticulously checking each suit of chain mail. Another task Christopher wasn't qualified for. Metal he knew, but whether the links would pinch or catch on the march, or yield too easily to a thrust, were facts learned only by hard experience.

"My Lord Vicar, I would like to ask a favor," Karl said. Words Christopher had never expected to hear from the young veteran.

"Of course, Karl. Anything." Only after he spoke did he realize he meant it. He owed Karl everything, certainly anything that was in his power to give.

"Though I am bound to the draft, and thus not free to dispense with my future, I would like permission to marry. It may grant the child a pension, if the Saint sees fit; at the very least it will allow him to inherit my name."

Christopher could not stop himself from meddling. He never could. "Is that all? Is that the only reason you want to marry her?"

Karl quirked an eyebrow. "Isn't it sufficient?"

Christopher sighed. "Of course. Yes, you are free to do whatever you want. I just wanted you to . . . want more."

"One woman is very much like another," Karl said. Christopher thought of all the women he'd known Karl had been with, and the many more he didn't know about. He thought about a handsome young man growing up in a world where women outnumbered men by two to one. "She is as good a woman as any, peasant though she may be," Karl finished, and Christopher thought to detect the tiniest sliver of defensiveness.

"I didn't mean . . ." Christopher couldn't argue with Karl's misunderstanding, without naming it and thus making the offense real. In that moment he realized what he was looking for was already there. Karl could have had any woman he wanted. A prettier wife, a town wife, a daughter of a wealthy craftsmen. He could even have had a noblewoman, if he wanted. But he had chosen a girl from his own background, a poor, farm-bred orphan. He had chosen a woman he was comfortable with.

"I didn't mean to question your judgment," Christopher said. "I just want you to be happy."

Karl looked up from the armor in his hands, his rifle slung over his shoulder, standing inside a building dedicated to arming and defending the common men of his county. Everything he had wanted, and more, from the day he had first turned down promotion in hatred of the hierarchy of rank. Everything he and Christopher had built.

"Happiness is not possible in this life," Karl said. "But I am content, if that is any consolation to you." He shrugged, in manly dismissiveness, and Christopher was too embarrassed to reply.

He went in search of Helga instead, and found her in the village. She had rented a room now that the chapel was no longer her home; Svengusta had been staying at the inn. Christopher watched the lady of the house bowing and scraping to his lordly rank, and concluded this arrangement had to change.

"I need to build a house, don't I?" he said to Helga.

She adjusted herself on the narrow bed that served as her living quarters. She had been given a place of honor in the house, to one side of the stone fireplace. The other side comprised the kitchen. The best spot in the house, directly in front of the fireplace, had been given over to one of Christopher's Franklin stoves, its tin chimney leaning crookedly over to the flue. The peasants had adapted to the efficiency and cleanliness of the stoves, but they still hadn't gotten around to rebuilding their houses around them.

"A manor, my lord. This is a house." A crude wooden ladder stood in one corner, leading to the loft where the children slept. "You need a manor like one in town, with fancy glass windows and a proper staircase."

"And a staff of servants to run it," he said with a grin, picturing Helga in the house of her dreams.

"You already have a staff," she answered. "Half the women of the town work for you."

"And a guest room, of course." He was thinking of Svengusta. The man shouldn't have to live in an inn just because Christopher had evicted him from his chapel.

"Tom could build you one," she said. "He has a very nice house in town."

Christopher had been to that house before. It wasn't that nice.

Helga saw the doubt in his face. "Not his old one. The new one he had built when his son was born."

"He's building houses now?" Christopher couldn't remember how much he was paying the man these days.

"On the cheap, he claimed, since he had so many of your workmen and not enough dirt for them to shovel."

Apparently he was paying Tom more than just money.

"Sure," he said. "Have Tom build us a house. But no fancier than his, Helga. I'm not a real lord. I only have a village, and the boys in it still throw snowballs at my head."

She giggled until she had to stop, putting a hand over her belly. "He is kicking all the time," she said. "It will be any day now."

"I told Karl he could get married."

Helga smiled, like a sunbeam. "I knew you would. He didn't want to ask, but I knew you would say yes."

That meddlesome spirit clawed its way up Christopher's spine to seize control of his throat. "Is it what you want, Helga?"

She looked at him with more frank wisdom than he had imagined possible.

"I know I do not have his heart," she said. "I never will. That is given only to you. But I have the rest of him, and that is enough for me."

Christopher struggled for something to say, but Helga cried out. "Oh!"

"What?" he exclaimed, but the lady of the house was already there.

"It is the baby, my lord." The housewife called out commands to the household, imperious as an admiral. "Goodwoman, breathe deep. Daughter, fetch the priest. Lord Vicar, please go away."

He had no training for this. It wasn't part of combat healing. He caught up to the woman's daughter outside the house. "I'll get Svengusta," he said. "You can, uh, boil water." Weren't you supposed to boil water for babies?

The little girl looked up at him as if he were insane. "I'll check the inn. You look into Fenwick's; sometimes Pater likes to visit there." She ran off, leaving him no choice but to follow her instructions.

Svengusta was indeed at Fenwick's, playing a game of stones with the youngest of the Goodman's herd of boys. Christopher rushed out his message. The old man nodded sagely and climbed to his feet.

"Leave the board, lad, and we'll finish it up later."

Christopher frowned, nervous. Svengusta wasn't washing his hands, or changing into clean scrubs, and Christopher was pretty sure he wasn't going to.

"Is she going to be okay?" What he knew of childbirth was blood and pain and hospitals.

Svengusta stared at him in amazement. "Do you think me so ready for the pasture, then?"

"No, of course not. I just mean . . . is it safe?"

The old man harrumphed. "I haven't lost a mother or child since . . . well, since ever. Not one in fifty years, boy, not one. The Bright Lady may not be all that on the battlefield, but in the hearth and home her power is unparalleled."

Of course. The healing magic that made limb-severing duels non-fatal would render birth equally safe. No woman would bleed out here. Even infection would invariably yield to the power of a Curate.

Christopher was unable to reconcile this tender mercy to the innocent with the incessant bloodbath of the thresher. Until he remembered that children yielded no tael. The dying only started in earnest when the tael was ready for the harvest.

The reconciliation soured him. Seeking isolation, he went to the chapel, the only empty building in town.

Even it was occupied, though. Lalania stood alone in the middle of the room, bales of cloth and spools of bunting piled haphazardly around her.

"Christopher," she said. "Are you ready?" His part in the wedding was to say a blessing. Purely ceremonial, Lalania assured him, as the beneficial effects would only last a few minutes until the magic evaporated, but it was traditional.

"Helga's having a baby," he said. "And marrying Karl."

She nodded. "An auspicious day. The peasants like to marry on the same day as a lord. And to be blessed with a child, as well. Sweet Helga could hardly ask for more."

She could ask for romantic love, Christopher thought. But he didn't say anything. He knew Lalania would be even more dismissive than Karl had been.

"Who's going to help you with all this stuff?" he asked.

"No one you know," she said cryptically. "Though I suppose you should observe. Or rather, I cannot deny you. But please, promise me you will not speak of the magic I show you."

Lalania gave him a look charged with warning, expectation, and excitement, and then turned to her lyre. He had heard her play it before, but this time she did something different, speaking softly in her magical language, striking a chord he had never heard before. He wasn't even sure it was possible to hear.

White tendrils of mist floated up out of the ground at the lyre's call. Christopher's hand went to his sword, an automatic reaction he no longer tried to fight, but Lalania was enraptured with triumph, so he did nothing else. The mist formed itself into figures, ghostly and vaguely shaped with arms and torsos. As she played the unreal chords, sounds he heard only as a reflection from some unknown place, the figures began to move. They seized cloth and tools, hammers and scissors, and began to work. With each passing second they moved faster and faster, until the room was a blur of flying mist, flapping cloth, and buzzing scissors. In a moment their work was done, the ghosts coming apart into strands and motes and then nothing at all. The chapel was left transformed, a festive banquet hall cloaked in streamers and drapes, choked with garlands of flowers, the floor swept clean and every stone polished to a gleam.

"Wow," Christopher said. It seemed like a much bigger effect than the minor magic he had seen her use before.

"A shameful use of power, I know," she admitted. "But I could not resist a trial." She didn't seem at all ashamed. "It would be best, though, to not mention this to anyone."

Curious that she felt the need to warn him twice. The bards were always secretive, though, even about trivial things. Christopher shrugged, rendered useless once again, and went to find somebody he could safely annoy. Fenwick's boy seemed like a good choice.

He didn't know the ceremony, so his contribution was limited to the spell. Svengusta stood at the head of the chapel, leading Disa and Gregor through their vows. The girl wore a simple white dress, which Christopher belatedly realized was more a symbol of her Church than her purity—she and Gregor had never bothered to conceal their shacking up in the swamp. Gregor wore his shiny new chain mail and his glowing blue sword.

It was a war god's chapel they were marrying in, after all.

In the first row of spectators stood a handful of commoners, Karl and Helga and her baby among them. Svengusta waited after each stanza for the noble couple in front of him to recite it, and then for the three couples behind them to follow suit. Helga's baby cried only once, and the entire chapel wept with joy to hear the sound of new life.

At the end Christopher came forward and cast his blessing, the twinkling lights falling down on the shining couples. Never before had he spoken the words so earnestly. This was all just an adventure for him, one he hoped to go home from someday. For these people it was the rest of their lives.

The eating and drinking and dancing were easier to relate to. He'd done plenty of that since he got here. This time, at least, all of the attention was on someone else, so he could hang back and enjoy it.

His man Tom came up to pay his respects, his wife and her toddler in tow. "Congratulations," Tom said, perhaps automatically. He'd already said it four times, to the blessed couples.

"I didn't do anything," Christopher answered.

"You've married off a fistful of daughters, or close enough. That's something to celebrate." Tom could always find the bright side of any coin. "And I hear you're commissioning a grand new house for other people to live in while you're stinking in a swamp."

"Indeed," Christopher answered with a laugh. "Don't bankrupt me, though. It's a house for a village lord, not for a grandee of the realm."

"For now," Tom said with a wink. "For now. Also, I bring you Mistress Fae's heartfelt regrets. She was unable to attend, as she was deep in the pains of childbirth last I saw her."

Christopher remembered what Tom's wife had told him about wizards getting pregnant, and wisely decided not to ask Tom anything impolitic.

"A fine state for her, if you ask me," Tom went on. "Hopefully it will teach the witch a little humility."

"Do they know if it is a boy or a girl?" Christopher asked, trying to make conversation.

"They don't even know if it's human yet," Tom's wife said. "Gods know what kind of creatures that creature was consorting with. I've heard talk of wings from her window on starless nights."

"Hush, woman," Tom said. "The Lord Vicar doesn't want to hear your old wives' gossip. Still," he continued, tipping his head apologetically to Christopher, "it's clear the father is no man of the town. The witch has been as cold as ice since you elevated her to the gentry."

"No man at all," muttered his wife.

"Are you sure?" Christopher asked, meaning was Tom sure *he* wasn't the father, but Tom misinterpreted the question.

"Quite certain, my lord. It's not only the women's gossip. If there were a man bedding her, I can't imagine he wouldn't be bragging about it, and neither I nor any of my lads have heard a peep."

Christopher could think of one man Fae had slept with in the last nine months. But there didn't seem to be any purpose in mentioning it.

"I'm not worried about it, Tom. I don't think anybody else should be, either."

Tom shrugged good-naturedly. "That's good enough for me, then. And it will be for you, too," he said to his wife. "The Lord Vicar knows how to maintain his own stable."

"The Lord Vicar's not the one who needs minding," she said. "Every woman knows the quality of his household. It's the rest of you men what need be paying attention."

Tom gave him an aggrieved look, as if to say, *Look what you've started.* Christopher wasn't particularly sympathetic, so he grinned and bowed to the man's wife, which made the woman beam with pride and blush with happiness.

It was a wonderful sight, one of many that stayed with him for days. As he saddled up in front of the chapel on another frigid morning, men and horses stamping in the snow with steaming breaths, harnesses jingling and wagons creaking, he looked over his stone chapel and pictured the wedding it had held. Not just booty piled in front of the god for a change, but joy and hope. It warmed him inside, a secret fire he kept hidden from the rough soldiers cursing perfunctorily in the cold.

15

CAMPAIGN SEASON

The cold melted with every mile they rode. By Carrhill it was no more than coolness even in the dead of night. Christopher was annoyed, recognizing that this weather was wholly unnatural and therefore not subject to his analysis or understanding. A journey of a hundred miles should not turn Nordic snow into tropical rain.

The cloaks they had hugged tight a few days ago they now cast off, groaning under their weight. The boots were worse. In Knockford they had doubled their socks against the snow. Here they wanted to go barefoot. Christopher was of half a mind to let them, but he didn't dare. If hookworm broke out, he wouldn't be able to heal them fast enough. Leather-strap sandals would serve them better than boots. But where could he buy four hundred pairs of sandals while on the march?

The answer turned out to be magic. He accidentally let slip the topic in his obligatory meeting with the Lord Wizard of Carrhill, who could not be dissuaded from showing off. The wizard sent out for a dozen bullhides and a hundred yards of twine. When they were piled at the foot of his tower, he cast a spell, and purple-hued mist swarmed over the materials, leaving behind stacks of neatly crafted footwear.

Christopher recognized the effect as similar to Lalania's lyre, but he didn't mention that, confining his remarks to gratitude.

"I should thank you," the wizard said. "It's a tragically worthless spell. Who the hell needs hundreds of mundane objects in an afternoon? I can't imagine what the dark was going through the mind of the fool who created it. This is probably the only time I'll ever be able to make a profit off that cursed waste of ink."

The wizard charged him a hundred tael, which was tragically overpriced. As Christopher was leaving, he found he was expected to pay for the materials, too. The tradesmen waiting for him at the gate looked so unhappy that he didn't even argue. He'd robbed them of a profitable contract, after all, just to indulge a wizard's ego.

He left half the sandals in the stone barracks dedicated to the King's garrison. Gregor's regiment was still up in Knockford, forming for the march south, and they would appreciate getting the new shoes before they plunged into the swamp. The garrison was mostly empty now that his men lived in the fort, but it wasn't deserted. Several of Finn's teamsters stayed there, overseeing the stocks of supplies that flowed down from the north.

"Some of you are going to have to come out to the fort," he told them. "The King has ordered my regiments south, to engage the ulvenmen. The fort is going to have to become just another supply depot."

"Aye," their leader grunted. "Major Tom's already made that known. But the major said the men what went south would be given rifles? Is this truth?"

Christopher had no idea what the production schedules looked like these days. "If he says so, then it must be," he said, and hoped it was true.

They spent another two weeks improving the road from Carrhill to the fort. The men wanted a name for the place, now that it was at the end of a road. The only fort Christopher could think of was Fort Sumter. It wasn't really appropriate—he wasn't trying to start a civil war—but nobody here would understand the connotation. In a few days they had mangled it anyway, to Fort Sump. It was very much like a sump, the lowest place in the Kingdom where the noxious dregs pooled.

Then Gregor and his men came marching down the road, and the waiting was over. Wagons had preceded them, and more followed; indeed wagons rolled day and night, escorted by armed patrols to keep the dinosaurs at bay. Christopher's one military virtue was an over-abundance of supply. It was expensive, but the commerce drove the economy that let him print bonds, so in a sense he was getting it all for free. Or rather, at no more cost than his reputation. As long as the tael kept flowing out of the swamp, people would keep believing in his future, and they'd keep buying his promises. It all uncomfortably reminded him of national economics back home, so he decided not to think about it.

"Do we have any idea what we're facing?" he asked. Marching off to military adventures without proper planning also reminded him too much of home.

"We know enough," D'Kan said. "Well, enough for your purposes. A Ranger would slip down there in stealth with two or three trusted companions, locate the shaman, assassinate him in the middle of the night, and leave the rest of the ulvenmen to fight amongst themselves. But that's not your way. Your way is to make a huge noise and stink until every monster within a hundred miles gangs up on you."

"It's an efficient plan, you've got to give it that," Gregor said. "Fifteen hundred ulvenmen in a day is the sort of thing your Lord Rangers can only dream of."

"That's not combat, that's slaughter," D'Kan grumbled. "None-theless, it is what you have. So you will blunder about like a drunken bull until they attack. For that, the strategy is easy: go south."

"I would like to avoid any surprises like the Moaning Lands," Christopher said. His army would be all but helpless against an army of shadows.

D'Kan was unworried. "Easy enough. As long as you're being attacked by ulvenmen, you won't be attacked by anything else. Either the ulvenmen would have killed it, or it would have killed the ulvenmen."

"How far south?" Torme asked.

"A hundred miles, maybe less. Then the swamp ends. We know no further than that."

"Can you estimate the number of ulvenmen we will face?" Christopher asked.

The Ranger shrugged. "I am surprised the swamp could feed as many as we have already seen."

"So there may be surprises after all," Torme said. Christopher approved of the man's relentless cynicism. It was perilously close to logic.

"I would hazard that the shaman is the pin that holds the cart together. Remove him and the ulvenmen will revert to individual tribes."

Unless the shaman himself was a puppet of some greater force. Christopher looked at Lalania with concern, but she quickly shook her head. The *hjerne-spica* had no allies, she had assured him; the ulvenmen would be even less tractable servants than the erratic Black Bart had been.

"He must maintain that power through reputation," Christopher said. "If we march into his territory, he'll have to come and throw us out, or lose face. So that's our plan. We go down there and build a fort, and wait for him to come and get us."

Gregor laughed. "Madness, absolute madness. To sit and wait for your enemy to strike first is the height of folly."

"We can do little else," Karl said. "Our strength lies in size, not the keenness of our edge. We cannot maneuver an entire army like a band of heroes."

"Oh, I didn't say I disagreed," Gregor said. "It's such a stupid plan that no rational foe would even recognize it as a trap. Our only danger is if your shaman is completely insane. A madman might be able to see through your plot."

"The shaman will respond traditionally," Karl warned. "He will swarm our camp with soldiers, and when Christopher spends his magic to save the men, the shaman will strike at him directly. His previous failure will not dissuade him. Rather, he will use the knowledge gained then to strike more effectively. We must expect surprises."

"What surprises do we have left?" Christopher asked.

"You have a new rank, as does Gregor. Disa has three." Karl added up their advantages. "We have Cannan. And we have twice as many men, with a greater wealth of carbines."

"And me," Lalania said. "What am I, sour milk?"

"What if he ignores us and cuts our supply lines?" It was what Christopher would do. After all, he couldn't be everywhere at once. His men would be severely outclassed by an invisible, flying foe armed with lightning bolts. It would be as pitiful as pitting infantry against a stealth fighter plane.

"He will not spend himself in combat against commoners," Karl said. "He cannot be that stupid. You would lose a few dozen men, but eventually you would catch him in an ambush."

Torme agreed. "We can lose many men, and revive them. The ulvenman shaman can only afford to die but once. Every time he steps out from behind his horde he risks his fate."

The shaman was constrained by the same math that bound Christopher. Both of them had to hide behind their merely mortal servants. The difference was that the shaman did not seem to care how many of his servants he lost.

The other difference was that Christopher's men had guns. Lord Nordland could credibly threaten his entire company with just his sword and his wife; the King was arguably the equal of all the mundane regiments in the Kingdom. But a single troop of Christopher's cavalry would blast himself and his magic to pieces. Even the ulvenman shaman had ultimately retreated in the face of gunfire, despite protective magic. The age-old equation balancing a high rank against an army of mortals had been severely tilted by technology.

It remained to be seen if it was enough.

Once again Christopher rode his magnificent stallion through the swamp, looking for trouble, but this time he was in a much better mood. The ride was vastly more tolerable in chain than in plate. The ranked men rode at the center of a cloud of cavalrymen, so the track was well beaten and free of hanging branches by the time he rode it. The only difficulty was convincing his imperious horse to stop trying to take the lead.

There were over eighty horsemen now. Karl had been hiring steadily throughout the year, bolstering the ranks of the draft with mercenary veterans tempted back to battle by a commander who wouldn't leave them dead. Not just cavalrymen; Christopher had seen many older faces in Gregor's new regiment, a welcome seasoning to the greenest branch of his army. And armed contractors rode at the rear of his column, driving wagons and carrying rifles. This was the most professional army this realm had ever seen. He'd won two battles with his New Model Army. Now it would be seen if he could win a war.

Disa and Lalania also rode with the tiny knot of nobility—Christopher, Gregor, and the ever-present Cannan. The other priestesses were dispersed into the infantry, where their healing might save a life. D'Kan was with the horsemen, out in front where he preferred to be, but Torme and Karl had duties in the column. Christopher missed the presence of both men, but they'd already died for him. It was somebody else's turn.

The first day went as expected. They made half the distance they'd planned and shot twice as many crocodiles as they'd feared. They made campfires out of the reedy, gnarled trees, and pitched their tents on the dry patches. Christopher had an army of black-powder weapons with paper cartridges. Rain was his nemesis, and it rained every single night, sparking nightmares of hordes of ulvenmen in glistening fur.

If the mob that had broken on his fort attacked him on this open ground, he was doomed. D'Kan swore that even ulvenmen couldn't assemble such a force overnight, so they had a grace period—unless they got unlucky and stumbled into an invasion already in progress. Even then, D'Kan said they'd have a day or so to respond while the ulvenmen converged, asserting that their supply system—or rather, total lack of one—required them to spread out and forage on the march. Christopher wasn't so sure, remembering the *Triceratops* with houses on their backs.

The night passed with only a few gunshots, and in the morning they all got up and did it again. The highlight of Christopher's day was signing a requisition slip for more lard. Keeping the guns protected from moisture was a full-time job. He really needed to invent bluing. Or better, stainless steel. Or even better, bug spray.

"Is there some kind of gas cloud spell?" he asked Lalania. "Can we hire a wizard to fumigate this blasted swamp?"

She frowned at him sourly. "That would please the Dark, no doubt. A spell to kill an entire land. Fortunately wizards are limited to murdering people by the yard, not the acre."

Christopher thought about atomic bombs, whose killing radius was measured in miles, and kept the rest of his comments to himself.

On the fourth day they stopped marching and built a fort. Although it had taken them three days to get here through the mud, it would only take one day by road. Once they actually built a road, that was.

This fort was made of mud and scrub wood, but it still represented a huge advantage for his riflemen. They spent two whole days clearing the surrounding land, building walls, and digging ditches. The Romans had built a fort every single night on the march. Christopher couldn't quite match that, and he wasn't sure why. Maybe it was density. A legion had five thousand men, which increased their labor by a factor of ten over his two regiments, but only increased the circumference of their walls by some smaller number that he couldn't be bothered to work out. He needed to invent calculators, too.

Fort-building was even more boring than marching, at least for him. They were resting the horses, so there were no patrols, and the mechanics of ditch-digging and wall-raising were well understood, so there was nothing for him to do there. He spent the time leading Lalania around, explaining every detail and feature of the preplanned structure to her. She seemed to have concocted an intense interest in the minutia of fort-building. He concluded she must be even more bored than he was.

Once they had their fort, the infantry spent a day resting while the cavalry rode a wide circle. They had a brief moment of excitement when D'Kan discovered a circle of crude, dilapidated huts, but the Ranger declared them old and abandoned.

The next day they started the sequence over: march, march, march, and build. This time it was much more exciting. On the third day of the march the cavalry had been ambushed by a dozen ulvenmen. It was probably supposed to be a hit-and-run attack, but the ulvenmen didn't get a chance to run before the carbines cut them down. None of Christopher's men died, though several would have without Disa's healing. They let Gregor heal the wounded horses, for practice. That day the fort-building went off with considerably more alacrity and dispatch, seeing as how everyone was expecting a deluge of slavering dog-men by nightfall.

When the cavalry went out for patrol, they found another group of huts. To Christopher's untrained eye they were in as poor a shape as the others, but D'Kan swore they had been occupied only moments ago. Gregor lit a torch.

"What are you going to do with that?" Christopher asked him.

The knight paused, confused. "Our goal is to provoke them, I thought."

"Well, yes, but—"

Gregor held the torch against a straw-thatched roof, setting it ablaze. He handed the torch off to a cavalryman, who shared the flame with two others and set forth to burn the village.

Lalania twisted her mouth up. "This is warfare, Christopher, as the lords practice it. Eventually we shall damage the purse of the master enough that he sallies forth. Until then, the peasants suffer."

Disa tried to defend her man. "They aren't peasants. Each one of them is a warrior, and our enemy." The disquietude in her face belied her words.

Cannan's defense was more effective. "I could build a better hut in an hour. They'll spend less time worrying over this than you have."

There wasn't any particular danger that the fire would spread to the jungle. It barely consumed the village, and even that required a little help from Gregor's men.

The next day gave Christopher a reason to stop feeling sorry for the ulvenmen. The cavalry blundered upon a larger camp, and a short but savage battle ensued. The opening shot was the squeal of a horse, crippled in an ugly deadfall trap. While the men were still trying to help the animal, a dozen ulvenmen charged out of the swamp and fell on them with axes.

The ulvenmen were incredible. They cut through the men like firewood, chain mail shrieking under their blows. The men died almost soundlessly; usually, they didn't have a chance to even scream. A single blow was typically enough to reduce a man to dying meat. The ulvenmen were not so fragile. Christopher saw one take three shots from a carbine before it stopped moving. He realized that the previous ambush had been ineffective because the ulvenmen had started with arrows and had been prepared to flee. These ulvenmen, however, charged like axe-wielding rhinoceroses on fire, and Christopher's men fought to retreat this time.

The enemy advance broke on Christopher's knot of rank. He had time for one spell, and it was his new favorite, the one that made him as strong as Cannan. Between that, his horse, and his tael-fed vitality, he faced the beasts on more than equal terms. When the dog-men charged, snarling and chasing his fleeing cavalry, he, Gregor, and Cannan charged them back. Christopher ran one through, the blade sliding all the way up to the hilt. The ulvenman dropped his weapons and grappled with Christopher, biting, clawing, and climbing up onto the horse with him. Christopher twisted his blade inside the ulvenman's ribs, widening the hole until blood gushed out like a river. Then he kicked the thing off the end of his sword, and stood in the saddle to chop down at the next foe.

There wasn't one. The cavalry had reloaded, switching out their spare cylinders, and come back to save him. D'Kan was there, running from corpse to corpse on foot while his horse stood waiting, but then he looked over his shoulder and shook his head.

"The rest come. We must flee."

So they did, thundering away as fast as they could through the tangled brush. After a thousand yards they pulled up, and Disa healed those who were still alive. They had five dead men in the saddle, whose horses had stayed with the herd. Three more corpses were borne by cavalry men plucky enough to grab their dead comrades. D'Kan, ever practical, had five fingers in a sack.

Out of the patrol, only one was unaccounted for. Christopher felt a strange flutter in his stomach, a welter of grief and fear. The missing man was not just dead, he was gone forever. D'Kan assured him without mercy that the monsters would feast on the body tonight. When Christopher glanced speculatively back toward the camp, Gregor shook his head.

"No," he said with authority, and the troop turned toward home.

"We need bigger guns," Christopher complained. He was sitting close to the fire, trying to dry out. The stench of the ulvenman's blood had compelled him to dump a bucket of water over his head as soon as they had entered the fort.

"We have them," Karl answered. And they had. The camp was stuffed with cannons, both the little ones and the big five-inch Napoleons. The problem lay only in getting the guns to the enemy.

"We need more men," Gregor fretted. "Half the men must defend the fort, and we've already lost two score left behind as garrisons at our previous two forts. We lose strength with every step we take into this damn swamp."

They'd lost a quarter of their cavalry, too, in a single battle. The worst of it was that D'Kan claimed they faced a single tribe of ulvenmen. No more than a hundred, he swore, and probably only one or two of significant rank. Christopher was mystified how he could have thought killing ulvenmen was easy.

"We need better armor," Cannan said. His mail was rent in a dozen places, and Christopher's was no better.

"You need more carbines," D'Kan said. He was carrying one now, borrowed from one of the dead men. "Or a bigger wheel-thingy. If they could hold ten shots they'd be twice as valuable as holding six."

"We can't make the cylinder larger. The weight would be unbearable," Christopher explained, shaking his head. What they needed was magazine-fed semi-automatics. Or belt-fed machine guns. When the British had faced overwhelming armies of fearless warriors with spears, they had at least been only human.

"All we need is deliberation and caution," Karl said. "The ulvenmen thrive in the heat of battle. Force their pace to a walk and they will break apart. Tomorrow we will advance on foot, with cannon, and see how they like it."

The mood of the column of marching men was grim. Word had gotten around about the missing soldier. Half the men were scared of permanently dying, the adventure no longer a lark; the other half cast dark glances at those who had deserted their fellows in the field. The phrase "never leave a man behind" had taken on new meaning for Christopher. It was twice as important to his army's morale as it was to the US Marines.

The upshot of it was that the cavalry walked today, leaving their horses to rest in the fort. Still out in front of the column, they struggled through the brush they had bounded over on horseback. Their armor weighed them down, but no more than the cannons the infantry dragged through the same miserable scrub. Only Christopher's party was mounted. Only they would be able to retreat if everything went wrong.

Dismounting the cavalry didn't seem like a tactically sound decision to Christopher. He would have rescinded it, except he hadn't given the order in the first place. He wasn't really sure who had. It just seemed to happen, of its own accord, a spontaneous act of penance. Gregor dismissed his concerns, saying that the men had made the necessary choice. Christopher would have discussed it with Torme and Karl, but he lost trust in their dispassionate objectivity when he saw them flipping a coin to see who would stay to defend the fort and who would advance with the attack. Apparently Karl won.

It took them half the day to make the three miles to the ulvenman camp. This was worrying, since they wanted to be back in the fort before nightfall, but the army would move faster on the way home. They wouldn't be carrying so many tons of ammunition.

Nor would they be so cautious. D'Kan had issued poles for

probing suspicious ground. The ulvenmen made crude traps, but they were deadly nonetheless. The men in the front soundly thrashed every bush they encountered.

"Let us hope they apply equal energy to thrashing ulvenmen," Cannan said. Then he galloped forward and led for half a mile, displaying a singular unconcern for danger. Only when D'Kan threw up his hand and signaled that they were getting close did Cannan return to Christopher's side.

Now they were in the thick of it. The column spread out, forming a fat line, and they pushed the cannons with muzzles pointing forward instead of pulling them backward, despite the extra effort. The first rifle shot startled Christopher, which startled Royal, which caused Balance to prick up his ears and snort. But there wasn't a second one; somebody had just been trigger-happy.

"No complaints about noise now, Ser D'Kan?" Gregor grinned at the young Ranger, who held his carbine as if he intended to use it. The bow stayed in its scabbard in the saddle.

"Everything with ears already knows we're here." D'Kan had fallen back and attached himself to Christopher's group once their final destination was no longer in doubt.

"Well then," Lalania said. "Then you won't mind if I sing." She unwrapped her lyre from its protective sack and touched the strings.

It wasn't the unearthly music she had played before, but the effect seemed no less magical. The insanity of what they were doing, combined with the beauty of her voice and the lightness of her music, mixed together to produce a perverse pride in doing hard, stupid, scary things. Christopher could see his men perking up, shoulders squaring and necks stiffening, and a little more deftness to their step. Her song reached out across the swamp, clear and distinct despite the overhanging vegetation.

"Is that the effect of the new harp?" Christopher whispered to Gregor.

"No," the knight said. "She could always do that. You just never let her."

"Because it's stupidly dangerous," Cannan said. "It is not enough that everyone knows we are here; now the enemy knows exactly where your magic lies. The woman has painted a target on us a mile wide, and their ranks will strike unerringly."

"Do you despair?" D'Kan said. He seemed to needle Cannan by reflex these days.

"Not at all," Cannan replied. "At least this way I'll get to kill more than one ulvenman."

Only a few minutes later Lalania's song was joined by a percussion section, though it kept no sensible beat. Gunfire erupted from the left wing in spurts and bursts, one or two shots followed by a thunder of blasts, punctuated by ever-briefer silences. The men on that flank began to advance faster, reinforcing the armored cavalry scouts.

"Caution," Gregor bawled at the center. "Advance with caution." To D'Kan he said, "Get the right wing in motion," and the Ranger galloped into the brush to relay his orders. Gregor was trying to set up a crescent of fire, with the ulvenmen at the center.

Christopher started casting spells. The strength spell that made him a hero like Cannan made Cannan a superhero. Gregor didn't say no to it, either. Unfortunately, he could only cast a few of them each day. If only he could industrialize the production of magic, he wouldn't need guns. But that couldn't be done: better than him had tried and failed, as the books in the College's library had made clear.

He could hear a rising wave of sound from the left, like a swelling bubble. Suddenly a grenade exploded, and the bubble burst, resolving into the shouts of men and the barking of dogs, the clash of steel on steel. Under, over, and woven through was the sound of gunfire. Christopher found it comforting. He didn't need to worry as long as there were still rifles firing.

Then the boom of cannon. Christopher's horse stopped moving forward, and he realized it was because the men ahead of him had stopped. Three men pushed a small cannon past him, joining the wall that had formed in front. This was Karl's plan: to stand and fire when they spotted foes, and only advance when the field was empty. It was a good plan, as long as the ammunition held out.

Except for the smoke. The jungle was rapidly being suffused with white clouds. This reduced the effective range of the guns. On the other hand, it effectively hid the men, so the ulvenmen charged around blindly instead of in a targeted mass. Now there was fire up and down the line, and Christopher could no longer tell what was going on. Disa slid from her saddle to attend to a sudden incoming stream of men limping, crawling, and being carried on stretchers. Lalania shouted herself hoarse, her music still uplifting in the snatches you could hear of it. Something up ahead thrashed the trees like wind.

"Hold the center," Gregor bawled at Christopher. "Ser, with me," he called to Cannan, spurring his horse forward, and Cannan followed with only a single backward glance. They disappeared into the smoking jungle.

Christopher didn't know what to do. He had a terrible moment when he saw one of the young priestesses pass under Disa's care, but the girl leapt back to her feet after being healed and dashed off again. Lalania set aside her lyre and drew her sword, unable to compete with the roar of battle. Christopher drew his own, and waited.

The wave peaked, and then waned. The tattoo of gunfire dropped off, returning to single recognizable shots. Gregor and Cannan came trotting back, covered in blood, their chain mail rent into sieves.

Disa scrambled up, but Gregor waved her away. "It's not mine," Gregor said. "See to the men."

Cannan was carrying something bloody. An ulvenman's head.

"We got their leader," Gregor said. "Remember those dinosaur riders? There was only one. He must have been the chief. Fought like a dog, he did."

"And died like one," Cannan growled. "Drain this skull now, Christopher. It will be half your winnings from the battle."

Christopher looked into Cannan's face, concerned over the tone of that comment. Cannan looked back defiantly for a moment, and then looked away.

"Miracles are expensive," Cannan said, his voice pitched low enough that only Christopher could hear his excuse. But then, only Christopher was listening for one.

D'Kan came back for more orders.

"Let the smoke clear. Then advance with caution on all fronts." Gregor turned to Christopher. "Any excitement here?"

Two exhausted men dumped a stretcher at Disa's feet. The man in it was unmoving except for the blood pumping out of him. "I am done," Disa said, tears in her eyes. "I have nothing left." She looked up at Gregor hopefully.

"Oh, right," Gregor said. "Healing. I forgot about that. I used everything in the fight with the chief."

Christopher slid from the saddle and knelt at the soldier's side, converting one of his battle spells into healing.

"Only the usual," he told Gregor.

He spent the rest of the battle riding up and down the lines, looking for those too injured to seek out healing. Most of them seemed to be friendly fire casualties. The cannons had thrown out grapeshot without much regard for their fellow men. Those were the lucky ones: they were only wounded. The victims of the ulvenmen tended to be dead.

In half an hour it was over, the army half encircling the now-deserted ulvenman camp. Shortly after the death of their leader the remaining ulvenmen had begun fleeing.

"Now we should send the cavalry into the field to chase them," Karl said. "If only the fools had thought to bring their horses." Men were cautiously picking their way into the camp itself, without encountering resistance. "Chances are they did not go far. They expect to return here once we leave. They will lick their wounds, elect a new chief, and go on as before."

It was a losing proposition for the ulvenmen. Christopher had a dozen dead to their three score, a profit even before counting the leader's rank. Karl's plan had worked.

When Christopher congratulated him, Karl was dismissive. "It would have been better if the cavalry had retreated, instead of making us rush forward to save them. Also, they need to shoot less and aim more."

"You should have been in the center, Karl. Running the battle, not commanding a wing of it," Christopher said.

"I could not have cut down the dinosaur rider," Karl answered. "In any case, Ser Gregor did a fine job. Let him enjoy his victory."

The man in question called out, standing in front of a particularly sturdy hut in the middle of the ulvenman camp. Ser Gregor's face was troubled, and his voice was grave.

"Christopher, I am afraid you must see this."

16

HEART OF DARKNESS

Inside the hut was ugliness. Christopher raised his light-stone, but though it shed light, it only revealed the shape of darkness.

A dozen naked, filthy creatures cowered under his upraised hand. It took his eye a moment to recognize them as human. Another to realize they were mostly female, some clutching young children closely. All kept their gaze on the floor, save for one cringing figure who looked up at Christopher from the corner of his eye. Christopher deduced it was male only from the matted facial hair.

A baby cried, and its mother tried to hush it. Christopher instinctively stepped forward to offer some kind of help or comfort, and the woman shrank away, shaking in abject terror. The cringing man scuttled over and tried to take the child from her. She turned away from him, struggling silently, and he cuffed her brutally on the head.

The action released Christopher from his paralysis of horror. He leapt forward and pulled on the man's shoulder. Instantly the wretch collapsed to the floor, writhing in fear and hiding under his scarred arms.

The woman did not thank Christopher. She only acknowledged his existence by hiding the child, showing him her quivering back. He stepped back, forced to retreat by the strength of her fear.

"Dark fornicating gods," he swore, his breath short in his chest. He'd been trying to say something else, in English, but that was how it came out here.

"Indeed." Gregor was too distracted himself to notice Christopher's garbled speech, reacting only to the intent. His face was pale and still, the fire that animated it in combat completely quenched. "Dark gods indeed."

"Can you understand me?" Christopher said to the room. No one responded. The man on the floor still cowered under his arms.

"Lala," Gregor called out, a reluctant summons.

The bard approached with trepidation in her step, biting her lip. After her first glance she put her hand to her mouth and looked away.

"Can you talk to them?" Christopher asked her. "Do you know the ulvenman language?"

"I did not even know ulvenmen *had* a language until today," she said.

"Gods." Christopher shrugged, defeated. "What do we do with them?"

"Put them to the sword," Karl spat. "It would be an act of mercy. And you could put their tael to use killing ulvenmen." The young soldier had followed Lalania over, and now he stared into the hut without flinching. Christopher knew better, though. He could see the tightness around Karl's eyes, the only visible sign of the immense anger that burned deep inside.

"A season ago I would have agreed," Gregor said. "Now I do not know what to do. Brother Christopher, you are the head of the Church I have joined. What would Marcius have us do?"

"The best we can, whatever that is," Christopher muttered. He wasn't about to accept responsibility for theological doctrine. He had far too many real problems to solve.

"Then we turn them over to the Bright Lady," Gregor said. "It will cost you tael, instead of earning it, but the Saint may be able to do something for them." He motioned to Disa, and she cautiously joined them.

"Wife," Gregor said, "do what you can. The ones who cannot walk can ride on the gun carriages." He turned away, gruff and hard, and began bawling orders at the troops.

"Let us handle this," Lalania said to Christopher. "They may not fear a woman's voice as much as yours."

"Do they need healing?" Christopher asked. "I only have one spell left."

"I doubt it," Disa answered. "They were not in battle. Whatever ills they suffer can probably wait until tomorrow. What they need is food and tenderness."

"And cleaning," Lalania muttered. But she had her lyre out again, and began a gentle, soothing melody.

Christopher turned away, relieved to be relieved of this burden. The Saint had magic to fix a man's mind, like the spell that fixed Torme and Cannan. Perhaps he would be able to fix these debased creatures. Perhaps they might, someday, have some kind of life.

"Karl," he said, "show me the cooking pots."

"I do not think that is wise." Karl wore his hard face, the one he used when he had to tell Christopher no. "You have seen darkness enough for one day."

"What?" Christopher said. "You told me that our cavalryman would have been eaten. I'm guessing they were sloppy about it." The entire camp was a testament to sloth. "All I need is a finger bone."

"And if you find other bones?" Karl asked. "Will you beggar yourself in random acts of kindness, reviving the remnants of slaves?"

Every attempt at a revival cost tael. Even the ones that failed.

"The slaves won't come back," Christopher said. "I know that. It's not even worth trying." Who would return to the horrifying world they had left? "I won't get the wrong bone, Karl. I've got a spell in mind for that." If he could find a ring he had seen once in a swamp, surely he could find a fragment of a man who had served under him.

Karl acquiesced in the face of magic. He led Christopher to a fire pit that seemed more garbage disposal than food preparation, and set soldiers to raking out the coals and exposing them to die in the warm, wet air. Then he left to supervise the taking of heads.

Christopher's spell worked, guiding his hand into a pile of ash to clasp a white shard. He could not recognize what bone it had come from, before it had been gnawed and splintered, not that it mattered. But his hand disturbed something else, something small and round and cracked. Something he could not fail to identify.

A small, broken, human skull, hardly bigger than a clenched fist.

He stood and turned away. The jungle hung in emerald strips under a cerulean sky, but the colors had no meaning to him. Everything was bleached in coarse shades of gray.

They left the camp unburned.

"Karl is right," he said. "They will return. And so will we."

Two days later Christopher thundered through the scraggly brush at the head of his cavalry. They were following Gregor's plan this time.

"The risk is necessary," Gregor had argued the night before. "They are still wounded, demoralized, and disorganized. We must strike while the iron is hot."

Every man they could put on a horse would swing north of the camp, accompanying Christopher and his entourage. They would descend onto the camp from the northwest, guided by Cannan's woodcraft.

Half the infantry would flank the camp from the south, led by D'Kan's unerring sense of direction. The other half would retrace their steps from the attack before, striking the camp from the east side under Torme. For speed they would take only their rifles, leaving the cannons and wagons in the fort. Only a single platoon would remain behind, guarding the supplies and liberated slaves.

If the shaman attacked now, he would destroy Christopher's army piece by piece. It was a gamble Gregor was willing to take. This assault would trap the ulvenmen in a net of gunfire from which there would be no retreat. The cavalry charge, fronted by the ranked men and bolstered by magic, would shatter any resistance. The infantry would pick off ulvenmen one by one.

When Christopher questioned the wisdom of leading with their best, that was to say, with himself, Cannan shrugged off the danger. "We killed their rank," he said. "They have nothing left to stand against us. They are dangerous now only to your common men."

The horses' hooves could be heard from a hundred yards away. When they pounded into the ulvenman's camp, the ulvenmen were waiting for them. They came running in a howling charge, and Christopher howled back at them.

Flanked by Cannan on one side, Gregor on the other, and Disa behind, the diamond-shaped knot of horses plowed into the line of ulvenmen and cut through it as if it were water. Christopher felt the blows on his chain mail like hailstones on a raincoat, but tael bound his flesh. He bled only steel links as he charged through the camp.

The cavalry did not follow them. Karl and his horsemen pulled up abruptly, discharging their carbines at the ulvenmen, and then retreated. The surviving ulvenmen barked in victory and chased after them, only to face a fresh rank of horsemen firing madly. As the charge stalled, the first group finished reloading, and rode back to the fore. Under this circle of continuous fire the ulvenmen broke and fled for the tree line, only to die from the infantry's rifle fire.

After forcing their way to the other side of the camp, Christopher's group paused while Disa healed them and their mounts. Royal's strength and weight deserved more credit for carving through the camp than his sword did. They turned back into the battle.

Christopher and his little group wheeled around the camp like a scythe blade, destroying everything in their path. Ulvenmen of all sizes and shapes fell under a storm of swords powered by magic, protected by magic. He spent so much preparing for battle that he hardly had any healing spells left. This was part of the plan.

"The faster we kill them, the less damage they can do," Gregor had assured him.

Now he and the two other swordsmen committed slaughter. Ulvenmen, unprepared and unarmed, tried to bite him, or snatched up weapons from the dead. There were smaller creatures that fought only with fangs and claws. At first Christopher thought they were dogs, until one leapt in the saddle and tried to bite his face off. He smashed it with his pommel, knocking it to the ground where it disappeared under Royal's flashing hooves. The goblins had little servants that they used for war, too, strange, deformed copies of themselves. Apparently it was a common stratagem.

When the ulvenmen drew bows, Christopher and his knights charged them and rode over them. When they drew axes and made a battle line, the guns cut them down. In a dozen minutes it was over. Nothing moved in the camp but humans, dispatching the wounded, cutting off heads, and smashing open huts. There were no casualties on their side. Gregor, Cannan, and Christopher had taken a dozen blows, rending their chain mail into tatters, but tael had bound their flesh. Christopher had been so angry, so eager to destroy these monsters that he did not even remember feeling the shock of being hit.

For an act of genocide, it was remarkably painless.

Christopher gazed over the carnage, watching the slave hut burn.

"How many more slaves do they have?" he asked. "How many more camps, with how many more people kept like cattle?" Not even cattle; the animals in barns and fields back home were treated with more gentleness than the ulvenmen had displayed. Several of the slaves they had rescued were missing various body parts, with only the marks of fangs left in their place. No farmer tortured his animals for fun. Christopher's peasants did not eat their livestock alive.

No one answered him. The men were busy. Only the women had nothing to do, and they were too gray and ill to speak.

The army formed up and marched out, leaving only smoke and

ashes behind. They had thrown the headless bodies into the burning buildings. D'Kan had wanted to leave them for the alligators to feast on, but too many of Christopher's men remembered clicking skeletons in the dark. They preferred to kill their foes only once.

"My lord, I have a message. The Saint says he will meet you and your fallen at Fort Sump, three days hence," Disa told him as they rode away.

That would save a lot of time and trouble. Christopher smiled in satisfaction. Apparently his stone fort was now considered part of the Kingdom, a place safe enough for the Saint to visit. Only after a moment did he wonder how Disa had known the Saint was coming.

"The Saint spoke to me," she answered, "in my mind. A sending."

"Why not just talk directly to me?" Christopher asked, trying not to feel left out.

"Plausible deniability," Lalania explained. "When news of your latest outrage reaches court, he can honestly say he hasn't spoken to you."

"What outrage?" he asked, but Lalania shook her head.

"You commit outrages like a man commits adultery. There will always be another one to take the last one's place."

Christopher looked askance at her, surprised by her bitter tone. She held a boot against her saddle, frowning, scrubbing at it with a bit of cloth, trying to clean something off it. Blood.

He let it pass.

The cavalry rode with him on the long trek back to the edge of civilization. The draft horses followed in a herd, each one burdened by two or three dead bodies. Christopher and Karl were alone again, almost, like old times, if you ignored the grim horsemen that shielded them from every direction. The rest of the rank stayed in the swamp. Christopher was considered safe enough with the cavalry, as long as they kept moving.

"That cavalry tactic you did, Karl. It has a name." His memory had been jiggled and jogged over the days, and the word had come back to him. "A caracole. When the cavalry fires and withdraws to reload." If he recalled correctly, the otherwise brilliant king of Sweden, Gustavus Adolphus, had considered the tactic useless and ordered his cavalry to stick to the traditional lance charge, softened up by a single round of fire. But the Swedish cavalry had lame wheel-lock pistols, not revolving carbines. Also, the Swedish cavalry didn't fight giant man-eating dog-men.

"You should not call them cavalry," Karl said. "It will only confuse people, who will expect nobles with lances and plate mail."

"Carabineers, then." That couldn't confuse anyone, since from their perspective it was a made-up word.

"Good enough," Karl said. "Now that I have a word for it, it will be easier to hire more. You should have a hundred of them."

Christopher glanced over at Karl, questioningly.

"Between the chain mail and the carbine, they are the equal of a first-rank knight," Karl explained. "A man with a hundred knights at his back need not fear anything."

Except bankruptcy. Feeding that many horses was a challenge, let alone feeding the men. And their guns. The carbines ate powder like a man drank beer.

A stray fact came to Christopher. Lalania had said once that the King had a hundred knights. Christopher glanced at Karl again, but this time there was no explanation forthcoming.

The men of the previous fort had been very happy to see them, and very disappointed that they had stayed only a few minutes. Christopher looted their stores of barley and promised them a rotation soon. Whether they were nervous about sitting alone in the swamp or bored because they were missing all the action was impossible to tell. Maybe it was both.

Fort Sump was different. With stone walls, massive supplies, and a visiting Saint, it felt like civilization. Captain Steuben was there, along with a quartet of knights, the Saint's formal escort.

The Captain of the Wizard's Guard was also present. He appeared uncertain at first, but as he watched Christopher handing the Saint a ball of purple, he seemed to reach a decision.

"It is true, then, that you have won another great victory over the ulvenmen?" he asked Christopher.

"I suppose you could call it that," Christopher said.

"The Lord Wizard told me such. He also instructed me to discover the secret that allows common men to slaughter ulvenmen like dogs."

It wasn't that much of a secret. "Remember those rumors you heard? Well, they're true."

The Captain grimaced. "I deserved that, Lord Vicar. But my master has instructed me to swallow my tongue and apply to you for succor. He desires that I arm my men as yours are armed."

"You want to buy guns?" Christopher said, surprised.

"The Lord Wizard wishes to buy guns," the Captain corrected him. "I beg you recall your relationship with his lordship when you set the price, and forgive the clumsiness of his servant."

Christopher had wanted to sell to the lords, but he wasn't sure this was the one he wanted to start with. On the other hand it figured that the wizard would be an early adopter of technology. He had less to lose from the diminishment of the power of the sword.

And Christopher had promised him a chance to be on his side.

"Sure. I'll write you a letter to my shop master." The letter would say rifles only, at a hefty profit. No grenades, carbines, or cannons. Not yet. And he'd set a price for gunpowder that was high enough to discourage stockpiling. If push came to shove, Christopher could cut off the supply of ammunition and shut down the wizard's army in a matter of weeks.

The Captain seemed surprised at his easy victory. Perhaps he had expected Christopher to gloat over their reversal of roles. Or, more likely, expected to be robbed like he had robbed Christopher.

"Don't worry, Captain," Christopher said. "I'll be making a fortune off you."

"Off my Lord Wizard, you mean."

"Not really," Christopher said. "The guns are going to be expensive. You know your boss won't want to hear the details, so you're going to have to loosen up on the cut you take to pay for them all. I predict a tight purse for you for a while."

"Thank you for the advice, Lord Vicar." The Captain didn't sound very thankful.

"Look at the bright side," Christopher said. "When the ulvenmen attack again, you'll look like a genius for having bought guns."

"When?" the Saint asked. "Not if, but when?" He had listened so far without comment, but interrupted on this choice of word.

"Probably," Christopher said. "The supply of ulvenmen seems inexhaustible."

"We can kill many," Karl added. "But not all. Some will escape into the swamp, and in a generation or two they will return."

Christopher was uncomfortably reminded of his conversation with Friea. From the point of view of the ulvenmen, this must seem like a black harvest of its own.

The Saint was inspecting Christopher closely. "A thankless task, one that might drive any man to despair."

"No," Christopher said. "Not me. I have a wagonload of despair coming for you."

"If you can wait two more days, my lord Krellyan. They could not travel so fast." Karl took over explaining for him. "We rescued victims of the ulvenmen. The Colonel wants you to heal them, at his expense, as much as you are able. He has unlimited faith in your powers."

"And you do not?" the Saint asked Karl, with gentle irony.

"You have not seen them," Karl said flatly. "Even Torme blanched. Nothing this broken lives in our realm and calls itself human."

Christopher wasn't so sure Karl was right. Karl had never seen into the dungeons of the Gold Apostle. He imagined what kind of misery might live there, and seethed. But he could not reach the Apostle. Not yet.

The ulvenmen, on the other hand, had no one to protect them but themselves. And no one to blame, either.

They didn't leave Fort Sump right away. Christopher woke up the next morning to a dull, sporadic drumming. At first he thought it was the return of the ulvenmen, and he leapt out of bed faster than his feet and wound up on the floor.

He calmed down once he noticed the absence of gunfire. Threading his way through the fort, he found Cannan in front of a makeshift forge hammering away at a metal coat. Gregor was watching him dubiously.

Cannan lifted the coat to inspect it, and Christopher saw that it was made of overlapping scales mounted on a leather backing.

"Where did you get that from?" he asked.

"The last dinosaur rider," Gregor answered. "Ser Cannan wishes to dress like an ulvenman."

"Better than we," Cannan muttered, fiddling with the scales.

Christopher could see his point. After the last battle their chain mail had been reduced to rags. The scales looked somewhat hardier.

"Here, let me," he said, when Cannan returned the coat to his makeshift anvil, intent on welding a cracked scale. Reaching down to mend it with a spell, Christopher noticed with surprise that the scale was elaborately engraved. It seemed remarkable workmanship for the primitive conditions they had seen.

"This is fine work," he said. "Surely we can figure out who made it." The patterns would be like a signature, revealing which smith had labored so long over such an unusual item.

"It's no work of the north," Gregor said. "Not that any smith I know would even make such an odd design."

"The Rangers would," Cannan said. "They lack the forge-craft to make plate, and the coin to buy it."

When both Christopher and Gregor stared at him in concern, Cannan shrugged.

"Ask the boy."

Christopher called out, summoning his senior staff. One after another, Torme, D'Kan, and Karl examined the armor and declared it foreign to their respective areas, south, east, and west.

"That leaves nowhere," Christopher said.

"Nowhere but the center," Lalania announced. She stood outside the circle of men in a carefully idle pose, subtly castigating them for failing to have called on her expertise. "There are many smiths in Kingsrock. If you want to know where to buy fashion, you need but ask."

"What smith would hammer out a death sentence under the shadow of the King's own window?" Gregor asked. He held the coat in his arms, examining it from different angles.

"Perhaps he did not know for whom he toiled. The contract could have been placed through an intermediary—the same one who sold the ulvenmen human slaves."

Despite her words, Lalania's frown as she examined the armor told them her theory was untenable. She traced her hand over the leather backing, still smooth and supple.

"Does this not seem remarkably cared for to you?" she asked Gregor. "Soft leather in this swamp?"

Gregor's face revealed surprise as his eyes followed her finger to the detail he had overlooked. Christopher, who knew to the copper piece how much he spent on castor oil to keep his men's boots and saddles intact, was equally surprised.

Gregor bawled out a call for his wife. Lalania gave him a sour look. "So quickly have you forgotten my talents," she said, and Gregor went silent, his mouth trapped between apology and rebuke. Lalania ignored him and cast a spell.

Then she leapt back in surprise, her eyes wide. Gregor dropped the coat and stepped back hastily. Cannan, of course, drew his sword.

"What?" Christopher said, mostly because he understood almost nothing of what had just happened.

"It is enchanted," Lalania gasped.

Now Christopher stepped back, concerned. But for once Cannan's face almost betrayed a smile.

"And to think I doubted myself," the big knight said. "No wonder the beast-man stood so long against our swords."

"Indeed," Gregor agreed. "That does explain much. Lala, what rank?"

She concentrated, tracing patterns in the air with her finger. "All I can say for certain is that it is greater than first."

Having just destroyed an evil artifact, Christopher was deeply suspicious of stray magic items. The other men were not. They began to display acquisitive leers. D'Kan knelt to pick up the armor, frowning only at its weight.

"Is that safe?" Christopher asked.

"It did no harm to the ulvenman chieftain," D'Kan said. "And there is no shame in making use of the arms of the enemy where we can."

Karl took the armor from D'Kan. "Nonetheless we will ask the Saint to inspect it first."

"While he does that," Torme said, "how shall we share out the spoils?"

"Simple enough," Cannan replied. "Gregor and I will dice for it."

It made sense that one of the high-rank warriors would wear it, as they were always in the front line. Except, so was Christopher. He opened his mouth to object, but Torme was already speaking.

"Perhaps it will not come to that," Torme said. "Didn't we slay a dozen of those dinosaur riders just a season ago?"

"The scrap pile . . ." Christopher said, and everybody rushed outside.

The armor and weapons from the defeated ulvenmen had been tossed into a mound at the foot of the hill. Theoretically they were supposed to be carried by the empty supply wagons back to his forges in Knockford for recycling, but the draymen preferred to rest their horses on the journey home. They only took a load of scrap when Christopher remembered to remind them. Now the nobles dug through the pile with alacrity, searching for anything not rusted or rotted to ruin. Since a thick layer of filth lay over everything in the pile, it was not obvious which was mundane material or magically enhanced. Lalania repeated her spell, but it only ran for a few minutes, and the pile was four feet tall. Cannan began winnowing the coats with a pitchfork; anything that didn't come apart under the assault was carefully checked by Gregor and Torme.

By the time they reached the bottom they had recovered two more scale coats. The pile had once stood at least eight feet; there was no telling how many pieces of enchanted armor had gone into the forge unnoticed, to suffer the same fate as the ring. Lalania's theory of destroying magic items for immediate gain hardly seemed necessary anymore, given that he had been destroying them through simple ignorance, despite their unnatural hardiness.

The armor was far too broad across the shoulders for a human frame, and hung to the ground on everyone but Cannan. Gregor and Cannan took the suits back to the anvil and commenced to make alterations, cutting down the armor in length and breadth, and repairing what damage had been caused by rifle or grapeshot. Disa used her magic to rejoin the edges of the armor to its new, smaller shape.

Christopher went through the pile of discarded scales, mystified. He cast his own detection spell, so he could see the enchantment lying on the scales on the coat; as each scale dropped to the ground, its aura faded away. Yet when Gregor took a scale from the pile on the ground and used it to replace a broken scale still on the coat, the newly placed scale regained the aura. What, precisely, did the enchantment lie on, if it was not each individual part? He would have said the leather backing, but at one point Disa joined in a new panel, and the leather took on the same glow.

When they brought it inside for his inspection, the Saint studied the armor somewhat longer than Lalania had.

"It seems safe enough," he finally said. "A simple third-rank enchantment, with no surprises that I can detect. But its mere existence is surprise enough; there are few in the Kingdom who can do such work. I am one, but you need not ask; I assure you this is no enchantment of mine."

"The Gold Apostle is another," Lalania suggested.

Krellyan frowned at her. "Even I cannot casually inquire as to whether or not an Apostle has been arming the King's enemies."

Cannan shook his head. "You overthink this. Some adventurous party, from days of yore, wandered south, fell into a bog, and drowned. The ulvenman shaman, guided by magic, dug them up and handed out their gear to his loyal lieutenants. Indeed, the tael from their heads probably made him the chief shaman in the first place."

"Does that happen?" Christopher said. It seemed improbable to him.

"All the time," Gregor answered. "For that matter Baron Fairweather surely had a blade of rank on his person when he disappeared. Who knows what has become of it? Wandering out into the Wild to recover the treasure previous wanderers have lost is half an adventurer's life."

Perhaps no more improbable than the fact that he had almost

left the same treasure to rot in a scrap heap. In a hundred years the other metals would have wasted away, and some lucky sod would have stumbled over a fortune literally lying on the ground. How improbable would that seem?

"More to the point," Lalania said, "what else did the shaman uncover?"

Christopher thought about the wand of fire he had taken from Flayn and given to Fae.

Gregor shook his head. "It can't be anything too dramatic," he said. "Otherwise he would have already used it against us, back when we were kicking his ass the first time."

"You could break these like you did the ring," Lalania suggested. "They will yield less tael than that powerful enchantment, but your pocketbook will not complain."

"Or we could wear it, and fashion be damned," Cannan said, getting to the truth of her objection. "I do not fancy charging into an ulven camp wearing a nightshirt again."

"One for each us," Gregor agreed. "A few pieces from Kingsrock to round out the missing bits, and—with the strength of that enchantment—it will serve us better than plate."

Christopher, at a loss, looked to Karl for guidance. The young man nodded subtly, indicating his approval. Lalania gave them both an annoyed look but held her tongue.

"Okay, then," Christopher said. "But somebody needs to show me how to put it on."

17

A FORTIFYING MELODY

The combined tactics of caracole and overwhelming firepower served out Christopher's retribution on the inhuman slavers so effectively that the new armor was barely put to the test. The carabineers knew how to engage the ulvenmen with minimal losses now. Once they had located a camp, the infantry would push to envelope, cannons at the fore, rifles and carbines on the flanks. When they had exterminated all the camps within a day's march of their fort, they marched deeper and built a new one.

In two camps they freed more slaves. Three others were without, although D'Kan found evidence of human bones in them. The smallest camp had been to the west, so now they marched east, trying to find the center of the ulvenman realm. They had pushed as far as they could during the last three days, and pitched a tight, cold camp on a spot of slightly drier-than-usual ground. The plan was to march four days before building a fort, instead of three. It meant an extra night in the wild, unfortified, but Christopher's anxiety for the human slaves pushed him to reach farther, and his men agreed. Building a fort was two days they didn't spend killing ulvenmen.

There was an unusual amount of gunfire the night after their extended march, as sentries picked out spies or just movement in the bushes outside their perimeter. Perhaps they had surprised the ulvenmen by moving faster than usual. In the morning they broke camp, loading their supplies on wagons, saddling and hitching horses, and fell out in a long column, the carabineers ranging far ahead of the march under Gregor and D'Kan's guide.

In the middle of the day, when Christopher was thinking about lunch, he heard the muffled sounds of rifle fire far ahead. He hadn't sent a scout in the air yet, so he called out for a volunteer. Charles rushed to shout out his name, forgetting that Kennet was with the carabineers and thus, for once, not the automatic winner of any volunteer request.

Charles flew off, leaving the moving column behind in seconds, and returned in only seconds more.

Christopher wondered if the boy had forgotten something. Then he saw his face.

"Something's coming!" Charles shouted, over and over again, almost blubbering. The gunfire in the distance increased. Men up and down the column noticed.

"Report, soldier!" Christopher barked at Charles, trying to return him to sensibility.

"They're coming, Colonel. The ulvenmen are coming."

"How many?"

"All of them. And they bring night with them."

A rifle fired from the head of the column, followed by another.

"How long?" he asked Charles, and the boy trembled, seeking self-control.

"Minutes? Half an hour, maybe." The act of calculation seemed to calm him. "I saw a broad swath of movement, and something shrouded in darkness. Our horsemen flee before them. They will be here soon."

They would arrive exhausted and disordered, and possibly out of ammunition. And they would be followed by a horde. Already the edges of that flood were encountering Christopher's army, as the occasional shot showed. His men, sensing trouble, began to look around nervously.

He had to choose. Stand and fight, or retreat to the nearest fort. Neither option was tenable. The last fort was three and a half days behind them. Even if they abandoned their baggage, they could not travel faster than ulvenmen. And standing their ground without a wall would be suicidal if the entire ulven nation was truly on the march.

Lalania dismounted, skipping forward, bowing to Christopher as she passed him. "Now, my Lord Vicar, you will not regret the price you paid for me," she called out.

"What the— Lala, get back on your horse," he said to the woman, annoyed that she had chosen this moment to turn cryptic and strange. She ignored him, unsheathing her lyre as she ran forward.

"Sir, what do we do?" Charles asked. But Christopher was watching Lalania.

As the sound of her lyre floated over the jungle, white mist rose from the ground. Like he had seen in the chapel, the mist separated into figures vaguely man-shaped. This time there were many, many more. Lalania struck her notes forcefully, loudly, commanding them. They responded with a chant, low at first but gaining in volume as more and more figures appeared.

Suddenly the figures streamed toward the column, streaking to the supply wagons. Horses and men began to panic, but Christopher shouted them down.

"Hold your ground! Stand still and do not interfere!"

The misty figures flowed into the wagons. When they came out they were carrying tools: axes, shovels, hammers, and saws.

"Work!" sang Lalania.

"Ho!" called back the misty figures, their hollow voices resigned and resilient, the echo of common working men. The axes fell against trees; shovels bit into ground.

"Work!" sang Lalania, increasing the tempo.

"Ho!" they called back, matching her pace. The tools moved faster and faster until they blurred, the sound of metal biting wood turning into the static buzz of a chainsaw. Sawdust and dirt floated up from the ground over a hundred yards. Trees began to fall, and Lalania disappeared in the cloud.

"Work!"

"Ho!"

Her music continued unabated. Christopher forced his attention away from the spectacle.

"Guard the perimeter!" He didn't know if the ulvenmen could disrupt the process, whatever it was. He didn't want to find out the hard way.

Men ringed the cloudy area, shooting occasionally. The ulvenmen were like the foam of the surf, a trickle preceding the flood.

Shouts from the front. His horsemen were returning, their mounts lathered and steaming. They rode around the mysterious cloud, staring at it suspiciously. If it weren't for Lalania's voice coming faintly out of the center, he was sure they would have attacked it.

"What the dark is that?" Gregor called.

"Lalania," Christopher said, shrugging. "How long do we have?"

"Ten minutes, maybe less. Do we flee or fight?"

Christopher threw him a look. It was way too late to flee.

Cannan snorted. "He means, do *you* flee. Your army will buy you time. Your horse and magic will buy you ground. Rank can still flee this fight and live, Christopher."

"Do you want to go?" Christopher asked him.

Cannan looked at him, a level gaze that nonetheless suggested reproach. "My place is between you and death."

"We're not going to die here," Christopher said, stung by the well-deserved rebuke. He had only meant to ask Cannan's tactical advice, and instead managed to insult the man's courage. He looked again at the cloud. It seemed to be clearing a bit, and he could see no treetops peeking out from it. Meanwhile, the gunfire was becoming more frequent.

"Finish up, Lala," he called out.

The dust settled rapidly, leaving behind a magnificent fortification of wood and earth. A large double gate faced Christopher, swinging open by the efforts of two misty figures that sank into the ground as soon as their task was done. In the doorway Lalania bowed, smiling triumphantly and covered in leaves, dirt, and sawdust.

"Enter and be welcome, my lords," she said.

"You heard the lady," Gregor bawled. "Get your asses in there!"

The troops stampeded the fort, dragging wagons and horses after them. They poured onto the walls, throwing block and tackle onto the waiting frames, winching cannons into place. The fort was a clone of the plan they had been building to for the last few weeks. They knew the layout from memory, the defense through practice. Christopher could feel hope soaring.

"Could she always do that?" he asked Gregor.

Gregor was not amused. "Nobody can do that. Even your dark damned Lord Wizard can't do that. I have no idea what in the nine hells she did, and I don't think I want to know."

Lalania was not available to discuss the issue, being otherwise engaged. She was singing the morale-boosting song, the one that made everything seem possible despite all odds.

The last of the men dragged the gate closed behind them, lacing it shut with thick rope in place of bars. The gate was made out of layers and layers of the scraggly jungle trees, so well fitted and tightly bound that no gaps showed. It wasn't iron-bound timber. It would fail against a battering ram or siege engine. But against a horde of axe-wielding monsters, it would buy them sufficient time to empty their carbines and reload. That was enough.

Dead ulvenmen began piling up around the fort. New ones kept coming, a rising tide. Christopher went to join his command staff in the center of the fort. Their only job was to wait until the shaman appeared.

"Does anybody know why they are attacking during the day?" he asked.

Gregor had an answer. "They hoped to catch us on the march."

"But they failed. So why are they still coming?"

"The price of ill discipline," Gregor answered. "The charge has been sounded. If the shaman calls his horde off now, they will melt into the jungle and disappear. This is his one best shot."

"That means he is coming for you," Cannan said. "You must prepare."

Christopher nodded, agreeing. It felt odd to pray while standing, with a sword in his hands, but that was the way of a war god.

A general cry of dismay rose from the front of the fort, unchecked by the booming of cannons. Christopher glanced at his team. They squared their shoulders, drew their weapons, and followed Cannan to the forward wall.

After mounting the top, Christopher could see something out over the smoke-covered battlefield. It looked like night, as Charles had said, a patch of darkness moving purposefully toward the fort, towering over the scrubby trees.

The darkness also towered over his fort. Whatever it was had to be stopped before it breached the walls. Cannons fired into the darkness, as futilely as firing at a cloud. Karl's suspicion was borne out. The shaman had indeed prepared a surprise for them.

"Light-stones," Disa said. "Light-stones may counter the darkness." She went back to hiding behind the lip of the wall.

Immediately Gregor lunged forward, hurling the stone he carried. It fell short, bouncing off an ulvenman's head. The ulvenman snarled and gestured rudely. Christopher almost apologized out of habit, but then somebody shot the beast.

Cannan tossed a light-stone in his hand, weighing his chances against the range. D'Kan snatched it out of the air, bound it to an arrow with a bit of cloth, and shot it into the middle of the cloud.

The flickering light vanished in the dark.

Next the stone Gregor had thrown winked out as the darkness advanced over it, a seashell buried under the inrushing wave.

From the depths of the shadow came the inevitable lightning bolt. Christopher was already prepared. The bolt flared golden on his shield, while D'Kan and Cannan stood a safe distance away and returned fire with blazing carbines, aiming at the point of emergence. The darkness advanced unimpeded, and Christopher took an involuntary step backward.

The nearest cannon stood silent, its twitching crew held steady under Gregor's direction as he commanded them to wait for something to shoot at.

The range was now close, and Christopher had only a few seconds to act. He unleashed the spell of dissolution at the heart of the cloud, trying to dispel the dark magic.

The darkness failed, and Christopher almost wished it hadn't. A tower of festering, rotting flesh was revealed, with tiny forearms and a head the size of a Volkswagen. The monster roared, soundlessly, its vast fanged mouth opening like the Beltway Tunnel framed with stalagmite teeth. A foul wind swept out, leaving no doubt that the creature that came for him was already dead, had been dead for days. The shaman rode its shoulder like a sparkling parrot.

Gregor shouted his gun team into action, but the monster was quicker. It whipped its head to the side, smashing the gun platform into splinters of wood, flesh, and bone, snatched the cannon in its teeth and flung it across the fort.

Christopher held up his sword and chanted beautiful words in Celestial, the ones that had driven the soul-trapped abominations out of his chapel at Svengusta's side. He had not even known what he was doing then, as a lowly Pater, and it had worked. Now he was a priest of high rank.

Not high enough. Black and purple haze invaded his sight, crushing him to his knees with a backlash of evil. The light in his sword faltered and went out.

Another jagged, brilliant bolt. Christopher's shield burned out, leaving a few thousand volts to arc through him. Cannan stood ready nearby, his sword prepared to strike, but the monster and the shaman were out of his range. D'Kan was standing his ground, shoveling charges into his carbine. Gregor was bending down at the smashed gun port, presumably trying to heal the crew, but Christopher knew it was a waste of time. Mundane flesh and blood could not have survived that terrible blow.

The *Tyrannosaurus rex* turned its attention to Christopher, its beady eye sockets glowing purple. Christopher raised his sword in futile defense, scrambling to regain his feet. His earlier boasting now seemed amply punished: he did, in fact, fear the king of thunder.

Gregor threw a grenade over the wall, igniting the boxes of cannon ammunition he had been dumping. The explosion rattled the wooden wall like a wind chime. Christopher fell to the deck as the undead dinosaur collapsed to one side, unbalanced by the loss of a leg.

In its absence the shaman hovered in the air, hanging like a metallic Christmas ornament. Again golden lightning sparked from his fingers, reaching down to where Christopher lay helplessly.

Cannan charged across the wall, shoving Christopher out of the way like a hockey puck. The heroic act left no defense for the knight. Yellow fire burned through him, knocking him off the wall and into the bowels of the fort.

Christopher responded with his last spell of dissolution, aimed at the shaman, trying to undo his formidable defenses. The sparks of bullets bouncing off the invisible shield in front of the creature showed he had failed. But not completely. With a yowl of outrage the shaman fell from the sky, landing on the wall only a few feet away from Christopher.

The gold-and-silver-scaled ulvenman was shorter than Christopher had expected, no taller than a human being. He was armed with a glowing double-headed axe. Christopher smiled in grim satisfaction, clambered to his feet, and set his sword to glowing with its own killing light.

The shaman took the opportunity to cast a spell of his own. Apparently he felt embarrassed by his moderate stature. He sucked in a deep breath, blew out his cheeks until he turned purple, and began to swell, growing to twice his original height, a veritable giant now. His axe, already wickedly large, disconcertingly grew with him, becoming positively massive.

For crying out loud, Christopher thought. He lunged into the attack desperately, cutting down into one of the gigantic thighs. The ulvenman returned the favor, smashing Christopher with his oversized axe. Christopher flew backward and slammed against the wall, almost going over the top. If not for the thick scales of his coat, he would have been split in half.

Another blow like that would finish him, despite his armor and tael. He had no way of telling what unnatural life remained in the giant. Bullets still bounced off its invisible shield as men in the fort fired at it, and none of the cannon could be turned to face inside the wall. D'Kan must have been paying attention during the strategy lectures, because he had crept up behind the giant's shield. Furiously he emptied his carbine into the giant's back, every shot sparking on the metal scales. The giant leaned and swung awkwardly, stretching out with its axe in one hand to reach the Ranger. At the last second D'Kan backflipped out of the path of the deadly blade. It would have been a fantastically impressive feat if only he had pulled it off. His flip ended on his head rather than his feet, and he fell off the wall and into a watering trough.

Something touched Christopher on the back of the leg. Disa, white-faced, healing him. Growling, he threw himself back into the duel. Nobody was healing the shaman.

With a high downward stroke he tried to sever the leg he had cut before. The ulvenman parried with his axe, one-handed; with the other hand he reached out and shoved Christopher, sending him flying on his back like an adult pushing a child. The giant advanced in his wake. Now Disa was exposed to its wrath, crouching at its feet.

The ulvenman threw his shoulders back and roared. Golden scales splashed out in the wake of Gregor's sweeping blow as he cut into the ulvenman from behind. Christopher scrabbled forward on hands and knees, trying to shield the priestess. Distracted but not dissuaded, the ulvenman aimed at the soft target. As the axe came down Christopher got his sword in the way, turning the blow from the defenseless girl. The axe slashed into the walkway, flinging out splinters of wood as long as his arm. Christopher struggled desperately to his feet.

The giant raised a massive paw and stomped on the walkway, setting it quivering like a bowstring. Christopher fell again, clutching at anything to stop himself from falling over the edge. This was absurd; he would have to have a word with Lalania about the quality of her construction. Disa's hand found his, saving him, but the effort cost him his sword, which went spinning down into the fort. Gregor stumbled as well, dancing crazily. The ulvenman raised his axe to swing again, and Christopher shielded Disa with the only thing he had left. His body took the blow, crushing him against the girl, his scale mail parting under the force. Now he was only an inch from death, the unnatural vitality of his tael an empty memory. Gregor threw himself forward, sacrificing any chance of keeping his footing to bury his sword in the giant's back. Copious blood splashed in its wake, unstaunched by tael. The giant was also one stroke from death, if there were anyone to deliver it.

A helmet appeared on the walkway ladder. As it rose it revealed the bulky figure of Cannan, smoking, burned, and angry. With a deep-throated growl he swung his massive black blade through the giant's ankle, severing its paw. The monster fell, finally, onto Gregor, who grappled it around its massive head. Together they rolled off the wall, taking Cannan with them.

Christopher crawled forward and looked down. The giant was gone. In its place was the little ulvenman shaman, its neck twisted at an impossible angle, missing a foot, covered in golden scales and red blood. Cannan rose to his knees like a marionette on strings, violence still fueling his movements, and hewed its head off for good measure. He raised his sword again, preparing to mince the body, but finally ran out of steam, collapsing to the ground in a heap.

Gregor leapt forward and touched the fallen knight, speaking a healing spell.

"He lives," Gregor said. "Where is my wife?"

Disa clambered down the ladder and bent over Cannan. Gregor crawled up, handing Christopher his lost sword.

"You might want to hang onto this," he said.

"I was hanging onto Disa," Christopher replied. "How much healing do you need?"

"Not as much as you. Recall that Cannan and I are knights first, Christopher. Though we are not your equal in rank, we are harder to kill. And easier to replace."

That reminded him. He leaned out to make sure someone pulled D'Kan from the trough before the Ranger drowned.

Christopher spent the rest of his spells undoing the damage the shaman had inflicted on his flesh and his armor. He did not save healing for his army. That was what the priestesses were for.

The ulvenmen continued to fight with savage fury for the rest of the day, but the outcome was already decided, despite the staggering numbers that poured out of the woods. Their attack was spirited but unorganized. They had not prepared for the fort, and even its simple dirt-reinforced wood walls were too much for them. Most of them seemed unprepared for any battle, armed with sticks, stones, and scavenged weapons. Many of the little doglike creatures fought too, scrabbling up the walls or being thrown over the top by the larger ulvenmen. All of them died in waves while Christopher watched, trying to estimate when his men would run out of ammunition.

Paradoxically, nightfall ended the battle. Restored to their senses by the comforting dark, the ulvenmen slunk away, and quiet reigned, save for the roaring in his ears from so many guns.

The cost of the battle was surprisingly low. Christopher was unnerved to realize he was measuring lives in terms of the tael it took to restore them. This was not a perfect equation: three of the previous batch of casualties had remained corpses. The failure rate was highest among the mercenaries. Men who had already fought for a lifetime were perhaps disillusioned enough to not want to return to more war.

Christopher sympathized with them. Only the promise of seeing his wife again had brought him back. Or so it would seem: Christopher could not remember his own death, or being dead, even though Krellyan had carried on a brief conversation with him. Or possibly with a seeming of him, like the shade of Stephen he had talked to under the hanging tree. It was a complicated bit of theology that no one seemed to understand very well. In any case, Krellyan had employed the lure of his wife to drag him back to this world, with its blood and noise and endless porridge.

For men used up and cast aside by this cruel feudal system, there might not be a strong enough line. Captain Steuben remained impressed at how many did return, even while Christopher felt the loss of every single one. The man he had plucked out of the ulvenman's fire pit was one of the returned, which was a real comfort. On the other hand, one of the permanently dead had been raised once before, which was mystifying. Who would come back once, but not twice?

Ruminating on that mystery was considerably more pleasant than facing the fact at hand, which was that he owed this particular victory, including his life and arguably the tael from the battle, to Lalania. Her magic had turned disaster into triumph, a triumph measurable by the fat rock of purple in his hand. The shaman had yielded a fantastic prize, equal to the cost of making a viscount out of a commoner, yet its tael was only a shard of the stone drawn from four thousand dead ulvenmen.

The destruction of the ulvenman horde had made Christopher fabulously wealthy again. Assuming he, rather than Lalania, owned the reward. With a little trepidation he brought his council together to discuss the issue.

Karl dismissed it instantly. "Your army did the killing. And in any case, the minstrel is your sworn servant. You need not pay her by the spell."

"It would be a princely fee for a single performance," Lalania agreed. She was still very satisfied with herself. "Nonetheless if you offered me a rank or two, I would not turn it down."

"There are better things to spend this on than pretty girls," Cannan growled. "Christopher must take another rank."

"I concur," Karl said. Christopher understood their reasons. Both of them stood to gain only if he achieved his goals. He wasn't so sure why everybody else was nodding in agreement, though.

Gregor offered an explanation aimed at Lalania. "He'll need all the rank he can get when the King finds out you two have stolen from him."

"I did not steal anything," Lalania huffed. "I do not *steal*. I took what was mine, with the King's permission. Christopher is my undoubtable witness to that. The White cannot lie."

"Actually, it's not quite that straightforward," Disa said, visibly alarmed at Lalania's words. "What is this talk of theft?"

"We took that lyre out of the castle," Christopher recalled. "The King gave Lala permission to fetch her lyre, but I don't think that's quite what he meant."

"It is mine," Lalania declared. "It belongs to the College. It has belonged to us since the day Varelous handed it to his daughter. It has remained ours for all the years kings have kept it locked in Kingsrock. Every Skald for three generations has sworn that the lyre belongs to any bard with the wit and nerve to reclaim it. The lyre is mine, by every legal right."

"The King won't see it that way," Gregor said, rather dryly.

"Then I suggest you do not be the one to tell him," she snapped.

"Why was it there in the first place?" Christopher asked.

"To defend the city," Gregor explained. "You have seen the effects firsthand; as you can imagine, such magic would void the efforts of many siege engines."

"When was the last time a trebuchet threatened Kingsrock?" Lalania argued. "In any case, the College would not fail to defend the capital."

"Assuming the bard who held it were present. Or on the King's side. Or still alive." Gregor turned to Christopher. "I suspect the reasoning was that leaving such an artifact in the hands of adventurous young women would only lead to its being lost or damaged."

"So to protect it, they lock it away where it does no one any good at all," Lalania objected. "Can you not imagine what the Lyre of Varelous could do for the realm?"

"It could bankrupt a lot of carpenters," Christopher mused aloud. "I'm not sure that's a good thing."

"It could build a lot of roads," Lalania said. "Roads you build to the profit of the realm, but at only expense to yourself."

That was a good point. He didn't get to collect tolls on the roads he paved, but he still had to build them to support his army in the field.

"Just how many roads?" he asked, imagining four-lane highways stretching from one edge of the realm to another.

"It will be a week before the magic recharges," she said. "It is only a minor artifact, not the harp of the gods."

Karl shook his head dismissively. "We can build roads at our leisure. Creating forts on demand is rather more valuable. Eventually the King will hear of this, and ask for his property back, and Christopher must have enough rank to say no."

"I also concur," Torme said. "Every rank you gain puts you further from the reach of the Dark."

Christopher looked at D'Kan, the only member of the group who hadn't spoken yet.

"I care not," the Ranger said. "My only proviso is this: if you promote *him*"—and he jabbed his finger at Cannan—"then you must promote me."

"He will promote who he wills," Karl automatically objected.

"You need not worry, boy," Cannan said. "He will never promote me."

The two men glared at each other, D'Kan fiercely and Cannan with distant impassivity.

"I have another reason," Disa said cautiously. "If you promote yourself, you will be able to do sendings, instead of waiting for someone to contact you."

It was a compelling argument. A new rank would open new levels of magic to him. The attraction was perverse. The more his industrial empire grew and his technology improved, the more he became dependent on the power of magic.

And, of course, his ultimate goal involved staggering rank. He had finally studied the Cardinal's books. The spell that would take him home could only be cast by a Prophet. Nine ranks did not sound so far from six, but the cost of every step doubled. He would need to destroy six more ulvenman hordes to earn his ticket home, assuming there were even that many left. The impossibility of the task was daunting. Sometimes he pretended that his industrial empire would earn him enough gold to buy the rank; other times he imagined the wealth he would extract from the Gold Apostle's head. Mostly he dealt with it the same way people dealt with their mortgage, by simply not doing the math.

And in any case it seemed like a terrible price to extract from this world just to leave it. He would need to leave something behind that was worth the cost. An honest and stable government, the knowledge of not just firearms but democracy and equality, a world in which men did not die before the age of nineteen: these were the only things he had to give. Giving them would involve taking away some things, like feudal privilege, from the people currently in power. Doing that would require rank.

He sighed, defeated by circumstances. The only path to fairness that he could see required him to take all the profit from the labor of others. It was too convenient.

"There will still be plenty left over," he said.

Cannan shrugged, unconcerned. "There are still ulvenmen to kill. Only the brave died today. The weak and the cowardly remain to be seen to."

18

YOUNG MEN AND OLD DOGS

The remaining ulvenmen did not seem to know they were weaklings and cowards. At each village they were unreasonably surprised to see Christopher's troops emerging from the woods, but they fought with unbridled fury, and now always to the death, with almost no thought of retreat. Their resilience forced Christopher and his armored swordsmen into every battle; their reckless charges cost him a few men each time, a price he was willing to pay since it was reimbursed. In any case, by the third death the men usually stopped dying. The chief cause of death was fear, after all: freezing or fleeing in the face of slavering fangs. The men who stood their ground and calmly aimed and shot tended to survive. Christopher reckoned that at some point his entire army would consist of thrice-raised men, tallow boys transformed into tin soldiers by the Saint's magic.

If only he could use the same magic on himself. Outwardly he appeared a clockwork doll of destruction, a metal-scaled windup toy with a scything blade. But the steel was only skin-deep; inwardly, he quivered like a sponge.

He went into each battle terrified of the surprise or ambush that would kill him, lain by whatever new shaman had emerged from the shadow of the high rank he had killed. He left each battle exhausted with the trembling rage every slave hut and cooking pit bone pile ignited inside him. Emotionally he tried to become a machine that dispensed vengeance without reflection. It worked, for a while.

Eventually his analytic mind reasserted itself. The facts that flickered around his consciousness thickened until he could not ignore them. Wandering through a defeated camp, overseeing his men as they dispatched the wounded and took heads, he stumbled across a scene his tattered denial could no longer mask.

One of his soldiers held a hissing, spitting dog-thing, smaller than usual. The man laughed as it snapped and bit at him, displaying the antics of the creature for the amusement of a small group of soldiers who watched him with mixed expressions.

Christopher, disgusted at this petty cruelty, strode over and cuffed the man behind the ear with a mailed fist. The man staggered, dropping the doglike animal to flop a few feet away but unable to flee on its broken legs.

"Just kill the damn thing," he growled. Drawing his sword, he raised to strike, when motion caught the corner of his eye.

An ulvenman lying close by, wounded but not yet dead, stretched out a paw and whimpered. But not for mercy or vengeance; its attention was not upon Christopher. The ulvenman was reaching for the dog.

In that moment truth came crashing in, flooding over the barriers of his rage and drowning righteous fire in cold, sad horror. The world tilted and spun, although nothing moved at all, and in an instant the scene before him was cast anew, though nothing had changed.

The dog-sized creatures were not animals. They were children. The ulvenman before him was not just a vicious, man-eating beast. It was a mother.

His sword slipped from his paralyzed hands and fell to the earth.

The soldier, rendered insensitive either by constant battle or Christopher's lax discipline, grumbled.

"Just a bit of sport, sir. You didn't have to hit me unawares."

Christopher's rage boiled over, escaping from him in hyperventilating bursts of breath.

Someone else, not so foolish, moved quietly into view, shielding the soldier. Christopher could not make out his face through the red flare in his vision. Christopher stepped over to one of the silent, gaping watchers and forcefully took his rifle. He spun on his heel, stepped over the dying ulvenman, and leveled the barrel at its head. It ignored him, staring only at the pup. He pulled the trigger with all of the mercy left in his body.

Automatically he broke open the rifle, ignoring the blood spattered across his legs. Someone, somewhere, said something he could not hear through the blood pounding in his ears.

"We are not savages!" Christopher screamed in response. Or perhaps in denial. "We must kill, but we do not torture!"

The interloper stood up from where he had knelt over the pup. The small creature was still, its throat slashed in barbaric mercy. Christopher recognized the man's face. Karl, severe and grim.

Karl turned to the soldier, advanced with the bloody knife, and slashed the stripes from the man's shoulders. He knocked the rifle out of his hands, letting it fall discarded to the ground.

"You are dismissed," Karl said.

Shocked, the soldier looked over his shoulder to the hostile swampland. He opened his mouth to argue, but Christopher cut him off.

"Get out! Get the dark out of my army, you filthy animal. Go!"

The soldier stepped back, pressed by the gale force of Christopher's anger. "But—"

Christopher turned to the soldier whose rifle he had taken. "Give me another round."

Silence descended over the camp. The soldier dared to glance aside, no doubt looking to Karl for help. What he saw could not have comforted him. Slowly, clumsily, he began to extract a paper cartridge from the box at his hip.

"It takes twelve seconds to load a rifle," Karl said to the doomed fool, his tone jarringly conversational. "I suggest you begin running now."

"But—"

Karl shrugged.

The man bolted, running for the tree line, sobbing and cursing.

Christopher fumbled with the gun. He didn't have a lot of practice loading them. He hardly ever touched one. And something was wrong with his eyes; the world was blurred into broad swatches of color, all detail gone, though the ugliness still remained.

He stopped, closed his eyes, and concentrated on breathing. When he was calmer, he opened his eyes and finished charging the weapon. Looking up from his task, he saw no sign of the target of his ire. Wordlessly he handed the rifle back to the man he had taken it from.

He collected his sword from the ground and walked away with it in hand, unable to trust himself to any more complex action. There was no danger of accidental damage from the bared blade; his men kept their distance.

His anger protected him the remainder of the day, on the long march back to their fort, while he dismounted and stabled his horse, even through a tasteless dinner. Only after the sun had long sunk and the jungle made its night music did righteousness desert him. He sent for Karl, intent on reversing the doom he had meted out.

Karl refused him.

"No," the young soldier said. "You cannot change your mind now. It would destroy all discipline. What soldier would obey a hard order if they thought you might rescind it but given a little time?"

"He'll die," Christopher said. "Sending him out alone and unarmed into that swamp is a death sentence." A permanent one, since the body would likely never be found.

Karl shrugged, the same movement he had made in answer to the miscreant's argument.

"It was my fault," Christopher argued. "I shouldn't have lost my temper."

"You are wrong," Karl said. "They need to love you, but they must also fear you."

"It has to stop. That kind of behavior cannot be tolerated. They can't do that, Karl. I can't let them."

"I assure you, Colonel. You will not see such mischief again."

Something in Karl's choice of words troubled Christopher.

"I won't see it . . . not that it won't happen? Is that what you're telling me?"

Karl almost shrugged again, but Christopher's piercing glare would not be evaded.

"Soldiers are creatures of violence," Karl said. "They necessarily deal in pain and death."

"Hardly any of them are soldiers," Christopher objected. "They're just farm boys with guns."

"Farmers are hardly any more gentle. To scratch a living out of tears and dirt leaves little in the way of sympathy. The cow that nursed your infant child is sent to the butcher the first day her milk fails.

"And you must remember," Karl added before Christopher could respond, "they are from a White county, but they are not White. Many find your doctrine almost as incomprehensible as that of the Black."

The vast bulk of Christopher's army was Green. Karl himself was Blue. Only the priests had to be White; there could be as few as seven people in the entire army who would put any intrinsic value on the rights of others, particularly when those others weren't human.

"But I can't allow it." Regardless of the morality of his men, he was the one in charge.

"You do not allow it. You do everything in your power to prevent it. Nonetheless, it may occur. And I will deal with it before you find out."

"You'll tell me, then?" Christopher asked, but Karl wasn't nodding in agreement. "How many other times has this already happened?"

"You ask, so I can refuse. But do not order me to tell you, because I will not. If the men see that I tattle every event to you, then they will stop telling me. And at least one of us has to know what is actually going on."

"Wait a minute," Christopher said. "I can't do this. I can't sit here, knowing that I don't know what crimes my men are committing, and go on as if nothing were wrong."

"Then disband the army," Karl barked.

Christopher gawked at him, surprised by the harshness of his tone.

"I can't do that, either," Christopher sighed. His moral duty to the slaves of the ulvenmen was only one of many reasons.

"The cynic says, 'White won't stay White long on a battlefield,'" Karl said. "But I and the men will do everything in our power to prove it wrong. We will shield you from the blood and bile with our bodies and our souls. Because you are our only hope. Your purity is the shelter that covers our kith and kin. Your dream of utopia is the only dream we have."

It wasn't utopia he was after. Even Christopher wasn't that optimistic. All he wanted was to make things better, not perfect. But from the perspective of the peasants, the luxuries and rights common Americans took for granted was a fairy tale. From the perspective of oppressed serfs like Torme had been, it was even less believable.

"Is it your dream too?" he asked Karl. "Do you think we can make a better world?"

Karl almost smiled. "I believe you believe it."

At the next ulvenman camp Christopher annoyed his soldiers by ordering them to hold their fire. His new rank had given him new magic, and now he could cast the spell that Krellyan had used to talk to him when he had first stumbled through the Saint's door. For a brief time he could extend his magical grasp of language to cover all spoken tongues. It was not as useful an effect as one might suppose, since the entire Kingdom spoke the same language except when casting spells.

But in this case it allowed him to treat with the ulvenmen. He dismounted and walked forward while Royal snuffled in loud disapproval. He suspected the rest of the army felt the same way, but apparently they had better manners than the horse.

The howls and barks from the camp ahead of him resolved into words and sentences. The transformation was not particularly enlightening: mostly the ulvenmen seemed to be working themselves into a battle frenzy by trash-talking. "I kill many and feast on brains!" and that kind of thing.

"Attention!" he shouted. Or at least he tried to; what came out was a short, savage bark. When it had no effect, he moved closer and shouted louder.

Finally an ulvenman stuck its head out from around a hut and answered him. "Be silent, man-pup. The warriors are speaking."

Not quite the response he expected, but he soldiered on. "I have come to speak to the warriors. Instruct them to attend to my words." The spell translated his meaning into the appropriate idiom for his audience, which in the ulvenman case seemed both formal and blunt.

The ulvenman laughed at him. "You will be eaten first for your presumption." Its head disappeared back behind the hut, and after a moment the noise from the camp subsided into a conversation Christopher could not overhear.

A few more ulvenman heads popped out, inspected him, and disappeared again, followed by urgent whispering.

"Ahem," Christopher said.

The sounds of a brief struggle, and the ulvenman was shoved into view again. Like a dog it tried to turn tail and run, only to be blocked by a harsh bark.

Reluctantly the ulvenman faced Christopher. "The warriors wish you to instruct me with your words. I will then carry your words to the warriors."

"Tell the warriors to come out and speak to me directly."

The ulvenman stood patiently, scratching its ear with a long-fingered paw.

"Why do you not do as I request?" Christopher demanded.

"Is that the entirety of your words?" it asked.

"No, of course not. I wish to deliver my words directly to the warriors."

The ulvenman suddenly flopped down on its haunches to scratch more vigorously at its ear with its larger, stubby-toed foot. When it was satisfied it stood up and addressed Christopher again.

"The warriors wish you to instruct me with your words."

Christopher growled in his throat. The spell did not need to translate this universal sign of exasperation. The ulvenman grimaced, which on its long snout came out more like a hyena's smile.

"Understand, you are over there, but the warriors are over here. If you came over here then you would be closer than the warriors, and I would do what you say."

"You could come over here," Christopher said.

Another hyena smile.

"That is not a good idea."

Christopher could tell that other ulvenmen were watching him. He could feel the pressure of their gaze, peeking out from the straw-and-mud huts and possibly even the long grass.

"Tell the warriors blarrguuhhhh," he said. It didn't come out as intended because halfway through his sentence someone shot him in the throat with an arrow, neatly bypassing all of his magical, heavy armor.

A larger, more impressive ulvenman stood up from the grass, bow in hand. "The god-man is silenced!" it shouted. "*Attack!*"

It was most disturbing. Although the arrow did not threaten his life, thanks to his tael, it still prevented him from speaking in any intelligible manner. He could taste blood and iron in the back of his throat every time he exhaled a breath. As ulvenmen burst out from the huts and up from the grass, he marveled at how close they had crept during the brief conversation.

Then he began to feel fear. He was out in front of his army, alone, on foot, and unable to cast spells. The monsters could quite conceivably overwhelm him and pull him down. If they dragged him into their camp, they could gnaw on him till his tael failed and then quite possibly eat him before his army could rescue his corpse. Or, worse, throw him into the fire.

The ulvenman he had been talking to was dancing with glee at his predicament. When it caught him staring, it threw back its head and barked in mocking laughter.

Then somebody shot it.

From behind Christopher came the sound of thunder, followed by a rolling cloud of sulfurous stench. Ulvenmen fell before him, but not all of them died. Christopher tore the arrow from his throat, his tael blocking the agonizing pain that would have dropped him like a sack of potatoes and sealing the gash in his arteries that would have bled him out in seconds, but he still could not speak. The flesh was intact but not entirely functional.

Automatically he tried to cast a healing spell. But that required speaking. He started running instead, turning his back on the ulvenmen and lumbering through the grass. He didn't have to outrun the ulvenmen. He just had to give his army time to reload.

He didn't quite make it. Something plowed into his back, and he went facedown into the dirt. Claws scrabbled at his neck for a moment while he struggled ineffectually. He had not cast the strength spell before this battle. Now he was pinned underneath several hundred pounds of rabid dog-man.

The claws stopped grasping, and Christopher's danger was reduced to ignominious suffocation. Before that sorry fate claimed him, the dead weight was dragged free.

Gregor extended his hand and helped Christopher to his feet. The knight-priest touched Christopher's throat and cast a minor healing.

"Thank you," Christopher said, trying not to be too humiliated.

"It was a good effort." Gregor patted Christopher on the shoulder. "I don't know that I would have been so trusting, but that's why I'm not head of our Church. I'm learning from you. Now pray tell me the lesson is over."

Christopher thought of the cooking pits, and what he was likely to find inside this camp.

"It is for today," he said, and drew his sword.

Another camp, another day, and again Christopher tried to parley, but this time he did it from atop his horse with bared blade.

"Send out your slaves!" he demanded. The ulvenmen barked at him, so he had a cannon blow up a hut.

There was a commotion in the camp, but the ulvenmen didn't swarm out and attack immediately.

"And if they do send out their slaves, then what?" Torme asked him.

"I don't know," Christopher said. "Do you have any ideas?" Gregor and Torme were servants of Marcius, too. They should be figuring this stuff out as much as he was.

Torme looked over his shoulder to the rear lines where the young priestesses waited to begin their healing. "I begin to see the attraction of the pacifism of the Bright Lady," he said.

Disa and the other priestesses had refused to even discuss the issue with Christopher. "The hand that wields the blade must choose the cut," she had told him. "This is between you and your Patron."

Christopher didn't rebuke Torme. He felt a similar regret. But once he had picked up a sword, there had never seemed to be a chance to lay it down.

An ulvenman sauntered out of the camp bearing a large sack. Christopher held up his hand to still his army's impulse to shoot everything that moved. The ulvenman didn't walk in a very straight line, but eventually it got within a few yards of Christopher.

"That's close enough," Christopher said. "But I don't want tribute. I want your slaves."

The ulvenman nodded vigorously and upended the sack.

Human heads rolled onto the ground, bloody and fresh.

Christopher's horror was blocked by sheer confoundedness. Out of simple shock he said, "Where is the rest of them?"

"We brought you the heads, undrained, as you demanded," the ulvenman said, clearly irritated at his question. "But there is no sense in wasting good meat."

Utterly defeated, Christopher banged his head on his horse's thick neck.

"Colonel?" said Karl, looking for instruction. Christopher waved his free hand at the direction of the camp. This was sufficient for the army, and gunfire began in earnest.

Once the artillery realized they did not have to worry about collateral damage, they systematically obliterated every structure in the camp before the infantry advanced. Consequently this camp had cost the army not even a single casualty, which pleased Karl immensely.

"What about the slaves?" Christopher asked, but Karl shook his head.

"I would rather destroy slavery than free a handful of slaves," he said, and Christopher could not argue. In any case, the fault was Christopher's alone.

The next time he gave the ulvenmen a chance to send their women and children away to safety. His army grumbled at seeing so much tael escape, and grumbled even more at having to take the camp hut by hut instead of shelling it into rubble, but they accepted the price after taking the slaves alive. Christopher enjoyed a bit of pride, handing out I-told-you-so looks for free. D'Kan rolled his eyes at such sensitivity to monsters. Two days later they came across another camp, and D'Kan paid him back in spades.

This camp had refused to send away their dependents, and after the battle D'Kan had an explanation. In the cooking pits he found many fresh ulvenman skulls, large and small.

The women and children from the last camp had sought refuge here, and had been eaten instead.

"It is to be expected," D'Kan said. "They can barely feed themselves, let alone scores of mouths that cannot fight or hunt. No doubt they took a selection of the youngest females, and tossed their old ones into the pot. And of course the tael from those sacrifices accounts for why this camp had so many ranked warriors."

Christopher almost turned his army around and went home. He knew that if he let himself hate the ulvenmen for no worse a crime than being ulvenmen, he would not remain White for terribly long. Yet the perfidy of the beasts was indefatigable.

"Is there no other option than genocide?" he asked, not expecting an answer.

"This is not extermination," D'Kan said, "merely culling. I assure you that some sneak through our fingers to hide in the swamp until we leave. In a generation all will be as before, and in need of pruning again."

Christopher stared at the Ranger in horror. What was the difference between the *hjerne-spica* and what he was doing?

"Not quite the same," Lalania said, reacting to Christopher's palpable dread. "If we are thorough and exacting, they will learn not to take human slaves."

"Perhaps we should stop the misery at its source," Gregor mused. "The King ordered you to solve the problem once and for all; would not a final battle be more merciful than this endless suffering?"

D'Kan turned to the knight with his own horrified expression. "Obliterate their entire race? Solely for your convenience? I thought the White prided itself on stringent morality."

"I'm just saying," Gregor said, embarrassed.

"You're okay with us killing any individual ulvenman, but if we kill all the ulvenmen you have a problem with that?" Christopher asked the Ranger.

"Death is a part of life. The ulvenmen certainly understand that. But to exterminate an entire race is a crime against nature. Surely you theologians can understand that."

It was a valid point of view, if you didn't think personal rights were terribly important.

"In any case," D'Kan added, "if there were no ulvenmen, something else would move in. Who knows what horrors they hold at bay? And not only by force of arms. If a dragon thinks of this swamp as its larder, and we denude it, then perhaps it will transfer its attention to us. For this reason alone you should continue to cast a loose net and let some fish escape."

"Can I make a truce with them?" Christopher asked Lalania. "Can we at least have a peaceful border?"

The minstrel shrugged, always unhappy at having to admit ignorance. "I don't know. Absent some form of centralized authority, the best you can do is terrorize the entire population into fearing humans." She was graceful enough to not point out that Christopher was responsible for that absence.

"You think too highly of yourself if you think you could have made a treaty with the shaman," Karl said to her. "He would only seek to lull us into carelessness."

"More to the point," Torme said, "the manner in which the shaman would have enforced a treaty is precisely the kind of violence you are trying to avoid."

Christopher turned to face his expert on the methods of

madness. "So either we kill the ulvenmen, or the ulvenmen do it themselves?"

"Yes," Torme said. "And left to their own, the ulvenmen would kill humans as well, and worse. At least under our hand they die quickly."

From the faces of his council, Christopher could see that logic was sufficient for them.

"Then we will do it D'Kan's way," he said. "Do not pursue the ones who flee."

"But those are the cowards," Gregor objected. "You will create a nation of weaklings."

"No, I'll create a nation of ulvenmen smart enough to run away from people with guns. And maybe, someday, they'll be smart enough to make peace."

Thin gruel for his starving conscience, but there was nothing else on the table.

Christopher changed tactics for the next battle. He did not fully surround the camp, instead leaving one side open. Then he addressed the ulvenmen.

"Any ulvenman don't wanna get killed better clear on out the back. And leave the slaves."

Unsurprisingly, it had little effect on the outcome. Most of the ulvenmen preferred fighting and dying to running. Christopher found this mystifying, given that the jungle seemed like an easy place for a giant dog-man to make a living. He had to remind himself that they weren't human beings. They clearly had a different set of values. Indeed, the chief source of dissatisfaction among the ulvenmen seemed not to be dying, but dying futilely. When they were engaged in hand-to-hand combat they fought with savage glee and excited barks even while they were being cut to ribbons. But most of the time Christopher's men shot them down at range, and the howls of outrage were heartbreaking to hear.

Sympathy drove him forward, into the thick of battle. Gregor followed his lead, perhaps eager to release the flame that seemed to drive him in combat. Cannan, of course, required no excuse for reckless assault. Together they swept through the ulvenmen like a lawnmower through grass. The faces of his targets were obscured by his helmet and his rage, rendering them impersonal objects to be struck. The speed of the horse carried him past the damage he caused before he had to see its effect.

Afterward Disa put them back together again. Christopher did little healing these days, spending his magic to make his swordsmen even more supernaturally enhanced than they already were. The effects of his spells were only temporary, so choosing the time and place of battle was necessary to maximize their impact. Gregor's comments about the stupidity of waiting to be attacked made sense now.

His men seemed heartened by his bloody role, looking at him with awe and perhaps pride, even while Karl objected.

"Do not expose yourself too much," he said. "There may yet be surprises left in store."

"Wise advice," D'Kan agreed. This kind of full-frontal warfare was not what he considered strategy. Unlike the knights, he had been trained to strike and withdraw, choosing targets after careful consideration. "And in fact we may have found one for you."

The Ranger led Christopher and his command party out of the open edge of the camp. A hundred yards beyond the camp lay a curious sight.

An old ulvenman, the oldest Christopher had ever seen, gray-muzzled and hunch-backed, was tied to a stake in the ground by a long rope, looking for all the world like a dog on a leash. He—or it; Christopher hadn't figured out how to tell the difference between males and females—was unarmed. Which also meant naked, since the ulvenmen only seemed to wear armor, never clothing.

Intrigued, Christopher dismounted, but D'Kan paused him.

"Ware, my lord. I cannot see any trap or ambush, which implies that the danger is magical." The young man had a pretty high opinion of his abilities.

"I will go first, then," Cannan said. He leapt from his horse, strode up to the ulvenman without hesitation, and tapped it lightly on the forehead. Christopher couldn't decide if this reflected an equally high opinion of his own indestructibility, or perhaps merely a low opinion of the value of his own self-preservation. Most likely it just reflected a desire to upstage D'Kan.

The ulvenman yipped and tried to bite the hand that touched it. Christopher could see from its reactions that it was completely blind. And all but toothless.

"Nonetheless," Lalania said, "do please cast some kind of detection."

He didn't have much left, but on the chance it would reveal something, he cast the aura spell. Perhaps to a dual purpose: he was relieved to see that Cannan remained the Blue he had been in the Cathedral. Their late orgy of violence had not shaken the man's moral development. Christopher really wanted to examine himself, but the spell was not capable of that. His only clue to his status was that his avatar continued to grant him spells every morning.

He blinked, and stared again. The glow around the ulvenman was clearly green. Pale, shot through with streaks of red and blinking motes of yellow, but still green. There would be men in his own army who would be no better. Or even worse.

He looked away to clear his sight. Also, unwittingly, to spy on his comrades. Gregor's White burned even brighter than Torme's. Karl's Blue seemed softer than he remembered. Lalania subtly gave him a gesture that could only be interpreted as unspeakably rude. Embarrassed to be caught in the metaphysical equivalent of eavesdropping, he forced his attention back to the scene.

"It's Green," he told Lalania. "How is that possible?" The behavior of all the ulvenmen he had encountered had been solidly in the camp of violence for violence's sake, a hallmark of Red or even Black.

"It's staked out like bait, so I'm not sure its moral status has any relevance to the status of ulvenmen at large," she answered.

His one concession to conscience had been to keep the translation spell in memory in case it could be of use, even though it meant one less spell to bolster his killing machine. Now he felt vindicated. A tiny, tiny bit, but every drop counted these days.

He came forward and addressed it in the most respectable terms the ulvenman language would allow him.

"Toothless one, why are you left out as an offering to wild animals?"

The ulvenman sniffed the air once, in Christopher's direction.

"You speak with authority, cub of man. Are you the god-man who leads the fire-stick horde?"

It was always interesting to hear one's self described by others. "I am."

"Then I am left as an offering to you. The chieftain said no more food could be wasted on a useless storyteller, and the god-man likes to talk, and so here I am."

"Your chieftain is dead," Christopher said. "He cannot deny you food anymore." It wasn't quite the words he had meant to say, but the intent was close enough.

"The joke is on you," the old ulvenman replied. "I die soon. Even when the females chew my food twice I can no longer keep it down. You will get no stories from me."

"I only want one story. Tell me how to forbid the ulvenmen from killing men."

It barked, mockingly.

"Send us home. Send us back to Kotikoria, where the two moons leave the night dark sometimes, and the game runs plentiful and free. Where magic does not make terrible foes out of puny, hairless monkeys. Send us home, human, and we will forget about your stinkings and bad taste and horrible, sharp metals."

Christopher sighed. "I cannot." The ulvenmen, like the goblins and the humans themselves, were castaways here, their ancestors brought over by whatever capricious magic had delivered Christopher. He would need towering rank to find his own planet; he could never find their alien world. Perhaps no one could.

"We know this. No one can send us home. Our god Jumala has banished us to this place, to kill all or be killed. Today you win. I smell the blood of my kin on your hands. But tomorrow you may not win, and ulvenmen younger and stronger than I will feast on your bones."

"No," Christopher said. "That will never happen. If I cannot forbid the ulvenmen, then I must kill them all. Your shaman forbade and was obeyed, so tell me how to do the same." There didn't seem to be a verb for "command," only "forbid," which was not a promising sign.

"Keisari was a fool. I told all that no good could come of dabbling in magic, but the warriors no longer listened to my wisdom, even though many had cried out excitedly for my stories when they were but pups. Many times I said that some brave warrior should sneak into his tent and cut off his head while he slept, but fear of his golden fire-bolts was too much for them. It would not have been so when I was young."

Christopher had been on the receiving end of those bolts, and he didn't think they qualified as mere dabbling. "Has someone taken his place?"

The ulvenman shrugged. "We have not heard from the big camp since the great battle. Nor have we sent speakers to the big camp. Our new chieftain was not beholden to the big camp, and we were all tired of sharing our treasure anyway."

When the tax system broke down, you knew you were dealing with complete social collapse.

"Tell me how to find the big camp." Maybe he could influence the choice of replacement leader, toward someone more controllable. Or at least sane.

"You must go west, and north at the quickwater. Then west again. But it will do you no good. Destroy that canker and only stronger ulvenmen will result."

"I hope for wiser ulvenmen." If one old ulvenman could reach Green, who was to say more could not? "Like you, toothless one."

"I am only wise because I am weak. The strong do not need wisdom. When I could hunt my own food and thrash my foes, I did not need to care for the good opinions of others. You will find no weak ulvenmen in the big camp. Keisari killed them all."

"Keisari is dead," he reminded the ulvenman. "You outlived him."

The ulvenman shook his furry head in denial. "We all die. Life is to be lived hot, like blood. I should have died seasons ago, when I could no longer fight, instead of clinging on with stories for pups. Twenty years is too many."

"What?" Christopher cried out. "What? How old are you?"

"Twenty, man-pup. Twenty times the floods have come and gone since I was whelped. More than any ulvenman I have ever heard of. But not as long as our human slaves, which grow and breed as slowly as trees. To live in servility is bad; to suffer it for so long is unthinkable. Your race must have displeased your god even worse than we did ours."

"What?" Christopher said. "How old was Keisari?"

"Fourteen he was, still hale, but past his prime. He should have been slain by stronger and younger before you faced him. Perhaps a real hero could have defeated your god-magic."

Christopher had felt crushing remorse at discovering that he had killed ulvenman children. Now he faced the dreadful fact that *all* of the ulvenmen were essentially children. How could he expect moral reasoning out of grade-schoolers armed with fangs and claws?

Too full of despair to speak, he simply stared at the ulvenman.

Its weathered face, marked with scars; its knobby body, contorted, twisted, and thin. The ulvenman was suffering the ravages of decay at an age where a man would be starting his real life, marriage and career and adulthood.

"I can't do this," he said. But it came out in English, so no one understood.

"I have told you many stories," the ulvenman wheezed, struggling to stand up. "Even of Kotikoria, our most sacred story handed down from warrior to pup for more generations than we can count. Now give me a boon, young pup. Give me the warrior's death I should have had. Free me from this wretched leash and let me die fighting."

The hollowness inside Christopher was disorienting. Wordlessly, sightlessly, he drew his katana and cut the rope in one smooth motion. Cannan, standing by impassively throughout the interview, ripped his great black sword from its scabbard as if by reflex. With the ringing of freshly drawn metal still hanging in the air, the ulvenman lunged forward, snarling pathetically.

Cannan severed it in half with a single stroke.

"They're innocents, Cannan." Christopher spoke to the knight in helplessness. "They're all innocents. Even the guilty ones."

"To draw breath on Prime is to ride the wheel of fortune. There are no innocents here." Cannan cleaned his blade with no visible sign of emotion, but he did not meet Christopher's gaze.

19

A WOMAN OF VALOR

Over the next few weeks Christopher drove his army mercilessly, marching miles a day in search of the fabled "big camp," and destroying everything in their path.

He rode into each battle with the aura spell active, but all he found was a sea of Red. His ferocity in these assaults first enthralled, then terrified his men. He threw himself into the attack, trying to offset his guilt by exposing his body to the ulvenmen's wrath. Knowing that the source of his battle ardor was sympathy, not hatred, would have only confused his soldiers. To be fair, it confused him. But an honest and quick death in battle was all he had to offer the ulvenmen.

When they broke and ran, he called off his troops and let them go. He was perpetually amazed at how few would flee even when given the chance. In some ways it was comforting; he could pretend that what he was doing was consensual. When that stopped working, he concentrated on finding the capital so he could peacefully end the war. Between the two he stayed busy fighting. Since both lies were so threadbare, he spent a lot of time fighting.

His advisors would not let him march willy-nilly into the swamp in search of his final objective. He had a supply line to maintain, food—for men and horses—and guns. The army traveled only as fast as it could build roads and forts, which was measured in single digits of miles per day and hours of itching frustration. Lalania's lyre remained silent, saving the magic against need, so every foot of road and wall was built by human hands.

The quick-water turned out to be a river, and pinning his march along the banks reduced the number of camps they encountered. The camps were smaller, with less warriors but more slaves. This simplified Christopher's life. Every camp he destroyed liberated more human wreckage, which fueled his rage for the next assault. Disa and Lalania began giving him sidelong glances, perhaps using their magic to check his aura. It was a relief to everyone when the Ranger announced that the big camp was now within striking distance.

They built one last fort. It was a good fort, perhaps the best they had ever made. Either they were getting better with practice or they felt a subconscious desire to impress their foes. Christopher felt the same pressure. He feared a trap, of course, but he also feared a massacre. If he could not make a treaty then his men and the ulvenmen would eagerly turn to bloodshed. Even more he feared actually making a treaty. What did he know about state diplomacy? How would he recognize a good treaty, or an enforceable one? He had no idea how to balance the competing interests of the ulvenmen, the army, the King's orders, the human slaves, and his conscience.

Knowing that a bloodbath would suit everyone but himself was no comfort.

"Whatever happens tomorrow, you have done by them fairly," Gregor told him. "If you came into our Kingdom and asked for a treaty, we would respect that."

"Some of us would," Lalania said. "Others would vow resistance to the death, and still others would pretend to yield while plotting treachery and deceit. And when the invader properly chastised the wicked, many would demand rebellion. No, I think if Christopher marched an army into Kingsrock, the numbers of dead would be legion."

"The numbers are already legion here," Christopher said. D'Kan had estimated that they killed some eight thousand ulvenmen over the last year. When asked how many were left, the Ranger shrugged and said the swamplands should only have held two thousand to begin with.

In the morning his men were eager, assuming that this great battle would break the back of the ulvenman resistance. Christopher did not bother to explain that a campaign of smoking the remaining dog-men out of jungle camps would be as painful and unrewarding as Vietnam had been for the American army. The men formed up into a solid battle column, taking their wagons of supplies with them. They expected that the night would see them in a fort built by Lalania's magic, surrounded by dying ulvenmen. Christopher was afraid they were right.

But the landscape changed as they marched into the heart of the ulvenman kingdom. First were the fields, rice paddies neatly terraced in walls of mud. Second were the slaves, large barns of dirty, ragged people who gawked in awe at the freemen. One white-bearded man stumbled forward, babbling, and only after a moment did Christopher realize he could understand his speech without magic.

The slaves so far had been younger, though the ravages of their existence made it hard to tell. As best as could be determined, they had all been born into slavery, implying that the ulvenmen had been keeping human slaves for at least thirty years. They spoke no language other than the ulven one; they remembered no history other than the jungle. The people captured in the last great raid against Carrhill ten years ago had apparently been judged too difficult to tame and thus useless for any other purpose than food. It was a testament to the darkness that clouded Christopher these days that he sometimes thought they had been the lucky ones.

The man groveling at the foot of his horse had white hair and human speech. Lalania and Disa knelt beside him, offering comforting touches like a pair of beautiful, grieving angels. The man looked past them to the only solace he could accept: the sight of a man clad in steel.

"Praise the gods, my lord," he babbled. "All praise to you, my lord."

"Why do you speak our language?" Christopher asked. Looking from the outside, he was shocked at the harshness of his own voice, but from the inside he was a welter of wildly inappropriate emotions. Disgust, that a man who had been educated as a human being had accepted life as an animal; anger, that he had to confront the misery of the slaves face-first instead of as an abstract quality; fear, that he could not provide what this supplicant asked for; shame, that he had taken so long to effect a rescue.

"I was born in Balenar. For forty years I grew wheat for the Gold Throne. I was headman of my village, as my father before, and as my son would be in my turn. Then the monsters came in the middle of the night and carried off my entire village. Those who fought were slain instantly. When they ripped my boy's body from my hands I vowed I would live long enough to claim justice."

"Be calm, father," Lalania said, putting her arms around him. "You are safe now. Think only of that." The way she pressed up against him, any man would be hard-pressed to think of anything other than her presence. Christopher wondered at such solicitude; it seemed more intent on distraction than comfort.

The old man blinked, but pushed away from her, his words a flow that could not be stopped by such mere distractions.

"Lord, whatever county you rule, whatever gods you serve, I claim the right of justice. The Golden Prophet took our wheat and tael for naught. His protection was like the wind, a promise that vanished as soon as the night fell. He has forgone the lord-right, and my servitude is unbound. I vow to serve you, my lord, if you would but claim me. The lands I farmed for generations will flower under your hand. If you but claim them."

The old man fell to his knees, trying to kiss Christopher's stirrup. Lalania let him go, a look of failure on her face.

"You wanted a cause for war," Gregor said, looking on from horseback with dismay, "and now you have it. If those words were said within the bounds of the Kingdom, honor would bid you challenge the Gold Apostle within the hour."

"Or see the old man hung," Lalania said. "The more usual outcome, I can assure you."

Christopher flinched. "Let's do none of those today. Please stop that. Somebody make him stop."

Lalania struggled with the man, who seemed to have latched onto Christopher's boot like a shipwrecked sailor with an oar. The contest began to become undignified, until Lalania whispered a word into his ear. For the first time, the old man noticed her; now he followed her gentle lead, trusting her completely with his fate.

"These are serious charges," Disa said, standing white-faced while Lalania led the old man away. "Merely to speak of this would count as a challenge."

"And well deserved." Gregor scowled. "A lord who cannot defend his peasants is a fraud. Losing an entire village is incompetence on a grand scale."

"Or worse," Torme suggested. He stood in the old man's place, having dismounted and come up to help Lalania before she solved the problem with magic.

"What could be worse?" Gregor asked.

"A village not stolen, but sold."

"Please stop talking," Disa begged. The young priestess looked as if she was going to throw up. "Speak no more words we cannot unspeak."

"Did you notice," Gregor mused aloud, "he mentioned the Gold Prophet? So, he has been gone from the Kingdom at least five years. How coincidental that the Gold Throne should purchase enough tael for another rank after suffering the loss of an entire village."

"Those were specifically the words I was referring to," Disa said, glaring at her husband.

"Why would anybody even do such a thing?" Christopher asked.

Black Bart had burned whole villages for tael. Who would sell one for gold?

"A good peasant is worth more than the tael in his head," Torme answered. "No doubt the old man was expected to pass on his farming skills. And what would the shaman do with a pile of gold, out here in this swamp? The Gold Throne no doubt got a good price for its goods."

"And those words," Disa said. "One might almost think we were accusing the Gold Apostle of treason."

"If the shoe fits . . ." Gregor started to say, but Disa interrupted him.

"Are we the cobbler then, to boot the demon's hoof?"

Christopher had a less metaphorical question. "Where would the shaman get a pile of gold?" The swamp did not seem like gold-mining territory.

"The same place he got his armor and his rank," Gregor said with a shrug. "Just the coat you are wearing is worth a small village."

Christopher had thought the chief allure of wandering around in the swamp was turning people into tael. If there were treasures this great buried out here, that meant he owed the late Baron Fairweather an apology for the low opinion he had formed of the man's financial planning. No doubt the Baron had been disappointed to discover that the shaman had found the hoard first, and used it to make the Baron part of the treasure for the next lucky adventurer. If that was what had killed the missing Baron. D'Kan seemed to think there were a million other ways to die in the swamp.

"Are we going to find Baron Fairweather as a prisoner?" Christopher asked, largely at random. His ability to redirect conversations was a pale shadow of Lalania's.

"No," Gregor said. "Nobles are not peasants or craftsmen. Their only value is in their heads."

Lalania had returned alone, having passed the old man off to the lesser priestesses. Christopher looked at her, an unspoken question on his lips. Was this the work of the *hjerne-spica*?

"No," she said, shaking her head sadly. "This is no more than ordinary, mortal evil. You need not invoke theology here."

She was reminding him to speak circumspectly in the midst of so many witnesses.

"Nothing has changed," he said. "We still have to subdue the ulvenmen. I still have to . . ." He had been about to say, *Destroy the Gold Throne before they destroy me.* But Lalania's example had put some sense into him. "I still have to walk the path of good without upsetting the applecart."

Torme made a dubious face. "You evidenced some difficulty walking past a cabbage cart at Joadan's door, with far less provocation."

"He has greater rank now," Lalania said. "No doubt power and time have led to wisdom and restraint."

Lalania's words had another meaning. The higher his rank, the closer he came to calling out the Gold Throne openly. He looked forward to where the remnants of a great treasure still waited for him and urged his horse forward.

For all of a hundred paces his vengeance carried him on. He sat straighter, his horse stepped higher, and the looming possibility of violence began to take on a silver lining. Could the deaths of the ulvenmen be redeemed by the destruction of the Gold Throne? Would removing that cancer tomorrow justify this slaughter today?

Fine theological questions, to be undone by the simplest of arguments hammered out on dull iron. Riding into a clearing surrounded by a thicket of huts he came upon an ulvenman working at a forge. The creature was shaping a spear point; it looked up only long enough to snarl, and then returned to its work with only the slightest increase in tempo. For sheer courage the ulvenmen could not be faulted. Christopher already empathized with their other positive qualities: simple honesty, passion for life, and a casual disregard for authority. The sight of one engaged in his own profession undid all his battle ardor.

There but for a completely different genetic code go I.

Someone spoke, a liquid and pleasant voice that rendered the barks and growls of the ulvenmen almost dignified. The smith threw down his tools in annoyance and scampered off. Christopher, dislodged from his introspection, finally noticed what the rest of his army was gawking at.

An oddly attractive girl, slim and pale, with wide lavender eyes and silky white hair that looked as if it had been artfully blow-dried, sat on a rock at the edge of the forge. She was bound by a thin gold chain to a heavy, misshapen lump of gold lying on the ground. The girl was covered only in a scrap of cloth that she wore with such innocent simplicity as to render her twice as alluring as if she were naked.

D'Kan's reaction was startling. He sprung from his horse and rushed forward, stopping ten feet away and staring intently. Haltingly, he spoke some kind of challenge in the language Niona had used for magic.

The girl listened attentively, and helpfully corrected his pronunciation when he stumbled over a difficult vowel. That was too much for the Ranger. He dropped to one knee and bowed his head.

"Ser," Gregor called out, "explain yourself." The knight had a hand on his sword. So did Cannan, Torme, and Karl. Really, everyone with experience or a lick of sense was uneasy. Nothing spelled danger like the unusual, and nothing spelled unusual like a pretty girl in the middle of a jungle. Only the common farm boys ogled.

"My lord." D'Kan's voice trembled in awe. "We are blessed. The noble Lady before you is an elf."

"Or," Christopher said, "she just looks like one." He'd seen magic that could do that. "And talks like one." He'd seen magic that could do that, too.

"I am indeed an elf," the girl said. Her voice was sweetly melodic, and Christopher could feel Lalania's annoyance from twenty feet away. "I did not think it necessary to prove, but if there is anything I can do to ease your mind, please name it."

"How is it you speak our language?" Christopher challenged. This was becoming a thing. Maybe he should have it printed on a card he could hand out to random unlikely strangers.

"I know many languages," she answered. "The human tongue is but one of them. It may please you to know I also speak the ulvenman language, if parley is on your mind."

The twitch in Lalania's cheek was so pronounced Christopher fancied he could hear it.

"It is, in fact. But I do not understand your position with the ulvenmen, since you wear a chain."

"I am currently a slave," she acknowledged. "As the property of the shaman Keisari, I brought him entertainment. As the property of his successor, the chieftain Rohkea, I brought prestige. Now I am yours, given as a gift in the hopes of bringing peace."

Christopher glanced at Lalania for help. The bard wore a frown that was either suspicion or jealousy, but in either case kept her silence. As the principal he was expected to do the speaking. Stalling for time, he asked a question at random. "Tell me about this new guy."

"He is a young warrior. Strong, of course, as all rulers must be. But also more curious than the usual of his type. He is . . . manageable, I think."

No one who viewed this coolly self-possessed woman sitting half naked between an empire of inhuman slavers and several hundred rowdy young men could imagine, even for an instant, that she was a slave. Now she had admitted to being more.

How much more remained to be seen. Christopher's hand reflexively drifted to his sword. The Skald had spoken of monsters who stood behind thrones and guided kingdoms like shepherds herding sheep to the slaughterhouse. True, she had described them as figures of nightmare, but she had also taught Christopher that seeing was not believing in this world. Magic could put a beautiful face on anything.

"So . . . have we now met the true power in this damned swamp?"

"Not as such," she said, shrugging delicately. "Ulvenmen are not much swayed by entertainment and prestige. But if you are not intent on wholesale murder, I would like a chance to try."

A perfect ploy, to offer him the one thing he desired most. A chance at peace. Doubt mastered his tongue, and like any fool, he said exactly what he was thinking.

"How do I know you're not a *hjerne-spica*?"

She raised her eyebrows in surprise, while D'Kan exploded in outrage.

"My lord! You cannot be so blind as that!"

"Hush, boy," Cannan said. Even with all of his attention fixed on the mysterious girl he could not pass up a chance to chastise D'Kan.

"Well," the girl said, "there are a dozen ways to check, depending on your resources and patience. The easiest would be a Lens of Perfect Acuity. If you happen to have one, I will gladly submit to your inspection."

He didn't even know what that was. He had to glance at Lalania, just in case it was one of the spells he hadn't bothered to study yet. She shook her head sadly at either his ignorance or his poverty.

"Start with the simplest," Lalania suggested. "For my part, I am already convinced."

"By what?" Christopher asked.

The bard shrugged. "I can think of a dozen better ways I would seek to lead you into a trap. This is none of them."

It occurred to him that Lalania might not actually feel that way. If she did think it was a trick, she might well play along until she could figure out how to trap the monster back. She would expect him to have already guessed that, and to trim his sails to the wind, which-ever way it might blow. So many roles to play, until the curtains came down and the actors were forced to reveal their true faces. He really missed the Skald's null-stone now.

All this plotting made his head hurt. He cast the aura-detecting spell, the only non-killing spell he kept in memory other than the gift of tongues. The girl's aura blazed white with a purity that put Gregor and Torme to shame.

When he reacted to this fact by raising his eyebrows, she spoke a sentence in Celestial.

"Perhaps you should contact your Patron directly for advice."

A good bluff on her part. He could hardly admit he had no idea how to do that. Maybe he could ask Disa about it later.

"Assume I believe you. Now what?" A safe assumption, he did believe. The sophistication of this ploy seemed wholly unlike the crude play of force the *hjerne-spica* had displayed so far. If they had enough magic to fake an aura and two holy languages, then they could have just as easily knocked him to the ground and forced a ring onto his finger. Or, more aptly, replaced Lalania with their own doppelganger. Their power had to have limits; he could not doubt every juncture, or he would go mad. Indeed, that would be the ultimate plot: to make him doubt every stroke of good fortune, every potential ally, as merely another stab from the dark. He decided not to fall for that one, which, necessarily, meant embracing this one.

The girl rattled her chain, and returned to the common tongue. "First, you strike this from my body, to show the ulvenmen that you decide who is free and who is not. Then you force Rohkea to swear obeisance to me in your stead. Then you leave. I will deal with the creatures as best I can. Should I fail, either through chaos or death, you will be free to exterminate the tribe."

"You want us to turn the ulvenman kingdom we just conquered over to you?" Gregor asked, his voice flat and hard.

"What remains of the ulvenman treasure lies at my feet. The rest of the swamp is of little value to you. You cannot run it like a fief. Nor will your affiliation let you keep it as a royal park, hunting ulvenmen like animals for your profit and amusement. All you can do is kill them, and then come back in a decade to kill them again."

Torme had heard a different part of her words. "You would put your life on the line for these monsters? You would bind your fate to theirs?" She had said that failure to tame them might lead to her death.

"Yes," she said obliquely, "though perhaps not in ways you understand."

"It doesn't matter," Lalania said. "The King will never accept this. March home and tell him you left the ulvenmen under the supervision of a slip of a girl? He would hang you before you finished the story."

"Not a girl," D'Kan said. "A Lady Elf."

Lalania shook her head. "That only makes it worse. Even if you could convince the King that elves were real, it would only be read as collusion with the druids, whose loyalty is already suspect."

The lady in question spoke up. "I have been told that kings are convinced by tael. You have conquered the ulvenmen; by tradition you may demand a tax. Will not your King be satisfied with this?"

It had worked so far; Christopher kept buying his way out of his faux pas. There was no reason to think he couldn't buy this one off as well.

"And you have to free the slaves," Christopher said. "No more slaves. Of any race."

She nodded. "That accords with my own plan. Also their fecundity must be contained. On these foundations I will be able to build a stable social order."

"Will you make them all Green?" Christopher asked her. "I met a Green ulvenman once." He did not add, *But then I had to kill him*. Perhaps it was obvious.

The girl looked at him with slightly more respect. "That is my goal. I hope in time to breed a race of Greens."

"That could take a while." Christopher wasn't sure the girl really understood the pace of evolution.

"Perhaps," she conceded, "but I think it a good use of my time."

"You speak as if we have already agreed to your scheme," Gregor said.

But of course they had. The girl could surely read it in Christopher's face or, for that matter, Gregor's tone of voice. Here, once, was a chance to lay down the meat cleaver. Even if the scheme were doomed to failure, the fact that the girl was willing to risk her life meant that Christopher could not balk at risking his prestige.

"Do you really think you can do it?" he asked her.

Her answer was simple and direct. "I have to at least try."

Christopher's answer was equally direct. He nudged his horse forward and drew his katana. He could not bear the thought of more slaughter, and babysitting a race of dog-men while breeding them into a semblance of humanity was not what he had been brought here to do.

The girl raised her hands, the chain stretched between her wrists. Christopher had been planning something practical, like cutting the chain against the stump, not this absurd display of prowess.

Stifling a sigh, he cast the weapon blessing. After that he had the confidence to lash out with the sword, sundering the chain in a squeak of metal. The girl didn't blink.

She stepped forward and bowed at the side of Christopher's horse. Royal snuffled welcomingly to her. When she stood up the horse swung his head under her hand, eagerly accepting her friendly scratching. Christopher felt betrayed. First his scout and now his mount were smitten with the girl's charms.

"Order me to call Rohkea forth," she said.

"Okay. Call forth Rohkea."

She turned and barked imperiously at the camp. Christopher didn't have the speech spell up yet, so the scene was ludicrous. Briefly he wondered if he looked that silly when barking, and then he cast the spell. He wanted to hear this conversation with his own ears.

A huge ulvenman crept out, ducking its head in caution. A dozen more followed behind it. Christopher's men shouted and cocked rifles, but Karl was already bawling at them to stand down.

When the monsters were within a dozen feet, they ducked lower.

"Tell the god-man we do not wish to die today," the huge one said. With such mastery of diplomacy, this had to be Rohkea.

The elf spoke sternly. "The god-man questions whether you deserve to be chief of all clans."

This resulted in angry barking. Not words, just barks. Eventually Rohkea calmed down enough to argue.

"I hunt better than any in this camp. It is known. Who else could lead?"

"Hunting and leading are not the same. Your hunting skills will not send this army away."

Rohkea glared at the girl, a sinister red tongue thrashing about in a forest of fangs. "You said that your gifting would bring peace."

"There is peace," she said. "The god-man has not killed you yet. But for peace to continue the ulvenmen must listen to the forbiddings of the god-man in all things."

"Do we live to be servants of these puny creatures?" Rohkea asked, pulling his lips back in disgust.

"Or servants in death."

Rohkea looked like he was considering it. Royal flattened his ears, and Christopher was comforted that he had not put away his katana. That the ulvenman could project such menace even while unarmed and facing an entire army was impressive.

But the elven girl had picked her champion well. After a moment of low growling, Rohkea capitulated. "What does the god-man forbid?"

"He forbids the hunting of men, or in man territory. He forbids the keeping of slaves. He forbids more than one female for each male."

With each commandment the ulvenmen had snarled louder, and on the third one they broke into angry howls. Christopher allowed himself a grin at the expense of the poor creatures. Even the human Kingdom did not enforce such a Spartan rule.

The girl put her fingers in her mouth and whistled, piercingly. Biting at the air in frustration, the ulvenmen quieted.

"The god-man also gives to me the power of forbiddance, to use as I see fit. I will stay, and the god-man and his army will go away. But if I am killed or unheard, the army will return and kill all."

Rohkea huffed a few times. Then he asked, "What will you forbid?" Christopher was impressed again. Asking about the terms of service before swearing to them was more than he had managed.

"A few things, here and there. Nothing so hard as the things the god-man has demanded. Now you must choose. Do you hear the god-man in these things or not?"

"If I hear the god-man, then I will be chieftain of all the clans. You will forbid in his name, but I will forbid in mine." Rohkea made it a statement, not a question.

"For as long as you are able," the girl promised him.

The huge creature roused itself, standing upright. At eight feet tall it could look Christopher levelly in the face even though he was on horseback. Rohkea stalked forward, walking in the stilted gait that his dog-legs compelled. Christopher did not feel sorry for him; when the ulvenmen ran their clumsiness disappeared, replaced by supple speed.

He did feel sorry for his horse, who was trying to go into fight mode. Royal had never been this close to an ulvenman without running into or over it. Christopher started to have a real battle of control, one he was losing, until the elf looked at Royal and made a gentle shushing sound. The horse quieted instantly.

Rohkea, now within arm's length, exhaled heavily, his breath washing over Christopher. For a moment the two locked eyes. Rohkea was looking for fear, even a shred, a simple flinch. Christopher steeled himself and stared back.

Kneel or I will have to become the butcher again.

The ulvenman knelt, placing his furry head under Christopher's boot and pushing up. It was such a doglike action that Christopher almost reached out and petted him.

"Now go," the girl said. "Bring forth all the slaves, without harm or wounding. Deliver them to this spot. I will go and speak with the god-man and learn his other forbiddings."

"I will look foolish to be giving away so much treasure," Rohkea complained.

"Then kill anyone who barks at you," she said.

Rohkea answered by baring his teeth. He trotted off into the camp, followed by his pack. Only the pack threw backward glances at Christopher's army. Rohkea was too proud and too aware of status to do so.

"You have signed yourself up for a lot of killing," Christopher said to the girl. Ruling this realm would require an iron fist in a steel glove, and the death penalty would be handed out like Halloween candy. He wasn't sure how she could remain White under such conditions.

"Only what is necessary." She glanced behind him, where his men stood ready. "You should withdraw the bulk of your army. To do less would be to show fear. Also, if it is convenient to you, I would like to discuss some specifics of our arrangement."

Apparently he wasn't going to hammer out a treaty from horseback.

"I'll wait for the prisoners," Gregor volunteered. "Leave me the cavalry and the priestesses. If anything goes wrong we can quickly retreat."

"If any ulvenman disrespects you," the girl said to Gregor, "kill them. But please do not pursue further vengeance, or kill without provocation."

Gregor blushed furiously and muttered something that might have been, "Of course not."

Christopher looked back the way they had come. "I guess we should pull back to the fort. It's a fair distance." He turned to the elf, realizing he didn't know how to address her. "Can you ride?"

She answered him with a look. A stupid question; she had mastered his warhorse with a single word.

"Take mine," D'Kan said. He led his mount to the girl and offered the reins. She smiled at him, and while he melted she studied the strips of leather that bound the horse.

"I do not understand these restraints," she said. "Can you remove them?"

Blushing, D'Kan extricated the bit and bridle from his horse.

"And this," she added, pointing to the saddle.

D'Kan leapt to please, unbinding his horse and taking the heavy saddle onto his shoulder. The girl whispered to the horse and gently sprung onto its naked back. The creature shook its head in freedom and walked away, bearing the girl toward Christopher, and leaving D'Kan to stare dumbstruck after her.

Christopher felt a little empathy for Lalania. He'd worked hard to master the respect of his men and animals, yet only Cannan seemed undazzled by this slip of a woman. The elf had the same effect on men that Karl had on women: Christopher became invisible.

Sighing, he turned his army back to their fort, the men alternating between grumbling over the lack of a battle and mooning over the spoils.

20

PEACE CONFERENCE

He examined his new subject from the other side of his dining table. The subject was the Lady Elf Kalani, the name she had finally provided with a small smile as if it were a quiet joke, and the title a gift from D'Kan. The table was a plank set on two barrels; the chairs, short kegs or stumps destined for the fire. Roughshod, but the army felt the high-ranks needed a dignified place to eat. The men, including the officers, ate from their bowls while standing or sitting on the ground. The exception was Karl, who ate at the table despite having no rank. Although this could arguably be explained by Karl's close personal relationship with his lord, Christopher chose to interpret it as the beginnings of his republican reformation.

Taking on a feudal vassal would be a step in the wrong direction, but there was no other way to describe the arrangement the girl was proposing. Christopher could not pretend it was an alliance when the tael only went one way. And how, exactly, could the master of a village engage in foreign treaties for the whole Kingdom? Lalania assured him he could not.

But he could still take the allegiance of a lesser lord, because that would make her a subject of the King, via his own vow of fealty.

"Except, of course, the King will not accept a nonhuman as a subject. Let alone a tribe of them. Nor will you be able to keep the peace, Christopher." Lalania continued to expound on the many reasons this would not work. "Other lords will ride down here and hunt for sport. If ulvenmen are killed, you are shamed as too weak to defend your property. If lords are killed, you are shamed as having failed the King's orders to pacify the region. Either outcome leads to the destruction of the ulvenmen, once the lords realize they are easy pickings."

"It is true," Gregor confirmed unhappily. The slaves had been turned over quickly, and had fled from their captors in such haste that the cavalry struggled to keep up and maintain order. Their column had returned to fort only moments after the infantry arrived. "The mystery of the jungle kept the free-booters at bay. When even high-ranks like Baron Fairweather could disappear without a trace, few cared to hunt in such an inhospitable land." He paused to slap a mosquito, an act so automatic no one noticed it anymore. "But now that you have broken the back of the beast, the lower ranks will rush to feed on the scraps."

"Normally this is considered a boon," Karl said. "The lower gentry gain a rank or two, and the land is cleared of stray monsters. The next step is for you to raise a castle and import peasants to work the land. You gain a fief, free and clear; the realm expands, gaining a peer and a county."

Everyone stared at the young soldier. Such political knowledge seemed out of place for one so unconcerned with promotion.

"Once, when young and foolish," Karl confessed, "I may have looked into it."

"Nobody's going to want to build farms down here." Christopher wasn't even sure they could, the ulvenman slaves' efforts notwithstanding. "And I'm already a peer."

Disa did not say anything, but she laid her hand on top of Gregor's.

"Gods no," Gregor said in alarm. "Surely I've done nothing worthy of such a banishment. Also, there is still the matter of the ulvenmen."

"You care for the beasts?" D'Kan asked, incredulous. No one had ever formally invited the Ranger to these meetings, but he seemed to assume he was entitled to attend. For all Christopher knew, he was.

"Care is perhaps too strong of a word," Gregor answered. "Still, I find myself in a dilemma. I cannot justify their wholesale slaughter, at least not as long as there is a chance at another way."

"I concur," Torme said. "Not just because I am a loyal servant of the

Lord Bishop. My affiliation compels me to speak against any course of action that does not give due regard to the Green we once saw."

"A servant of who?" Christopher asked, alarmed.

"You, idiot," Lalania said. "Did you forget your new rank gained you a new title?"

"Oh." Christopher had forgotten.

"You're all idiots," she continued. "You sit here and discuss the moral rights of man-eating monsters, apparently oblivious to the realities. You cannot defend these creatures, and they cannot defend themselves."

"Give us but a little time," Kalani said, the first substantive words she had spoken since the conference began, other than "please" and "thank you" when offered water and food. She had turned down ale, but accepted dried meat, which had surprised Christopher. He had expected vegetarianism to accompany that hairstyle. "Within a few weeks Rohkea will have subdued the remaining clans. From that tael I will build a force of ranked warriors that should be proof against any but an army."

"That's even worse," Lalania exclaimed. "When the King finds out you've ranked monsters, he'll name you traitor in a breath."

"So don't tell him," Christopher said, but he knew it was stupid as soon as it left his mouth.

"Then what's the *point*? If people don't know there are opposing ranks, then they'll come hunting. And die. Either way, you'll be blamed for creating monsters."

"But they'll be monsters under our control," Gregor objected, his voice trailing off as if he realized the weakness of his argument even while it was still being birthed.

Lalania just rolled her eyes, too exasperated to speak.

"Do not dismiss such a claim so quickly," Torme said. "The King tolerated Black Bart, and surely he was little more than a monster under the leash of the Gold Apostle."

"And the Lord Wizard of Carrhill," Disa added. "Few even consider him human."

"So what we need," Christopher said, "is a force that the lords will recognize as dangerous, but that the King will recognize as fully under my control. One that doesn't involve rabid dogs with ranks."

"How can I tame the clans, or even defend myself, without rank?" Kalani asked. Her tone was simple curiosity, with neither outrage nor sarcasm. Christopher wished he could be so diplomatic. Or innocent. Whichever it was, really, would be an improvement.

"If all you need to do is kill things," Christopher said, "I think I have an answer."

He watched the group carefully, interested in seeing how quickly each of them figured it out. Karl and Cannan showed no reaction, one because he had probably already seen it coming and the other perhaps because he just didn't care. Gregor and Torme were next, the knights turned priests grinning in amusement or irony, as their respective natures warranted. Disa and Lalania were almost last, the priestess making a small "O" of shock with her mouth and the minstrel making a large "O." At least it kept her from speaking for a moment. D'Kan was the final domino to fall, releasing a veritable fountain of outrage.

"You cannot be serious!" the Ranger barked.

"You forget yourself, Ser," Torme was saying to the Ranger, but Christopher interrupted him.

"It's okay, Torme. It's a shocking idea."

"Please enlighten me," Kalani said. "I do not understand your private jest."

Christopher tapped his fingers on the table for emphasis. "Lady Kalani, you may have noticed that my regiment of common men has had little trouble in destroying entire ulvenman armies."

"I was aware, to some extent," she agreed. "But I put the credit to your account. Although I do not know what the title 'bishop' signifies; I assume it is an advanced rank."

"Not that advanced," Christopher said. "Judging by the tael we took from the shaman, he outranked me."

She looked at him with a more personal interest than she had so far shown. "And yet you defeated him?"

Christopher realized he took an inordinate amount of pleasure in exceeding the expectations of sophisticated and beautiful young women.

"You may ask how," he began grandly.

"Thank you," she said. "How?"

Apparently elves didn't do rhetorical questions.

"Um. Guns. The answer is guns."

She nodded in understanding. "Rohkea complained of the fire-sticks. I confess I did not fully believe his remarks. I assumed that he exaggerated the strength of your magic to excuse his failure. Although I am glad to see that it was nothing less than overwhelming power that made him flee."

"He fought us?"

"Twice, actually. Once at a stone fort, though he was only a first-rank hunter then. A second time at a wooden fort, as a full chieftain. Despite his battle-lust, he retained the sense to retreat when defeat was obvious. You can see how rare a find he is; I would have been sorry to lose him."

"You care for the beast?" D'Kan said, scandalized instead of shocked this time. Christopher wondered what precise temperature of porridge it would take to please the man.

"He is far-thinking, for his kind. In any case he is capable of morality, should he choose to apply himself, and should be treated as such." She didn't seem to grasp the essential jealousy of D'Kan's complaint, or perhaps she chose to ignore it. "On his own terms he is worthy of respect."

"On his own terms I am entitled to kill him," Gregor said, perhaps making sure of where the land lay.

"Yes," Kalani agreed. "Having lost, he does not expect any less. But you saw how he behaved, how he cared to stand taller than his fellows even when unarmed. I believe I have convinced him of the power of opinion. Such is the start of a code of honor."

"You are going to school these creatures in honor?" Lalania said, either outraged or surprised. Christopher wasn't sure there was a difference for the self-assured bard.

"Over time. There are many steps to the program: population control, restricted access to breeding females, a labor economy in which goods and favors are exchanged instead of taken. Eventually the ulvenmen will cooperate out of desire to gain. Then they may learn to desire the esteem of others, not just their fear."

"They may learn to ask, not just to take," Christopher said. "To expect more than merely noninterference from others." The peculiarities of their language would appear to be more than arbitrary.

"Yes," Kalani said. "As you know, it is possible for them. But few individuals of any race could obtain high affiliation in their current social conditions."

Christopher looked at the elf. Her comments were of a kind he had stopped being used to. The moralities of her concerns he still recognized—Disa was as gentle, and Gregor as inured to necessary suffering—but the way she talked was unique for this world.

"You set yourself to an ambitious campaign," Gregor told her, though with respect rather than disapproval.

"It will require that I gain a certain amount of rank of my own," Kalani said apologetically.

"How much?" Torme asked.

"At least fifth. That is one good deed Keisari left me: the ulvenmen are intimidated by lightning bolts. I will need to take my promotion out of any taxes. But if your weapons are strong enough then I will not need to promote other hunters or chieftains."

"What about healing?" Christopher asked. To his mind healing spells were a lot more effective for maintaining a society than light-ning bolts. "And disease? Or can your shamans cure disease?"

"None of the other shamans were of any consequence. Keisari would not tolerate competition, only toadies," she answered. "In any case, my first advice to Rohkea was to eliminate them. But yes, the ability to heal sickness will be a boon, although honestly ulvenmen rarely succumb to plague or infection. Also being able to change my shape will further intimidate the ulvenmen, and grant me some small chance of escaping should my plans fail."

Christopher counted on his fingers. "Lightning, healing, shape-change . . . You can do all that at fifth rank?"

"Of course," D'Kan said. "She is a druid."

Once again Christopher wondered if he wouldn't have been luckier to stumble into a chapel on the other side of the Kingdom.

"What does any of this matter?" Lalania asked. "You cannot arm these monsters. The King will view it as an act of treason, as will most. Even your own army."

"Arming them is the best thing I can do," Christopher said. "Think about it. With guns they won't need to spend tael on ranks. Instead they'll buy ammunition with their tael. If they try to attack us, we'll just stop selling them powder, and they'll be weaker than they are now because they won't have any ranks. Giving them guns makes them dependent on us, while keeping them as a buffer against the Wild."

His staff looked dubious, but Christopher knew it would work. It had worked on the Native Americans. Within a hundred years of the European's arrival the tribes could no longer feed themselves without gunpowder.

Of course, in the end, it hadn't worked out all that well for the natives.

"This is the only way we can avoid murdering them all," he pointed out.

That argument convinced everyone but Lalania.

"For now, Christopher. But what happens when you die? What happens to the ulvenmen then?"

He shrugged. "Either Kalani has tamed them into true allies, or my successor will cut off their supplies of powder and then massacre them."

Lalania shook her head in rebuttal. "Or they'll attack while they still have ammunition and do untold damage."

"Then maybe the King shouldn't let me die."

For a moment no one had anything else to say.

"Unbelievable," Gregor said. "Had you told me a week ago that I would be selling rifles to ulvenmen I would not have believed you. But I am sick of killing women and children, no matter how fanged and furious they may be."

"Technically we will be selling guns to an elf," Torme suggested. "I find that view somewhat easier to swallow."

Lalania threw up her hands. "I do not think the King will swallow any view. You cannot convince him with logic, Christopher."

"I know how to buy the King's acceptance," Christopher said. "A fistful of tael, and the promise of more." Christopher had garnered a staggering fortune over the last few weeks. He didn't even know exactly how much. Shame had stopped him from counting it.

A soldier approached and saluted. "Colonel, some of the prisoners need healing."

"I thought I asked for them unharmed," Christopher said, frowning.

"They were, sir. But some of them ran themselves half to death on the way back."

"I can help," Kalani said, and she accompanied Christopher and the priestesses as they worked through the mass of refugees. Christopher watched her interactions with the victims closely, looking for a slip of the mask, but they responded to her as if she were one of them: a fellow slave, not a member of the oppressing government, or even a resented and pampered pet. The elf had shared their suffering, and yet she was prepared to risk her life to redeem their—and her—torturers. He did not fear the King's wrath as much as he feared the shame she could put him too, if he did not give her at least a chance.

At the end of the long day Christopher collapsed on his cot in his command tent, exhausted by the misery that had passed through his hands. Kalani, apparently unfazed, leaned against the center pole of the tent. She was wearing some clothes of Disa's, soft white robes that amplified her innocence.

"How did you stand it?" he asked, not really expecting an answer.

"I was somewhat lacking in choice," she said. "Still, though I was prepared for the savagery of this world, I did not expect it to be so . . . senseless."

He had the opposite problem. He could almost make sense of it; they were monsters, after all. It was the sheer brutality that disoriented him. He had no idea how anyone remained sane through it all.

"And yet you choose to stay?" He still marveled at it.

"In a different capacity. Although there will still be savagery, it will at least be directed to a purpose."

"I will support you as long as I can," Christopher said. He sat up and started unlacing his boots. The heat made his feet sweat, but he couldn't wear sandals under the sabatons and greaves. "But I have to warn you, I don't know how long that will be."

"It is appreciated," she said.

He stopped messing around with his boots. After opening the silver vial around his neck, he paused. "What rank are you now?"

"Third," she answered, watching him.

He carved off a rock and put the rest away. "Here. If you fail, it won't be because I failed to do everything in my power to help you."

She came forward, softly. When she reached out to take the rock from him, their hands touched.

"You are most generous," she said, staring down at him with wide eyes. "I am in your debt."

The artlessness of her seduction was endearing but ineffective. Lalania had raised his expectations to a ridiculous level.

"You should probably get back to the camp, keep an eye on your beasts," he said. Harmless as her flirtation was, he was too tired and depressed to deal with it.

"Do you not wish me to stay for the evening?"

"No. Not really." He shrugged and went back to wrestling with his laces.

Now she was perplexed. "I was told high-status human males expressed their standing through sexual dominance."

He stopped fighting with his boots. Any desire he might have felt was quelled by the distinct feeling that he was just another interesting creature for her to study.

"Told? By who?"

"My teachers. They are quite knowledgeable, I assure you. At this juncture we should mate, both to establish your leadership and to cement our alliance."

After a moment he realized his mouth was hanging open.

"Lady . . . it doesn't work that way."

"Are you certain?"

"Let me rephrase. It doesn't work that way with *me*. But if you're really hard up, I'll assign one of my men. Like D'Kan, for instance." Assuming the boy could get past his goddess-worship to actually touch her.

"No," she said, "I have no particular desire for such an act. Nor am I against it, if it would advance my cause."

"Well, then, you've learned something." He grinned. "Your teachers don't know everything."

She was unimpressed with his logic. "That seems highly unlikely."

"I can think of one thing they didn't know. Where you were. Otherwise they would have rescued you."

"Your inference is unsound. My location is no secret to them, and I was not in need of rescue."

He dropped the ends of his boot laces. This conversation apparently required all of his attention. "I thought you said you didn't have a choice."

"I was trapped, yes. But that does not mean I needed rescuing. However, I am grateful to you for furthering my program. Keisari was too corrupted by power for me to manage. Having captured me, he could not take any advice from me. I feared I would have to wait until he died of old age."

"Why didn't your teachers help, then?"

She gazed down at him, her pert eyebrows arched coolly. "I told you this was *my* program."

Christopher looked at her white hair and violet eyes and pointed ears, and reminded himself, *This creature is not human.*

In fact, now that he thought about it, she had said "this world." Implying she had once been on another world.

"Where are you from?" he asked.

"Álfheimr, of course. Where else would I be from?"

His magical grasp of the language provided a translation: elf-world. Well, duh.

Still, this was the first person he'd met who had traveled here from another world. Presumably she knew how to travel back to her world; possibly she might know how to travel to his.

There was a quick rap on the pole next to the tent door, and Lalania stepped inside. The bard had a knack for interrupting just when things were becoming interesting.

"It is getting dark," she said. "Lady Kalani, our leader needs his rest. I have prepared a place for you in my tent, if you would care to sleep."

"No thank you." Kalani shook her head politely. "I shall return to the ulvenmen. They have short attention spans, so it is best I do not let them forget me for too long."

"I don't think I want to send a patrol out in the dark," Christopher said. Rifles were a lot less effective when you couldn't see your opponent until one was standing in front of you with a giant axe.

"I do not require an escort," Kalani said. "This is my domain now."

"You can at least take a gun," Christopher offered. "In fact, take several. We'll give you a hundred rifles to start."

Lalania shook her head. "Gods, Christopher. You'll disarm your army at that rate."

He shrugged. "Not really. We're going to give them the old-style rifles." He figured the extra weight wouldn't bother the ulvenmen, and the men would be pleased to be upgraded.

"I am thankful, but I confess myself surprised that you would sell such powerful magic at so low a price," Kalani said carefully.

"They're not magic," Christopher objected. "Just machinery."

"I confess that is an interesting distinction."

"Something else your teachers don't know," Christopher said. "Maybe they should talk to me and find out what else I know that they don't."

Kalani pursed her lips. "If they want to talk to you, they will. You might not find the result entirely to your taste, however. They are quite set in their views."

Christopher had found this interview with the young elf unnerving. Imagining a skald-aged version did not lead to an improvement of his mood.

"I don't know why you're surprised," Lalania said. "We apparently sold whole villages."

"That was . . . unexpected," Kalani admitted. "Keisari had uncovered a treasure hoard; the weapons and armor bought him the loyalty of the chieftains, while the tael bought him rank. The chests of gold just sat in his hut until he got tired of tripping over them. Then one day he bragged to me that he had made a deal with a devil even worse than he. He seemed to think that importing your peasants would make his slaves more productive. It failed, of course. The tribesmen found the new slaves disobedient and ate most of them."

Her tone was entirely too casual for Christopher's taste. "Those were people you are talking about."

She looked back at him, unperturbed. "Forgive me. You discussed the thousands of ulvenmen you slew in the same terms. I thought it merely your way of speaking."

She and the Saint had something in common. Namely, they made you wish you'd kept your mouth shut.

"As long as we're speaking frankly," Lalania said, "I have some questions. Such as, how did Keisari find such a treasure hoard? And whom, exactly, did he bargain with for the villagers?"

"Your questions are unprofitable," the elf answered. She cast an eye outside the tent. "The hour grows late; if you would excuse me?"

"Of course," Christopher said, standing up. She slipped out before he could bow, or open the tent flap, or whatever act of politeness he thought he was supposed to do.

Lalania watched him with a hint of amusement. Chagrined, he waved a hand in the departed elf's direction.

"Should I bring her back and demand answers?"

"I think you've suffered enough for one day," Lalania said. "I already know the answers, anyway. I was just trying to get rid of her before dark. It is important that your soldiers see her leave your tent at a seemly hour."

"You already know?"

"As much as needed. The Gold Apostle would not deal in person, nor would he leave tongues to wag; I would not wager a copper that the men who made the exchange are still alive. And the hoard, obviously, came from Kalani. At least we can assume she only helped him find one; if she had planted it, there wouldn't have been any useless gold."

He sat down again. "How can you possibly know that?"

"Because it's what I would do. Except if I bought a ruler a throne, he would stay bought. We'll chalk it up to her inexperience. Presumably she has learned, and will do better with this one."

"Wait a minute, you're saying she's responsible for—" He stopped talking because Lalania put a finger on his lips.

"I am not saying that. There is no value in saying such a thing, which is why she did not answer you in the first place. Nor is there value in thinking it. She did not intend that particular end. We all make mistakes, after all."

The bard's mistake had involved burning down an inn while he was still in it. Apparently there was a certain sympathy between schemers and plotters. No doubt that was the source of Lalania's forgiveness; if he could not hold Kalani's missteps against her, then surely he would have to hold Lalania blameless for hers.

Lalania, having made her point, moved on.

"Meanwhile, I concur with Lady Kalani: you don't really want to meet any more elves. Even Varelous had a low opinion of their meddlings."

Christopher tried to argue, perhaps out of habit. "D'Kan doesn't."

"Yes, but *you* have a low opinion of *his* opinion, so I think it comes to the same in the end. Now I will send Karl to tuck you into bed, so the rest of us can stop worrying about your virtue and get on with our jobs."

She went out and Karl came in. Christopher began to wonder if his boots would ever get the attention they required. They had a quick discussion about logistics, during which Karl gave him less argument than Lalania had.

When they were done, Christopher brought up the other issue weighing on his conscience, sparked by thoughts of forgiveness and redemption.

"Karl, that man I sent into the swamp. Is there anything we can do?" The rage had passed, burned out in weeks of violence.

"Not this again," Karl said.

"I'm not sure I was right. It's not like he violated an order. We never said, 'don't do that.'"

Karl shook his head. "You wear the White. That speaks louder than mere words could ever do. Nonetheless, I will put your mind at rest if you promise me to never broach this subject again."

Christopher paused, but he knew Karl had already won.

"Okay," he said.

"The fool was begging food from Fort Sump last week. He has thus returned to the borders of the Kingdom, alive, which is more than he deserves, but his fate is now out of your hands."

"How did he survive so long?" Christopher asked.

"The chief dangers of the swamp were ulvenmen and dinosaurs," Karl said. "Most of whom now reside in your pocket."

Christopher thought of another danger born of their time in the swamp. "Karl . . . would you lie to me?"

Karl shrugged. "Only if I had to." Then he left.

21

YOU CAN'T GO HOME AGAIN

The ulvenmen learned with frightening speed. Kalani stood by Karl and translated his instructions, but it wasn't really necessary. The ulvenmen mimicked his every move until even their clumsy, clawed hands could manipulate the paper cartridges, although often with the help of their amazingly long and deft tongues. The rest of the drill—aiming and shooting—they got on the very first try.

Watching them, Christopher felt a pang of indecision. Was it really wise to arm these warlike monsters? Right now it was only Rohkea's posse, but eventually Kalani would have an army that snuck better and shot straighter than Christopher's. And her soldiers couldn't usually be killed with one shot. Worse, the greatest weakness of Christopher's army was close combat, but the ulvenmen had not abandoned their great axes. Once the battle turned to melee they would become even deadlier. Christopher wasn't entirely sure what the ulvenmen army's weakness was.

Karl stood beside him and watched as Rohkea went through the training drill a second time on his own, barking orders at his squad.

"He is a hell of a leader," Christopher said.

"The ulvenmen do learn fast," Karl agreed. "To be fair they are somewhat more focused than our farm boys usually are."

"Is this a good idea, Karl?" The ulvenman's tongues shook with glee every time the guns went off. Raw power was intoxicating to them.

"As long as they come when you whistle," Karl said.

They would have to. Their weakness, of course, was logistics.

The thrill of explosives was one thing. The tedium of making paper and powder was something else. The ulvenmen could barely maintain a dry place to sleep, let alone the lack of contamination necessary to chemical manufacturing. The heat of a forge burned out impurities; they could make iron even in a swamp. But any technological advancement beyond that would require precisely the cultural revolution Kalani was trying to foster.

Kalani joined them to say good-bye. She would send regular couriers to Fort Sump, bearing reports and requesting supplies. The ulvenman capital had lain at the far end of their territory; in getting there Christopher's threshing machine had swept across almost all of the land inhabited by the ulvenmen. He strongly suspected D'Kan was somehow responsible for this wide path, but had no proof. In any case Kalani did not seem upset at the knowledge that little remained of her new kingdom to be conquered.

She had modified Disa's robes to acknowledge the fact of the omnipresent jungle heat, shortening the skirt, opening the cleavage, and dyeing it in camouflage stripes. She also wore a necklace of fangs and carried a spear with a stone head that nonetheless looked painfully sharp. Though she wore the accoutrements comfortably, to Christopher she looked like a New England college anthropology student playing at being native. Leaving her in a swamp full of monsters seemed wildly irresponsible.

"Feel free to visit whenever you like," she said, unconcerned with his unease. "The ulvenmen will do well to learn to tolerate a human presence. But please do not summon me to your court unless the need is dire. My place is here, at least for several generations."

Rohkea stood aside, watching. Christopher cast his spell and spoke to the creature.

"You must not do what the Lady Elf forbids. Otherwise I must destroy all the ulvenmen. And I do not wish to do that."

"I do not understand," the ulvenman chieftain answered. "I wish to kill all humans. I would glory in such a slaughter. But rather than death you give us weapons against our enemies. Very well. I shall become a great chieftain of all the clans. With your fire-sticks we will kill all who challenge us."

"You will only kill those who the Lady Elf does not forbid you to kill," Christopher said, alarmed.

"Yes, of course," Rohkea agreed. "We will kill those who challenge you, too. You need but call out to the night sky, and your enemies will be our enemies."

Karl's comment made alarming sense now. For the price of a profitable trade agreement, Christopher had gained another army. Or so Karl seemed to think. Christopher was pretty sure using it in the Kingdom, even in the service of the White, would be too much for even the Saint to stomach.

"Do not forget," Christopher said. "You must not forget."

Rohkea gazed at him impassively, his comment either unheard or unnecessary.

He mounted his horse unhappily. It was time to leave, and there were still questions he wanted to ask Kalani. The elf had not been all that forthcoming on the topic of other worlds in their last conversation. He was unable to tell if she was hiding something or she just didn't know that much. Reluctantly he realized Lalania could probably tell the difference. She might even already know the answers. It was probably time to let her in on the truth of his origin. Of all the people he knew who could keep a secret, she was the next in line after the powerful Saint and Cardinal.

Turning back the way they had come, he called out to Lalania.

"Lala, speak to me in a language no one else here knows." As long as the translation spell was active, he might as well use it.

The minstrel concentrated for a moment and then laughed. She responded in the language the druids used.

"This will do," she said. "D'Kan thinks it is a woman's tongue, so he has never bothered to properly learn it, as demonstrated by his poor performance the other day."

"I have a secret. I—"

She cut him off. "Do not tell me anything you do not want the King to know. I am not a peer; I may still be called to question."

That settled that.

"I still have a problem, but one I cannot conceal from the King. Namely, tael."

She looked at him curiously.

"I have a lot of it. A *lot*. I want to ask the others what to do with it, but I'm afraid they'll tell me to promote myself again, to a Cardinal. Yes, there is enough for that."

The minstrel whistled softly. "I knew the treasure was rich, but I dared not hope for so much. My answer is the same, Christopher. You must promote yourself, now more than ever. Cardinals of your Church can revive the dead. That is a power so necessary to the Kingdom that it will excuse almost any crime."

"Cardinals of the Bright Lady can revive the dead," Christopher corrected her. "I am a priest of Marcius."

She waved him off. "Don't be concerned with details. Certainly no one else will be. In any case, at the rate you're going you'll be raising angels in another year or two. The fact remains that having another high-rank priest can only make the Kingdom stronger. Even the King will see that."

"The Gold Apostle won't."

"The Gold Apostle will have plenty of explaining to do once these slaves start talking. You leave him to me. Your only concern is the King. And your only answer is one he can understand—rank for yourself and tax for him. The sheer success of your actions excuses them more than any logic you can muster. Or so we must hope; your cursed conscience has left us no other path."

Christopher looked around for the faces of his council, but they were busy getting his army on its feet.

"Don't bother," she said. "You know they will agree with me. Do not save your fortune against future need when you could spend it insuring you'll be around long enough to have a future."

After consuming his promotion and setting aside his taxes he wouldn't even have enough to make another priest. At the time his gift to Kalani had been a pebble from a quarry. Now it would represent almost all of his remaining wealth. He realized he had already taken Lalania's advice. He had spent tael on Kalani because it was the right thing to do, without calculating how much he would have in the future.

"I still have to ask their advice," he told Lalania. "But this time I won't argue."

"Promises, promises," Lalania said.

The march home was unpleasant. It was hot during the day, wet in the evening, and cold at night. The bugs only stopped for the rain, and there were no sudden attacks or terrifying monsters to relieve the tedium. The freed slaves were like babes in the woods, hurting themselves every time you took your eyes off them. Eventually they were confined to the wagons while the soldiers carried the supplies, because it was just easier on everyone. Arriving at Fort Sump, the army disembarked like grumpy children after a long car ride.

"Tomorrow I will announce the leave roster," Karl shouted, and the bad mood evaporated in steamy clumps. The men had not been to town in many weeks. They would have gold to spend and stories to tell.

Christopher appreciated a night in relative comfort, and the chance in the morning to fill his head with something other than spells designed to kill things. The first spell he wanted to try was the infamous sending, available to him since he had become a Bishop but unused as he had always had better uses for his magic in the middle of a war.

He thought about whom he wanted to reach out to and touch. It was a high-rank spell, so using it like a prank phone call would result in a lecture on the Value of Magic from the Cardinal. Which made the choice obvious.

He fixed the image of the Cardinal's bushy bearded face in his mind and concentrated on releasing the spell. This one took minutes to take effect, like waiting for the other party to pick up the phone. He wondered if he could invent a spell that worked more like e-mail.

Then he could feel the Cardinal's presence, as if the man were standing right in front of him. He spoke out loud.

"Defeated ulvenman nation. Took low casualties, freed more slaves, promoted myself to Cardinal. Met an elf and sold her rifles. How are things up there?"

The reply came a few seconds later.

"Your message is incomprehensible. If the ulvenmen are pacified, then report to the King at once. Do not wait for rumors to steal your thunder."

He felt a lot better about leaving this time, because Gregor and Disa were staying behind. The army would have healing and rank. Only Lalania and Karl were coming with him to face the music. And Cannan and the inescapable cloud of cavalry, of course. Kalani might not need an escort in her own domain, but Christopher did. One would almost think the civilized lands were more dangerous than the Far Wild.

They went to Knockford first to make sure Jhom understood the urgency of supplying rifles. The looks on the faces of the gate guards surprised him; they seemed frightened at his approach. Too late he understood their fear was for him. A man squatting against the gate stood, corking his bottle of wine and wiping his mouth. The length of the sword at his hip identified him as a knight, though the swagger of broad shoulders would have been enough.

"Lord Vicar Christopher," he said. "You are summoned before the King on a charge of high treason."

"Begging your pardon, Colonel," said one of Christopher's cavalrymen. "Should we shoot him?"

"Sadly, no," Christopher said. "But please, Ser, explain yourself."

"I thought my speech clear enough," the knight said. "The King whistles and you come running. Don't darking matter why he whistles, does it?"

Christopher fumed silently for a moment. And then another one.

"No," he finally said, "I suppose it doesn't."

Out of idle curiosity, which was a welcome distraction from the worry that harried him as he led his escort back up the road toward Kingsford, he asked the man how one lone knight expected to arrest a high-ranking priest surrounded by his own loyal army.

"Your Saint stands hostage for your honor," the knight answered. "Although to be fair it is why I did not try you in the swamp. An 'accident' there might have been too tempting even for you lily-livered Whites. I believe the party that headed south was at least ten strong. Now, of course, they have sore arses for nothing, and I have the King's favor."

It was such an honest answer that Christopher paid for the man's lodging at the inn in Fram.

The next day he and the horsemen toiled up the long road to the city—or, to be fair, the horses toiled while the men sat. The column moved in silence; Lalania had run out of words and plots. Cannan never said anything unnecessary.

Karl had only spoken once. When they mounted that morning,

fresh from breakfast at the inn, he had asked Christopher a single question.

"Are you sure?"

Christopher thought about it, but there was really no option. His army could not hold out without supplies from Knockford, nor could it defend Knockford against any army the King could raise. He wasn't entirely sure it could defend Knockford against the King. A man was a small target to hit with a five-inch cannon, and nothing less would be sufficient.

"Yes," Christopher said, and Karl apparently put all thoughts of rebellion out of his mind. For now.

Now they approached the castle, and Christopher began to wonder if his choice was the right one. But there had been no other. There never had been, really.

The formalities were minimal. Karl and the cavalry could not accompany him, of course, but Cannan and Lalania's right to be at his side was not questioned. They followed their captor over the draw-bridge and into the great main hall.

Treywan was waiting for him, flanked again by purple, white, and yellow. The hall was full of armored men this time.

"My dear Vicar," the King bellowed. "You won't believe the most astonishing tales I have had of you. Most astonishing!"

Christopher dropped to one knee and bowed his head. Now he wished he had listened to Lalania so long ago and invested in fancy court clothes. Instead, he had worn his armor without thinking. In the swamp it aroused no comment; here, surrounded by men in plate and chain, his strange scales made him look . . . Wild. He could feel the unspoken question in the gaze of the crowd. It was time to remind them that he was one of them.

He raised his head and looked the King in the eye. "With all due respect, my lord, it is 'Cardinal' now."

The King blinked. "Truth?"

Christopher extracted the silver vial that hung around his neck and poured out his taxes. The effort left the vial pathetically empty.

The King stalked forward and took the purple plum from Christopher's open palm. He held it high and gazed into it like a crystal ball.

"Do not be diverted, my lord. He cannot bribe his way out from this." The Gold Apostle put on a brave face, but it was pretty obvious he feared the King was indeed about to be bribed.

"And the ulvenmen?" the King asked. "Do they still threaten us? Although with a treasure like this, I do not see how any of them could still be alive."

"Some still live, my lord, but they are not a threat. I left them under the rule of a Lady Elf, who guarantees their good behavior. Should she fail to keep them in line, I will return and exterminate the race."

The King weighed the purple stone in his hand. "We can only hope. Still, tell us why you did not kill them all in the first place."

"It did not seem to be your command," Christopher said. He was trying not to sweat too visibly. "You ordered me to resolve the ulvenman threat once and for all. Rather than destroy them, and risk missing a few who would breed into a new threat in only a few years, I decided to make them our servants instead of our enemies. Now the southern border is protected not only by your armies, but by the ulvenmen themselves."

"Those armies are there to protect the border *from* the ulvenmen, but no matter. Answer this far more serious charge: have you sold arms to these foul creatures? My lawyer assures me that we made that a capital offense many years ago."

Christopher was losing his battle of perspiration. "My lord, I did not know that. But the answer is no. I sold some weapons to the Lady Elf, for her servants, but they are under her control."

"A good answer, is it not?" the King asked. The room murmured its assent. "I knew you'd have good answers, priest. You're full of the damn things. I bet you can even answer this: did you arm foreigners against the realm?"

It sounded like Christopher might actually be doing okay. "Not against the realm, my lord. The Lady Elf cannot be anything but an ally. In any case I only sold rifles, the same weapons my common militia wield. I did not sell swords or armor."

"See? See?" the King said. There was a mild round of polite applause. Christopher started breathing normally again.

"Just one more question, priest. I know it's hard coming up with these fantastic answers, but I have just one more question. Tell me: is this Lady Elf *human?*"

Christopher felt the sudden shift from comedy to deadly menace, like ice cracking underfoot.

"No, my lord. She's an elf." He swallowed, hard. "But she's a good elf. I mean, she's White."

"Priest," the King said, "that is not a good answer. That is not an answer that will keep your head from the chopping block. *Try again.*"

There was nothing else to try. Lalania had been right from the beginning. Christopher had argued with her until she changed her mind into either underestimating the King's hostility or overestimating his sanity. Christopher could not think of a thing to say, and Lalania, trembling and white, was not allowed to speak. Cannan put his hand on his sword. Though his face did not change, his eyes communicated a distant regret at what was to come, and what the outcome must surely be.

Christopher shook his head. He could not fight his way out of this. Nor would the gloating Gold Apostle make the same mistake twice. This time they would burn every shred of his body and scatter the ashes. And if the Saint spoke up in his defense, it would only mean that the White Church would burn with him. There was no defense against treason, and treason was anything the King said it was.

But by the gods, he was not going down alone. He stood up, the better to deliver his charge against the Gold Apostle. The two of them could share the same gallows.

"My lord," he said, but he didn't get any further.

A knight stumbled into the room, shouting. Men rushed to stop him, but once they got close enough to understand his ranting, they joined him. A growing knot of madness was sweeping toward the King.

"For the sake of all that is Dark and Light," the King said. "Is this one of your damn stratagems, priest?"

Even now Christopher could not lie. "No, my lord. Although I wish it was."

Treywan drew his sword. The men around him, in their colored cloaks, moved back in fear. Save for the Saint, who stood directly behind the King and laid a hand upon his shoulder. Christopher figured that had to be worth a few brownie points.

"Hold!" cried a nearby man Christopher recognized as Ser Morrison, although it was the real one this time. The man blocked the crowd's rush to the King with his body, backed up by a handful of other knights.

Unnecessarily, since the crowd stopped at the edge, spilling forward the provocateur.

"My lord," the man cried, his anguish too deep and real to be feigned. "My lord, I beg for royal vengeance. I have ridden three horses to death to fall at your feet and beg for vengeance."

Christopher's stomach began to twist. The man was wearing blue armor. Bright, beautiful blue armor stained with blood and dirt.

"Vengeance for who?" the King asked, because he had to.

"Vengeance for my Lord Duke Nordland," the man cried. Tears streamed down his face. "The most valiant Duke, my lord, and his lady wife. My wife. The town. It is all fire and ash!"

"Speak clearly, man," the King growled, fearsome as a thunderhead about to break. "You make no sense."

"Castle Nordland burns," the man said. "A dragon has come."

"They will think it is your doing," Lalania said. "I know better, because I know you cannot lie, and yet even I find myself thinking it. How terribly convenient, that at your trial for treason, your worst enemy should be obliterated by terrible force."

They had retreated to the Cathedral, temporarily forgotten in the confusion. The King, after turning several shades of pale, had thrown Christopher a murderous look and then stalked off to muster his army. Haste was pointless, of course, and everyone knew it. The dragon would have already burned everything, had burned everything days ago. Still, for the sake of appearances, something had to be done.

"He wasn't my worst enemy," Christopher said. "The Gold Apostle is. If I had a pet dragon, I would be sending it there, not against Nordland."

"As always, you are sensible, and yet insensibly surprised when others are not." The Saint shook his head in dismay.

"There is a way out of this rumor," Lalania said. "If the King slays the dragon, and yet Christopher's power remains unabated, then it will be clear that the dragon was not the source of his power."

"If?" Christopher said, unclear on why there was uncertainty. Cardinal Faren had traveled with the army, offering his phenomenal healing power and Captain Steuben's markedly less phenomenal fighting power to the effort. In addition, the Gold Apostle, the King's wizard, and a horde of lesser knights, priests, and wizards had joined the short march north. It was an awe-inspiring collection of prowess, and there were still the peers and their armies to summon.

"He has killed one," Saint Krellyan said. "Why should he not kill another?"

"He has?" Christopher exclaimed. That was even more amazing news than that he might or might not kill this one. Why didn't anyone ever tell him this stuff?

"It's not just a dragon. It's a goblin horde. Apparently they got tired of waiting for Nordland to fall into their trap, and brought the trap to him." Lalania, as usual, was more informed than anyone. "First reports imply that the monsters have retreated, but that could be a ruse."

"Or an effective ploy," Krellyan said. "The King will now feel bound to pursue the monsters into their own realm to administer justice. This may lead him into the traps set for Lord Nordland."

"This is nuts," Christopher complained. He might not like the ruling class of the realm, but he wasn't prepared to replace it just yet. If the King died, civil war seemed inevitable. The druids would secede, the Black would destroy the White, and the Greens would destroy each other. "We've got to stop him."

"How?" Lalania said. "Unless you're volunteering to do it for him."

That was a thought. But he couldn't, not yet. He had finally paid attention to the books in the Cathedral's library; he knew what spells came with his next rank, what pinnacle of power he had been fighting so hard for.

"One more rank," he said, sighing. "One more rank and Marcius has to keep his promise. Then I could kill dragons." Then he wouldn't need to, because he wouldn't care about the King's life.

Lalania stared at him, her attention speared by his words. He didn't care anymore. It was way past time for keeping secrets.

"Do you speak truly?" Krellyan asked him. "If you could travel home, you could return and save our Kingdom?"

He thought about what Earth had to offer. Automatic rifles that made his weapons look like hobbyist's toys. An anti-aircraft gun to reach up and claw that dragon out of the sky. Artillery that could deal destruction at ranges measured in miles instead of yards.

"Yes," he said. "A few sacks of gold would buy more than everything I have made here."

"Is death all you would bring us?" Krellyan asked sadly.

He thought about other things, like democracy and women's rights and chocolate.

"Not all. But for now, it is what we need."

The Saint looked older and grayer than Christopher had ever seen him.

"I do not know if this is the right thing to do." The Saint spoke uncertainly. "Yet I cannot pretend the decision is not mine to make. There is a clear signal, a pressing need, an obvious path. Every fact but tradition and caution drives me forward."

"What?" Christopher asked. "You were right to stay behind." Although the Saint had even more healing than the Cardinal, he was too valuable to risk. There was only one person in the realm who could revive a savaged corpse, and everyone agreed that death by dragon was likely to be savage.

"Not that," Krellyan said. "This." From a cord around his neck he produced a silver flask, and from the flask he produced a rock of tael so large that Christopher was practically blinded. It was equal to all the tael he had ever seen in this world.

"The Church has saved long and hard for my replacement, and yet it still must save another thirty years. And yet, if the realm perishes, of what value is all this saving? Brother Christopher, if you can truly save the realm, then I must lend you the means if they are at my disposal."

"You would make him a Prophet?" Lalania asked. "This trouble-some, mysterious stranger, who rattles our entire realm like a drum even though he has been here a scant two years?"

"If he is a drummer, then the music would appear to be written by a god," Krellyan said. "What else accounts for the rhythm of our lives of late?"

Lalania shot Christopher a triumphant look that clearly said, *I knew it*. So many times he had professed his ordinariness to her, only to have it all stripped away as a lie here in the Cathedral, under the shadow of the Bright Lady. He fought the truth, out of habit if nothing else.

"Lord Krellyan," Christopher argued, "I can't accept this." He had already printed a fortune in bonds he had to be responsible for. This amount of debt was too much for him to conceive of.

"You cannot refuse it," Krellyan said, "if your words are true. The safety of the realm is more important than your conscience."

Maggie. He would get to see Maggie. It would be short and hurried. He would be unable to rationally explain where he had been, or why his nose was straight now, or why he was spending gold coins on heavy weaponry. But he would get to see her again.

"It's not what I planned. But it will speed up my plans." He could only carry armloads, but that would be enough. A shoulder-mounted rocket launcher to kill this monster, and then blueprints for factories and machines. The Chinese had made AK-47s in conditions that didn't include running water or regular electricity. He could bring back calipers and drill bits, tools that he could use to make other tools. He wouldn't need magic anymore. "I'll need gold."

"Gold is the least of our worries," Krellyan said. "The spell will let you carry ninety pounds; will that be sufficient to your needs? If so, I have that much in our vault and easily to hand."

At a thousand dollars an ounce, that was over a million dollars.

"Yes," Christopher agreed. "That will do for now."

"Then begin," Krellyan commanded, "before I lose my nerve. Gain your rank today, and tomorrow we will send you home to do what you can do."

Christopher took the lump of purple and ate it before he lost his own nerve. It was not just a contract for a staggering debt, but also for changing a world.

"Look at the bright side," Lalania said weakly. "When you kill the dragon you'll be able to pay the Saint back."

He had forgotten that part. It was also a contract for killing a dragon.

The next day they waited fretfully for the rank to manifest. It was ironic. Christopher had finally achieved the pinnacle of power in this world—he could revive the dead now—and yet the first spell he would cast would be to leave it.

"It will take me days," he warned them. "Stall the King as long as you can."

"He will not invade the goblin lands without mustering the peers," the Saint assured him. "This will give you a week at least. In any case you can send to me, and I to you. Do not spoil your mission through false urgency."

Christopher had forgotten about the sendings. There were probably lots of things he was forgetting, but right now it didn't matter. He was going to go home and find Maggie and squeeze her until she burst.

He picked up a thick leather satchel in each hand, holding a combined ninety pounds of gold. Heavy, but no worse than the plate armor he had once worn, and his time in this world had made him strong. Chanting the unfamiliar words, he prepared himself for the unimaginable. Although, come to think of it, his first trip through a portal had been so subtle he hadn't even noticed it. Suspicious, he looked around to see if he had already made the transition, but he was not on Earth. Or in the Cathedral. Instead, he stood in an unending field of soft white mist curling around his ankles like cotton, under a dull white sky that stretched out forever.

"I am here to keep my promise," Marcius said. "Though honestly you should have contacted me before jumping into the spell. Still, we can't fault enthusiasm."

"Right." Christopher nodded. "You promised me the key to my home. So bust loose. I've got places to go and important people to kill."

"Very well, but before I tell you the secret, promise me you won't add me to that list."

Christopher cocked his head. Marcius sighed.

"The key to your home is you. You, and you alone, can contact

338   JUDGMENT AT VERDANT COURT

the ancestral plane of man. I give you nothing, because you require nothing. Anytime you try to travel to your plane, you will succeed."

"Why can't other people?" Christopher asked.

"Because they were not born there. You can only reach the plane because you came from it. The way is blocked to any other, including even I."

"So . . . I am special." Lalania would be glad to know a god had said she was right.

"Only by an accident of geography," Marcius said.

Christopher thought out loud. "That explains why no one else goes there. That explains why Earth isn't constantly being invaded by curiosity-seekers wanting to buy technological marvels."

Marcius had a different viewpoint. "It also explains the lack of murderous invasion by *hjerne-spica*."

"Ha," Christopher said. "They'd be pretty cheesed off to discover they had wasted their time. There isn't any tael on Earth." Dead people didn't give off purple stuff when you boiled their brains. If they did, he was sure somebody would have noticed by now. The AMA, or the CDC at least.

"They might well do it for mere sport," Marcius said. "But that does not matter now. The terms of our bargain are fulfilled. So I wish to take this opportunity to thank you for all that you have done for our world."

"I'm not finished," Christopher objected. "Don't thank me yet. I still have time to screw it up."

Marcius smiled wryly. "Nonetheless, you have sown the seeds of change, and I hope for the best."

"Like I said"—Christopher grinned—"you ain't seen nothing yet. But before I go, can you answer one quick question? I mean, I can figure it out once I get there, but I'd like to know as soon as possible so I can start planning."

"One question is not out of line," Marcius agreed.

"Can I revive the dead over there? I mean, on Earth." It had finally occurred to him that raising the dead—indeed, even merely healing cancer—would be worth more than any amount of gold he could carry.

"No," Marcius said carefully. "As you noted, there is no tael on Earth."

"Damn." Christopher frowned. "I'm not looking forward to making more trips weighted down like this. . . . Wait a minute."

He stared at the god's inscrutable face.

"Wait a minute. Spells don't work on Earth. You just said spells don't work on Earth."

"That is correct," Marcius said.

Christopher gaped, at a loss for words. Logic and desire warred inside him until curiosity won.

"Then how can I come back?"

Marcius smiled, so sad and noble that Christopher wanted to cry. Or punch him. Or both.

"You cannot. Your power will let you open the gate to your world from here, but it cannot reach from the other side. Once there, you will not be able to cast magic of any kind. But consider: you will keep your regenerated body. You will keep your fortune in gold. You will be reunited with your wife, after only a few years. We consider these gifts small payment for all you have done for our world. If you choose to go home now, the gods will not blame you."

The gods might not, but plenty of other people would. The Saint, who had just invested the future of his Church in him. Cannan, who had been promised a miracle. Karl, who had learned to hope.

And himself. He could not walk out on these people, who had fought and died for him, who had believed in him even when it made no sense to do so. He could not do that to himself.

"I can't do this," he said. "I can't quit on them. Why did you let me believe I could go home when I can't quit on them?"

"You can go home," the god told him, "whenever you want.

The spell will even let you take your horse. You just can't take your obligations."

"Was it all a lie?" Christopher asked. "Was it all a lie from the beginning?"

"No," Marcius said. "There is still a way in front of you. And there is still more I hoped you would do. But all of the challenges you have defeated will be like paper lions before the challenges that lay ahead."

"And I can quit anytime. You're betting on a horse that can quit the race anytime."

"I am not betting," Marcius said. "I am hoping. It is an entirely different kind of beast."

The god began to fade. Christopher knew he had to make a decision, a decision he would have to keep making every day until it wore him down into a broken nub. And why would he go home then? Who would want him then?

He let the spell die on his lips, its beautiful syllables an inaudible good-bye to the woman he loved. The mist cleared and left him standing in the Cathedral, dropping heavy bags of gold to the floor in a defeated clatter. Krellyan and Lalania stared at him in alarm.

"What happened?" Krellyan asked.

"I met a god," Christopher said. "He gave me some advice for travelers lost far from home. 'Do not make promises.'"

ACKNOWLEDGMENTS

Thanks for the encouragement of the Loyal Crew who have been with this series since the beginning: nephews David, Alex, Dylan, and honorary nephew Fletcher, and compadre Josh, half a brother half a world away; to my agent Kristin for her inexhaustible patience; to my copyeditor Jeffrey, for counting missing fingers among many other clarities; to my editor Rene, for making me look in the interesting corners; to Sophie, for finally starting prep so Mommy and Daddy can have writing time; and always, to Sara.

ABOUT THE AUTHOR

M. C. Planck is the author of *Sword of the Bright Lady* (World of Prime, Book 1) and *Gold Throne in Shadow* (World of Prime, Book 2). After a nearly transient childhood, he hitchhiked across the country and ran out of money in Arizona. So he stayed there for thirty years, raising dogs, getting a degree in philosophy, and founding a scientific instrument company. Having read virtually everything by the old masters of SF&F, he decided he was ready to write. A decade later, with a little help from the Critters online critique group, he was actually ready. He was relieved to find that writing novels is easier than writing software, as a single punctuation error won't cause your audience to explode and die. When he ran out of dogs, he moved to Australia to raise his daughter with kangaroos.

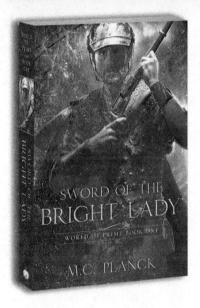